Making The Reata

A Novel

Terry Tallent

Silver Spur Publishing

ISBN: 061551815X
ISBN: 13 9780615518152

LCCN: 2011963217

Silver Spur Publishing
Ojai, California

The front cover image is from a lithograph of the
Ojai Valley by A. H. Campbell, circa 1854.

The map of California's South Coast was created
by the author and Tina Drennan in 2011.

For Hildegard,
And my fellow writers of The Ojai Novel Focus Group:
John, Tina, Sharon, Jon & Nancy

This is a work of fiction. While based on historical fact, the author has reserved the right to alter the people, places and events to accommodate the story.

There was a boy…
A very strange enchanted boy.
They say he wandered very far, very far
Over land and sea,
A little shy and sad of eye
But very wise was he.

Eden Ahbez

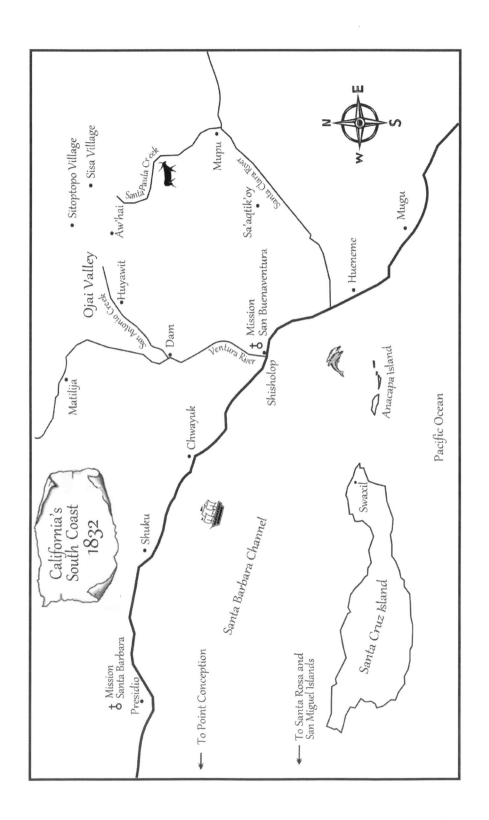

California's
South Coast
1832

Mission
Santa Barbara

Presidio

Shuku

Chwayuk

Matilija

Ojai Valley

Huyawit

San Antonio Creek

Dam

Sitoptopo Village

Sisa Village

Aw'hai

Santa Paula Creek

Mupu

Sa'aqtik'oy

Santa Clara River

Mission
San Buenaventura

Ventura River

Shisholop

Anacapa Island

Hueneme

Mugu

Swaxil

Santa Cruz Island

Santa Barbara Channel

Pacific Ocean

To Point Conception

To Santa Rosa and
San Miguel Islands

N
E
S
W

Making The Reata*

* A reata (ree-ah-tah) is a braided rawhide rope, or lasso. It was used in the early days of California for working livestock. Americans later named it the "lariat," after the Spanish term, *la reata*.

1

THE FLOOD

Inigua was awakened just before dawn by a gurgling sound, and then the hiss of coals drowning in the fire pit. He drew his blanket aside and sat up stiffly on the mats of the sleeping platform. He could sense his wife awake there beside him.

"Islay," he said, "do you hear it?"

"Yes. The river is rising."

"Are the carrying nets ready?"

"Yes. Everything is ready."

"Then we must go. Quickly."

Inigua set his leathery feet down on the earthen floor. His age-worn joints creaked in protest as he stood up. "*Aiee*," he intoned as he felt cold mud squeeze up between his toes.

In the dark, he and Islay slipped into their serape-like *cotons*. By the time they shrugged the carrying nets onto their backs and adjusted the straps so they rode across their foreheads, the water was already up to their ankles. Inigua draped a blanket over his wife's head, like a shawl, and did the same for himself.

The old couple sloshed through the tarry darkness of their sleeping enclosure. A faint, gray light filtering through the smoke hole helped guide them along the curved wall of the hut. When they reached the doorway at the eastern end, Inigua untied the inside mat and then pushed aside the outer one. Torrential rain was falling. The old couple groaned at the sight, for they knew that before long they would be soaked to the skin. Despite this, they were relieved to see that dawn was breaking. At least there would be light enough to travel.

Inigua knew that their escape would not be easy. They should not have stayed the night here. If Islay had not been so ill the day before he would have taken her away then. But she'd been too weak to travel. He could only wait and hope her strength returned quickly, or that the rain stopped. But neither had, and now the river was rising rapidly. They had no choice but to flee now. Inigua took his wife by the hand and led her out into the pelting rain. They headed west towards the hills that lay beyond the broad river valley.

Inigua and Islay had lived here at the mouth of the Ventura River for several years now. Their traditional dome-shaped hut was made of bent willow poles lashed together and thatched with tule. Nearby, at the river's edge, they had built an earthen sweat lodge. They eked out a living by offering the use of it to neophytes from Mission San Buenaventura across the river. Some of the older neophytes liked to go to the lodge in the evening after work and have a sweat and then bathe in the river. They liked it because it was refreshing, and it reminded them of the way things were before the Spaniards came. In payment, the neophytes brought the old couple food, or an armload of firewood, or perhaps a little wine purloined from the mission cellars. Inigua had grown quite fond of wine.

The winter of 1831-32 had not been a good one for sweat baths. It had rained far more than was normal in southern California. The usually sleepy, meandering stream in the riverbed had awakened and flowed vigorously all season long, earning once more the name of River. So robustly had it flowed that the fallen tree trunk that used to serve as a footbridge from the mission fields had washed away, as had the sandbar that once dammed the river down by the beach. It was thus difficult for the neophytes east of the river to reach the sweat lodge. If they came at all they had to use the plank bridge farther upstream, to the west of the mission complex, and then slog down through the mud and rocks of the river basin to the river mouth. Many of the older neophytes found this too troublesome, and did not come.

It had been a lean winter. Inigua and Islay seemed always to be hungry. They tried to live off the land, as they used to do. But it was not easy, given their ages. Inigua caught fish with his casting net when the surf was not too high. At other times he worked the river. He also hunted small game with a bow and arrow in the thick undergrowth at the river mouth, or set deadfalls and snares in the underbrush where he sometimes caught rabbits and birds. Islay tended a small garden and kept a few chickens. Besides these, she carefully hoarded a cache of acorns and seeds left over from those they had gathered upriver in the fall. Islay made them into soups, or hot mush, or cakes.

The old couple could have gone to the mission and had all their needs met. The padres had always been kind to the elderly. But Inigua vowed to have nothing more to do with the mission. He stubbornly refused to go there, not even to attend mass, and he would rather go hungry than ask the padres for food. Inigua had grown more truculent than ever in his old age.

The Ventura River had not flooded for seven years, and in that time a forest of trees and brush had sprung up along the western reaches of the river delta. It was through this thicket that Inigua and Islay now struggled. They hurried as best they could for they both knew that they must travel a good distance before they reached the high ground. Meanwhile, heavy rain continued to fall.

Inigua was glad to hear the sounds of the river diminishing behind them. Given time and luck, they just might make it to the hills. But shortly, he and Islay heard the ominous clatter of river rocks up ahead. Inigua knew that before them, just beyond that line of brush, lay a broad, dry barranca. He feared the river might have risen high enough to breach it. If that was true, there might be two channels now – one in front and one behind them.

When they reached the source of the sounds, his fears were confirmed. A wide rift of swift flowing water filled the barranca. In the gray light of dawn they could see scrub brush, torn branches, and dead wood streaming down towards the sea. The water was not quite waist deep, but Inigua was reluctant to attempt a crossing. Islay was too weak to stand against it, and besides, if they were snagged by the fast moving debris they could be swept off their feet.

Inigua peered upstream, searching for a place where they might cross. But he could see none. He turned away dejectedly and led Islay downstream.

They both realized their situation was even more desperate than before. They had to find a way out quickly. Staggering under their heavy loads and the driving rain, they presently came to a stand of cypress trees, beyond which the hurling stream to their right rejoined the main river to their left. The combined force of the waters was now sweeping away a broad stretch of beach. Up and down the coast, ugly brown storm waves pounded into the flood.

They found themselves isolated on a long, narrow island in mid-stream, and they could see that the waters were rising steadily around them. Inigua turned to face Islay. His beloved old wife looked back at him, blinking through the rain. She was in her early seventies, nearly as old as him, ill, and in no condition to be trudging about with a full pack over rough terrain. Islay knew as well as he did that if the river continued to rise, they just might die today. She tried to appear strong, and indifferent to the danger, but he could tell she was neither.

"We can't get around the water, old woman," he said.

"It doesn't matter," she answered. "We are already wet."

"We will be wetter still if we don't do something. Do you think you are strong enough to climb one of those trees?"

She frowned at the cypress and then at him. She said, "If you can climb, old man, so can I." Her familiar gruff bravado sounded hollow to him now. It carried no conviction, and its emptiness disturbed him. He felt something cold inside, something hard and sharp pricking at his spirit.

He turned away so that she would not see the fear of it in his eyes, and led her into the stand of trees. They examined them carefully, searching for one that would be easy to climb, was large enough to hold them both,

3

and, hopefully, strong enough to withstand the flood waters.

Meanwhile, seven miles upriver, the dam that spanned San Antonio Creek was about to give way. The rock and mortar dam which walled the large creek off from the river had been cracked and weakened by time, earthquakes, and previous flooding. Faulted as it was, the main wall could no longer withstand the pressure of the mounting reservoir behind it.

The dam gave an almost human groan. This was followed by an eerie rending sound, and then a boom as the main wall exploded. Huge chunks of it tumbled down into the gorge, shaking the earth as they did so. The pent up waters in the canyon roared through the gaping hole.

Below, the already swollen Ventura River gasped at the sudden lateral onslaught. Staggered, the river took a long moment to swallow the vast, muddy surge. Then, bloated with a new urgency, it swept on towards the sea.

Back near the river mouth, above the sound of wind and rain and rushing waters, the old couple heard the low, angry rumble of its approach. Their eyes darted upriver. They saw a great wide swell, like a broken wave, sweeping down the breadth of the river. Torn vegetation boiled along at its forefront. Nothing seemed capable of withstanding such force.

Inigua felt the cold, hard, sharp thing from before. It stabbed insistently, cutting deeper.

"Islay!" he yelled, "Follow me! Hurry!"

He flung off his blanket and climbed into the lower limbs of the cypress they had chosen. Slipping off his carrying net, he hurriedly placed it in the crotch of a limb higher up. Then he reached down and took Islay's net and did the same with it. The nets carried food and their most valued possessions.

"Hurry!" he screamed above the din. "Leave the blankets. There is no time." But Islay insisted on passing the blankets up to him first. He tossed them over the limb next to the carrying nets. Then he took Islay's hand and pulled her up next to him with a grunt.

"Higher. We must go higher," he shouted.

He glanced at Islay. He saw that her strength was nearly gone. He could feel his own strength fading too. But he could not give up. He must try to save them. He heard the flood-surge roaring down the island towards them. He struggled up to next higher limb. He sat down on it, held on to the main trunk with one hand, and reached for Islay with the other. She looked up at him dejectedly.

"I can't," she said. "It's too high."

"You must try," he said, "Give me your hand." She smiled up at him, seemingly amused at the urgency in his voice. It reminded Inigua of the way she used to smile at him when they were young. At last she sighed, and raised her hand wearily towards him. He took it and pulled with all his might.

4

Just as she was getting her feet under her on the limb below, the massive flood-surge slammed into the tree. The cypress tilted back violently, flinging their blankets and carrying nets into the boiling flood. The tree shivered and jerked at its roots, but somehow held. Inigua felt the power of the water dragging heavily at Islay's body below him. His rain-slickened clasp on her began to slip. He looked down in desperation.

She looked back at him with a disconcerting calm. He saw no fear in her eyes now, only a mixture of sadness and tired resignation. Then, their hands slipped apart and he watched helplessly as she was dragged under.

"Noooo!" he cried.

He felt the hole in his spirit widen, and he tried to close it by screaming her name, "Islaaaay!" Twisting around on the limb, Inigua gaped downstream, willing her to bob up, somehow clinging to a log or floating along with the rolling surge. He waited, holding his breath.

Nothing. Nothing but the endless flow of churning caramel water. She was gone. Islay was gone! He could feel the black hole grow and deepen inside of him. He cried out when it broke through into the lower world, the world of the dreaded *Nunashish*. A dank wind blew up out of there, carrying with it the smell of dead things, and the sound of mournful howling and the hiss of slithering snakes. Inigua averted his eyes so that he might not see down in there.

A large section of the shattered plank bridge came sweeping down in the flood and rammed into the cypress. It jolted Inigua, nearly tumbling him off the limb. He grasped the main trunk with both hands and hung on. He was stunned, immobilized by shock. Everything he cared about in the world was gone. He sat and stared at the bridge as it peeled off to one side and sped on towards the sea.

The rain continued to pour down on his bowed head, and the river to rise until it sucked greedily at his knobby feet. He didn't attempt to climb any higher. He just sat there shivering and staring down into the muddy water. He didn't care now if the river claimed him too. He was all done struggling.

The great flood of 1832 was long remembered around Mission San Buenaventura. Neophytes who kept vegetable gardens along the eastern side of the river had scrambled out of their huts, much as Inigua had done on the other side, and run for the nearby hills behind the mission. Some of them didn't make it. Those that did looked back to see their houses washed away, their furniture, tools and implements lost, their tidy plots of land swept clean and buried by the flood.

Further east, the broadening river dissolved and carried away adobe walls that protected mission fields. Berms and footpaths and roads were erased. Irrigation ditches filled up with mud. Along the coastal plain, freshly plowed fields awaiting spring planting were inundated and smothered under a thick layer of goo. Fishing boats resting on the shore were swept out to sea. A heavy toll was taken on livestock and wildlife along the river, and an unknown number of neophytes were drowned or buried by mudslides.

Beautiful San Miguel Chapel, founded by Junipero Serra down by what would become the corner of Thompson and Palm Streets in Ventura, was completely demolished. In the Indian rancheria near the mission, numerous dwellings and storehouses were destroyed or damaged. The water rose so high that for a time it threatened the main church and the mission quadrangle itself. Though these structures survived intact, as did the vineyards and orchards on the high ground, the flood was a devastating blow to the mission, a blow that sent it reeling towards its ultimate demise a few years later. To the 700 muddy and bedraggled survivors, whether Chumash, Mestizo, Mexican, or Spaniard, it seemed as though a spiteful God had turned his back once and for all on 'The Mission-By-The-Sea.'

2

PADRE-SUPERIOR

Two days after the flood, Father Francisco Xavier Uria, the Padre-Superior of Mission San Buenaventura, rode a white burro down the tree-lined lane that led towards the beach. The river had by then retreated to its bed, and a canopy of brilliant blue had supplanted the leaden skies. The padre rode forth to determine the full extent of the damage to his mission.

Padre Uria, a native of Cantabria in Spain, was a short, portly man of sixty-two. He wore the course, gray robe of the Franciscans, full-skirted and full-sleeved, with a cowl hanging between the shoulders behind. A broad, stiff, round-brimmed hat, gray to match his robe, protected his bald head from the morning's strong sun. Circled twice around his generous waist was a heavy, twisted white rope. From the left side of his waist-rope depended a long rosary chain with large wooden beads and a wooden crucifix. Padre Uria rode a burro instead of a horse in obeisance to the late Junípero Serra's admonition to go humbly about the Lord's work.

Beside the padre, towering above him on a handsome black bay rode Corporal Sanchez, the newly-appointed mayordomo of the mission. He was a lean and leathery Mexican soldier, a veteran of the Mexican war of independence. He wore a sombrero, and a faded and much-patched military uniform with trousers that flared over his boots. His boots were old, but of good leather, with rowel spurs attached. Cradled in the crook of his left arm was an aged army musket.

Following Corporal Sanchez came the *alcalde*, Luis, one of the mission's four annually elected Indian constables. At his side rode his burly deputy, the *regidore*, Felipe. Bringing up the rear was a thirteen year-old mestizo boy, Pablo, the padre's personal servant. The two Indians and the boy wore the typical dress of the neophytes: loose-fitting smocks called cotons, and trousers made of unbleached muslin. The cotons were worn outside the trousers and belted with a red cotton sash.

The riders' mounts picked their way gingerly through the mud, which in places was knee deep. The morning stillness was broken by the disagreeable sound of hooves squishing into and sucking out of the glutinous muck. Above, in a cloudless southern California sky, a scalding sun burned down on a scene of glazed and steaming desolation.

When the riders reached the collapsed remains of San Miguel Chapel, Padre Uria reined in. The usually light-hearted priest sighed deeply and made the sign of the cross over the ruins.

Although the venerable old chapel had been relegated to only occasional use since the main church by the quadrangle had been completed some twenty years before, this place still held great historical significance and symbolic value to the mission. It was here that Junípero Serra founded this, the ninth of the Spanish missions in California. It had been the last mission Serra founded, for he had died two years later. The reverend father had served the first mass here on this spot on Easter Sunday, fifty years before. And it was here that the first heathen savages had later been baptized into the fold.

Padre Uria looked sadly at the collapsed adobe walls, the flattened roof, and the broken and scattered tiles. Although a relative newcomer to San Buenaventura, he knew that the chapel had undergone major repairs after being damaged in the great earthquake of 1812. But seeing it now, he could tell that it was finished. The mission no longer had the time or the resources to rebuild, or for that matter, was there any great need for the chapel any more.

Staring down at it, Padre Uria saw something of himself lying there in the ruins. Though not quite finished himself, he was worn out and suffering from painful maladies accrued during his thirty years of zealous toil in five different missions up and down *El Camino Real*. He had already applied for retirement to the current Padre-Presidente of the California missions, and was now just waiting for a replacement to be sent. Although it might be many months before a new priest arrived, Padre Uria knew his own career was nearly over. He no longer had the will or the energy to rebuild this revered chapel. The glory of its success, even its very existence, would one day be forgotten. Just as he and his work would be.

"Corporal Sanchez," he said to his mayordomo, "in a few days, when the ground has dried, send some men and a carreta to salvage the roof tiles. Have them taken to the mission and stacked behind the quadrangle. We may have use for them one day."

"Sí, Padre."

"Do the same with any good timbers you find. Cut up the useless ones for firewood. Salvage any useful items you find in the rubble. Then level this site. We might as well put it under cultivation."

Then nudging his burro with the heel of his leather sandals, the padre led his entourage beyond the ruined chapel towards the beach.

As they rode forward, they could see the Santa Barbara Channel sprawled there before them. The wide stretch of sea did not wear its usual cloak of shimmering blue, but seemed rather to be shrouded in a sick, dull glow. The water was the color of a deep bruise. Twenty and more miles out to sea, seen through the pristine morning air, the bleak and silent Channel Islands floated like bloated purple bodies.

As Padre Uria and his followers neared the shore they caught the stench of corruption and decay curling in on the sea breeze. Mounting a low bluff, the five riders beheld dirty, debris-clogged waves breaking thickly along the shore. The waves sounded weak and phlegmatic, like a pneumonic cough.

Along the beach, a wide strip of glistening clay dwelt where once a swath of white sand had lain. Great heaps of driftwood and steaming kelp now littered the dismal strip as far as the eye could see in either direction. Gulls, vultures, and condors scavenged through the jetsam, feasting on dead things washed down by the flood. Here and there among the ravaged wood and torn roots scurried rats and other rodents, stalked by hungry and disoriented snakes deposited there by the flood. Above the wracked scene hummed clouds of fat, sated flies.

From the direction of the river the five riders suddenly heard a cracked, high-pitched howl. They looked to the source and saw a mud-caked specter of a man hobbling along the shore. The apparition waved a crooked staff at a condor whose talons were imbedded in a lifeless, furred body while its beak tore at the flesh.

The man-thing shouted. Words flew forth, some of them emanating from deep down in his throat, others off the very tip of his tongue. The words sounded foreign, primeval, filled with strong, halting gutturals, glottal stops and clicking noises. The neophytes accompanying Padre Uria glanced furtively at one another. They recognized the words as belonging to the esoteric *'antap* language of the Chumash. The savage, for that is what he seemed, stooped for a stone and hurled it at the condor. The stone missed by inches, and the condor squawked angrily, spread its wings a full nine feet, and loped ungainly away, running to gain enough speed to become airborne.

From a distance, the men watched as the savage seemed suddenly to swoon. He leaned heavily on his driftwood staff, and sank to his knees. The fleeing condor looked back and saw its tormentor fall. The great bird stopped running, furled its wings, and circled behind a toppled tree trunk from which vantage point it eyed the man furtively. It would relish eating his eyes.

The savage seemed spent. He barely managed to remain upright by clinging to his staff with both hands. He was naked; his bone-thin frame smeared with mud and dried blood, the latter seeping from open wounds and abrasions on his hands, elbows and knees. His tangled white hair, dirty and matted, hung in disarray about his stooped shoulders. The haggard face, with a nose as prominent as a hawk's beak, looked cracked and disfigured, though in fact it was only plastered with dried mud. The man's piercing eyes looked crazed, the madness there tempered only by exhaustion.

"*Ay Dios mio!*" uttered Fray Uria as he urged his burro forward. When he and his companions had carefully picked their way through the debris and drawn up to the man, the padre said, "*Buenos dias*, poor fellow. May God take mercy on you."

The kneeling man slowly raised his head and squinted up into the sunlight at the riders. It took him a few moments to reconcile himself to their

9

presence, and to decipher the padre's Latinate tongue.

"Ah, it is you," he replied in Spanish. "Hallelujah. The holy goddamn padre and his running dogs are here."

The riders stiffened. Corporal Sanchez scowled down at him and said, "Be careful what you say, old man, unless you want to add a flogging to your misery."

The side of Padre Uria's face twitched uncontrollably, but he still looked down kindly on the Indian scowling up at him from the mud. "Never mind, Corporal," he said. "He is in a bad way, this poor wretch. He doesn't know what he's saying."

To the man kneeling in the mud he said, "What is your name, my son? Do you belong to the mission?"

"Do not call me son, Francisco. I am not your son. I am older than you. Why, I am old enough to be your father. Hee, hee."

It was then that Padre Uria recognized him. "Inigua? Is that you?" He raised his right hand to the sky. "Praise be to our merciful God in heaven! We thought that you and your wife were lost for certain. I should never have let you leave the mission for the river. What are you doing down here, Inigua?"

"I am looking for Islay." Inigua's haggard head twisted and he looked away towards the river in the distance. "She is here somewhere. Of that I am certain. But I must have missed her somehow. She may be sleeping somewhere along the beach and did not hear me calling her."

He raised his withered arm and pointed. "The river caught up to us and she was swept away. I spent a whole day and night in a tree. Yesterday I had to swim out into the ocean to get around the river. I almost drowned a second time out there. I came ashore and looked for her everywhere. I walked all the way to the Santa Clara River and could not find her. She is probably tired and thirsty, as am I. Today I will cross the Ventura River and search to the west. But I cannot understand how she could have ended up over there. The current flows this way."

Padre Uria shook his head sadly. "I do not think you will be searching any more today, Inigua. It is too dangerous here. There are rattlesnakes and other things. Besides, you are a sick man. Anyone can see that. You are tired and thirsty. I think you had better come with us.

He turned to the boy. "Pablo, give him a drink of water."

His servant, a handsome and intelligent boy, slid nimbly off his pony and walked timidly to the grizzled old man. He held out his leather *bota* of water, in a gesture redolent of offering Holy Communion.

Inigua looked sharply at the boy, his harsh black eyes burrowing into his like those of a bird of prey. Pablo blanched at the scrutiny, but gamely stood his ground, his arms frozen in a gesture of presentation. After a few tense moments, Inigua's look softened. He said, "*Haku*, little man," and took the bota. He tilted his head back and drank deeply.

10

When he was done he wiped his mouth with the back of a clawed, mud-caked hand. He looked up at the priest and said, "I am not going with you, Francisco. You cannot tell me what to do. I am no longer one of your stinking neophytes."

"Don't call me Francisco, Inigua. Call me Padre."

"But do you not remember, Francisco? Five years ago, in 1827. The Mexican government released us from your slavery. They let us go. Hee, hee. Not only that, Islay and I were too old to be of any use to you Spanish scum any more – except to gather wood for your infernal ovens."

The three neophytes gasped. Corporal Sanchez scowled again and very deliberately took his musket into his right hand. They all looked at the padre, expecting him to set them upon the scoundrel. But the padre, who had a reputation for having a very quick temper, only chuckled at this blatant insolence. His companions saw, however, that the spasms that had mysteriously appeared on the right side of his face in recent months, had suddenly grown more pronounced.

"Ho, ho, you call us names," he said to Inigua. "I can call names too, you bastard spawn of a heathen cuttlefish. It is true the upstart Mexicans made the ill-advised decision to grant our neophytes their independence. But, Inigua, you still have eyes do you not? You must have seen that hardly any of your people left the mission. In fact, some have even joined us since then.

"I let you and Islay go to live at the river because you wanted to go there. And no one else wanted that land. And I was happy to be rid of you. You were always a trouble maker.

"But you should know this, my friend, I never signed the Oath of Allegiance to the Mexican government. I am a Franciscan, and a Spanish priest, and I do not agree with their decrees nor do I follow their orders. And I am thinking that now, by God, you must come back to the mission."

"You cannot make me go there, fat boy."

The padre's men could hardly contain themselves on hearing that, but the gray-clad priest on the white burro raised his hand in a gesture of restraint.

"According to mission records, you were once baptized," he said to Inigua. "That means you will always belong to the Catholic Church. Technically, you are still a neophyte. So there is an end to it, old fellow. Ho, ho, ho."

"By the drizzling shit of your overburdened burro," said Inigua. "You damnable Spics are all the same. You think you own everything."

Padre Uria's followers saw the priest cock one eye in mock surprise, and then smile. To their consternation, he seemed to be finding these insults amusing. They restrained themselves out of their love and admiration for him. One of the reasons they loved him was that Padre Uria was not dour and stern like most of the other padres they had known. They knew that Padre Uria was not a frivolous man, however. He took his work, his religion, and his mission very seriously. But he could not help being what he was, a happy, jovial man at heart. He was addicted to pleasantries and jokes, and he loved to laugh. These traits endeared him to them.

Padre Uria's fellow riders could not, however, keep from glaring at Inigua. They had never known another Indian at the mission to dare talk to any priest that way, much less the padre-superior. They were eager to fall upon him.

The padre spoke, "I see you haven't changed your misguided opinions of us since I saw you last, Inigua. You are still the rebel with a tongue as sharp as a skinner's knife. You have learned nothing from your many visits to the whipping post.

"But never mind, poor fellow. Come with us now. We will take you to the mission and bathe you and dress your wounds and feed you. Then you must rest."

"Blessed father," said Inigua, "*beso ma cula.*"

There was a collective gasp. Luis, the alcalde, was the first to speak. "Let me beat him now, Padre. Or, if you prefer, I will wait until he has recovered and can feel it more sharply."

The padre shook his head. "Neither, Luis. Just put him on the back of Felipe's horse and take him to the mission. Felipe, take Pablo with you. See that this poor man is taken care of. Bathe him, give him some clothes, nourishment, and see that he rests. I will send for him when he has recovered."

"No!" shouted Inigua. "Leave me alone. I must find Islay."

"Inigua," said the padre, kindly. "I do not think you will find Islay. And if you were to find her, I do not think you would be happy doing so. Do not worry. I will send people out to search for her. But if she were alive, I think that we would know it."

"Please, Padre. Leave me alone. I must find her."

"No.

"Felipe, you and Pablo take him to the mission. And Felipe, send some riders out to search for his wife. Corporal, you and Luis, come with me."

Padre Uria turned his burro to the west and he and the two men rode on towards the Ventura River leaving Felipe and Pablo to place the feebly resisting old Chumash on horseback.

When the padre reached the river he saw that it was much lower now, though it still ran hard and fast, disgorging great quantities of muddy water and flotsam into the sea. Looking upstream, he saw no trace of the plank bridge that had once spanned the river. This meant Mission San Buenaventura was cut off, possibly for days to come, from any help from her sister missions to the west: Santa Barbara, Santa Ynez, and La Purisima. It also meant that all travel up and down El Camino Real would end here.

Either here or at the Santa Clara River to the east, which was probably impassable as well.

He and his companions turned north at the river mouth and struggled along its soggy banks up the river valley. Not quite a mile to the east, at the foot of the coastal hills, sat the mission complex. The large white church with its red tiled roof, massive front buttress, and soaring bell tower dominated the assembly of low buildings around it. Along the far side of the church extended the long front wall of the quadrangle. It was there that the padre lived. Soldiers of the mission guard were quartered in barracks just to the east of the quadrangle.

To the west of the church lay the *campo santo*, then the *monjerio*, and on the near side stood the long rows of apartment-like adobe dwellings of the single male neophytes. Scattered irregularly around the quadrangle, and at varying distances, were many little structures. Some were square and made of adobe. Others were round and made of tule. Padre Uria and his companions could see the path of destruction the river had cut through the perimeter of the little community. Only those dwellings huddled closest to the mission had been spared.

Other houses and huts had dotted the river valley. They were all gone now. As the three riders continued alongside the river, they looked up at the steep slopes to their right where the hills lined the eastern side of the river valley. They saw where mudslides had filled or carried away sections of the *zanja*, the main canal from the reservoir. This was very bad indeed. Restoring it to service would be both time-consuming and difficult.

The zanja, of course, was connected to the rock and mortar dam at the mouth of San Antonio Creek, some seven miles upriver. The dam, built many years before, walled the creek off from the river. The dam, and the considerable reservoir behind it, was the main source of the mission water supply. Water was directed from the reservoir into the stone-lined zanja which carried it along the base of the hillsides on the eastern edge of the river valley. Cobblestone and mortar aqueducts arching over several lateral canyons continued the water uninterrupted on its way. As it flowed along its long, sloping journey towards the mission (a drop of nearly five hundred feet) water was diverted into a network of irrigation ditches that fed the fields and orchards bordering the river and eventually to those gardens and fields in front of the mission along the seashore.

Near the end of its journey, water for human consumption entered a settling and filtration tank on the brow of the hill behind the mission. From there clay pipes carried it down the hill and into a stone-lined reservoir behind the main quadrangle. This was the mission's primary cache of potable water.

Fray Uria and his men continued up the river valley. They were relieved to see that the orchards and vineyards on the high ground away from the river had survived with only minimal flooding. Everything close to the river, however, was gone. As they rode on, the valley narrowed with each passing mile.

Rounding a bend in the river, the men were shocked to find no trace of the assistencia, or sub-mission, which served the inland Indians and the vaqueros of Rancho Ojai. The Chapel of Santa Gertrudis, near what is now Foster Park, was gone, as were the tule huts of the neophytes who maintained it. The ground where they once stood was swept clean but for a scattering of river rock and odd bits of jetsam.

These revelations were distressing enough, but the men were absolutely overwhelmed when they reached the dam site further up river and saw that it had failed. Until then they had thought mudslides cutting the zanja were responsible for water not reaching the mission. But now they realized the entire dam was gone. This was indeed a major catastrophe. They stared down in disbelief as torrents of water rushed down San Antonio Creek unimpeded into the Ventura River.

The three men knew that the restoration of the water system was absolutely essential to the mission's survival. Without water for irrigation nothing could be made to grow in the dry southern California climate. It was evident, however, that nothing could be done about the dam until both San Antonio Creek and the river subsided. That might take days – even longer if more rain came.

Padre Uria knew he would have to direct his flock to carefully conserve what water remained in the reservoir behind the quadrangle, and in a secondary reservoir two and a half miles north of the mission. He knew that after these reserves were gone, and until the dam could be repaired, the neophytes would have to laboriously transport water from the river itself. And that water was now contaminated. The padre feared another outbreak of cholera if river water was used.

And how, the padre wondered, could they rebuild the dam and repair the canal and irrigation ditches and the bridge over the river, and still have time to plow and replant the fields for this year's crop? At last count there were 668 neophytes to feed, clothe and care for. There was also some forty *gente de razón* to be supported, as well as himself and Father Cuculla, and the half-dozen soldiers of the mission guard.

And how could they spare the manpower from *La Matanza* (the cattle slaughtering season) coming up in June? The roundup must be accomplished somehow, and the branding, the killing, the skinning, the hide-curing, the rendering of tallow. In the meantime, there was all the ongoing work at the mission shops – the carpentry, the tannery, the saddlery, the pottery, the weavery. And then there was the winery, the mill, and the limekiln to operate. So much work, and so few neophytes to perform it all. Of the four hundred-odd males, many were either too young or too old to be of much help. The padre had perhaps two hundred able-bodied men to rely on.

14

Of the 276 female neophytes, again, many were too young or too old to help. Those that were healthy and of working age would be busy with their usual tasks of weaving and sewing, washing and dying, food preparation and child rearing. Few could be spared.

Prior to leaving the dam site, Padre Uria ordered the alcalde, Luis, to follow San Antonio Creek farther upstream and try to reach Rancho Ojai. Rancho Ojai was located in a mountain-encircled valley some fifteen miles north of the mission. If Luis could make it to Ojai he should take stock of conditions there and tell the mayordomo of the rancho to send down all the men and horses he could spare. If possible, the mayordomo should also bring the weekly twenty head of cattle with him. This, along with an additional twenty head from Rancho Piru, was the usual number processed at the mission each week.

When Luis had departed, he and Corporal Sanchez turned their mud-splattered mounts towards home. Padre Uria's head hung low as they rode in silence down the river valley. A leaden depression fell upon him. He felt altogether daunted by the sheer extent of the flood damage and the labor it would require to repair it. He wondered why the Lord had chosen to lay this heavy cross upon his already tired and ailing shoulders. Why, after so many years of devoted and arduous service, had God chosen this time to burden him so? Were he a younger man he could have risen so much better to the challenge. But now, in his twilight years as a Franciscan missionary, it was a struggle for him even to perform the routine, daily obligations of the office of padre-superior. The effort of rebuilding seemed beyond his capacity.

He prayed to God for the strength to persevere.

3

THE MISSION

Having returned to the quadrangle, Padre Uria had a late lunch with Padre Cuculla, his fellow Franciscan at Mission San Buenaventura. Cuculla was younger than his superior, and of a more fervent, serious, and sober demeanor. Lean to the point of cadaverousness, Cuculla had a sallow complexion from which dark, deep-set eyes glimmered with the intensity of a saint or a madman. A taciturn man by nature, he listened closely as Padre Uria apprised him of the extent of the flood damage and the threat to the mission's continued existence. Cuculla was stunned speechless. He made a hurried sign of the cross with a lean, long-fingered hand that vaguely reminded one of a claw.

After lunch the two padres retired to their separate quarters to pray for guidance, and to take their usual siesta. Meeting again later that afternoon over mugs of thick hot chocolate, they were joined by the mayordomo, Corporal Sanchez. The three men worked out a plan for the coming days.

It was decided that until the crisis was over, Padre Cuculla would bear the greater part of providing both the spiritual and temporal needs of the congregation. He would offer holy mass, hear confessions, baptize the newborn, perform marriages, give last rites and preside over burials, as well as provide the daily mid-morning religious instruction for the children. With the help of the alcaldes, he would also oversee the day to day operation of the mission: food preparation, the ongoing work at the *lavenderia*, weavery, tannery, candle shop, etc.

In the meantime, Padre Uria would devote himself almost exclusively to the restoration of the mission water supply, and to the building of new plank bridges. Construction projects, and the organization and supervision of work parties were where Padre Uria's true talents lay. And although these duties were the traditional responsibility of the mayordomo, ever since the uprising at Mission Santa Inez, Padre Uria had been distrustful of mission guards and of the military in general. There was far too much work for Corporal Sanchez to oversee anyway. Besides, Padre Uria had always taken a keen, hands on interest in all mission construction projects.

Padre Uria had over thirty years of experience in building, farming, and animal husbandry. He began his service at Mission Santa Barbara in 1797. He later served at postings in San Fernando, Santa Cruz, Santa Inez and Soledad, before eventually coming to Mission San Buenaventura in 1828. As padre-superior of this last mission for the past four years, he had come to know it well, its people and its resources. With all due respect to

16

Corporal Sanchez, Padre Uria knew there was no one better qualified than himself to direct the difficult job of rebuilding.

It was decided to divide the reconstruction forces roughly in two. One group headed by Padre Uria, perhaps a hundred men in all, would begin unearthing and, where necessary, reconstructing the stone-line zanja that snaked along the steep slopes above the river valley. Once the canal was repaired, the mission's water supply could be restored by installing a *noria* at the dam site. A noria was an endless chain of buckets that would bring water up from the creek and deposit it in the zanja. The padre-superior would have his carpenters suspend all other work at the mission and begin constructing the components of it at once. The pieces would be hauled to the dam site by ox-drawn *carretas* and assembled there.

The steep terrain around the dam precluded the use of mules and a horizontal turnstile to operate the noria once it was installed. That meant the neophytes would have to propel the contraption by treading on a vertical, stepped, wooden wheel. The wheel would pull the chain of buckets up the steep incline. It would probably have to be worked twenty-four hours a day to supply enough water. But the drudgery of such a task could not be helped. Until the dam was rebuilt and the reservoir filled, it was the only way to insure a steady supply of water.

The second group of workers, also about a hundred strong, headed by Corporal Sanchez, would concentrate on clearing the roads, irrigation ditches, and fields in preparation for planting. As each field was cleared it would be plowed with teams of oxen. It was now the end of February. Hopefully, planting could be done sometime in April, and the water system would be functioning sufficiently by June or July to meet the irrigation needs.

Once the river subsided, Padre Uria would draw neophytes from other projects, and with the aid of carpenters and the gente de razón, would rebuild the bridges across the Ventura and Santa Clara Rivers. These bridges were a vital link with missions to the northwest and to the south. Without those bridges, travel along El Camino Real would be severely curtailed. Only men on horseback could make crossings. For the time being, no wagons or *carretas* would be able to pass until the rivers subsided fully, or the bridges were in place.

Padre Uria made a point of telling Corporal Sanchez that he would be ordering the vaqueros from the ranchos, and all able-bodied gente de razón, including the soldiers of the mission guard to assist in the recovery work. Corporal Sanchez eyes widened when he heard this, for he knew it would be a difficult order to enforce. These gentlemen did not believe in working with their hands. They would not take this order well. He knew they considered any work that could not be done from the back of a horse to be beneath them. He felt the same way himself. The corporal saw a difficult time ahead trying to enforce this order. He told the padre he saw morale and

17

discipline problems in the future if this order was given.

Padre Uria replied, "Corporal, as you must surely know, this mission has just experienced perhaps the worst catastrophe of its existence. It is in danger of total collapse. Without everyone's help, this mission just may cease to exist. And then what is to become of you and your men, and the high and the mighty gente de razón?"

The padre went on to tell him that he would write letters asking for help from the other missions. As soon as the two rivers subsided he would put the letters in the hands of vaqueros who would deliver them on horseback. He would ask for help from the three missions to the west, as well as from San Fernando and San Gabriel to the south-east. If those missions sent neophytes to help with the work, only then would the gente de razón and others be relieved. Until then, the gente de razón would just have to swallow their pride. Corporal Sanchez went away grumbling.

At five o'clock, Padre Uria presided one last time over evening devotions in the mission church. The nave of the church was long and high ceilinged, but somewhat narrow, as at all the missions. This was because the width of the building was limited to the length of the timber used as joists to span the ceiling from sidewall to sidewall. At Mission San Buenaventura, the timbers had been cut from huge pines in the mountains above the Ojai Valley. The interior walls of the church were painted and decorated by the neophytes using locally made dyes and paint. Some decorations were applied using stencils, while others were applied freehand with a brush. Candles along the sidewalls illuminated the fourteen canvas paintings of the Stations of the Cross that had been brought from Mexico.

As usual, the barefoot neophytes stood, kneeled, or sat on the tile floor of the nave as the mass progressed. This evening's service was a special mass said for the souls of those who had perished in the flood.

Padre Uria spoke to his congregation from beneath the canopy of the beautifully carved pulpit that projected from the right wall. Behind him, the pilasters of the canopied Romanesque altar were finished in heavily gilded imitation marble. On the wall behind the altar were fixed the sculpted images of the mission's patron saint, St. Bonaventure, flanked by the Immaculate Conception and St. Joseph with the Infant Jesus. The elaborate altar pieces included gilded mirrors, silver crucifixes, and oilstocks. All these were bought and transported at great expense from artisans in Mexico and the Philippines.

During his sermon, the padre-superior reminded the congregation of the Old Testament story he had shared with them the evening before: the story of Noah and the Flood. He reminded them that, just like Noah's family, they must now be prepared to go forth after the flood and honor almighty God by working hard and rebuilding what had been lost. Members of the congregation looked at each other and sighed.

18

Continuing, he said, "There is another tale from the Old Testament that tells the story of our merciful Lord saving a man from a watery grave. It is the story of Jonah and the Whale."

Padre Uria told them the story of how Jonah was thrown overboard by sailors during a terrible storm and was then swallowed by a whale sent by God to save him. After three days, Jonah was cast out onto dry land. Jonah repented for his earlier rebelliousness and became obedient to God's will.

When Padre Uria had finished the story, highlighting its attendant moral, he announced to them what many had already heard by rumor: a flood victim had been recovered that morning.

A subdued buzz of interest hummed through the Chumash congregation when they heard Inigua's name. Most of them knew him by sight, but many were too young to know much about him. They knew that he was one of the oldest of their race, and that sometimes, when he looked at them, his eyes were filled with scorn. At other times his eyes seemed to overflow with pity. Because of this, many neophytes felt uncomfortable in his presence.

They knew that Inigua had left the mission several years ago (an extremely rare occurrence, especially for one so advanced in years), and that he had been living down by the river mouth with his wife, Islay. She was remembered as a weaver of beautiful baskets, and as a knower of healing plants.

The congregation knew these old people were among the few to have known pagan life before the coming of the Spanish. It was rumored among them that the old couple still practiced some of the heathen ways and the mysterious secret rituals. This made the younger neophytes wary of them. They had been taught to be good Christians, work hard for the mission, and to despise all things heathen.

Padre Uria recited a solemn prayer for the departed soul of Islay and the other victims, and then a prayer of thanks for the safe return of Inigua, the modern-day Jonah. God had plucked him from the jaws of death and from out of the clutches of the flood.

Padre Uria did not share his own thought, however, the thought that perhaps God had a reason for sparing Inigua. The padre knew that God sometimes works in mysterious ways. And what could be more mysterious than saving a scoundrel like Inigua?

Concluding the sermon, Padre Uria informed the congregation of the true extent of the flood damage, quelled the many false rumors circulating among them, and emphasized the need to restore the canal system and rebuild the dam as quickly as possible. He told them that tomorrow they were to assemble as usual after breakfast in front of the mission church. They would be given new work assignments at that time.

After the service ended Padre Uria hobbled painfully on swollen ankles to the kitchens to check that the women had completed cooking the evening *atole*. Then he ordered the ringing of Saint Mary of Sopopa's bell signaling that dinner was ready. Under normal circumstances each neophyte household would send a family member with a container to the kitchen. Hot atole would be ladled from the cauldron into their containers to be taken to their homes in the Indian rancheria. The families would dine there, often supplementing the atole with beef (which was always plentiful), fish or wild game, or seasonal produce from their own gardens.

But now, because of the flood, some of the neophytes had no containers to bring and no homes to take them to. Padre Uria directed the alcaldes and regidores to arrange for those who still had homes to be served in the usual way. The homeless were to line up outside the kitchen. As they filed passed the door they were given bowls of atole and a tortilla. These neophytes were then to take their food out into the quadrangle to dine on the walkways under the interior arcade, or simply sit down cross-legged in the garden. They could quench their thirst at the fountain at the center of the quad.

Later, those who had relatives in the Indian rancheria were to try to somehow squeeze into the already crowded domiciles. Those who had no place to stay would be temporarily housed either in storage rooms in the quadrangle, or simply camp out with blankets under the arcade.

When this was arranged, Padre Uria retired to his quarters adjacent to the church to dine with his cats.

4

CURATEL

The setting sun shone through the oaken bars of the guardhouse window and painted striped shadows on the opposing adobe wall. Below, on the hard-packed earthen floor, Inigua lay curled in a woolen blanket, fast asleep. His head rested on a pair of muslin trousers rolled up like a pillow. The old man's eyes began to flutter as a dream came to him.

He saw Islay swimming in the ocean. Her sleek, gray body slipped effortlessly through the water. She looked happy and healthy. From time to time she breeched from the water like a dolphin. In fact, she had the body of a dolphin. Her eyes and her smile were her own, but she had the fins and fluke of a dolphin.

Inigua was glad that Islay was alive, and that she was a dolphin. There was little danger of a dolphin drowning. And dolphins were revered beings. The Chumash people believed that dolphins were their brothers and sisters. Inigua knew well the legend of how that came to be.

His people were created a long time ago, from the seeds of a Jimsonweed plant that grew on Mi'chumash Island – the largest of the Channel Islands, the one the Spanish called Santa Cruz. Their mother was *Hutash*, the Earth Goddess; their father was Sky Snake, the Milky Way.

Sky Snake could make lightning bolts with his tongue. One day he decided to give his children a gift. He sent a bolt of lightning down to the island and so sent fire to the old ones. The people of Mi'chumash Island used this fire to warm themselves and to cook their food. They lived well and multiplied because of this fire, and in time many villages sprang up around the island. But before long the place became very crowded.

The noise of all those people began to annoy Hutash. It kept her awake at night. She decided that some of the people would have to move off the island and over to the mainland. So she made a bridge for them out of a rainbow. The Rainbow Bridge stretched from the highest mountain on Mi'chumash Island all the way across the channel to the mountains of the mainland.

Hutash told her people to go across the Rainbow Bridge and to fill up the coast with humans. So the Chumash people started over the bridge. Most of them crossed safely, but some of the people made the mistake of looking down. They got so dizzy from the heights that they fell off the Rainbow Bridge and down into the water. Hutash felt very bad when she saw this. She didn't want her children to drown, so she turned them into dolphins. This is why the Chumash people always say that dolphins are their brothers and sisters.

And now, Islay was a dolphin. Hutash had saved her too! Inigua was greatly relieved. But now, in his dream, he saw Islay swimming away, swimming towards the place where old man sun settles in the evening. Inigua could not keep up with her because he was merely human. He could not swim nearly as fast as she. Finally, he found himself exhausted and alone, far out in the ocean.

Inigua floated there, resting, drifting, sleeping until he heard the ringing of the Saint Mary of Sapopa's bell at six o'clock. Its gentle knell was calling the mission neophytes to their evening meal. The bell seemed very close to Inigua, as indeed it was.

He opened his eyes and rolled onto his back. The place in which he found himself looked familiar. It had a damp, earthy smell, and hard, straight lines and sharp corners. It was not an Indian place, of that he was certain. Everything the Chumash made was round. Their houses were round, their sweat lodges, their sacred enclosures. They made them so because they understood that power works in circles. Everything tries to be round in the Indian world. But this place was square. It had to have been made by outsiders.

Inigua's eyes were drawn to the fading light in the window. He saw the bars there and realized he was in the *curatel*, the jail. He had been here many times before. He closed his eyes and remembered this last time. He had been brought here after those neophyte dogs had thrown him into the lavenderia and scrubbed him down with tallow soap and stiff brushes. To his credit, the boy, Pablo, had refused to take part in it. By doing so the boy had showed him respect. Felipe had become angry when Pablo refused to help him. He shooed the boy away and called another regidore, the one called Raimundo. Their rough scrubbing with the brushes had been painful, especially on his fresh abrasions. The boy had come back when they were done and brought cloth to bandage his wounds. Pablo had also brought him an old pair of trousers and a coton to cover his nakedness.

The regidores dragged him along to the kitchen where they helped themselves to bowls of pozole, a thick soup made of wheat, corn, beans and meat. They ordered the kitchen women to give Inigua some as well. The women did so. They also offered him a cup of cow's milk, but he refused indignantly. He hated milk. It upset his stomach and sometimes gave him diarrhea. He told them so, and demanded wine instead. Felipe boxed his ears for his presumptuousness. The women gave Inigua water to drink.

After his meal, while the regidores were outside smoking their pipes, Inigua tried to slip away and return to the beach. But that swine Felipe had seen him, caught up to him and knocked him to the ground. Then he and Raimundo brought him here to the curatel. A blanket was thrust into his arms and he was told to lie down and sleep. He had thrown the blanket back in

22

their faces and tried to break free, but they forced him back into the cell and bolted the door. For a long time he had yelled at them to open the door. But they had gone away. He yelled and begged and wept. But no one had come to let him out. Then, because he was so tired, he slept.

Inigua looked down at the thin outline of his body under the blanket. His body felt very heavy. How could that be? he wondered. His body did not look heavy. But it seemed as though the weight of it would not allow him to rise. It was as though his body wanted to settle down in a low place, a place even lower than the floor, a place where he could rest for a very long time. The heavy feeling was not confined to his wasted body, but to his heart, which bore a weighty burden. That terrible image of Islay slipping from his grasp came back to him. When he saw it he cried out as if he had been struck.

A cold wave of self-loathing washed over him. Oh, how he hated himself for letting her slip away. He hated his weakness. It had caused him to fail Islay. Guilt at his failure broke over him repeatedly, like waves over a half-submerged rock. If only he'd been stronger he might have held onto her.

Or if he'd done things differently she wouldn't have been in such danger in the first place. He should have gotten help and taken Islay away before the flood. He could have asked the shepherds in the nearby hills, or one of the farm families along the river. Either one would have helped him. But he'd been too proud to ask.

Inigua had lived along the Ventura River all his life. He should have known better than to build an *'ap* at the river mouth. How many times had he seen it flood in his lifetime? Five or six times at least. How could he have been so stupid?

He should never have left the mission. Life would not have been so hard on Islay if he hadn't dragged her away with him. And she would be alive today, alive and together with him. But now it was too late. Despite the dolphin dream, he knew in his heart that she was dead. He wished he was dead too.

Inigua pulled the blanket over his face, hiding his fractured visage from the dim light. He wept in shame for what he had done, and for what he had not done.

A new thought came to him, a new more dreadful thought to torment him – that of living on without her. The idea of being alone seemed to him unbearable. What would he do all by himself? His children were dead, all his relatives gone, and now his wife. How could he possibly go on? Where would he live? And how would he feed himself? There, under the blanket, fear and self-loathing ate at Inigua like sibling cougars gnawing on a fresh kill.

Utter exhaustion finally dragged him into a deep sleep. It was a dreamless sleep devoid of the pain and remorse that lurked in the shadows, lying in wait for his awakening.

23

5

VAQUERO

Padre Uria had always loved feline companionship. He had kept cats since childhood, and they had always been a great comfort to him, especially since coming to the new world. They were a refuge from the loneliness and isolation of his priestly calling. When he first arrived at Mission San Buenaventura, he'd brought four immense "blue" Maltese cats with him. They shared his rooms at the mission and spent their days hunting mice in the kitchen and storerooms, or stalking gophers in the nearby fields. As often as not they could be found simply lolling about in the garden of the quadrangle.

The padre's servant, Pablo, had already set the table with sturdy plates, bowls and cutlery. Three candles set in a carved wooden candelabrum burned at the center of the table, illuminating steaming pots and platters of food. Several more candles in wall sconces lit the rest of the Padre Uria's sitting room.

His four Maltese cats were placed on two stout chairs across the table from him – two cats sat side by side on each. They sniffed the air and looked with meek but expectant eyes across the table while Father Uria said grace. Pablo stood at the end of the table, his hands folded in front of him and his head bowed. When grace was said, Padre Uria nodded to him to serve the cats. Pablo placed a large plate of chopped meat in front of each pair of cats. The Maltese leaned forward eagerly and began eating.

Besides his usual bowl of atole, Padre Uria also enjoyed a huge slab of roast beef, a half-dozen tortillas with beans and onions, and a great goblet of his favorite red wine from Mission San Gabriel.

San Francisco, the oldest, largest, handsomest, and usually most sedate of the cats, broke the silence of their repast with a warning growl deep down in his throat. Santa Barbara, his chair-mate, shrunk back and lowered her ears. She was younger, smaller, and not so handsome.

"San Francisco!" said Padre Uria, reproachfully, "Leave your wife alone. Share your meat with her. You should know by now, for I have told you many times: Greed is one of the Seven Deadly Sins. I am surprised after your little operation a few years ago that you still have so much fight in you."

San Francisco blinked at him contritely and kept gnawing. More confident now, Santa Barbara eased back to the plate with her head tilted to the side. She pulled a piece of meat off warily, glancing from the padre to San Francisco and back again.

24

On the adjoining chair, their daughters Santa Clara and Santa Inez shared their plate peacefully. White-pawed Santa Clara was Padre Uria's favorite. She was the most lovable, and the one who enjoyed his attention most. And in turn, she was quite jealous of his affection. She would jump up and slap the others in the face with her white paws if they spent too much time in his lap. Santa Clara would follow the padre everywhere, like a dog, if he allowed it. The priest always had to remember to close her up in his rooms when he went to say holy mass. She had embarrassed him in front of the whole congregation more than once by prancing across the chancel to rub affectionately against his legs.

Santa Inez was the youngest and smallest of the Maltese, and the most mischievous of them all. She was always sticking her nose into places where it did not belong, and in doing so had used up more than half of her nine lives. She was famous for climbing trees and not being able to get down. Not only was she the major troublemaker, but she had the distressing habit of disappearing from time to time, sometimes for days on end. When she did, it caused the padre no small amount of worry. But this evening, both she and Santa Clara were quite well behaved.

Padre Uria conversed with his cats throughout his meal, treating them as if they were humans, humans who listened politely, but were too discreet to interrupt his erudite dissertation. He told them of his day's activities and complained to them that he was not feeling too well. His joints were achy, his ankles were swollen, and his butt was sore from all that riding.

Travelers along El Camino Real were often amused if, during a visit to Mission San Buenaventura, they overheard Padre Uria talking to his cats. It only added to his reputation as an eccentric. While a few travelers felt concern over the padre's sanity, most considered him a jolly, harmless sort, fond of a good joke, and fonder still of a goblet or two of wine. But there were no visitors this night. The swollen rivers prevented all travel to and from the mission.

Traveling Franciscans were often unsettled over the fact that Padre Uria named his cats after saints. Some considered it blasphemous. But since he was a long-standing member of their order, had worked zealously in California for so many years, and was nearly ready to retire, no steps were ever taken to chastise him.

Pablo, who had already eaten in the kitchen, was standing in attendance near the padre's heavy buffet table. He had been trained to stand at the ready to refill the padre's wine goblet or dish up additional helpings of food. He was also there to help handle the cats if they became unmannerly at table. Pablo was often amused and entertained by the padre's conversations with his feline friends. And he usually listened closely, for the padre frequently found a way to impart useful information to him during his tête-à-tête with his cats. But this evening Pablo seemed preoccupied. He paid little attention to the old priest's prattling.

Finally, during a lull, Pablo cleared his throat politely and said, "Padre, is it true that the vaqueros will be coming here from Rancho Ojai?"

Padre Uria raised an eyebrow and turned his head to speak around a wad of beef. "Yes, it is true. And others will come from Rancho Piru. They will be here to help us work. They will not like it much, but they will work."

"Why don't they like to work, Padre?"

The padre took a swig of wine and said, "Ha! Because they think the only work fit for a man is to ride horses, and to herd, rope, brand, or slaughter cattle. They are too proud for other work. They think they are too good to work standing on their own two feet. They are almost as bad as the gente de razón. But they will learn differently these next few weeks."

"Even though they will not like being here," said Pablo, "I am looking forward to their coming."

"Oh? And why is that?" asked the padre, scooping a spoonful of atole into his mouth, dribbling it down his chin in the process.

"Because they are great men, those vaqueros. They ride better than anyone. And people respect them. Even the gente de razón. I like their handsome moustaches and their dashing clothes and great broad hats and elaborate hatbands. They look *espléndido* with their shiny buttons, their rugged boots, their sparkling rowel spurs and well-oiled chaps. And I love the way they ride those magnificent horses. They make them fly like the afternoon wind along the Channel. They can twirl and throw the reata better than anyone, and lasso whatever they choose, even a snake. And those vaqueros, they fear nothing, Padre. They are very tough hombres, and they are allowed to carry knives, and sometimes even guns so they can protect the herds from lions and bears. One day I will be a vaquero too – just like them."

Padre Uria had dropped his spoon into his bowl, and was staring open-mouthed. "Ha, ha, my boy," he said. "You certainly have found your tongue tonight. I would never have guessed you wanted to be a vaquero."

"Sí, padre. More than anything in the world."

Padre Uria frowned as he rolled beans and onions into a flour tortilla. He did not much like the idea of losing such an intelligent, quick-learning boy. He considered Pablo an excellent servant. He didn't forget things like so many of the others he'd had. And he was diligent. He did things correctly.

When the cats had finished their meat, Pablo removed the plates and set saucers of milk in their places. The cats began lapping contentedly.

Glancing at the boy, Padre Uria noticed for the first time that Pablo was growing up. It was obvious the boy had too much potential to remain a servant much longer. Padre Uria knew that Pablo was an orphan. He had been born in 1819 to an Indian carpenter called Carlos, and a mestizo woman named Juanita. (Reportedly, his mother was the only child of a woman who had been raped by a Spanish soldier.) Pablo's parents had both died – the former having been killed in a fall while working on the bell tower, and the latter succumbing during the great measles epidemic of 1824. The boy had then lived with an aunt and uncle in the mission rancheria. But they too had died in a fresh outbreak of measles in 1828, the same year Padre Uria had come to Mission San Buenaventura. It was at that time he had chosen the boy as his personal servant.

"How old are you now, Pablo?" asked the padre.

"Almost fourteen," said the boy, trying to stand a little taller, but avoiding the padre's eyes. He had in fact just turned thirteen.

"And how do you propose to go about becoming a vaquero?"

"I do not know, Padre. Perhaps I can ask the vaqueros when they come."

"I doubt they will have much time to spend with you. I plan to keep them very busy. And besides, I don't want you pestering them with questions and keeping them from their work."

The boy's expression showed his disappointment. Padre Uria furrowed his brow in thought, and munched unconsciously on his burrito. After what seemed a very long time to Pablo, the padre swallowed the last of his food. He took a gulp of wine and patted his full belly. The cats, having finished their milk, were busy cleaning themselves.

Padre Uria gave a satisfied burp, and then turned to the boy and said, "I don't know why anyone would want to be a vaquero and spend the whole day in the saddle riding up and down hills chasing cows and eating dust. But if that is what you want, I might be able to help you. Since I am going to retire soon anyway, I suppose it is only right to see that you move along to some other kind of useful work.

"Tell me, Pablo. Where is Inigua?"

Pablo was surprised at this question. He wondered what the whereabouts of Inigua had to do with him becoming a vaquero.

"Felipe took him to the curatel," he said. At this the padre put his palms flat on the table and shot him a look of surprise and disapproval, as if Pablo were at fault.

The boy spoke quickly, "Felipe said there was no other place for him. All the storerooms are full of families who lost their homes. The quadrangle is crowded too. Felipe didn't want to leave him there because he would run away. So he took him to the jail."

Fray Uria rubbed his cheek to make it stop quivering.

"Padre," the boy added, "I think Felipe is very bad."

"Oh? Why do you say that?"

"He was rough with the old man. He didn't have to hurt him the way he did."

The padre frowned, "Felipe hurt Inigua?"

"Sí, Padre, though not badly. But it was not necessary for him to do the things he did. He was very hard on him. He struck him more than once, and I saw him pulling him along by the ear. He nearly dragged him to the

27

curatel." Pablo saw the twitching begin again on the right side of the Padre's face.

The priest drummed his fingers on the table, "Is Inigua all right?"

"The last time I saw him he was."

The padre sighed. "Well, perhaps the curatel is the best place for him right now. At any rate, I am too busy to do anything about it at the moment. Clear the table, Pablo, and then bring me my quills, ink and parchment. I must write urgent messages to the other missions before morning. And tomorrow, Dios mio, there is so much to do."

6

TARANTULA

Inigua awoke shivering in the darkness. A cold February wind blew through the barred windows of the curatel. He reached out and felt for Islay. It would be good to share her warmth. But she was not there. This is odd, he thought. She must have decided to sleep on my other side. Why would she do such a thing? He rolled over and reached out. He felt nothing there but the cold, hard floor. Where could she be? he wondered. Maybe she has gone to make water. I will wait for her.

He was still waiting when the muted light of dawn seeped into his small cell. As the gray light grew, he looked about him. He did not understand what his eyes were telling him. This was not his home. And then, slowly, with an awful sinking feeling, he realized he was in the curatel. Ah, no. Not again. This cannot be! And yet I am here. How have I come to be in this place? What have I done this time?

His once dependable memory now inexplicably failed him. He felt confused, and desperate for an explanation. He clenched and unclenched his fists, then breathed deeply, and tried to calm himself. Slowly, his weary mind cleared, and the nightmarish events of the preceding days came back to him. Ah, no... Now he remembered. He remembered everything. He remembered the flood, the endless searching, and the padre appearing, and the regidore bringing him to the curatel yesterday, and the torment he had suffered. His hands flew to his face. It was all true then. He had lost Islay. He began to claw at his face, gouging deep scratches with his torn fingernails.

"Islay," he moaned. "Islay. Islay."

The pain was intolerable... he must put and end to it somehow. He cast the blanket aside and rose quickly to his feet. He felt a sudden weakness, and his vision blurred. He should not have gotten up so quickly. Red flashes were followed by dark rings closing down his field of vision. He felt himself reeling. He staggered to the wooden door and braced himself against it with outstretched arms. He lowered his head, and in a few moments the dizziness passed. He watched, puzzled, as spots of blood dotted the floor below.

He raised his head and looked out the small slit-window of the door. The jailhouse from which he gazed stood in an open field about a quarter mile from the mission. In the still dim light Inigua saw a wide expanse of muddy field, and the double line of trees that led to the beach. To the left he could just make out the dark expanse of the Channel; to the right, the whiteness of the mission bell tower standing in stark relief against the predawn sky. He put his mouth to the window and cried out, "Hola! Is anyone there? Can you hear me?" There was no answer.

"Let me out! I cannot stay here. Do you hear me?" Again, only silence.

Inigua grew angry. He shouted out the little window repeatedly, and kicked the heavy plank door with his bare feet. The pain it gave him made him even angrier. He banged on the door with his fists. More pain, more anger. He staggered backwards a few steps, and then ran at the door, slamming into it with his shoulder, incidentally striking the side of his head. The impact sent him sprawling to the floor, stunned.

After a time, he raised his throbbing head and looked around the small, square room. His world had been reduced to this: a beastly world of confinement and pain. He could not live in such a world. If there was only a way, he would end his stay here right now. He looked about the bare room. There were two wooden buckets placed in opposite corners. One held drinking water, while the other was used for body waste. He could think of no immediate use for them. Then his eyes fell on the crumpled woolen blanket. "Ah," he uttered.

He crawled across the floor to the blanket. He took it in his hands and tried to rip it. If he could tear off a strip he could fashion a noose and hang himself from one of the two barred windows located high up on opposing walls. Inigua pulled as hard as he could, but try as he might, he could not render the blanket. He was too weak, and the blanket was new and tightly woven. He tried to gnaw at it, but it was too strong for him. He howled in frustration and defeat.

It was then that he heard the Angelus bell begin to chime from the mission tower. That infernal bell always rang at sunrise, calling the neophytes to morning mass. So began each day of life for the mission Indians. Inigua knew he could not bear another day of it, not life in this room without Islay waiting for him to get out as she had always done before. He wanted very much to die. But how? If he could will it, he would. But he had not the power to will it. He must think of another way.

The taste of the wool blanket made Inigua aware of his dry tongue and parched throat. He realized now how terribly thirsty he was. Here was yet another agony in a world that he had no use for. How he wished he could think of a way out of it. It might take some time to think of a way. But now he must do something about this thirst that was consuming him. It would be a good thing to drink, and perhaps then he could think more clearly.

He crawled over to the water bucket, and, lifting it shakily in his two hands, drank greedily from the rim. He paused to catch his breath, and then drank some more. As he was lowering the bucket back towards the corner, he saw something dark moving there. He set the water bucket aside, and peered down into the murky corner. Tilting his palm to reflect the light into the corner he saw the dark outline of a large spider cowering there. It was a tarantula.

"Ahhh," Inigua uttered with a malevolent shrewdness. Bending forward, he said in a low, confidential tone, "Haku, my little dusky friend. I see you are not quite full grown. What are you doing down there? You were hiding behind the water bucket, were you not? You must be thirsty too, eh? Or were you just waiting there for a moth or a cricket to come along? You were going to pounce on it, eh? And pierce it with those venomous fangs of yours? Ah yes, those venomous fangs. Hmmm, venom.

Inigua rubbed his jaw, and said, "I apologize for having to say this, my little hairy friend, but I think it is time for you to leave this life. For as you would eat, so shall you be eaten. Although you are not yet fully matured, I humbly ask you to give your life up to me. Believe me when I say, it is sometimes better to depart sooner than you like rather than to overstay your welcome. If you give your life to me, I will give mine in return. That is a fair trade, is it not? I thank you now for helping me satisfy this unholy hunger of mine. Come here, my little friend."

Inigua cupped his hands and trapped the tarantula in the corner. He clasped it about the abdomen between the thumb and forefinger of his right hand. As the hairy black legs splayed and waved, Inigua raised the spider up to the light and held it before his face. He looked into the multiple, glossy-orbed eyes, the two in front and the three on each side. He cocked his head to listen as the infuriated tarantula ground its jaws. Inigua dropped his gaze to the two curved and glistening fangs. The spider desperately began sweeping its legs across its underbody, and in doing so cast tiny black hairs up into Inigua's face, causing his eyes to wink and burn.

Inigua rubbed them with his free hand, and then angrily stuffed the tarantula in his mouth. It tasted both musty and bitter. The bristly body hairs stung his mouth and tongue. He could not bring himself to chew it, but resolved to swallow the spider whole. He felt the animal struggling as it slid down his gullet. Then Inigua felt a quick, sharp pain in his throat. It caused him to gag involuntarily. He could feel the creature pushing downward with its legs, attempting to back its way out. But Inigua was not to be outdone. He raised the water bucket to his lips and washed the beast down his throat and into his shrunken belly.

7

WATERWORKS

Padre Uria sat on a stool near the fountain, his chin angled toward the rising sun. His face was lathered with soap, and Pablo stood next to him, carefully gliding a straight razor up his chubby neck and under his jaw.

"I will be very busy today, Pablo. I am taking men out to work on the zanja. You must help me get ready. Ouch!"

"I'm sorry, Padre," said Pablo, "but your chin moved at the wrong time."

"Be more careful, you whelp. Now listen, I am meeting with mayordomo and the alcalde shortly. As soon as I am shaved, go to the kitchen and bring breakfast for us all: atole, bread, cheese, fruit, and some hot chocolate. And don't forget to bring milk for the cats."

When Pablo was done, the padre rinsed his face in the fountain. Then he took the cloth from Pablo's shoulder and wiped his face.

Drying his hands, he said, "You have my permission to absent morning mass. Please pray silently by yourself. And be sure to pray for our success in restoring water to the mission. After breakfast, go back to the kitchen and have them pack me a nice lunch. I will not be returning to the mission at midday. Then come and help me pack some things, including a blanket and my pillow. I will take my siesta in the field if I can find a nice shade tree."

Just then four lean, leathery men entered the quadrangle. They wore broad-brimmed hats, colorful short-waisted jackets and flared pants that hung over their boots. On seeing the padre they doffed their hats respectfully.

"Ah, good," said the padre, "the vaqueros are here."

"Buenos dias, *hombres*!" he called to them. They mumbled polite greetings.

"Come this way," he told them. "The letters are ready."

Pablo gazed at them with open admiration as they approached with a bowlegged swagger that caused them to tilt from side to side like ships on a rolling sea. Pablo loved the jingle of their spurs and the clomping of their heavy boot steps echoing along the hallway. He noticed that two of the men bore evidence of the hazards of their trade – one walked with a decided limp, while the other appeared to be missing a thumb.

The padre called to Pablo, "Hurry up, boy, to the kitchen. Don't just stand there dawdling." The boy turned away reluctantly.

Fray Uria hurried to his sitting room. As the men approached the door, he said, "Wait here." A minute later he emerged with five sheets of

32

paper, each folded twice and fixed with a waxen seal. Each letter was addressed to a different mission.

Handing three of the letters to one of the men, the padre said, "Ramon, you and Antero ride west along the beach. Deliver these letters to Santa Barbara, Santa Ynez, and La Purisima. Ride together as far as Santa Barbara, and then split up. One of you go on to Santa Ynez, and the other to La Purisima. Ride as fast as you can, and do not linger on the trail or at the missions. Put each letter into the hands of the padre-superior. I have explained everything in writing. If the missions can send neophytes to help us, lead them back here as soon as possible."

The padre handed two letters to another man. "Juan, you and Conrado ride east. Take these letters to the padres at San Fernando and San Gabriel. Do the same as I told these others, and then get back here, pronto.

"Any questions?"

"Sí, Padre," said Ramon, as he squinted at the handwriting on the letters. "I…well, none of us can read. How will we know which letter belongs to which mission?"

"Look on the back of the letters, *pendejos*," said the padre, irritably. The vaqueros did as they were told. On the back of each folded page the padre had drawn the cattle brand of the rancho belonging to that mission. "Ah," said Ramon, "I recognize this one. It belongs to Santa Ynez."

"Bueno," said the padre. "Do you all recognize these brands?"

The vaqueros studied them and nodded.

"Very well. I am entrusting you men with an important task. Do not fail me, or you will find something unpleasant waiting for you when you return. Do not soil these letters, and do not lose them. Carry them in your saddle bags. Put the spurs to your mounts, and report to Corporal Sanchez as soon as you return. Tell him everything you have learned. He will report it to me. *Comprende?*"

"Sí, Padre," they said in unison.

"Good, then it is time to go," he said. "*Adios*, my valiant riders. *Vaya con Dios*." Here the padre raised his hand and made the sign of the cross over the bowed heads of the horsemen.

A short time later the padre met with Corporal Sanchez and the alcalde Luis. They dined together as they finalized their plans for the day. Pablo had done all that had been asked of him, and now he helped the padre ready himself. When his preparations were complete, Padre Uria bid a lengthy and affectionate farewell to his cats. He then had the boy help him carry his things out to the front of the mission where his white burrow awaited.

On the way, the padre said to him, "After you have finished all your chores today, I want you to go to the curatel and see how Inigua is getting on. I am worried about him."

33

"But Padre, I must attend school this morning, and this afternoon as well."

"Never mind school. You already know how to read and write. If you are to become a vaquero you have no need of further schooling. I have informed Father Cuculla.

"Make sure that Inigua has plenty of water. And see that he has something to eat. Tell him I will send for him when things settle down around here. Maybe tomorrow or the next day. Come to me this evening and tell me how the old fellow is getting along."

By the time the St. Peter's bell rang at nine o'clock the padre and his work crews were ready to depart. Assembled in military marching order, the Chumash workers were barefoot and wore only *taparrabos*. The mild day and the muddy work to come made other clothing superfluous. Many of the men carried shovels, hoes, and picks over their shoulders like rifles. Others carried wooden buckets for earth moving, or large botas of drinking water. The padre mounted his white burrow and led a crew of men up the steep switchback trail that mounted the hill behind the mission. Their destination was "*El Caballo*," the settling and filtration tank of the mission water system. El Caballo was named for the horse-head shaped waterspout connected to the tank's control box.

Alcaldes and regidores led a second, larger work party. They headed west around the hill and then north up the river valley. Groups of men from this second party would work on clearing the secondary reservoir two and a half miles north of the mission. Others would fan out along the zanja, clearing mud from the canal and preparing the groundwork for the repair of damaged sections.

Meanwhile, Corporal Sanchez had broken his men into small work crews and sent them out to begin the tedious and dirty work of clearing roads, paths, and irrigation canals. Each crew would be supervised either by a soldier from the mission guard or a gente de razón.

The padre's crew would start by cleaning and restoring the filtration tank and then move north along the zanja, clearing, cleaning and repairing until they joined with the other group working south. Work at the dam site would have to wait until the creek and river subsided.

Padre Uria never ceased to marvel at the ingenuity of the mission water system. It had been designed by Father Pedro Cambon, a Franciscan priest who helped Junipero Serra found Mission San Buenaventura fifty years before. Padre Uria knew that Cambon had learned how to build water systems by consulting a Spanish translation of a series of books by the ancient Roman architect Vitruvius: "The Ten Books of Architecture." Besides explaining how to design and construct water systems, one of these books described the process for making 'Roman Cement,' an incredibly strong and long-lasting form of concrete. Roman cement and river cobblestones were used to construct the dam, parts of the seven mile-long

34

zanja, the aqueducts, El Caballo, and the storage reservoirs. Padres Vincente de Santa Maria and Francisco Dumetz supervised Chumash Indians in constructing the water system. [The complex system was so well designed and built that it lasted for over seventy-five years until finally destroyed by mudslides during the famous sixty-day deluge of 1862.]

Padre Uria knew that El Caballo, the large settling and filtration tank on the brow of the hill behind the mission, was a vital element of the system. Housed in a concrete and brick building shaped like a short loaf of bread, El Caballo was fifteen feet long by eight feet wide and eight feet tall. The tank's purpose was to filter water for domestic use. The loaf-shaped building kept the tank free of wind-blown debris and out of the weather. It also kept the interior dark, thereby eliminating the growth of algae in the tank. The bottom of the tank held a mixture of charcoal and crushed granite through which the water filtered. Clean water left the settling tank via underground terracotta pipes that carried it to the mission reservoir, fountains, and to the lavenderia where Indian women did laundry.

Attached to the western corner of the main "loaf" was a smaller loaf-shaped control box. Water from the zanja entered the control box from whence it filled the tank. Excess water in the control box gushed from the horse-head spout and entered a basin that led to canals and pipes where gravity carried it down the hill to mission fields and gardens.

* * * * *

When the clamor and confusion of the work parties' departure eventually subsided, Pablo returned to the padre's quarters. He carried the dirty dishes to the mission kitchen, and then went back to clean and tidy the apartment. When he was done, Pablo stepped out into the quadrangle to enjoy the soft morning air. A mild winter sun shone down on the quiet, empty garden. All the neophytes were out working, and the children were at work or in class with Padre Cuculla. Pablo could hear the gentle sound of water dripping in the fountain, and the twittering of birds as they flitted about the fruit trees and shrubs. A rare moment of peace had settled over the usual bustle of the mission.

Pablo was cheered by the quiet beauty of the day. He felt elated too at being free of all his petty chores and obligations. All but one, that is. He must still pay a visit to that renegade Indian, Inigua. The thought of it darkened his mood somewhat. He was not looking forward to it. Inigua was an angry and dangerous person. He scared Pablo. But even as the boy resisted the idea of visiting him, he felt a strange pulling at his heart at the thought of the old man lying alone in the darkened curatel mourning his wife. Pablo was all too aware of what it was like to lose someone you loved.

He remembered seeing Inigua on the beach the other morning – how ravaged and tortured he looked. The sight of him had shocked Pablo. But he

35

was even more shocked at how the old Indian had spoken to the padre. He had never heard anyone talk so insolently to a priest. He knew that if Corporal Sanchez had had his way that day, he would have shot Inigua dead on the spot. Pablo didn't understand why the Padre was so fond of Inigua, or why he was so indulgent of his disrespect.

But Pablo had to admit that he was oddly attracted to Inigua as well. He was like no one else the boy had known. It was obvious that Inigua had been punished often in his life. Pablo remembered watching as Felipe and Raimundo were scrubbing him down in the lavenderia. He saw the awful scars laced across Inigua's back. He must have been whipped many times to be scarred so deeply. Pablo wondered what he had done to deserve such punishment.

This spurred Pablo's curiosity. He wanted to know what Inigua had done, and why he was the way he was. It was obvious to him that there was something very unique about Inigua. Pablo wondered what it might be. Perhaps it is his wildness, his rebelliousness. Giving it some thought, he decided that, no, it wasn't Inigua's wildness that appealed to him. Maybe it was just the way he held himself. It was something that had nothing to do with what he did or said. It wasn't anything that you could explain. There was pride there, and a kind of dignity and grace that dwelt alongside a good deal of courage. Pablo could still see Inigua standing there on the beach and challenging the four men on horseback who wanted to take him away. Pablo's heart went out to him.

8

ISLAY

Inigua felt a great weariness. He lay down on his back and covered himself with the blanket. He rested his head on the floor, laced his fingers together over his thin frame, and settled down to die.

Though his mouth and throat still prickled and burned, the tarantula now lay at peace in his stomach. Inigua closed his eyes and murmured, "Wait a little longer, Islay, and I will join you on the journey to *Shimilaqsha*."

Like the Chumash of former days, Inigua knew that Shimilaqsha, the Land-of-the-Dead, lay across the western sea. It was a happy place where food was abundant. The people spent their time singing and dancing and feasting, and they never got old. But Inigua also knew that before beginning their journey to Shimilaqsha, the spirits of those who had died continued to inhabit the land of the living for several days. During that time they visited the places they had known in life. Afterwards, they traveled up the coast to the cape that the Spanish named Point Conception. From there they journeyed west across the sky-path, the Milky Way, to Shimilaqsha. Inigua felt certain that Islay, his long-suffering wife, was still lingering hereabouts. She might even visit this place, for she knew it well.

But then, to his sudden chagrin, he recalled another, darker, memory. According to Chumash legend, those who die of drowning are not allowed to enter Shimilaqsha. They are consigned to wander the sea for eternity, swimming endlessly, never to touch land again.

He forcibly dismissed this memory from his mind. It was too bleak even to consider. Now that he was in the last moments of his own life, he would rather think of Islay as she once was. He would rather think of the times they walked the earth together.

He remembered the first time he ever saw her, when he was very young. It had been up along the Ventura River, near the place called *Aw'hai*, the mystical, mountain-embraced valley some four or five hours walk from the coast. He and a small group of other boys from his village were returning from their coming-of-age ceremony, which had taken place in a secluded canyon high up in the headwaters of the river. Several shaman, members of the priestly 'antap society, had accompanied them. They were following the Indian path bordering the river that led down to the coast and their home in *Shisholop*. Traversing the deep ravine, they saw smoke rising from the cooking fires above the village of *Matilija*. The village was located on a wooded slope above the river basin.

The sight of the smoke and the thought of food made the boys' mouths water, for they had not eaten in a handful of days. They had been taught that one must fast before undergoing the coming-of-age ceremony. It was a vital part of the ritual.

They saw a group of young girls, accompanied by a few old women, walking from the direction of one of the side canyons. As the two groups neared one other, the most beautiful girl Inigua had ever seen came into view. She, like the other women, wore only a milkweed waist-belt from which depended two scant deerskin aprons, one in front and one behind. Her budding breasts peaked out from behind the long, dark hair which hung down in front. She wore bangs, which were neatly and evenly trimmed by using the glowing ember at the tip of a twig, as was the custom of her people. Her body was smooth and lithe and strong, and although her hips were still narrow, she swung them provocatively as she walked. She looked radiant and in high spirits. When the two groups drew close, her eyes met his. She smiled, showing perfect white teeth. He knew even before she smiled that he had to have her, and that one day she would be his wife.

The older 'antap men gave a friendly greeting to the party of new women, and then spoke with the older 'antap women with them. They learned that the girls had just undergone their own coming-of-age ceremony, and that they lived in Matilija. The 'antaps of Matilija invited the new men and their shamans to stop at the village. They would be given food and allowed to rest. The men readily agreed.

Inigua managed to maneuver himself so that he walked close behind Islay as she mounted the steep Indian path that led to the village. When she glanced back, he smiled at her and said, "Haku, lovely one. What is your name?"

She grinned, but answered saucily, "My name is my own, stranger."

"Forgive me," he said. "That was disrespectful of me. My name is Inigua. I come from the village of Shisholop."

"You give your name readily. You can call me Islay."

"You are a woman now?"

"Yes. And you are a man."

"When you drank the *Momoy*, did you sleep? And did you dream of your totem?"

"Yes, I slept. And I dreamt of a Grizzly bear."

"Ah, that is a powerful being."

"I think I dreamt of a Grizzly because I was afraid before the ceremony; and bears always frighten me. There are many of them around here, and in the valley and hills of Aw'hai. Last summer and fall they threatened us many times when we were out gathering. They don't like us because we eat the same food as they. One time my family's dogs saved me from being killed. If it weren't for them I would not be here today."

"I am glad you are here. You are too pretty to die."

"Oh, go on, you flatterer. You boys from the coast have such watery tongues. What totem did you dream?"

"I dreamed of a dolphin. I don't know why."

"I think I do."

"Why?"

"Perhaps you are like a dolphin. You are obviously clever, and your body is sleek like a dolphin's. And you seem to have that silly grin of theirs on your face all the time. You are probably graceful in the water, although I have not seen it. Something tells me you are mostly good, but can also be very bad."

Inigua blushed. "How can you know these things?"

"I can see what is there for all to see if they will only look. Come to my family's *'ap*, young man, and I will give you a bowl of acorn soup. You look half starved. It is obvious you sons of fishermen don't know how to feed yourself when away from the sea."

Later, in the late summer of that year, she and others of her village traveled down to Shisholop to escape the heat of the inland valley, and to trade acorns and venison for fish and other products of the sea. Sometimes they traded for *ponca*, the shell bead money that was then the common currency. They would use this ponca to trade with Indians further inland. Her clan had stayed for several weeks in Shisholop, feasting on seafood and dancing and enjoying the cool of the coast. Inigua had found ways to spend time with her every day. And then there were the evenings. Yes, the evenings. The thought of them made Inigua smile now.

His throat was beginning to swell where the tarantula had bitten him. His tongue too was fat and unwieldy. He was finding it a somewhat difficult to breathe. But he told himself to just relax. After all, there was no need to get excited. This is what he had wanted: an end to the suffering and unbearable loneliness. He concentrated on breathing slowly and deeply. Other than the irritation in his mouth and throat, Inigua felt quite calm and content. All the pain that he felt in his body and spirit would soon be gone. He was still very tired however, and, quite unintentionally, he dozed off.

There was a dense fog hugging the coast, and he found himself walking along the misty shore. He saw a figure moving along up ahead. He quickened his pace to catch up. When he got close, the figure turned to face him. It was Islay! The sight of her brought such joy and relief in his heart. He wanted to go to her at once and hold her in his arms. But she looked back at him sternly and held up her hand, indicating that he should stop. She held his eyes in her own and shook her head solemnly. He could tell she did not want him to go with her. She lowered her hand and made a sweeping motion with her fingers, indicating that he should go back. He felt so sad when he saw that. His sadness produced a sympathetic smile on her face. They knew each other's expressions so well. He knew what she was trying to tell him: that it was not his time, that life was not over for him, that he still had things to do

39

on this earth, that he had to go back. From the expression on her face he could tell she still loved him, and that she wanted him to be brave. He felt better when he saw that, and he could think of nothing to do but turn back.

As he returned along the shore towards the land of the living he heard her voice call after him, "Do not worry, my love. Be patient. I will send you a gift; and a task to perform. And I will wait for you in the sea. It will not be for so very long, my love."

Saint Mary of Sopopa's bell began to peel. Inigua opened his eyes and studied the angle of sunlight through the oaken bars. It was noontime. He was shocked. How could he have slept this long? And how was it that he was not dead? He heard his stomach growl. He knew it was not the tarantula. It was hunger.

Inigua realized that for now he must go on living. The tarantula had not killed him, and Islay did not wish it.

Suddenly, he heard a voice outside the curatel, calling his name.

"Islay?" he answered, in a cracked and raspy voice. "Is that you?"

"No, señor. It is I, Pablo. I have come to visit you. Where is the guard? Is there no one here but you?"

"I know of no one here."

"All the soldiers must be out with work parties. Your voice sounds terrible. How are you, Viejo?"

"I am...I am alive."

"I have brought you food. And something to drink. It is a tea made from sage and the bark of willow. It will ease your pain, if you have any."

"I have it. Give me the tea."

"The door is locked, senor, and I do not have the key. I will pass it through this window."

Pablo poured some tea into a shallow cup and set it on the slit-window of the door. A gnarled hand grasped the cup and drew it into the dark interior. He could hear the old man slurping and gagging on the still-warm tea.

"You don't sound well, Viejo. Are you all right?"

"I will live. Have you seen Islay? Was it she who sent you?"

"Islay? No. It was the padre. He is worried about you."

"Hmmph. Tell that old *cabrone* he has no right to keep me here."

"I cannot carry such a message. He only wants to keep you safe."

"Why?"

"I do not know."

"What food do you have?"

"I have a small pot of pozole. Hand me your cup and I will put some in there."

Inigua drank the rest of the tea and passed the cup through the window. "How long will I be kept locked up in this place?"

40

"The padre said he will send for you when he is not so busy. He is out working on the zanja as we speak. He is also occupied each evening writing letters and talking with Corporal Sanchez and Padre Cuculla and many others."

Pablo filled the cup with pozole, a thick soup of vegetables and shredded beef. Inigua grasped it eagerly and pulled it inside. Pablo could hear him slurping the soup.

"I will rot in this place before he is no longer busy."

"I do not think so, señor. He wants to talk to you."

"Why?"

"I do not know."

"You do not know much, do you?"

"I am only a boy."

"That is no excuse." Pablo could hear the old man eating again.

After awhile the prisoner said, "I am sorry I spoke so. I do not mean to sound ungrateful. You are a good boy, I think, and I thank you for bringing the food, and the tea. The tea was good. My throat feels better already. Do you have any more?"

"Si, señor." Pablo added more tea to the proffered cup. "Are you sure you will be all right? You sound bad."

"I will live. There seems to be something I must do."

"What is that, Viejo?"

"We shall see. First I must get out of here, and then we shall see."

9

WINE

By the following evening Inigua was feeling stronger. Ever since his unholy communion with the tarantula, he had done little but rest and eat the food Pablo continued to provide. He now lay on the floor of the curatel with his hands folded behind his head, listening to the distant chiming of the De Profundis bell. He knew it must be eight o'clock. That particular bell, with a distinctive and plaintive voice all its own, rang every night at this time. It warned the neophytes the main gate was closing. Curfew was now in force and it was time for all to retire to their quarters – all but the mission guards, who would soon be making their rounds.

In the silence following the sounding of the bell, Inigua heard footsteps, the rasping of a key in the metal lock, the sliding of a bolt, and then the dry grate as the jailhouse door opened. He raised his head and watched a flickering candle approaching out of the dark. Behind the candle smirked the face of the Indian regidore, Felipe.

"So, *Malvado*," gloated Felipe, "I see you are not so full of fight as you were before."

Inigua sat up and glowered at him. It pained his throat, but he managed to hock up a gob of phlegm. He spat it at the man. Felipe saw it coming and quickly sidestepped. The wad sailed through the darkness and out the door. Felipe laughed wickedly.

Inigua hissed, "Get away from me, you licker of Mexican boots."

In the candlelight he could see the sneer on Felipe's face as he said, "I would like to go away and leave you here until your tongue swells up and turns black. Then you could not spit at your betters, nor curse your superiors. But unfortunately I cannot. The padre has ordered me to bring you to him. Do not give me an excuse to beat you, old man. Just come along quietly."

A short while later Padre Uria heard a polite knock at his sitting room door. He had already sent Pablo to bed, so he rose stiffly from his table and opened the door. He found Felipe standing there with his hat in his hand. Behind him in the dim light the padre could just make out the ghostly white halo of hair framing Inigua's head.

The padre said, "So, Felipe, you have returned."

"*Buenas noches* once again, Padre," said Felipe sheepishly. The priest had chastised him earlier for his mistreatment of Inigua. "I have done as you asked. Here is the old man. He came along peacefully, and I did him no harm. Please believe me, Padre, I am not responsible for the condition of his face. He must have done it himself."

42

Padre Uria peered past him at Inigua. The ravaged face of the old Indian looked back at him defiantly. The padre blinked.

"Gracias, Felipe," he said. "You may leave him here. Go home to your family. I will see you tomorrow."

"Si, padre. Buenas noches." The regidore turned and departed without looking at Inigua.

"Come in, *amigo*," said the padre.

Inigua shuffled into the room muttering, "Some friend you are, leaving me in the hands of that lunatic; not to mention locking me up for three days." His voice rasped like a horse plodding a gravel path.

Fray Uria cocked his ear at the sound of it, and closed the door. He motioned the old Indian to a chair at the oaken table. On the table stood a single candelabrum that illuminated a sheet of writing paper and a quill pen, ink, and blotter. The padre had been writing a *respuesta* to the mission headquarters in Mexico City. Beside the writing materials stood a glazed ceramic jug and two matching goblets. The cats where nowhere to be seen. They had been closed up for the night in the padre's sleeping room.

The padre said, "I apologize for leaving you in the curatel, Inigua. I have been so busy with this business of the flood that I had no time to see you. At any rate, I thought you might need some time alone."

"Hmmph," said Inigua.

As Inigua sat at the table, the padre had an opportunity to study his face in the candlelight. The skin was gouged with raw vertical lines which were beginning to scab over. There was a painful-looking bluish lump on his forehead.

"What happened to your face, old friend?" he said. "Did Felipe do this?"

"That overgrown slug? No." Then, waving his hand dismissively before his face, he said, "This is nothing. It is merely the way my people mourn the dead. Do not concern yourself about it."

"Have you had your evening meal?" asked the padre kindly.

"Yes. No thanks to Felipe and the despicable mission guard. I never saw them once. I think they planned to leave me there to starve. I would have too, if Pablo had not brought me food these last few days. Thank you for sending him."

Padre Uria clucked his tongue and shook his head. He had not been aware that Pablo had been taking him food.

Inigua peered across the table at the jug. "Is that wine?"

Padre Uria seemed to notice the jug for the first time. "Oh, why yes," he said matter-of-factly, "I believe it is. But of course you know that neophytes are not allowed wine." His eyes twinkled as he spoke.

Inigua scoffed. "Yes, but you know I am no neophyte. I'm a sick, tired old man, just like you, Francisco. Don't fool with me. My throat hurts. Give me some wine."

The padre chuckled, both at the reply and at the hoarseness of the voice. He shook his head and said, "Ah, well, old friend. I don't suppose it will do any harm to share a little wine with you. It is Saturday night after all. The work week is done and tomorrow is our day of rest." He moved his writing materials aside and sat down opposite Inigua. He poured wine into the goblets. As he did so, Inigua noticed that the padre's hand was unsteady, and that he spilled wine on the table.

"You look like you've had a few already, Francisco."

"So what if I have? And don't call me Francisco. It is disrespectful and rude. Call me 'Padre,' as I asked you before."

"But Francisco is your given name, is it not? You call me by my given name."

The padre sighed. "It is not the same. We are in different positions. Surely I do not need to explain this to you."

"But I am your elder," said Inigua doggedly. "Why don't you call me Señor, and I will call you *Muchacho*?"

"Don't be an ass. You are missing the point entirely."

"Ah, maybe so," said Inigua. "But I appreciate you having me here, amigo. It is good to be out of that cold and miserable jailhouse, here in a warm, lighted room." He raised his goblet with a leathery hand. He paused before he drank, and looked over the rim at the padre. He nodded his thanks.

"*Salud*," said Padre Uria, and they drank.

Inigua rinsed his mouth with the wine and swallowed carefully. Then he smacked his lips and frowned.

"What is it?" inquired the padre.

"This is not the good stuff, Francisco. This was made here at this mission. You must like to keep the San Gabriel wine for yourself."

Padre Uria laughed. "And since when are you such a connoisseur of wine?"

Inigua could feel the wine warming him. "I... well... I used to work in the mission winery when I was younger. Sometimes we had to taste the finished product to see if it was any good. And we had to taste the wine from other missions to see how ours compared. As you of all people should know, Francisco, San Gabriel makes the best wine in California."

"Ha, you old scoundrel. Is there no end to your villainy? And don't call me Francisco. Your manners leave much to be desired. Were I younger I might take the trouble of teaching you not to be so ungrateful of what the church provides."

"You would have no more luck than the others who tried. Padre Dumetz had no luck, nor did Santa Maria, not even the big man, Señan. I was always a slow learner. But my instructors left a deep impression on me. Would you like to see?" He moved his hand to the back of his head and made as if to pull up his coton.

Padre Uria waved his hand and said, "No, Inigua. That will not be necessary. And you know you were never a slow learner. I know all about your visits to the whipping post and all the rest. And I also know that the punishment did little to reform you. Besides, you were getting too old for the post anyway. That is one of the reasons I let you and Islay move to the river. How long ago was that? Three years?"

Inigua's face froze at the mention of his wife's name. He said nothing, but looked away and took another drink of wine.

Padre Uria pressed his finger tips together forming a steeple, and tapped his joined thumbs thoughtfully to his lips. As gently as he could, and in a low, confidential tone he said, "I sent riders out for two days in a row. They searched for miles up and down the coast. Alas, they found nothing. I'm afraid the sea has taken her."

Inigua's eyes fell to his wine and dwelled on the candlelight reflected there. After a long pause, and in a voice that cracked he said, "I know. She is gone now." He turned his face away from the light, so that the padre could not see it.

The priest looked away too, and was silent for a time. He gave the old Indian a few moments to compose himself. Then he said, "I'm sorry, old friend. Islay was a good woman. She used to bring me Yerba Buena and other herbs to ease my suffering. I'm sure that God will find a place for her in heaven." He saw anger flame up in Inigua's eyes, but it quickly dimmed.

Padre Uria drank some wine and observed another moment of silence.

He remembered having met Inigua many years ago on one of his first visits to San Buenaventura. Since then, he always enjoyed conversing with the old man whenever he had the chance. He learned early on that Inigua possessed a remarkable mind, and a memory that knew no equal. Inigua remembered everything, even conversations that had taken place decades before. And he was a whiz at languages. He knew nearly all the Chumash dialects; he could communicate freely with the Yokut, Tongva and other neighboring Indians; and his Spanish was nearly flawless. In addition, Inigua had a unique sense of humor that struck a welcome chord with Padre Uria.

But one of the things the padre could never understand was what made Inigua so rebellious and argumentative all the time. He'd been that way from the beginning. The man absolutely refused to accept the wonderful things the church and Spanish culture had brought to Alta California. He refused to acknowledge their superiority and he refused to accept their Lord God and his son Jesus.

The padre had seen such rebelliousness before in other Indians at other missions. But there was something different about Inigua's, something that gave the padre pause. There was a special kind of intelligence and pride nesting in the craggy old man. There was an inner dignity, even a kind of nobility there, something that refused to be conquered or subdued. That

45

something, whatever it was, and for whatever reason it existed, intrigued Padre Uria. For the life of him he could not understand where it came from.

He knew that Inigua had been baptized long ago, and that he had been trained and employed in many useful occupations during his working years: fisherman, mason, wood worker, leather worker, and most notably, vaquero. But the padre also knew that Inigua had incited trouble among the neophytes, and that he had run away from the mission on several occasions. At times the man seemed to be completely uncivilized and had remained, somehow, irreverent and combatant despite fifty years of mission tutelage. He remained true to some inner self, and he was the most unique neophyte Padre Uria had ever known.

Twenty years ago, Padre Uria would not have felt the same interest, curiosity, or compassion for the man. He would not have cared why this Indian was acting insolent and rebellious. He would simply have turned him over to the mission guards to be shackled, or placed in stocks, or flogged, or even killed if that was what it took. That would have solved the problem. The missions could ill afford to let one bad Indian undermine the whole process of conversion, education, and training of the great heathen masses. The mission's goal had been to convert the Indians, create useful productive citizens of them, and to secure Alta California and everything in it from interlopers, particularly the Russians. All of this was designed for the greater glory of God and Spain. And, for the most part, they had succeeded.

But now, with a long and productive missionary life swiftly drawing to a close behind him, Padre Uria was becoming more reflective, more philosophical. And the painful ailments from which he suffered in recent years had given his usual merry disposition a more serious bent.

The padre was amazed that the old man sitting before him now was in as good a condition as he was, despite the self-inflicted wounds. He knew that he himself would never have survived the ordeal Inigua had undergone. The Indian certainly looked tougher than he had several mornings ago, but he was obviously still suffering from exhaustion and grief.

When the padre saw that Inigua had recovered somewhat from the unhappy reminder of Islay, he said, "I have a favor to ask of you, Inigua."

"A favor? Of me? What could I possibly do for you?" He took a drink of wine.

"Two things, actually. One, I want you to spend some time here at the mission. I want you to spend a little time with me."

Inigua looked at him suspiciously.

The padre said, "I just need someone I can talk to, that's all. I want to talk to you."

"Talk? To me? Are you getting soft in the head, Francisco? What could you and I have to talk about? Why don't you talk to Cuculla or to those blasted cats of yours?"

"I do talk to them. But I want to talk with you. Everyone else just wants something from me, or expects something from me. I know you don't want anything from me, except for wine apparently, and you don't expect anything from me but the worst. We are both getting older, my friend. We see things differently now. I am curious about you, and I want to know what you think about things."

"Why?"

"Never mind why. That is only the first thing I ask of you. The second is that I want you to live here in the quadrangle and look after my servant, Pablo. He has his own room over there on the north side. It is sunny and warm there. You two can share it."

"Live here? No thanks."

"You must. I insist."

"*Mierda.* Why this boy?"

"He is an orphan, and a mestizo. His parents died some years ago."

"Do I look like a nurse maid? Give him to a woman. There are plenty here who have lost their children."

"He is too old for that. He doesn't need a mother. He is thirteen. I want you to spend time with him. I want you to help him achieve what he wants more than anything else in the world – to become a vaquero. You were a great one once. Teach him what you know."

"Why should I?"

"Because I ask it. And I think it would be good for you too. You cannot take care of yourself much longer. Please, say yes to what I ask. If you do this for me I will see that you have a rawhide bed and a warm blanket, three meals a day, and, from time to time you can share a little wine with me. We can sometimes talk in the evenings, you and I."

Inigua looked at him, and then down at the wine jug. He sighed. The fear and desolation he had felt in the curatel was fresh with him. Here at least he would not have to worry about how to feed himself. He would be looked after. He could do worse. He never thought it would come to this, but here it was.

"I will think about it," said Inigua. "And, perhaps while I think, you can refill my glass, Francisco."

The padre looked at him sharply.

Inigua smiled, and said, "*Por favor*, Padre."

The padre sighed, and said, "You are impossible. I will give you one more serving, but then you must go and sleep. You are still tired, and so am I." He refilled both their goblets.

"Where is the boy now?" asked Inigua.

"He is asleep in his room."

"Pablo is a good boy, I think. Even though he was raised at the mission."

"You like him, then? Does that mean you will do it?"

47

"Perhaps. But I must talk with him first before I decide. And if I help him, it will only be if I am free to do it in my own way, in my own time."

"You don't have that much time left, old man," said the padre. "Nor do I for that matter. Our time is nearly done."

"Speak for yourself, Francisco. I plan to be around when you are all gone." He took a drink.

"You will never see such a time, old friend."

"Oh, no? Then what are these rumors I keep hearing about the Mexican government? I hear they plan to shut down all these missions one day. They plan to return the lands to the people who were here first."

"What you hear cannot be true," said the padre. "And even if the Mexicans do close the missions one day, they would never return these lands to your people. They are too valuable now. But I pray that they do not close the missions. It would be a pity. No, it would be a travesty. All the work we have done. All those long years. All the sacrifices my fellow priests and I have made..."

"I think it is the Indians who made the sacrifices, Padre."

Fray Uria frowned. "Why do you vex me so, Inigua? I don't want to debate this question with you now. I am too tired, too worn out." He took a drink of wine.

"I can see that," said Inigua. "I am not surprised you are tired. You worked eight years at Mission San Fernando, did you not? Then seventeen years at Santa Inez, four more at Soledad, and two so far here. And now with all this flood damage to repair... It is no wonder you are worn out." He took a drink, as if toasting the event.

"Santa Inez was the best," reflected the padre, "despite the problems we had there. I built a whole new mission after the big earthquake destroyed it in 1812. And under my guidance the livestock and crops flourished like no other mission in California. And we had the best workshops. You remember them, don't you Inigua? You came there several times to trade for saddles. We talked back then on several occasions."

Inigua nodded, "I remember." He took a drink.

Padre Uria continued, "But the padre-presidente, he sent me away because of the unfortunate events that happened there, even though they were not my fault. I was sent to Mission Soledad. Soledad: the Siberia of Alta California. It was so difficult there, so lonely and depressing. I froze in the winter and baked in the summer. And the Indians, they were so hopeless. Soledad almost broke me. It broke my health, that is sure." He drank.

"Yes, you have had a hard time of it, Francisco. But not as hard as me."

"You have no idea how hard it was for us priests. We worked every day. We never had time off, not even the Lord's Day. There was always some work to perform. The only time off we had was when we were too sick to work. And for what did we work? Not for ourselves, but for others, and for

48

the glory of God. And we haven't been paid a peso in over ten years. Not since Mexico started their damnable revolution. And what were we doing all along? Working, working, always working. And now, no one seems to care any more." He drained his goblet.

Inigua crossed his arms and said, "I think you have had too much wine tonight, Francisco. You are just feeling sorry for yourself. You had better put yourself to bed. You need your rest, for tomorrow I am sure you have much to do, even though it is Sunday."

"I will put you to bed first, old friend. Come, I will take you to the boy. But you have to promise me you won't run away if I let you stay there."

"Promise? Why certainly, Francisco. I can promise you that," said Inigua, smiling. And then under his breath as the padre was rising, "For what that is worth."

"What was that?" asked the padre.

"Nothing, Francisco. Let us go to bed."

"Follow me. And don't call me Francisco. At least not in public."

10

PABLO

A throaty growl startled Pablo into wakefulness in the early dawn. His first thought was that some wild animal had somehow gotten inside his room. Holding his breath, he cautiously rolled over to face the sound. The growl sounded again, emanating from the single bed against the opposite wall. There was just enough light for Pablo to make out a human form under a woolen blanket. He was bewildered at first, but then he recognized the long white hair and the prominent nose of Inigua. The Indian's head was tilted back and he was snoring loudly.

Pablo let out his breath. How did the old man get in here? he wondered, and why is he here? He quickly donned his trousers and coton. He tiptoed towards the stiff rawhide door and pushed it open. He closed it quietly behind him and headed for the fountain in the center of the quad. He was in the midst of splashing cold water on his face when the Angelus bell began to chime in the church tower. Old Vincente rang that bell every day at sunrise, calling the neophytes to prayer service in the mission church. The blanketed forms of the flood refugees began to stir from their sleeping places under the arcade. They awoke to a crisp, clear winter day.

With cupped hands Pablo slacked his night thirst at the fountain. He looked up when he heard the creak of Padre Uria's heavy oak door. The padre's head emerged from the opening, the fringe of hair around his baldpate in disarray. He ushered his four cats out into the quadrangle.

Looking up, the padre said, "Buenos dias, Pablo. You are up early."

"Sí, Padre. It is because that old man, Inigua, he is in my room."

"Yes, I know. I led him there last night by candlelight. You were asleep, and we did not wish to disturb you. Come here. Come inside."

Once there, the padre told him, "My son, it has been decided that you are to share your room with Inigua for a little while. I hope you don't mind. I want you to spend some time with him. Comprende?"

Pablo was puzzled, but nodded, "Sí, padre."

"Inigua is in a bad way right now. He has lost his wife of many years. He is grieving. I want you to be kind to him, and to help him in any way you can. I know he can be difficult at times, but you will find he is not such a bad man in the end.

"Ay Dios Mio, my poor head. It pains me so this morning. I must do something."

As Pablo went about tidying the padre's sitting room, he saw the priest open his tin of snuff and take up a pinch. He held it under one nostril and then the other, inhaling deeply.

"Ah, that's better," he said. He stood before the wall-mirror and brushed his fringe of hair. He then limped over to the clock and wound it with the metal key.

Looking over at Pablo, he said, "Keep a close watch on Inigua. I don't want him wandering off. He is not to be trusted on his own. He is free to come and go as he pleases, but only if you are with him. If he should slip away, let me know immediately. See to it he eats and drinks plenty of water. Try to get him to take a siesta this afternoon. Don't let him come into my apartment though, and whatever you do, don't give him any wine."

"But Padre, why am I being given this task? I hardly know that man. Even though I feel sorry for him, he frightens me sometimes. He is strange, and I worry that he might even be dangerous. And, Padre, how am I to perform my other duties if I spend all my time with him?"

"Do not pester me, boy. You have been given this task because I want him taken care of. You will be relieved of most of your other duties in order to do so. And, Pablo, do not be frightened of Inigua. He would not hurt you.

"You are excused from mass again this morning. Stay around the quadrangle and see that Inigua doesn't disappear. I will be busy today, despite the fact it is Sunday. I have to finish my report, and will hold a meeting with the gente de razón. I must also make arrangements for a new servant."

Pablo looked at his master with stunned surprise. "Why are you replacing me, Padre? What have I done to displease you?"

"Nothing, you little fool. Don't keep bothering me with your incessant questions. All of this will become clear to you soon enough. And now I must go."

The padre left his quarters and hobbled to the church to assist Father Cuculla prepare for Sunday mass. Pablo dejectedly visited the men's lavatory behind the neophyte quarters west of the *campo santo* (cemetery), and then returned to the deserted quadrangle. All the neophytes had gone to mass. All but Inigua. Pablo discovered him sitting cross-legged in the morning sun, his back against the whitewashed wall of the arcade. The old man's head was tilted back and his eyes were closed.

Pablo called across the deserted square, "*Hola*, señor!" The old Indian lowered his head and squinted at him through the low sunlight.

"Haku, little man," came the gravely reply.

Pablo hurried into the padre's room and retrieved a tin cup. He then locked the oak door with the key the padre had left him. He made sure the cat's entrance, a small swinging door flap at the bottom of the door, was

51

unlatched, and then hurried to the fountain. He filled the cup and carried it to the old man.

"Buenos dias, señor? How are you feeling today?"

"Not bad, from the neck down."

Pablo held out the cup. "Would you like some water, senor?"

"Sí, *gracias.*"

As Inigua drank, Pablo eased down beside him and leaned his back against the wall. It had been a cold night, and the sun felt good. "I was very surprised to find you in my room this morning," he said.

Without turning his head, Inigua said, "You were sleeping so soundly last night you didn't hear the padre and I come in. We saw no reason to wake you. But I am surprised I did not hear you leave this morning. We Chumash are usually very light sleepers. In the old days we had to be. You could never tell when an animal or an enemy might sneak up on you."

He turned his head and looked at the boy. "You are mestizo, eh *joven?*"

"Sí, señor."

"Ah. That is a difficult thing. The Indians do not trust you because you are part-white, and the gente de razón do not accept you because you are part-Indian. It must be hard to be in the middle like that."

"Sí, señor. It is not easy. But in some ways it is not a bad thing to be mestizo. I understand both people and can get along with either one, even if they do not accept me as one of their own."

Inigua nodded. "The padre and I spoke of you last night. He told me you are an orphan."

"Sí," said Pablo softly. "My parents died when I was very young."

"That is a shame. A child needs the love and guidance only his parents can give. And you have no other family?"

"No, señor," said the boy looking down at his toes.

Inigua knew all too well what the boy must be feeling. He closed his eyes and put his head back against the wall. He felt the sadness hanging over the two of them like the shadow of a condor hovering against the wind.

It was some time before either of them spoke again. They listened to the murmur of neophytes repeating the *Doctrina* inside the church. The drone was punctuated by the twittering of birds visiting the fountain and fruit trees in the garden.

Eventually, Inigua said, "I was cold again last night. I am not used to sleeping alone. I slept lying next to a good woman for nearly sixty years. We used to keep each other warm." He put his hands up and gingerly explored his face. Scabs had formed over the scratches, and the swelling was nearly gone from his forehead.

"I can get you another blanket," said Pablo.

Speaking through his hands, Inigua said, "Gracias, joven."

52

After a pause, Pablo said, "Pardon me for asking, señor, but how did you injure your face? I did not see it when I visited you at the curatel. It was too dark inside that place."

The Indian lowered his hands and cleared his throat. "I did these things," he said. "In the olden times, we Indians did hurtful things to ourselves when a loved one died. We cut and burned our bodies, scratched our faces, chopped off our hair, and covered ourselves in ash. Some people broke their own teeth.

"But after the Spanish came to live among us, death came so fast and so often that we could not keep it up. We couldn't bear to hurt ourselves anymore. It made life too painful. Some of our people could not take the constant suffering. They killed themselves, or wandered off into the mountains, never to be seen again. Others just walked around here like empty baskets. Many of the neophytes are like that now. The gente de razón think they are stupid, but they are only empty baskets."

"You aren't going to hurt yourself any more, are you, Inigua?"

"No. I am over that. What would be the point, anyway? It would only make me more miserable than I already am. In the olden times we hurt ourselves to show the people how sorry we were at the passing of a great person. But now, who is there to show? They are all too busy licking their own wounds. And this state of affairs has diminished us all. There is no more greatness among the people."

"Excuse me for saying so, señor, but I cannot agree."

"Oh? You do not agree? You are indeed an outspoken boy. Tell me why."

"Because I do not believe things are as bad as you think. I believe there is still greatness in the world. I think you only say those things because you are feeling sad."

"Have I no right to feel sad?"

"Of course you do, señor. I felt sad too when my parents died. But people were good to me, especially the padre. He became a father to me. He took me in and taught me useful work, and gave me a place to live. He was more than a father. He was my friend. He made me laugh and helped me get over my sadness."

The Indian studied him for a moment, and a faint smile creased his lips. "And you no longer feel sad?"

"Sometimes I do. But I learned not to let it bother me so much."

"I learned that same lesson many times, when all of my family and relatives died one by one, year after year. After awhile you get worn down by that."

"I think you would feel better if you had someone to talk to, señor. Someone who was your friend."

"Oh, and who would be my friend?"

"I could be your friend, señor. Maybe you wouldn't feel so sad then. I know I am only a boy, but I could still be your friend."

Inigua looked away. He was certain now that this young man had been sent to him by Islay. It was the gift she spoke of in his dream. He turned to Pablo and said, "It is kind of you to make such an offer. You have an Indian heart. Perhaps you are right. Perhaps I do need a friend.

"Let me ask you a question, Pablo. Why is it that you want to become a vaquero?"

"I...I...I didn't know you even knew about that. I don't know why. I just do. I have wanted to be a vaquero for as long as I remember. That is why I asked the padre to teach me how to ride when I was nine years old. I am a good rider now. I love to ride."

Inigua gave a noncommittal shrug.

"One of the reasons I want to be a vaquero is that I want to do grownup work. I know I can do it, and I think it will be fun. I want to ride one of those quick, agile cow ponies that never seem to tire. I want to chase those long-horned cattle. And I want to learn to throw a *lazo* better than anyone. I want never to miss.

"And I want to wear dashing clothes and a fine sombrero like those cowboys I see visiting the mission. I want rowel spurs like them, and bright buttons on my pants, and a knife tucked in the back of my belt. I want to be tough like them too, and grow a mustache some day."

The old man smiled. The boy glanced at him and then away, his face reddening.

Inigua said, "It is good that you love to ride, for that is what vaqueros spend most of their time doing. It is interesting that you admire their appearance so much, but you need to understand that vaqueros do not always look so handsome. They don't dress like that when they are working. They only dress up in their fine clothes when they come to the mission because they are trying to impress the *senoritas*. You should understand that appearances are not everything, and that being a vaquero is not always fun. It is hard work, and often dangerous. I know, for I was a vaquero myself."

Pablo's eyes widened and he blurted, "You were a vaquero?"

"Yes, for many years, up at Rancho Ojai."

"Oh, señor, I have been waiting forever to talk with someone like you. Tell me everything."

"I can tell you this, Pablo, and it is something you need to understand: being a vaquero is difficult and dangerous work. I have known many vaqueros who were seriously injured, and not a few who were killed. Some lost their thumb or a finger or two when they lassoed an animal and got them caught between the saddle horn and the reata. One vaquero I knew was struck by lightning, and another killed by a Grizzly. Others met their end in falls, or at the tip of a horn, or were trampled in stampedes.

"But you are right about one thing. It can be fun. Of all the work I did at this mission, being a vaquero was the most exciting. I don't know why, but there is something very appealing about the danger.

"And you are correct in saying that vaqueros are tough. They are either tough or they do not remain vaqueros for very long. What I would like to know is this: are you truly intent on becoming a vaquero, or is this just a game, or a passing fancy, or maybe an excuse for you to get away from the mission? Tell me, please."

Pablo set his jaw and said, "It is not a game for me, señor. I am telling you the truth. There is nothing I want more than to become a vaquero. I have dreamed of it many nights."

Inigua nodded. "That you dream of it is a good sign. Our dreams tell us much. But dreams cannot always be relied upon."

"But I know what I want," Pablo said. "There is no doubt in my mind."

"Perhaps there is no doubt in your mind, but there is in mine. I need to know for certain."

It was getting hotter in the sun now. Sweat began to form on Pablo's forehead. He wiped it away with his hand. "Forgive me, señor, but why do you need to know?"

"Because the padre asked me to help you become a vaquero."

Pablo's face lit up, and he squirmed on his haunches.

Before he could speak, Inigua continued, "I told him I would think about it."

Pablo's face fell.

"I might be willing to teach you. If your desire is as true as you say, I am sure you can learn. But I am not sure you are tough enough to become a vaquero. It is not an easy life."

"I can be tough," said Pablo, squaring his shoulders. "I am also young and strong."

Inigua smiled. "You are not so young and not so strong. Before the Spanish came, we Indians were stronger at your age. We grew up fast, much faster than the youth of today."

"How can that be?" blurted Pablo.

"This much I will tell you: in those days a boy of your age, or a girl for that matter, had learned much. A boy already knew how to make a living for himself off the land or out on the sea. A girl knew all the things a woman needs to know. At your age children went through an arduous coming-of-age ceremony, and thereafter were considered adults. Some were even married at your age.

"But you are still a boy. That much is obvious. You live at the mission. Your meals are given to you. You sleep on a soft bed. You sit on a bench in the mission school learning things like Catholic doctrine and numbers and reading and writing. Most of your afternoons are spent dilly-

55

dallying around the quadrangle doing work that could be done just as easily by a woman. Your legs are weak. Your feet are soft. Your hands are soft. Your mind is soft from not being challenged by the realities of the world. You know nothing a man should know.

"The vaqueros out on the ranchos are the toughest men alive. If you were to go there now, in your condition, they would chew you up and spit you out like a sprig of licorice."

Pablo's mouth fell open and stayed open as he heard these things. He felt tears beginning to form in his eyes. Had his dreams been less vivid he might have sobbed at this blunt assessment of his worth. But instead he became angry. How dare this old heathen challenge his abilities? How dare this withered has-been dispute what he knew in his heart to be true? Inigua knew nothing. Pablo straightened his back and gritted his teeth.

He looked boldly into Inigua's eyes and said, "I am not as weak and soft as you think, señor. I have beaten boys older and larger than myself when they taunted me for having no parents or for being mestizo. I know that I have not done a man's work yet, but that does not mean I don't want to, or that I am unable. I don't care how difficult it is. I will do whatever it takes to become a vaquero. I will acquire this knowledge and toughness you talk about. I will not complain. I will learn all that I need to know. And I will be a vaquero one day. I can ride well already, and some day I will ride better than anyone. If you do not want to help me, or do not have faith in me, I will find someone who does." Then he folded his arms and leaned back against the wall again.

Inigua's eyes never left the boy's as he said these things. He was silent when Pablo finished, though an odd smile slowly spread on his lips. Pablo angrily swept the sweat from his forehead again. The morning sun seemed hotter than ever.

"I am glad you have spoken thus," Inigua said. "Your words are strong. I believe that you will at least try to be tough. I feel more confident that I would not be wasting my time with you. I don't have that many more years left, you know, perhaps only thirty or forty. I would not want to waste any of them."

Pablo smiled at this, for the padre had told him he thought Inigua was seventy-five years old. It was also apparent to Pablo that he had convinced him of his determination, and that Inigua might help him.

"I am very hot," Pablo said to cover his excitement.

"Stay a little longer," Inigua said. "Old people like the heat. Besides, you vowed not to complain. You said you would acquire toughness. You must learn how to take all the extremes of heat and cold. A vaquero rides in all weather and under all conditions. Console yourself by thinking how good it will feel when we go into the shade. It will be a little like the feeling you get when you come out of the sweat lodge and jump in the cool water."

"Sí, señor."

"You must understand that I come from a different world from you, Pablo. You were born and raised at the mission. I come from a world that contained no white men. Life is no longer good and easy like it once was here along the coast. The Spaniards have changed everything, and made work where there was no need for it before. They have made this land a living hell for those of us who are left."

Pablo said, "I do not feel that it is a living hell," as he wiped his forehead again.

"That is because you do not know any better. You do not know how good it was before. You only know what the Spaniards and Mexicans have taught you. I know other things. I know how it was before they came. It was good then. It was very good. It is my hope that those days will come again for the Chumash."

"I would like to know of those old times," said Pablo.

"I will tell you of them. I will do so because I think it will be good for you to know. It is important. Whether you accept it or not, you are a child of the Chumash. Just because you had one white ancestor does not mean you are not Chumash. I am sure your parents and grand parents would agree. Young people should know where they come from. They should know and they should remember. Soon, all the old ones like me will be gone. Then who will know what life was really like? And who will teach the young ones when the foreigners are gone from this place?"

"I want to know these things," said Pablo. "I have always wondered about my mother's people. They and my aunt and uncle rarely spoke of them. They were good Christians and spoke little of heathen life."

"Heathen? Ha! We Chumash had more religion, and lived it more spiritually than any Spaniard I ever met, except perhaps the padres. There are many things these high and mighty white men have forgotten, or perhaps they never knew. But enough of this. Let us move out of the sun now."

When they were comfortably seated in the shade, Inigua spoke. "If I were willing to help you become a vaquero, I want to know if you would be willing to do something for me."

"Of course. I will do anything. What is it, señor?"

"First of all, I want to tell you why I want you to do something for me. We Chumash have always been traders. We have trading in our blood. We like to make bargains. That was the secret of our wealth. Now, if I help you become a vaquero, it is only fair that you help me do something. Does that sound like a fair trade?"

"Sí, señor. But what is it you want from me?"

"I want you to teach me something."

"Teach you? What could a boy like me teach you?"

"Before I tell you, you must promise not to mention it to the padre."

"I...uh...well, all right. I guess...I promise."

"No guessing. You either promise or you don't."

"Sí, señor. I promise not to tell the padre."

"Bueno. Then I will tell you what I want. I want you to teach me to read and write."

"What? But I can barely do those things myself. The padres have been teaching me for years now, but I am not an expert. Why don't you ask Padre Uria? He could teach you much better than me."

"Because I don't want him to know about it. At least not yet. Will you do it?"

"Why…yes, if that is what you want. But why would a…a… man like you want to read and write?"

"You mean an old man like me?"

"Well, I…"

"Never mind why I want to learn. Teach me now."

"Now?"

"Yes. While the padre is in church."

"But you can't learn right now. It takes a long time."

"Not for me. Teach me now."

"But when will you teach me how to become a vaquero?"

"I will speak to the padre about it tonight. If you don't say anything to him about this little arrangement of ours, we can begin tomorrow, or maybe even today."

"*Excelente*, señor! But soon there will be many people here in the quadrangle. They have been staying here since the flood. If you want to keep it a secret, perhaps we should go somewhere."

"Let us go to the beach. I need a bath anyway. Can you get a horse?"

"Sí, señor."

"Bueno. Bring the horse. I will meet you at the front gate. If we hurry we will be gone before mass ends."

11

BEACH FIRE

Pablo hurried to the stables behind the guard's quarters just east of the quadrangle. His pony, *Rojo* snickered with eagerness as the boy quickly fitted him with a bridle and saddle. Rojo was a relatively small horse, but heavy-boned and sturdy. He had a thick red coat, and a friendly, child-like personality.

Pablo rode him to the front of the mission where Inigua was waiting. He found the old Indian standing on one of the whitewashed walls flanking the front steps. Inigua carried a blanketed bundle. The shoulder-high wall proved a convenient height for Inigua to mount the horse behind Pablo. That he did so with such confidence and agility surprised the boy. He had never seen a man of that age move like that.

Pablo turned the pony down the tree-lined lane that led to the beach. The still-muddy road was deeply rutted by carreta wheels. Rojo shied at the uneven footing, and Pablo guided him to level ground at the edge of the thoroughfare. They were half way to the beach when Inigua looked back and saw the front doors of the church swing open and the congregation begin to emerge. Soon after, they heard the ringing of Saint Mary of Sapopa's bell, calling the neophytes to breakfast.

"Don't worry about breakfast, boy. I went to the kitchen and talked with Encarnacion. I have known her for years. I knew her parents too. She gave me some food and water to take with us."

As the boy and the man rode between the twin rows of cedars they smelled the sodden smolder of debris fires. Here and there to the left and right, spires of smoke rose in the clear morning air. The fires looked implausible, burning as they did amid moist green fields, lush with winter grass, weeds, and the spawn of last year's wheat. For the past two days bulky logs and tree stumps had been gathered into piles by harnessed oxen. Smaller chunks were dragged there by horsemen using reatas. The piles were then set ablaze to clear the land for plowing. Leg-sized wood and smaller had been loaded onto carretas and carried off to feed the hungry fires of the mission.

"Is this your pony, Pablo?" asked Inigua.

"Sí, señor. He is 'Rojo.'"

"He is hot-blooded and has spirit. And you sit well upon him. Your body has good position and you sit low in the saddle, as one should. But I would make this observation: few riders understand the extreme sensitivity of the horse's mouth. Much of the communication between you and the horse comes through his mouth. You must keep just the right amount of tension on the reins. Too much and you give him discomfort and send wrong messages. Too little and the horse thinks he is free to do whatever he wants. I would say your hands are a little too far back. Unbend your elbows a bit, and grasp the reins further forward. That's it. See how your forearms now form a straight line from your elbows down to the reins and hence to the bit? Hold your hands about six inches above the pommel. Bueno. Now just remember to move your hands forward and back in time with the movement of Rojo's head, always keeping the same tension on the reins. Bueno."

As the riders approached the coast they heard the roar of massive waves pounding along the shore. Pablo reined in on the bluff overlooking the beach and stood Rojo sideways to the sea. Rojo's eyes grew large, and his ears pricked and pointed at the booming surf. The three figures watched as mammoth swells rolled in one after another off the Santa Barbara Channel. The swells curled around the projecting river mouth and cracked and roared as they fell like giant angry dominoes. They then swarmed ashore in great white masses of roiling confusion, filling the air with a fine mist.

Pablo turned his head and said, "Ay! Look at this, señor. The surf is huge!"

"Sí, Pablo. There is a storm out there somewhere. These waves are her children."

"They are magnificent, señor. I have never seen waves so big. Have you?

"Sí, *muchacho*, many times. Because of them our people did not fish or trade much at this time of year. The weather is too unpredictable, and this kind of high surf can come at any time. It makes it dangerous to enter and exit the sea. My people were very careful about their canoes. They did not want to damage or lose them. Canoes were the key to our wealth."

Inigua scanned the sea and sky. Then he said, "Look there," pointing to the south. "Do you see that low line of clouds forming out there? See how their tops tilt to the side? Soon the wind will rise. It will rain tonight, or maybe sooner."

Looking up at the perfectly clear sky overhead, Pablo said, "How can you tell, senor?"

"I know the ocean. My father was a canoe-maker, and I grew up in a family that lived by the sea. In fact, we lived right there." Inigua gestured behind them to an area along the shore. Pablo glanced over his shoulder but saw only barren wheat field.

"There are signs one can read," said Inigua. "My uncle could read them. He was a fisherman. He would study the color of the sea, and the shape of the clouds over the islands. He would watch the birds. He would smell the wind. And then, if you wanted to know, he could tell you what was going to happen in a few hours, or that night, or in a day. My uncle used his nose quite a lot. He said he could smell weather coming. I never fully understood it. But I took quite a few voyages with him when I was young and I learned a few things. I will tell you of them one day.

"But right now, let us go over there by the river. I want a sweat bath."

They rode along the clay bluff that hung a vertical five feet above the beach. As they neared the river mouth Inigua said, "Stop here, Pablo. See that little cavern down there where the bluff has eroded? That will make a good make-shift sweat lodge. There will be less wind in there, and it is not far from the river."

Inigua dismounted. "Why don't you take Rojo up along the river and see if you can find some soap plant or yucca. You know what they look like don't you?"

"I think so, señor."

"Bring me a few bulbs or roots if you can. Then go get a burning sprig from one of those debris fires. Meanwhile, I will gather wood."

When Pablo returned, Inigua had a large bundle of driftwood stacked at the mouth of the cavern. Inside the cavern lay a circle of stones surrounding a pile of dried leaves and kindling.

Inigua called to him, "Hobble your pony and come down here, joven."

When this was done, Pablo handed him the small branch with a glowing ember burning at its tip. Inigua got down on his knees and applied the ember to the dry tinder. He lowered his head and blew life into the fire. Before long, smoke curled up in the morning air. When the fire was well started, Inigua slowly began adding larger pieces of wood to the blaze.

"Have you ever had a sweat bath, Pablo?"

"No, señor."

"Good. Then this will be a new experience for you. From the very beginnings of the ranchos vaqueros have been using sweat lodges. They build them near a water source if they can. A stream or pond. Sweat baths are the best way to keep clean out there in those dry lands."

The man and the boy sat down near the mouth of the cavern to have their breakfast. Encarnacion had packed beans, carne asada, onions and peppers rolled up in flour tortillas. She also sent along a bota of water.

"Drink plenty of water," advised Inigua, handing the bota to the boy. "Sweat baths dry you out." Pablo looked at him questioningly. He was supposed to be telling *him* to drink water.

Before Pablo ate he made the sign of the cross and bowed his head. After a moment he lifted his head and took a drink from the bota. Then he took up his burrito.

"Do you always say grace before meals?" asked Inigua.

"Always, señor. Don't you?"

"Not the same kind of grace as you. So, you are a good Christian then?"

"Of course, señor. It is the way I was raised."

"Do you believe in the one and only Christian god?"

"Sí. Why shouldn't I?"

"No reason. I was just wondering. I suppose people have to believe in something."

"What do you believe in, señor?"

"Not much any more. All the Chumash deities seem to have deserted us, and I learned all I wanted of the Christian god. I decided I did not like him much. He did not seem worthy of my devotion." Inigua stood up then and went to feed more wood to the fire.

Pablo munched on his burrito and pondered this latest of Inigua's blasphemies. He did not understand how the man could not believe in the holy teachings. And he wondered how anyone could live so long under mission tutelage and not be converted. He was curious too about what god or gods Inigua might worship, if any. However, Pablo wasn't sure Padre Uria would like him discussing religion with this old heathen. He might fall under the spell of something unholy, something that might undermine his faith. He decided not to pursue the subject with Inigua. It would be better to just forget about it. Besides, he didn't want anything to spoil his own mood.

Pablo was happy and excited about being here at the beach. He was at last taking the first steps on the road to his dreams. He felt eager, and yet content, and best of all, free. He relished sitting here picnicking under the warm sun in the midst of the billowing mists and roar of the ocean.

When they had finished eating, Inigua said, "I want to let the fire burn down a little bit now. I put plenty of wood on it." Indeed, a veritable bonfire blazed behind them.

"Why don't we begin my reading and writing lessons now," suggested Inigua.

"All right," said the boy. "But I am curious. Why was it that the padres never taught you to read when you were a boy?"

"When I was a boy there were no padres here, and there was no mission. There were no white men. I was about your age when the Spanish first came to this place. That was in the year they call 1769. But they did not establish Mission San Buenaventura until thirteen years later. By then I was twenty-six years old. I was too old for schooling. But they decided I was not too old to work."

"Oh. I understand now. Well, let's begin the lesson, señor. I remember the way I was taught. We began with the alphabet."

"The alphabet. Ah, good. What is the alphabet?"

"It is system of signs or letters, señor. When you put certain of these letters together they make words. When you put certain words together they make sentences. That is how we talk, in sentences, and that is how we read and write too."

"Whatever you say, little man. Tell me more."

"First you must memorize the alphabet. That is what I did." Pablo picked up a driftwood stick which was about three foot-long. "I will draw the letters for you. There are thirty letters in the Spanish alphabet, señor. The first one is called A." He drew it in the sand with the stick. "It comes in two sizes: a big one and a little one. This is the big one. It is called a capital letter. Here is the little one." Pablo drew a small *a* in the sand below the capital letter.

"Is the big one the parent of the little one?"

"Ha, ha. No. The big one is used to start a sentence, or to begin a proper name. Otherwise you use the little one."

As the fire popped and crackled behind them and the sea roared in front of them, Pablo went on to name and draw all the letters for Inigua. They had to walk a way down the beach as the double line of letters got longer.

"This is strange," said Inigua. "Some of the letters are actually two letters. And look at this one. It looks just like the one that comes before it, but this one has a snake flying over it."

"Ha, ha. That is not a snake. That is an accent mark. It changes the pronunciation of the letter. That letter is an Ñ. By the way, the double letters are treated like one letter." Pablo pointed to each of them in turn. "This is *ch*, and *ll*, and *rr*."

"So these letters can be pronounced different ways?"

"Some of them can. But never mind that now. You must first memorize the letters. Let's go through them again." Pablo walked to the beginning of the line. He pointed and said, "A"

"A," repeated Inigua. And so they went through the whole alphabet again.

"Bueno," said Inigua. "Now it is time for our bath. Come, Pablo, help me close up the entrance to the sweat lodge."

Inigua retrieved the blanket he had brought with him. He placed one corner in Pablo's hand and held on to the opposite corner. He then bent over and picked up a rounded, foot-long stone. "Get yourself a stone like this one. There, that one over there." When Pablo held it in his free hand Inigua directed the boy to help him stretch the blanket out as they walked to the mouth of the cavern. "Put your corner up on the edge of the bluff on your side. I will do the same over here. Now we put the stones up there to hold the corners in place."

When the blanket was stretched tight across the top, it hung straight down with the bottom edge lying on the sand. "Now we anchor the bottom with more stones. That will keep the wind out."

When the blanket was in place to Inigua's satisfaction, the little cavern was enclosed on all sides, with the fire burning within.

"Bueno. Now we begin. Take off your clothes."

"Take off my clothes?"

"Of course. You don't want to get them all smoky and sweaty do you?"

"N...no, señor. I just...well...all my clothes?"

Inigua pulled off his coton, untied the draw string to his trousers and dropped them about his ankles. "All of them," he said. "Don't tell me you are bashful, Pablo, or ashamed. There is no reason to be ashamed of your body. What could be more natural than to be nude? You were not born with clothes on."

"I just feel, well, funny." Pablo looked up and down the beach. There was no one about. He looked up on the bluff above them and saw his pony looking down at him, its head tilted as if pondering these strange goings on.

"I'm going in," said Inigua. He picked up the bota of water and the two smooth, curved sticks that he had set aside earlier. He then gingerly pulled back one side of the blanket curtain. Pablo was distracted by the vivid scares on his back, but then glanced down at the old man's dangling penis and swaying scrotum. The boy's faced turned a vivid red as Inigua slipped behind the curtain.

After checking up and down the beach once more, Pablo sighed, and very slowly began to peel off his clothes. When he finally stood naked on the beach, he quickly moved to the opposite side of the curtain, eased it back a little and peeked in. Inigua was lying on the other side of the fire. Still blushing, Pablo slipped in, concealing his private parts with one hand. He quickly lay down on the opposite side of the fire.

"It is hot in here," he said, propping himself up on one elbow, but still covering his genitals with his free hand.

Inigua grinned. "Fires are generally hot, boy."

"What do we do now?"

"Just relax and wait awhile. Drink some water. Soon we will begin to sweat. Have you ever seen a real sweat lodge?"

"Sí, señor, but only from the outside."

"Then you know they are dome-shaped, usually covered with brush and earth, with a smoke hole in the top. The shape of them keeps the heat in, but lets most of the smoke out. Although we have no roof in this place, I think it will do."

Pablo concentrated on the fire. He was afraid to look at Inigua. He did not want to look at his maleness again. He could feel the heat seeping into his flesh. He could also feel the warmth reflecting off the earthen walls behind him. Before long he began to sweat.

Inigua spoke. "Did you know that before the Spanish came we Chumash men did not wear clothes at all?"

"No clothes? Didn't you get cold?"

"Only when the weather turned. Then we draped ourselves with capes or blankets. We did not feel "funny," as you put it, about our nakedness. It was perfectly natural to us. If nakedness is normal you do not

64

even think about it. Women were different of course. They wore a covering over their loins, usually deerskin. But still, they wore little or nothing on top."

"I cannot understand that," said Pablo. "The church teaches us that nudity is sinful, that we should hide our nakedness."

"I know what the church says, boy. But there is more to life than what the church dictates. You will discover that for yourself one day."

"I am getting very hot, señor. I am sweating very much."

"Good. So am I. Here, take this." Inigua handed the boy one of the foot-long smooth, curved sticks. "Do like this," he said. Inigua took his own stick and placed it near his shoulder. Then he ran the stick down the outside of his arm, sweeping the sweat before it. He then drew it down the front of his arm, and the back of his arm. Then he put the stick under his arm and swept the underside all the way to the wrist. Pablo imitated him. Next, Inigua swept the sweat from the other arm, then his neck and chest and sides and abdomen. Pablo followed suit.

"Now, do my back, Pablo, and I will do yours. This is the way we men did it in the old days. Be careful with my back, boy. The surface is…somewhat uneven, and tender…a little souvenir from the whipping post." Pablo squirmed in discomfort as he ran the stick over the bumpy back and sides of the old man. It reminded him of the washboard he'd seen women use sometimes in the lavenderia. When the two had finished, they sat down on opposite sides of the fire and swept the sweat from their legs.

"Now let us sweat again," said Inigua. "Drink more water. We will do this several times. The sweat cleanses the body, both inside and outside. The heat opens the tiny doors to your inside. Then the impurities come out. When we are done we will jump into the river. The cold water will close the doors and keep bad spirits out."

A half-hour later they rose and exited the sweat lodge. They ran into the river until they were waist deep, and then dove in. Pablo came up sputtering and gasping at the cold.

Inigua squatted so that his body was submerged to the neck, his white hair fanned out about his shoulders. "Where are those Yucca roots you brought? I want to wash my hair."

"I will get them," said Pablo. He galloped back to their campsite and retrieved them.

When they had finished shampooing their hair, the two returned to the cavern. Under Inigua's direction they took down the blanket and spread it out flat on the beach. By now Pablo had become less self-conscious of his nakedness. But he eagerly followed the old man's lead when he saw him donning his clothes. Then they lay down on their backs, side by side on the blanket. Inigua spread his hair out in the sun to dry. They both felt calm and pleasantly tired, luxuriating in their cleanliness. They shared the remainder of

65

the bota of water. Before long they fell asleep to the rhythmic drumming of the waves in the distance.

A blustering wind woke them in the afternoon. They rubbed their eyes, and sat up squinting at the sun, which was now obscured by a fine haze. Inigua shaded his eyes and measured the sun's height above the western horizon. He watched sea birds flapping towards shore. Then he turned his head to the south-east, towards the fast-approaching clouds.

He pointed at them and quoted, as if chanting some strange and barbaric litany, "A, B, C, CH, D, E, F, G, H, I, J, K, L, LL, M, N, Ñ, O, P, Q, R, RR, S, T, U, V, W, X, Y, Z."

Pablo looked at him, dumbfounded, his mouth hanging open like the gaping bag of a careless traveler. The old man rose to his feet and, looking out to sea, said, "We must go now. The storm, she is coming."

12

REATA

Dark clouds swallowed the February sky, and a red smear over Santa Cruz Island was all there was of sunset. Day's end went all but unnoticed by the dwellers of the mission, blending as it did so seamlessly with the coming of night. But the failing sun did not escape the vigilant eyes of old Vincente up in the bell tower. He watched the crimson light fade and then commenced to ring the Angelus bell, calling the faithful to evening prayers. Old Vincente was a devout Christian neophyte, honored for his ardent faith and long service to the mission by his appointment as bell-ringer. He was both proud and covetous of his position. As he hobbled down the narrow stairwell he heard the rain begin to fall. He clucked his tongue in disapproval, for rain during mass seemed somehow sacrilegious.

Down in the quadrangle, under the arched hallway of the arcade, Inigua stood in quiet conversation with Pablo. To the boy's invitation to join him at evening church services Inigua merely shook his head and said, "If the Padre asks, tell him I'm still feeling tired. Too tired to attend mass."

Inigua disappeared into his room until he was sure services were well underway, then made his way furtively to the mission kitchen. From the shadows outside the kitchen door he watched a handsome, thirty year-old Indian woman of ample proportions stirring a large vat of pozole. When she noticed him lingering outside the door, she handed her long wooden spoon to one of her kitchen crew and made her way outside.

"Haku, Inigua," she said, "How was your beach journey?"

"Haku, Encarnacíon. It was good, and we had a good sweat. Thank you for the food."

"*De nada.*"

"How is your family doing up in the valley?"

"Ah, I do not know. I have not heard from them since the flood. I am worried about them. I hope they are well, but I fear they may be suffering."

"I will be traveling up that way soon. I will check on them for you."

"Thank you, Viejo."

"Encarnacíon, I have come to ask a favor. Do you have any *Momoy*?"

She raised her eyebrows and shook her head. "'Sorry, I have none here at the mission. But my uncle has a good supply up in the *Aw'hai* valley. He is an *'antap*, as you probably know, and a member of the *Siliyik* Society. Why do you want Datura, Inigua?"

"I am thinking of performing a ceremony one of these days. But there is no great hurry."

"If indeed you go to the Aw'hai Valley, visit my uncle, Qupe. He lives in the village of *Huyawit*. Tell him I sent you. He can supply you with all you need. Maybe give him something in return. And please tell me all about my relatives when you return."

"I will do so. Gracias."

"Padre Uria has ordered a special meal tonight."

"Oh?"

"Yes. He is going to invite you to dine with him. I am roasting a leg of lamb. I am also grilling fresh steelhead trout netted in the river this afternoon. Why would the padre invite you to dinner? I have never heard of such a thing?"

"We have some business to discuss."

"About the boy?"

"Sí."

"What is going on? The padre asked me today if I would be willing to leave the kitchen and look after him. He told me to think about it. What's wrong with my little friend Pablo?"

"There is nothing wrong with him. But I cannot speak about this matter yet. Perhaps after tonight I can tell you more. And Encarnacíon, the less said about this, the better."

Inigua returned to his room and lay down on his bed to await developments. He tried not to think about Islay. He listened to the rain falling steadily in the quadrangle, and the unremitting trickle of runoff from the roof tiles. He wondered how long the rain would last, and whether the river would flood again. Then he could not stop thinking of Islay. Remorse and guilt revisited him, like those same cats returning to feed again on an earlier kill. He felt himself fall into a fathomless despair.

*   *   *   *   *

After a time, he heard voices and footsteps along the arcade, then the ringing of St. Mary of Sapopa's bell. Inigua's stomach growled. He had not eaten for eight hours.

Then he heard Pablo's voice calling from outside the door. "Señor? Are you there?"

The sound of the boy's voice, so young, so eager, revived his spirits. "Sí, muchacho," he said.

Pablo pulled open the stiff rawhide door and poked his head in. "The padre told me to invite you to dinner tonight. He wants to talk to you about something. I don't know what it is."

"It is about you."

68

"Oh? Oh, good. I am going now to light the candles and a fire in his room. Then I will bring the food. The padre will be there shortly. Can you join us in a little while?"

"Sí. But, Pablo, I want you to do something for me. Or rather, not do something. Please do not say anything to the padre about what you and I have discussed. In fact, do not say anything if you can help it. Just let me do the talking tonight."

"Sí, senor."

Later, when Inigua stood before the padre's door, he could feel the prying eyes of the displaced neophytes under the colonnade watching him. He quietly rapped on the door. Pablo opened it immediately. When the priest saw who it was he called out, "Come in. Come in, old fellow. Shut the door, Pablo."

As the door closed behind him Inigua saw that the table was set with ceramic plates bounded by pewter cutlery and cloth napkins. The wooden candelabrum glowed at the center of the table as on the previous night, but it now illuminated platters and bowls of steaming food. The smell of it made Inigua's mouth water. His eyes scanned the room. Candles burned in sconces along all four walls, lending a festive mood to the sitting room. A crucifix hung at the center of the east wall above the mantle. In the small fireplace below burned a cheery fire. From pegs along the south wall hung the padre's extra gray robe, a cape under a broad-brimmed hat, a leather apron, and miscellaneous pieces of tack. Inigua did not fail to notice a ceramic jug and two matching goblets on the sideboard by the dining table.

"Welcome, my friend," said the padre. "Your face is healing nicely. I hope you are hungry."

"I could eat," said Inigua.

"We missed you at mass. Where were you?"

"I was in my room. Resting."

"Since you are living among us now, I must insist you start attending church services. It would be a bad precedent for me to allow any neophyte to miss mass."

Inigua shrugged. "I can see how that might be a problem."

The padre gestured to the boy. "Come help me seat the cats, Pablo. And you, Inigua, sit down there at the end of the table. Let's hurry. I'm starving." When the cats were in place, two to a chair in their accustomed positions along one side of the table, the padre took a chair opposite them. He quickly said grace, and then ordered Pablo to dish up the cat's food: shredded bits of trout.

"Help yourself, compadre" the padre said to Inigua. "There is lamb and fish and pozole and fresh bread. There is even a salad of winter greens with olive oil and vinegar."

Inigua looked uncertainly at the cutlery. "After you, Francisco."

The padre took up a long knife and a fork. "I will carve the lamb," he said. "Inigua, you don't have to use a knife and fork if you don't want to. We won't stand on ceremony tonight, will we Pablo?" He began carving juicy slices of mutton from the leg.

"I can serve you," said Pablo.

"Do not bother," said the padre. "We are too hungry to wait. Why don't we just help ourselves? Sit down, boy." He stabbed a thick slab of lamb and placed it on his own plate.

"I like fish," said Inigua. He picked up a trout by the tail and laid it on his plate. "But it always seems to make me thirsty," he added, peeking over at the ceramic jug.

The padre groaned, "May the saints preserve us. Once more it begins. Pablo, before you sit, pour our guest and myself a glass of wine." The boy raised his eyebrows, but complied instantly.

"Muchas gracias," said Inigua, as the boy filled his goblet and moved to the padre.

"De nada," said the padre. Together they raised their goblets for a toast.

"To your continued health and long life," said the padre.

"And to yours, Padre," said Inigua. They drank.

Inigua smiled contentedly and smacked his lips. "Mmm. This wine is delicious." He winked at the padre. "My guess is that it came from Mission San Gabriel. It is so much better than the rotgut made here."

The Padre Uria paused in the act of ladling himself a generous bowl of pozole and said emphatically, "We do not make rotgut here, you rogue! Though it is true this wine comes from San Gabriel. I only bring it out for special occasions. You should be honored."

"Ah, I am. And the food, it smells delicious. Encarnacion is such a good cook." He glanced at the padre with a seemingly ingenuous look.

The padre looked at him suspiciously and then tore a hunk of bread from the loaf.

There was a long pause in the conversation as the three diners dished food onto their plates and began eating. Inigua gazed over at the four huge cats sitting next to him. They purred contentedly as they munched on their fish bits. Inigua took up his knife. As he separated a fillet from the backbone and ribs of his own fish he asked matter-of-factly, "Do these animals always eat at your table, Francisco?"

"Yes, unless we have important visitors. But my cats are not merely animals; they are my friends, just as you are. And don't call me Francisco. Call me Padre."

Inigua smiled and said, "Long have I puzzled over you Spaniards and your way with animals. You either kill them as if they were nothing, taking only the best parts and leaving the rest to rot, or you bring them into your house to live as if they were humans. I have never understood this."

70

The padre answered, "It is understood by all civilized people that the beasts of the forest and herds of the plains were put here by almighty God for our use. The holy bible tells us so. In Genesis 1:28 it says, 'And God blessed them, (meaning we humans) and God said unto them, Be fruitful, and multiply, and replenish the earth, and subdue it: and have dominion over the fish of the sea, and over the fowl of the air, and over every living thing that moveth upon the earth.' That is precisely what we Spaniards came here to do.

"And as far as pets, we Spaniards do not consider them human. They are simple, good animals, somewhat more intelligent than others of their kind, but capable of human friendship, even love."

Inigua nodded. "Even I, an ignorant savage, know that animals were put here for our use, although for us, different gods put them here."

The padre's face flushed and he spat accidentally as he said, "Do not blaspheme in my presence, old friend. I do not wish to hear of false gods while dining, or at any other time." The cats cowered at his raised voice.

"*Perdon*," said Inigua. "I did not intend to speak of gods, only animals. My people kept animals too. We had no cats and no horses, but our villages had many dogs. Our children played with them, especially when they were puppies. But we did not think of them as pets. Not really. We did not love them in the way you appear to do. Why? Because in lean years we might be forced to eat them."

Padre Uria nearly choked on a piece of bread. "Oh, how could you? How could you eat your pets?"

"We Chumash are... what is the word in your language?... pragmatic? Yes, that is it. We Chumash kept dogs for useful purposes. They raised the alarm when strangers approached. They ate our garbage so that it did not foul the village. They also accompanied and protected our women when they went about the fields and hills gathering seeds or firewood. We taught the dogs to help men hunt. To us, dogs were living tools. But they were the most handy of tools, for if you ran out of food, you could eat them."

"Good God," said Padre Uria, and took a swig of wine.

Inigua followed suit, then looked intently at the cats, as though he were a hunter spying fresh game. Still holding the knife, he licked his lips and reached over to stroke San Francisco's thick coat and then gently pinched his belly, testing for fat.

"Ho, ho," laughed the padre, nervously. "He is having fun with us, Pablo. Unhand that cat, you brute."

"No need to worry, padre. I see we have plenty of food. There is more food here than I could eat in a week. My, but this cat is big. He reminds me of a little bear cub.

"One time when I was a boy we found a baby black bear about the size of this cat wandering alone in the hills. His mother was nowhere to be seen. She must have died somehow. We took the cub home and kept him for

71

a while. He was cute and playful, as all young things are. We built a pen to hold him and to protect him from the dogs. We fed him our leftovers and garbage. But we did not keep him for very long. When he was fat enough, we ate him."

"Ha!" shouted the padre triumphantly. "I would expect no less of you. You savages used to eat everything in sight. I have been told that before we Spaniards brought you the light of reason and decency, you Chumash ate mice, rats, and gophers. Oooh. You also ate frogs and lizards and snakes. How horrible. Why, you even ate grasshoppers and other disgusting bugs."

"That is true. In lean times we ate almost anything. You can even eat skunk if you are careful in its preparation. But we did not find these animals horrible or disgusting. When prepared properly, they are all delicious. Take a nice gopher. Pulverize him with the skin on. Then roast him on a stick over an open fire. Ah, delicious."

The padre and Pablo made faces at each other.

Inigua took a drink and continued, "And if you've never tried roasted grasshopper you don't know what you are missing. But, as you well know, Francisco, we Chumash ate mostly seafood and acorns and venison. We also ate many seeds and berries. But no matter what we ate, we always asked the animal or plant's forgiveness and expressed our gratitude before taking them. We gave them the honor and respect they deserved, no matter what they were. Which is more than I can say for you Spaniards."

Here the padre drummed his fingers on the table. "Do not try to irritate me, old friend," he said. "You succeeded once, but will not again. I have heard all your rebel talk before. It falls on deaf ears now."

Pablo was surprised that the padre would take such insolence from his guest, and he thanked him in his heart, for he was anxious that the evening go well.

Inigua acted as though he hadn't heard. "And we wasted nothing," he continued. "The bear cub we killed not only fed the whole family, but we made tools and jewelry from his bones and teeth and claws. My father tanned the pelt with the cub's brains, and made it into a shawl for my mother. We fed the heart, liver, lungs and entrails to the dogs."

"Oh, please," said the padre, "I really must insist we change the subject. This talk of eating gophers and guts is making me lose my appetite."

After the padre had a moment to compose himself, he said, "So tell me, old friend, have you come to a decision about what we discussed last night?

"You mean about Pablo?"

"Yes, of course."

"Yes, I have. I am doubtful that I can help the boy."

Pablo put down his knife and fork and looked at him open-mouthed.

"But why?" asked the padre with a look of obvious frustration.

72

"Well, for one thing, I am not convinced that becoming a vaquero is the best thing for him. I myself did not at first want to become a vaquero. It came about as a result of being punished for one of my alleged misdeeds. First I was flogged by Sergeant Cota, then I was imprisoned and forbidden meat, and then I was put to work rendering tallow at that infernal whaling pot. But that did not last long. The alcaldes said I was a troublemaker. Can you believe it? They said I was a bad apple in the mission barrel. So Padre Dumetz had me sent to Rancho Ojai to get me out of the way. I became a skinner during La Matanza. Later, I learned to ride. I became an accomplished rider, which led to me becoming a vaquero."

"Yes, yes, I know your history," said the padre, impatiently. "But I don't see what the problem is. The boy says he wants to become a vaquero, and I am willing to support him in his efforts to do so. We both know you can do it, Inigua. Tell me – what is the problem?"

"May I have another goblet of wine, por favor?"

The padre rolled his eyes to the ceiling, then sighed in resignation and nodded to Pablo. The boy jumped to his feet and poured the wine for Inigua, and refilled the padre's goblet.

After Inigua took a satisfied sip of his wine, he turned his gaze towards the ceiling and, with his elbows on the table and his fingers laced together, he took on a studied, thoughtful, almost saintly look. A full minute passed while he ruminated. It was most excruciating for Pablo.

Finally, Inigua took another drink of wine and spoke. "I am quite flattered that you would think well enough of me, Padre, to entrust this young fellow to my charge. It is gratifying to an old man to know that his contributions and his knowledge have not been forgotten. I was a slave to this mission for nearly fifty years."

Padre Uria stiffened in his chair, and the strange twitching began on the side of his face.

Inigua glanced at him, and changed his tack. "I think this boy has potential. He seems to ride well enough, and his horse is satisfactory, although it will never make a good cow pony. I suspect that it would take the better part of a year to prepare the boy properly. Unfortunately, this would pose great difficulties for me."

Pablo's heart was pounding.

"Difficulties?" asked the padre, suspiciously. "What difficulties?"

"Well, as you might imagine, it is not easy for an old man like myself who has lost everything, to take on a task of this magnitude. I am afraid that without a good deal of material assistance I could not possibly teach the boy."

Pablo's heart sank.

But the padre was determined. "You know perfectly well that I am willing to give you any reasonable help that you need. You can stay here at the mission and have all your needs met."

"Alas," sighed Inigua, "I'm afraid I could not teach the boy while residing here at the mission."

"But why? I thought we discussed all this last night," said the padre. "What is wrong with teaching him here? Is it because I insist on you attending mass?"

"That is only a part of it. The biggest problem is that it is too crowded and noisy around here. It will be even more crowded when help arrives from the other missions. It would be impossible for him, and for me, to…to concentrate."

"But where would you go to teach him? And what kind of help do you need?"

Inigua took a drink of wine and rubbed his jaw. He said, "Well, I think it would be best to spend a good deal of time up in Ojai. There he could see close up what it would be like to be a vaquero. We could also travel around a bit, so he can get the lay of the land. It would enlighten him, give him an idea of distances, and toughen him up.

"But if I were to devote these precious weeks and months in the twilight years of my life to instructing the boy, I would not have time to fish or hunt game or gather food. So Pablo and I would need food to keep us going. And I would need clothing and footwear, a good horse with saddle and tack, a steer or two, and some tools and other supplies."

The padre responded, "I agree that it might be better to be near the rancho. And I can give you clothes. Food is not a problem, nor is the horse, and a steer. The mission has plenty of these things. But what tools do you need? And what are these 'other supplies' you require?"

"As I see it," said Inigua, taking a sip; "the thing that Pablo needs before anything else is a reata. Nothing worthwhile can be done until he has one and learns how to use it. Do you own a reata, Pablo?"

"No, senor."

"Then you must make one."

"But I don't know how."

Here the padre interrupted, "We have some old reatas here at the mission. He can use one of those."

"Oh, no, no, no," said Inigua, shaking his head. "After a horse, a reata is the most important thing in the world to a vaquero. Not only does his work require it, but his safety, and even his life depends on his reata. No self-respecting vaquero would use an old reata made by someone else. It could not be trusted. When reatas get old they dry out and break, and always at the worst of times.

"Besides, knowing how to make a good, strong reata is absolutely essential. It is the very first thing he must learn. He will carry this knowledge with him for the rest of his life. He will need to make himself a new reata each time his old one wears out. I can teach him how to do that."

The padre sighed in resignation. "All right, old fellow, what do you require for the making of this reata?"

Inigua took a sip of wine and said, "We will need two or three good knives: a sticking knife, a skinning knife, and perhaps a butcher knife. We will need two iron pots and a bucket or two. We need a sheep and two steers."

The padre raised his hand. "I understand that you need a steer for the hide. But why do you need two, and why do you need a sheep?" He took a sip of wine.

"The second steer we can use for making bridles and reins, and a saddle. The sheep I will be forced to eat so that I can use the bones to make a fid, and some other leather-working tools."

The padre leaned back and said, "You can have one steer, you old pirate. We have plenty of bridles and reins and old saddles here at the mission. Pablo can use them, along with his pony, Rojo. And if you only need sheep bones, I can provide them. We just killed a sheep today in fact. We are eating it now. There is no need for you to have a sheep of your own."

Inigua curled his lip as if he smelled something bad. "But how will he know how to make a saddle and tack?"

"There is no need. We have saddles and tack. He can learn that later anyway."

Inigua sighed and looked at the ceiling. "We will need plenty of salt, some old blankets or mats, a tent perhaps, and a good deal of firewood. A hatchet would come in handy."

"The salt you can have. One kilo. The blankets too. But beware, they might have fleas. As you know, we give out new blankets to all neophytes each year. We gather up the old ones. You can have as many of those as you want. I can lend you some canvas for a tent. As for the firewood, have Pablo gather it. It is for his benefit that we do this. Put him to work for you. You can borrow a hatchet."

"Bueno. Now we are getting somewhere. Perhaps I can teach him after all." Inigua grinned at Pablo. The boy was smiling so much his jaws hurt.

The padre went on, "I assume you wish to begin immediately, which presents a small problem. Our weekly allotment of cattle, sixty head, has not reached us because of the flood. I suppose I can let you have one of the dried trade hides.

Inigua said, "I would rather have a live steer."

The padre sighed, "And why is that?"

"I must show the boy how to choose a good one, how to kill it, and how to skin and butcher it. These are things he needs to know and experience. Every vaquero knows these things."

The padre thought about this and then nodded his head. "All right. Ride up to Rancho Ojai and pick one out. I will give you a note to give to the mayordomo up there granting you one steer. Leave the meat for use by the rancho."

Inigua curled his lip at this latter stipulation. "I want to keep the meat. I want to jerk it."

The padre looked skeptical.

Inigua took a drink of wine, and said, "The boy needs to know how to butcher a steer, and how to jerk meat. What do you think vaqueros eat when they're in the saddle all day? Jerky."

"All right," said the padre, "but you can't jerk a whole steer."

"No, but I know some Indians up that way who I am sure could use some meat. We can trade with them for other things we need. We will keep some of the fresh meat for our own use too. I, especially, want the head. Oh, and while we are speaking of necessary supplies, I require a demijohn of wine for medicinal purposes. Making a reata is hard work and it will be hard on this old body."

"No," said the padre, firmly. "You can have a bota when the reata is completed. That is the most I will offer."

"That is unsatisfactory. It will take two or three weeks. The pain will be too great."

"Drink some medicinal tea. That will stop the pain."

Inigua looked at him and arched his eyebrow. "No," he said. "I need the wine to complete the work. No wine, no work. I have spoken." He crossed his arms in front of his chest.

An audible groan escaped Pablo's lips.

The padre continued to eat, glancing as he did so from Pablo to Inigua. He sighed as he chewed and rolled his eyes to the ceiling. "You make it hard for me. I will give you one small bota of wine to begin, not a demijohn. In a week, if there is good progress, I will give another. I will give you one bota a week, as long as the training progresses at a good pace. I have spoken." The padre crossed his arms over his chest and looked Inigua in the eye.

Inigua smiled and nodded and unfolded his arms. "Bueno," he said, and took a drink.

Then Padre Uria raised his finger for emphasis and said, "But no one must know of this last arrangement. Keep silent about it, both of you. And, by the way, Inigua, it will be wine from this mission, not San Gabriel. There is absolutely nothing wrong with our wine.

"And now that that is settled, and before we put this subject to rest, is there anything else you require?"

Inigua said, "I am well pleased by your generosity, Francisco. There is one other necessity. When we have gathered all these things we will need a way to transport them. We cannot carry them all on our horses. We will need a pack animal."

"You can have the use of a mule. Return it and all the other things to the mission when you have no further need of them."

"Bueno. I agree. The boy and I thank you."

The padre nodded, and then turned to the boy. "Pablo," he said, "as of tomorrow you are relieved of all your duties here at the mission. I will arrange to have someone take your place. Your schooling is now finished. I am pleased that you have learned how to read and write. You should be grateful. It is a great gift you have been given. It is a pity your education will end here. It is a shame that you will waste it by becoming a vaquero. But if that is what you want, so be it.

"I hereby place you under the care of Inigua. I admonish you to obey him, and to listen to him closely. If you do not apply yourself you will be returned to the mission and flogged.

"And as for you, you old reprobate, I order you to take good care of this boy. Do not fill his head with that foolish insolence and rebelliousness of yours. Do not waste time. Do not become drunk. Do not waste the mission's assets. I will be keeping track of you. You are to report to me each week on this night. Send the boy if you have legitimate requests, or if you have any messages for me."

Inigua's eyes were slightly glazed by now. He smiled and said, "You can count on me, Francisco."

13

PROVISIONS

Dawn found Pablo standing under the arcade watching the tail end of the storm streaming north towards the mountains of the interior. As daylight grew, patches of blue began to show behind wisps of fleeing clouds. The boy had been too excited to sleep in. He was eager to begin preparations for their upcoming journey. Inigua seemed unperturbed, however. He was still sleeping soundly in the room behind him. Pablo attended mass and then went to the mission kitchen. He collected two bowls of atole and carried them to their room in the quadrangle.

After the two had eaten and visited the men's facilities, they set out to gather provisions. They carried with them slips of paper listing the things they required. Each slip bore the waxen imprint of Padre Uria's signet ring.

Their first visit was to the corral and stables just east of the quadrangle. There they encountered the fifty-year-old stable master, José Sabino. He was a short, bow-legged Indian who bore a leather patch over one eye. José recognized Inigua immediately and walked towards him smiling, his hand extended. "Buenos dias, Señor *'Anakuwin*," he said. Pablo was puzzled by the greeting. He had never heard the old Indian called by that name.

Inigua smiled back. "Haku, José. It has been a long time." They shook hands, or rather arms, for they clasped each other by the forearm. They then embraced warmly. Pablo guessed this was the traditional, brotherly greeting of Indian vaqueros.

"'Such a long time, señor," said José. "It is good to see you." Then his expression fell. "I was saddened to hear of your loss," he said. "How are you getting along, Inigua?"

"Ah, sometimes good, sometimes not so good. What happened to your eye, my friend?"

José's face reddened and he lifted his hand to the patch covering his left eye, revealing an empty socket. "Ah, this. I had an accident some years ago… out on the rancho. I lassoed a young bull at branding time, and just as my reata pulled tight the bull twisted his head and caught it with the tip of its horn. My reata must have been weak there, for it parted as though cut with a knife. It flew back in my face and the tip whipped my eye out just like that." He snapped his fingers. "I found myself looking at the ground from this missing eye as it dangled in front of my chest. My compadres, they tried to put it back in, but it would not go. After a time, the cord began to wither and my sight to fade. Soon I could see nothing out of it at all. My friend, Jaime, cut the cord with his knife, as you do the castration of animals."

Inigua grimaced and said, "I am sorry, José."

"Ah, well, what can one do? I learned soon enough that I could not see to throw the lasso any more. Sometimes I threw too short, sometimes too long. I could not judge the distance. So now I am the stable master."

"That is not a bad thing," said Inigua. "But it is a pity about your eye. You were a fine vaquero."

"Gracias, señor," said José. "I owe much of it to you. You taught me many things. What brings you here?"

"We are going on a journey, this boy Pablo and I. He is taking his pony, Rojo. I need a good mount with tack and saddle. We also need a pack animal, a mule with bridle and pack rack. We have permission from Padre Uria. See? Here is his marker."

José barely glanced at it. "You can have whatever you want, señor. There is a nice chestnut gelding here you might try. See him? Over there in the corral, the one with the star on his forehead. He was a good cow pony once. He is fifteen years old now, but still has plenty of spring in his step. He is strong and sweet tempered. I recommend him, if you aren't planning to work him too hard."

"No, not hard. I trust your judgment in horses, José. What is his name?"

"They call him *Tabaco*."

"I will come and give him a try tomorrow. We will not be leaving for a day or two."

"He may need re-shoeing," said José. "Go see that big grouch Albino. He is the head blacksmith. And for your tack and saddle you must go to the leather shop over there next to the stables. Speak to the gente de razón, Señor Morales."

As Inigua and Pablo slogged across the muddy paddock towards the leather shop, the boy asked, "Why did the stable master call you Señor Anakuwin?"

"Oh, that is just a nickname my family gave me. It means 'little coyote' in Chumash."

"Why did they call you that?"

"Oh, I guess it had to do with the way I acted when I was young. Nicknames were common in the old days because we Indians did not like strangers to know our real name. If they turned out to be enemies they might put a curse on you if they knew your real name."

They arrived at the long, low adobe building that housed the leather shop. As they entered through the open door they were enveloped by the rich, almost sensual smell of tanned leather. When their eyes became accustomed to the dim interior light, they discovered two disheveled Indian men sitting on low benches. Using greasy rags, the two were methodically rubbing tallow into strips of leather. One of them, the older of the two, glanced up at them with a weary expression and muttered a vague, "Buenos dias."

"Buenos dias, señor," said Inigua. "How are things with you?"

"Terrible. All this rain. It is no good for the leather. You see up there, where the roof leaks? There, and there. The water comes in and wets the floor. That makes everything damp in here. Señor Morales ordered us to wipe down everything every day. If we do not do it, the mold begins to grow. And look at all this. Look at all the things we must look after."

Inigua and Pablo scanned the large collection of leather goods hanging from pegs along the walls, and from hooks under the roof beams: tack of every size and description, reatas and tether ropes, hobbles and botas and leather bags. There were a dozen or more saddles straddling long wooden benches aligned across the room. Some saddles were new, others old and in various stages of disrepair. Against one wall stood shelving upon which perched sandals, crudely made shoes and boots. In the adjoining room stood several work benches. Along the wall behind them hung wooden mallets, metal leather-working tools, and an assortment of fids and awls and balls of twine.

"Where is the gente de razón, Señor Morales?" asked Inigua.

"He is not here. He is sick. He has the grippe, or so he says. My name is Lorenzo"

"We need a saddle and some tack, Lorenzo, and a few other things."

"Fine. Take what you need."

"We have permission from the Padre. See. Here is the list with his sign."

"I cannot read, but it does not matter. It is not my place to make decisions. I believe you anyway. Take what you want. It will mean less work for us when it is gone."

"Bueno. We will do as you say."

Inigua and Pablo spent a good deal of time in the leather shop. They carefully selected all of the things that they needed, and helped themselves to some other things not on their list, including an old reata. They both found belts and sandals in their sizes. Then they made arrangements with the heedless neophyte to pick their gear up later.

In the afternoon they visited the blacksmith shop. The head man was a huge, powerfully built Indian with a surly demeanor. Albino was his name. He was christened thus for his complete lack of pigmentation. A former mule skinner, Albino had in the past suffered perpetually from sunburn. Mercifully, he had been re-assigned to indoor work. He was taught blacksmithing by a gente de razón from Sonora, Mexico. Albino proved an apt student, and his prodigious strength served him well in his new employment. He was now a proud and accomplished metal worker, and had been appointed head blacksmith. The real man in charge, Señor Jacinto, only came into the shop occasionally now. He came to give orders and to inspect the finished work. He otherwise led a life of leisure.

"So, you tell me you need knives and a hatchet?" said Albino, after Pablo had read the list and showed him the waxen seal. "What would you two *rateros* need with these cutting tools?"

"That is not your concern, señor," said Inigua. "You saw Padre Uria's mark, did you not?"

"I saw it, but I have no knives to give you right now."

"Then make them," said Inigua. "We are in a hurry. They are needed by tomorrow night. We also need a fine honing stone – something light that can be carried about."

Albino looked down his nose at the old man and the mestizo boy. "So, you think you can walk in here and tell me to drop everything I am doing and make you three knives?"

"Yes."

"I think I will be making your knives when I am good and ready, *viejito*."

Inigua sighed and said, "I will carry your message to the Padre. But I do not think he will be pleased to hear it. After all, it is for him that we make this request. But I understand. You are looking tired and overworked. You could probably use a few days in the curatel to rest and regain your strength. Although it will be hard to regain your strength after the flogging I see in your future."

Albino's red eyes flared and he stepped forward. "Who are you to threaten me so?"

"I am no one," said Inigua, stepping back and bowing. "Only a humble messenger. Come, Pablo. I can see we will find no satisfaction here. It is unfortunate, both for us and for him." They turned to go.

Albino looked after them. "Uh, perdon, señor," he said. "I… mmm… now that I have thought about it, I realize I may have a little free time tomorrow. Perhaps I can work on your knives then. I think I have a hatchet around here already. Come tomorrow afternoon and I will have them ready for you."

"Ah, that is good of you, Albino. Muchas gracias, señor. Oh, and by the way, we have a steed or two that need shoeing."

"I don't do horseshoes any more. But bring the beasts tomorrow and I will order one of the younger men to shoe them. I only do the finer work now."

"You are a true artist, Albino. We look forward to cutting with your beautiful sharp blades. Buenos dias. See you tomorrow."

They went to the mission kitchen next. There, Encarnacion supplied them with a sack of dried beans, a sack of oats, some sugar and salt, beef jerky, dried fruit, and other consumables for their journey. Encarnacion had a soft spot for Pablo, and made sure to include several balls of ponocha, a thick brown sugar candy.

That night, by candlelight, the boy began teaching Inigua how to write. Using a quill pen and a small jar of ink liberated from the Padre's quarters, Pablo guided the old man in writing the alphabet on the back of the slips of paper which listed their supplies.

The following morning they visited the trade warehouse located about a block south of the mission on what is now Figueroa Street. It was a large adobe structure where both hides and manufactured goods were stored. In the summer and fall of each year, it was common for Yankee ships to ply the California coast. They came to trade manufactured goods for mission products, principally cow hides, tallow, and sea otter pelts. The Americans then sailed home to Boston or other east coast cities where the hides were turned into leather products, the tallow into candles, and the pelts into fine hats, coats and shawls.

The gente de razón, Pedro Olivera, was in charge of the warehouse. He was a heavy-set Mexican with a smug, well-fed look about him. When Inigua and Pablo entered the building, Señor Olivera glanced up at them from his account book. He studied them for a moment, and then returned to his work. He continued making meticulous entries in the account book. The two visitors waited patiently.

Several minutes passed. Inigua cleared his throat.

Señor Olivera ignored him. After another minute had passed, he lay down his quill pen and sighed. "What do you want?" he said, not looking up from the ledger.

"We have been sent by Padre Uria," said Inigua. "We have a list of things he wants us to collect."

"Let me see this list."

Pablo stepped forward and handed it to him.

Señor Olivera spent a full minute studying the list and meticulously examining the wax seal. He turned the sheet over and blinked at the scrawled alphabet on the back. "What is this?" he said.

"Oh, that is nothing," said Pablo, nervously. "It is only the front that you need to see."

Señor Olivera shook his head. "This is most irregular." He turned the sheet back to front and back again. "I will have to verify this with the padre."

"That will not be necessary," said Inigua. "You have the list and his seal. We need these things now. The padre sent us to collect them at once."

Señor Olivera raised his eyebrow. "What is your name, viejito?"

"My name is Inigua."

Señor Olivera looked at him for a long time. Then he said, "You had better be telling me the truth, Inigua. It would be a very serious offense if you were to acquire these items without proper authority."

"I commit no offense in collecting what the Padre has requested. He is the head of this mission, after all. And you report directly to him, do you not?"

"I know my position well. It is not your place to remind me, you insolent cur."

"I beg your pardon, señor. I mean no insolence. I only ask that you do your duty and give us what is on the Padre's list."

The Mexican clenched his jaw, and a large blood vessel began to pulse on his broad forehead. His eyes narrowed and he stared at Inigua for a long time. Slowly his anger melted, and his eyes took on their usual calculating look. Grudgingly, he turned his head and called out, "Ramaldo!"

A thin, worried-looking neophyte appeared in the doorway to the main storage room. "Sí, señor?" he said.

"You can read, can't you, Ramaldo?"

"Sí, señor."

"Take this list and bring the items on it for these two *pinacates*." Señor Olivera then rolled down his shirt sleeves, stood up from his desk, adjusted his pants up around his ample belly, and walked towards the rear door with his head held high.

A short while later, Inigua and Pablo emerged from the warehouse burdened with pots and pans, tin plates, cutlery, a large roll of canvas, a compressed brick of salt, and other assorted items. They took them to their room in the quadrangle and deposited them there. The quad was deserted now, the neophytes having been put to work in the fields and zanja despite the muddy conditions.

The two then walked past the campo santo which lay behind a low adobe wall just west of the mission church. In the graveyard were buried departed neophytes, often lying one on top of another, three and four deep in each grave. The waist-high wall surrounding it kept the dogs out, dogs that would otherwise dig up the bodies that lay nearest the surface. Pablo made the sign of the cross as they passed the cemetery. He said a short, silent prayer for his parents who lay buried there.

Just beyond the cemetery rose the high walls surrounding the *monjerio* compound. Within dwelled neophyte girls and unmarried women. To the west of the monjerio stood lines of long apartment-like structures that housed unmarried men and boys. Neophytes who were married and had families, on the other hand, lived in individual houses scattered around the little community that had grown up around the mission. Inigua and Pablo mounted the steps of the monjerio and knocked on the sturdy oak door.

After repeated knockings, they heard the sliding of a bolt, and then the door swung open to reveal Sister Ugolina, the matron in charge. She held the door with one hand, ready to slam it shut if necessary.

She peered out suspiciously at the old man and the thirteen year-old boy. "What do you want?" she said.

"We have been sent by Padre Uria," said Inigua.

83

"If it is about those boys who climbed over the wall the other night, I know nothing about it. We only know they were here because they left their makeshift ladder behind."

"We have only brought a list of things the Padre requires," said Inigua.

"Does he want to know the names of the girls who got up in the middle of the night to meet the boys? I swear, I do not know who they are. Dios mio, how am I to know? I was asleep the whole night. The girls must have stolen the key while I slept. I beseech the Padre to have mercy on me. It is not my fault. I work so hard all day that when darkness comes I am worn out. I lock every door and window and count all the girls. Then I go to bed and sleep like those that lie yonder in the campo santo. Is the Padre going to put me in the stocks?"

"Not if you cooperate with us by giving us the things we came for."

Sister Ugolino looked at them suspiciously. "You cannot visit any of the girls. Especially not him," she said, jabbing her finger at Pablo.

"We do not want to see any girls. We only want some blankets from the weavery, and a few items of clothing. And two hats. See here? We have this list, and here is Padre Uria's mark." The woman looked at it skeptically.

"I cannot read," she said.

"Never mind. Let us come in and we will pick out what we need."

Sister Ugolina twisted her hands together uncertainly, glancing to the left and right and behind her. Once more she sized up the two males standing at her door. Then she said, "You can come in, old man. But not the boy. I'll have no young boys in the monjerio. Not ever again." Young Pablo stood open-mouthed, looking at her with innocent indignation.

Inigua agreed to her demand, and so Pablo spent the next half hour mumbling to himself and fidgeting on the steps of the compound. When Inigua emerged, his arms were piled high with blankets and clothing. They returned with their booty to their room in the quadrangle.

At midday, as Pablo was about to go to the kitchen to fetch their lunch, Inigua made an odd request. He told the boy to ask Encarnacion for a few raw carrots. Pablo returned later with two hearty bowls of pozole and a handful of raw carrots.

After eating, the man and boy returned to the corrals. They conferred briefly with José Sabino, and then Pablo watched Inigua step into the corral with a carrot concealed in one hand. The horses, seeing a man enter their enclosure, retreated to the far end. They bunched together, jockeying for the center position. Those on the outside turned their hind ends to the outside. The horses glanced nervously over their shoulders at Inigua.

In a calm, firm voice, Inigua called out, "Tabaco."

The mature chestnut gelding raised his head. Inigua gave a quick whistle and held the carrot up for him to see. Tabaco separated himself from the herd and walked cautiously towards the man with the orange tidbit.

84

"Buenas tardes, Tabaco. Here is a little treat for you. Come on, boy." When the horse stood before him, Inigua took a slow step to the side and offered up the carrot. The horse took it and chewed contentedly, eyeing the man as he did so. Although Pablo could not make out the words, he heard Inigua talking to the horse. Tabaco swallowed and then looked at his benefactor's hands. Inigua showed him that they were empty, then stepped forward, talking calmly all the while, and patted the horse on the shoulder and ran his hand along his sides. Tabaco seemed to like being touched and petted, and seemed mesmerized by the old Indian's words. Inigua checked the horse's teeth. He then ran his hand down the horse's front leg and lifted the foot. He inspected the hoof, and then went on to the other hooves. Over his shoulder Inigua said to Pablo, "His teeth are fine, although worn, which is understandable given his age. His hooves are in good condition, but he needs shoeing. What about Rojo?"

"His shoes are fine, señor.

After a few more minutes of acquainting himself with the horse, Inigua walked to the corral fence and retrieved the hackamore he had draped over one of the rails. "Come here, Tabaco." The gelding came to him and stood quietly as Inigua slid the harness over his head and fastened it in place.

Inigua called to the boy and had him enter the corral and help him mount the horse with cupped hands. He then ordered the boy to open the gate. He rode Tabaco out along the main thoroughfare that would one day be Main Street, and headed east along the base of the hills. Pablo waited for a half an hour, and at the sound of hoof beats he turned to see Inigua smoothly transition from a canter to a trot to a walk. The boy swung open the gate and Inigua rode the horse through and dismounted in the corral. He removed the hackamore from Tabaco's head, talking to him all the while, and then offered him another carrot, which had been concealed in the pocket of his coton.

"Bueno," Inigua called to José Sabino, who stood watching from the stable door. He is a good mount, a fine animal. I will take him to the blacksmith for shoeing."

The last place Inigua and Pablo visited that day was the winery. The winery had been dug into the hillside to form a kind of cave. The walls were lined in stone. It had the strong, but not unpleasant smell of fermenting grapes. There they met Segundo, a middle-aged neophyte with a somewhat bored expression and blood-shot eyes. After showing him the slip of paper with the Padre's sign, he asked Segundo for a bota of wine.

"At last, someone is here asking for wine," the man said. "Ever since the flood I have had no business here. All I do is sit here and watch the wine ferment. What kind of wine do you want?"

"Do you have any of the San Gabriel?"

"Yes, we still have a little left. But we have plenty of wine from this mission."

"Which do you prefer?" asked Inigua.

"Why the San Gabriel, of course, although I am particularly fond of our pear brandy."

"Pear brandy?"

"Yes. It is the preferred beverage of knowledgeable and discerning imbibers. It is the best this mission has to offer. Gente de razón, and even the padres from the other missions, always ask for it when they pass by on El Camino Real."

"Can you give me a little taste?"

"I see no harm in it, as long as you are here on the Padre's business. I might even join you. It is almost time for me to go home anyway." Segundo produced two small ceramic cups. He filled them from an oaken barrel, and handed one to Inigua.

They toasted one another and then sipped from their cups.

"Aiee," said Inigua. "It is sweet, but has a real bite to it."

"Sí, señor. It will give go to your head in no time. Caution must be exercised, however. If too much goes to your head it will leave you with a headache like no other." The two men chatted amiably in the Chumash language and drank until their cups were empty. Pablo sat outside and looked out at the distant ocean. He was bored stiff.

"Perhaps you could give me a little of this brandy to take on my journey," said Inigua. "I leave tomorrow."

"You seem like a decent fellow to me. And even though I am not authorized to do so, I will give you a little to take along. Here is a little ceramic flask of it with a cork. Please make no mention of this to the Padre. There is always the possibility that he might disapprove."

"My lips are sealed, compadre."

"And you require some wine, señor?"

"Si. The wine we want has been requested by Padre Uria. Which does he prefer?"

"The San Gabriel, of course."

"Bueno. Then give us the San Gabriel. You can put it in this new bota."

"As you wish, señor." When this was done, Segundo wished them a pleasant journey and swung the doors of the winery closed.

14

DEPARTURE

Pablo and Inigua were up at first light, on this the last day of
February. They dressed quickly and stepped out into the quadrangle to find it
even more densely populated than before. Over the two previous days, help
from neighboring missions had begun to arrive. Soldiers, vaqueros and gente
de razón had quartered in private homes, in sheds and storerooms, and even
in the curatel. Neophytes settled into the mission church, but the overflow
had been forced to camp out in the quadrangle. Pablo and Inigua had to step
over and around numerous sleeping forms as they made their way out of the
quad. They went directly to the mission stables where they set about
grooming and feeding their mounts. They did the same for the mule, a sturdy,
even-tempered beast named Chico. The Angelus bell sounded as the animals
contentedly munched their feed. When they had had their fill, the man and
boy saddled the horses and harnessed the pack frame to Chico's back. They
then rode to the front of the mission and tied the animals at one of the
hitching posts.

While mass was underway in the church, the man and boy carried
their provisions from their room and loaded them onto Chico's strong back.
Later, they ate bowls of atole for breakfast, and then went to Padre Uria's
sitting room to say their farewells.

Tears welled up in the padre's eyes as he hugged Pablo to his ample
belly. "Take care of my little Pablito," he said to Inigua. He ran his hand over
the boy's head and ruffled his hair. Pablo blushed at the unaccustomed
affection. "Come back next Sunday and we will dine together that evening.
You will probably need a good meal by then.

"We shall see," said Inigua.

"But I want to know what you are doing. Come on Sunday."

Inigua said nothing.

"You had better be here," said the Padre. "Do you have enough food
with you?"

"Plenty," said Inigua. "We have everything we need. Do not worry,
Francisco, we will be back one of these days."

"Not one of these days. Sunday."

"As you say."

The padre walked them out to the front of the mission. On the way
he handed Inigua a small slip of paper. "This is a voucher with my marker.
Show it to Fernando Tico up at Rancho Ojai. It gives you permission to take

one steer. Show it to him before you do anything. And here. Take these." He handed Inigua a small leather pouch.

"What is this?" asked Inigua. The padre shrugged. Inigua opened the pouch and poured the contents out in his hand. It was seven little silver coins, Spanish *reáls*. "There is no need for this, padre. Where would we spend money anyway?"

"You never know. These coins might come in handy. Take care not to lose them." He watched closely as Inigua secured the pouch's drawstrings to his belt.

They said their final goodbyes on the mission steps, and then the old man and the boy put on their new hats and mounted up. Inigua could see that Pablo was close to tears. The boy bit his lip to keep them at bay. As they turned down the tree-lined lane they looked back to see Padre Uria weeping openly and making the sign of the cross over their departure.

Inigua, clucking his tongue, took the lead, and Pablo followed leading the mule by its tether.

"Which way do we go?" called Pablo.

"This way, to the beach. I want to check the weather."

They rode to the low bluff overlooking the shoreline. Inigua sat on his horse, gazing out at the sea and sky. Presently he said, "It looks good, eh, Pablo? There are no clouds in sight, and no wind. The air feels warm. It is a good day to travel."

Just then a movement out in the water caught Inigua's attention. He lowered his hat brim to shade his eyes, and spied a pod of dolphin streaking through the blue water just beyond the breakers. Pablo followed his gaze and saw them too. He watched as they jumped from the water, then swam and jumped again, their sides glistening in the low morning sun.

Pablo heard Inigua say something in a low tone, seemingly addressing the dolphins. The boy cocked his ear, straining to hear what the old man said. But he could not make it out, and then Inigua fell silent. The Indian sat on his horse intently watching the dolphins make their way to the west along the beach until they finally disappeared from view.

Puzzled and anxious at the delay, Pablo said, "What are we waiting for, Inigua?"

"Nothing. We ride now." Inigua urged Tobaco on towards the river. Once there, the two turned north along the old carreta road. They could see where work crews had cleared the path, which, though still muddy from the recent rain, was firm underfoot. Spread before them lay the wide river valley. The river, evenly dividing the fertile valley, sang lustily from its rocky bed as it rumbled down to the sea. The vegetable fields bordering the eastern edge still lay buried in mud, but here and there virgin growth had sprung up out of the ruin. Further east, on the higher ground, tidy orchards and well-pruned vineyards looked prim and expectant in their winter bareness. Rising to the left and right of the valley climbed steep hills, green and lush with winter grass. Directly ahead, in the middle distance, bush-covered hills rose like a staircase into the blue mountains of the interior.

Gushing, Pablo said, "It is beautiful, is it not, senór? Everything is so green."

"Sí, Pablo. But I cannot get over the land being so naked. There used to be many trees on those hills, mostly coastal oaks. When the Spaniards came they cut them all down for timber and firewood. Then they burned the hills of brush to provide pasture."

"Ah, look there, señor." Pablo pointed to the west of the river. "*Oveja*." On the long, broad hill that sloped towards the coast a flock of a hundred or more salt and pepper sheep grazed under the watchful eye of an Indian shepherd and his dog.

As Inigua and Pablo rode forward they glanced to the east to catch one last glimpse of the mission church and quadrangle squatting at the foot of the steep hill behind. The whitewashed walls gleamed in the morning sun, and the red terracotta roof tiles blazed as though fresh from the kiln. Up on the hill above the mission, on a plateau midway up, stood a large, whitewashed wooden cross – standing as a beacon, a sign, and a symbol. Inigua knew it could be seen for many miles out to sea. The man and boy watched as several hundred neophytes began assembling in front of the quadrangle. Presently they would be divided into crews and given work assignments by the mayordomo.

"I am glad we are out of there," said Inigua.

"Me too," said Pablo. "How long will it take us to get to Ojai?"

"Have you never been there?"

"No. I have only gone as far as the Chapel of Santa Gertrudis."

"Then you are in for something special. To answer your question, the Ojai Valley is about fifteen miles from here. But we must go further than that today. We must go to Señor Tico's, to his wooden house in the upper valley. It is higher up and some miles to the east."

"Oh, yes, I know of this man Tico," said Pablo. "I have seen him several times. He comes to the mission when someone is to be punished. He is in charge of the whipping post."

"I know. He is also the mayordomo at Rancho Ojai."

"Did he ever…well…you know…?"

Inigua looked sharply at the boy. "No, he never laid his whip across my back, if that is what you mean. Not that he would not have wanted to. But Tico is from Santa Barbara. He only came to this mission a year or so ago. I was too old by then. They do not whip old people much any more. The Spanish used to do it, but too many died because of it. Now the Mexicans just put them in the curatel for a few days without meat. I have heard talk about this man Fernando Tico. They say he is a hard one."

The two rode side by side through muddy fields and the orchards of olive, pear, apricot and other fruit, including pomegranate. Soon they came abreast of *Cañada del Diablo*, a steep canyon that ran down out of the hills across the river and emptied into the valley. Pablo made the sign of the cross as he looked up into its twisting, shadowy interior.

"Why do they call that the *canyon of the devil*?" asked the boy.

"Oh, it is just another Spanish superstition," said Inigua. "Those Spaniards, they like to scare themselves. It is a long story, but I will tell you this much: many years ago soldiers from the mission were chasing a bad Indian on their horses. The Indian went up into that canyon, and when they tried to follow him, the Indian started a fire. The wind was blowing very strong that night. The wind blew the flames down the canyon and into the faces of his pursuers. The soldiers turned and fled. They were convinced the flames were the fiery breath of the devil himself. At least that is what they told the padre when they returned empty-handed."

Pablo thought about this story for awhile, and then asked, "Who was that bad Indian?"

Inigua looked over at him. He shrugged, smiled enigmatically, then looked away.

As each mile passed under their horses' hooves the valley gradually narrowed. Pablo gazed over at the aqueduct on their right as it snaked along the base of the hills. Some portions of it, those running over hard ground, were nothing more than open trenches. Porous sections were lined with river rock and Roman cement. Other places, places under steep inclines, were provided with masonry flumes to protect the ten-by-thirty inch channel from falling debris.

When the riders got to *Cañada Larga*, a wide canyon dipping down out of the hills from the east, Pablo admired the tall Roman arches spanning the creek bed at its mouth. The arches held the aqueduct fourteen feet above the ground in order to maintain its proper grade and to allow the canyon to drain underneath. The columns and arches were six feet thick at their base, and were supported by massive buttresses of cobble and mortar.

"Oh, señor, that is magnificent, eh?"

"Magnificent to look at, yes. But not so magnificent if you had to carry river rock across the valley in order to build it. I was one of the unfortunate ones who did. But I must admit, that bald-headed padre, Pedro Cambon, he knew what he was doing when he planned it. And after he left, Dumetz and Santa Maria brought trained neophytes from San Gabriel to build it. They had worked on such projects before. Those Christian Indians from the south thought they were better than us. But we Chumash showed them we could work harder than them any day. We were such fools back then."

Beyond Cañada Larga, the river valley veered to the west and began to narrow drastically as the hills closed in on either side. Pablo and Inigua saw purple-blue Lupin blooming on the slopes alongside colorful patches of Wild Peony, Indian Paintbrush, Chamise, Gallitos, and Wild Lilac.

But the ruins of the Chapel of Santa Gertrudis drew their attention down and away from the hillsides. The four-roomed, U-shaped adobe structure had once stood here on the level plain between the hills and river, some five miles north of the river mouth. The rooms were arranged around a central patio or courtyard. Orchards and vineyards had dotted the fertile ground about it. Padres riding here on horseback had served Sunday mass for the Christian Indians, vaqueros and shepherds of the interior.

But now, Santa Gertrudis was no more than a memory. Only a few tumbled sections of walls remained. Debris and roof tiles lay scattered over a wide area. There was no sign of the fourteen neophytes who had lived in tule huts nearby, and had maintained the chapel and orchards.

As they rode slowly by, Pablo could not take his eyes from the ruins. He had such clear memories of attending mass here. Inigua, on the other hand, after a brief, satisfied perusal of the remains, seemed far more interested in a large sycamore tree that stood up ahead near a bend in the river. To Pablo, his mentor seemed rather callous about the tragedy which had so recently taken place here.

"See that tree?" said Inigua, pointing. Pablo looked up ahead at the noble hundred foot-tall Sycamore. Barren of leaves in winter-time, its mottled gray and white trunk stood in stark relief against the sky where the hills closed down on either side of the river. Though the ends of several low limbs had been twisted and broken, the tree had suffered little damage from the flood.

"This is a sacred tree," said Inigua. "It is the Gatekeeper, the one who stands between the hill country and the coast. It has stood here since ancient times. My grandfather said it was here long before he was born. We Chumash revere it as one of the old ones. When our people travel between the hill country and the coast we always stop and speak respectfully to it. We sometimes hang a little token or gift from one of its limbs. But I see nothing there now. The flood must have taken them."

Inigua rode forward until he was abreast of the massive Sycamore. He hailed it, and gave a short greeting in Chumash to make his presence known. Then the old man urged Tobaco forward until they were under the wide-spreading limbs. He took the little pouch from his belt and hung the drawstrings over the tip of a low-hanging branch. He secured it there so that the wind would not blow it down.

Pablo shook his head. That was the money the padre had given him.

Inigua said to the tree, "Gatekeeper, please accept this as an offering. Please hold it for someone who needs it more than me. Thank you, oh ancient one. *Kiwa'nan.*" Then he urged Tobaco forward and through the narrow gap in the hills through which the river flowed.

He turned his head to the boy and said, "I want to tell you something, Pablo. We are now entering the back country. There are many wild animals up here, and we will come across them sooner or later. I want you to pay

91

attention to your pony. He will tell you if he senses something. Be prepared to keep him under control. Do not let him bolt. It is in the nature of a horse to run away at the first sign of danger. Your job is to keep him from doing so, both he and the mule."

Pablo swallowed. "Sí, señor."

"If we see a bear or a mountain lion we will stop and wait for it to move away, or try to go around it. But even a little animal like a bird or a squirrel can scare the horses. There is a lot of brush up where we are going. The horses cannot see to determine what is out there. If they smell or hear something their first instinct is to run away. Do not let them."

"I will try, señor."

The river thundered over the rocks to their left as they passed the narrow gap. The horses climbed a low rise above the river. Signs of the recent flood were everywhere: downed trees, ravaged brush, great heaps of driftwood and torn vegetation. They kept to what was left of the trail, picking their way through debris as they went. When they topped the rise, Pablo heard Inigua gasp.

"What is it, señor?"

Staring down the slope ahead of them, Inigua said, "Ah, no. It is as I feared. *Las Casitas* is no more."

"Las Casitas?"

"There was a village here, boy. Many small houses. Twenty or so. They…they are all gone."

"The padre said the dam broke."

"Yes. These poor people, they had no chance." The riders descended the low hill and picked their way through the desolation. Inigua scanned the area with a solemn expression. About a mile further on they came upon the jagged jaws of the dam. They drew to a halt and watched San Antonio Creek vomit jetsam through the gaping throat.

Pablo drew abreast of Inigua. He glanced at the old man's face and saw that it held a savage, angry look. "Are you all right, señor?"

"This is what caused it all. This is what took Islay from me. Her, and so many others."

Pablo could think of nothing to say.

Inigua lowered his head and sat in silence, staring at his hands crossed over the pommel. After a time, he looked up and down the canyon through which the creek flowed. He studied the contours of the land.

Then he sighed. "I had thought we might follow San Antonio Creek up into Ojai. It is the shorter way. But it does not look good. See? The trail has been eaten away in places and buried in others. See all that wood and rock blocking the way. I do not think it would be safe for the horses to try it. We had better cross the creek and continue following the river."

He urged his mount down along the creek to a spot where it widened and was shallower. He guided Tobaco into the rushing water. The old horse moved forward obediently, but placed his feet carefully among the rocks. When Pablo urged Rojo after him, however, the pony balked. "Go on, boy," said Pablo. But Rojo refused to enter the water.

"Señor, my pony will not cross."

Inigua halted his mount in midstream and looked back. "He should be used to following my horse by now. Come, Rojo," he called to the pony. "Come on, boy." As if echoing him, Tobaco nickered.

Rojo, hearing the other horse, and seeing that man and mount were unharmed, reluctantly placed one foot into the water. He lifted it and shook it.

"Go on," urged Pablo. Rojo snorted and stepped gingerly in the rushing stream. Inigua continued on towards the far bank. The boy and his mount followed. Chico came along without hesitation, and the little group crossed with no further difficulty.

Ahead of them rose a steep, brush covered hill. Inigua angled his mount to the left, towards the river, to get around it. Pablo followed leading the mule. A little ways north of where the creek emptied into the river, the effects of the broken dam and subsequent flood diminished, a well-traveled trail emerged alongside the river. They moved along it, climbing into the foothills. The two riders passed dense growths of Deergrass, Milkweed, and Bay Laurel along the river. Above them, Live Oak and Maple clung to the steep hillsides amid great swaths of Manzanita and brush. Rojo's eyes widened and he looked anxiously all around him at the unfamiliar terrain.

"Rojo is scared," said Pablo. "He is not used to all these strange plants and the tall hills."

"Just talk to him," said Inigua over his shoulder. "Tell him everything is all right. You see how Tobaco is calm. He has been here before. Your pony will look at him and be reassured.

"'You see this trail, Pablo? This used to be just an Indian foot path. But when the Spanish started the Rancho up here they got the Indians to widen it. The first thing we did was to set a fire. We burned out this whole river valley. Then we chopped back all the growth along the old path to widen it. Now this trail is used every week to drive cattle down to the mission."

About a mile further on they came upon a small group of people approaching on foot. They were Indians. They had a defeated, hungry look about them. Their clothes were nothing more than rags. Upon their gaunt faces was written the signs of a hard winter. They scuttled off the trail to let the riders pass.

"Haku, young ones," said Inigua, reining in as he drew abreast of them. A young man and woman stood with their hands on the thin shoulders of their two tired-looking children, aged about six and eight.

"Haku, my elder," said the man.

"Where do you go?" asked Inigua.

93

"We go to the mission. We do not want to, but we must. There is no game. The deer have all but disappeared from our home ground. My children are hungry, and it has been a cold and wet time for us. We go to the mission to beg for food and a place to stay."

"I am sorry to hear it," Inigua said. "But I fear you will have a hard time finding a place to stay down there. There are many people there visiting from other missions. They came to repair flood damage."

"Aiee. That is not good for us. But we have no other place to go. Our village up in Matilija Canyon was flooded out. We lost all our stored food. All of our neighbors have scattered."

Inigua said, "The padre will only let you stay at the mission if you are baptized into the church. Is that what you want?"

"No, señor, but we will do it if we have to. We only need a little help now. When spring comes we will return to our home. We can gather seeds and fruit and hunt deer as we always have done. When summer arrives there will be new acorns to eat."

Inigua turned to Pablo and said, "Get some of that beef jerky from Chico's pack. Give it to them." As Pablo went about doing this, Inigua turned to the man and said, "I have an idea, young fellow. If you had a little money, you would not have to go begging. I hate to see anyone beg. With money you could pay for a place to stay and you could buy a little food. You could find some work to do in the town and get by for a month or two. Then you would not have to join the church."

"But we have no money, grandfather."

"Do you know the great tree at the turning place of the river? The Gatekeeper Tree?"

"Yes, of course."

"Go to that tree and you will find something in the branches to help you on your way."

"Gracias, grandfather."

"It is nothing."

When Pablo had remounted, the two groups said their farewells and went their separate ways. Pablo looked back to watch the family walking down along the river, their fists to their mouths, their strong teeth eagerly tearing at the strips of jerky.

94

15

THE OJAI VALLEY

Inigua and Pablo followed the river for several more miles till they came to a place where the hills flattened out to the east. They dismounted there and watered the horses. The chaparral-clad mountains to the north loomed much closer now, their highest peaks dusted with snow.

Inigua looked up at the sun. It was just past midday. The sky was clear, and a light breeze had begun to blow up the river from the sea. They took some jerky and dried fruit from Chico's pack and sat down on the riverbank to eat.

"How are you feeling, Pablo?"

"I feel good. But my rear-end is a little sore. I'm not used to riding this far."

"Our butts will be on fire before this day is done. We are only half way to our destination. Soon we will enter the Aw'hai Valley. If you do not know it, Aw'hai means 'Moon' in our language. The valley runs east to west following the path of the moon. At the far end we must climb steep hills to reach the upper valley. Tico's place is further still. Our animals will be tired. They are not trail-hardened. But we need to keep pushing in order to reach his place by nightfall."

"And how are you feeling, señor?"

"I feel fine. It is good to be in the saddle again, and good to visit these lands once more. We should fill our water bags. The water is clean here.

"Now that we are leaving the river, Pablo, I want you to ride abreast of me. I need to know where you are at all times. Ride to my left, and keep Chico close to your left. We need to keep our eyes open for wild animals: coyote, cougar, and bear. And we need to be aware of the cattle too, especially the bulls. Their rutting time is over, but some of the young bulls do not know it yet. They may view us as rivals. One rule you should always follow when you are on the rancho: do not dismount unless it is absolutely necessary."

"Why is that, señor?"

"It is for your own safety. These long-horn cattle are as wild as deer, but unlike deer they can be very aggressive. When you are on your horse you are bigger than them, and they respect your combined size. And if, despite your size, they come after you, you can easily elude them on your pony. But if you are on foot you are smaller than them and not nearly as fast. On foot they are not afraid of you and may attack you. That is why vaqueros only dismount when there are no cattle nearby."

"Gracias, señor. I will remember."

The two mounted their horses, and guided them up the riverbank. They climbed a gradual incline, following a well-trodden trail. They rounded a low hill on their right and came upon an area of flat land running north and south. To the north, along a plateau above the river, spread a dense forest of live oak. It ran for several miles to the very foothills of the mountains. To the south, in a depression formed by two hills, lay a small lake surrounded by bull rush and thick brush. The unruffled surface of the lake reflected a flawless upside down-view of the sky and surrounding landscape.

Inigua gestured about him. "The Spanish named this place *Mira Monte*. They called it that because you get your first view of the mountains of Ojai from here. That lake over there is a good place to snare duck and geese. There are several other shallow lakes in the valley, all of which disappear in summer."

As they advanced onto the higher ground, the mountains surrounding the Ojai Valley sprang into view like a series of vast ocean waves frozen in time, their crests flecked with snowy foam. The ridges of the mountains rose one behind the other and bent themselves into a great oval bowl enclosing the ten mile-long by three mile-wide valley.

Pablo's breath caught at the spectacle spread before him. His eyes were drawn to the most prominent of the mountains far to the east of the valley: a great wall of horizontal, striated rock that stood like the rampart of some mythical city. "What is that big rocky mountain up there?" he asked.

"We Chumash call it *Sitoptopo*, which means cane or grass. It looks a little like a bundle of cane lying on its side. The Spanish could not pronounce Sitoptopo, so they called it Topa Topa. Those Spaniards had such bad ears and such lazy tongues. They could not pronounce Aw'hai either, so they call it Ojay, or Ojai. We used to try to correct their pronunciation, but they did not like us doing it. So we decided to let them live in their ignorance."

The riders advanced, threading their way between two hills. Another lake came into view. This lake was shallower than the first, long and slender, and filled with reeds. They skirted the lake, and at last entered the Ojai Valley proper.

Pablo felt very small in the face of the gigantic mountains towering thousands of feet above him. Their imposing presence intimidated him, and their brooding silence was unnerving. He could not get over the feeling that he was being watched and listened to.

He scanned the sky and saw a giant condor soaring overhead, its wings dipping and lifting as it carved a great circle against the endless vault of blue. To the east, and much lower down, he saw buzzards making smaller, tighter circles as they descended upon something that lived and breathed no more.

Inigua said, "In Chumash legend these mountains were once living beings – giants called *Molmoloqika*. They were the first residents of Aw'hai. But when the great flood came they all drowned and their bodies came to rest here. They are the mountains. If you look closely you can see some of their faces."

Pablo studied the mountains. He saw one peak that indeed looked like the head of a reclining Indian seen in profile. It was uncanny. And regardless of the fact the padres had taught him to discount heathen superstition, he struggled with the persistent and disturbing sense that these mountains somehow presented a threat to him. The steepness of their ascent made him wonder if they might tumble down at any moment, crushing everything below, including himself. But he told himself he was being childish to think so. These mountains had probably been standing here since the beginning of time. Maybe God had designed them as a barricade, a fortress formed by powerful stone guardians protecting this valley and all it contained. Perhaps rather than feeling threatened he should feel sheltered and safe. Despite his mixed feelings about these great monoliths and the valley they enclosed, he knew he had never seen such a beautiful, strange, and eerie place in all his life.

He noted that the valley floor sloped slightly towards him from the east, and that its flat expanse was broken here and there by low undulations and shallow watercourses. Groves of trees lined the streams and the low places which were separated by wide open fields. Pablo could see what must be a thousand long-horned cattle scattered about the valley and up onto the slopes, their heads bent to the lush winter grass. He was mystified to see the many charred remains of tree stumps and scorched brush amid all this green.

Sensing his puzzlement, Inigua said, "My people have long practiced the burning of brush here in the valley and along the river. They used to burn it every few years. Clearing the brush allowed grass to grow, which attracted deer, rabbit, and other game. It also made it easier for we humans to travel cross-country. Fernando Tico has learned this lesson too and has continued the practice so as to provide forage for the cattle.

"We will follow this path down the center of the valley. It leads to the track we will climb on that brushy incline at the far end."

They rode on in silence, enjoying the scenery and the warm day. Cattle paused from their grazing to watch silently as they passed. After a time, Inigua observed, "We Chumash always considered this valley a sacred place. Many shaman make their homes here. Some of them live here in the valley, others are recluses. They live in hidden places high in the mountains."

"How do they feed themselves up there?" asked Pablo.

"Oh, they have their ways. They eat what they find. Sometimes they run down deer. Their families help them too. But those antap know many things. They spend their days thinking about the ways of this world and the way of things beyond this world. They drink Momoy and commune with the spirit world. They paint their visions on overhanging rocks and in caves."

Pablo was looking ahead and saw two spirals of smoke rising in the east. "What is that smoke up there?" he asked.

"Those are probably cooking fires from villages, or rancherias, as you know them. The village in the distance, on the left, is called Sitoptopo, after the mountain behind it. The one on the right is Huyawit, which means Condor. It is hidden among the oaks. We may visit there before we climb the hill. There is a third village here in the lower valley. It is behind us, up the Ventura river beyond where we left it. It is called *Matilja*, or what the Spanish called Matilija. That is another word they could not wrap their tongues around. I did not take you to Matilja because it was out of our way. There are a couple of villages in the upper valley as well: Aw'hai and *Sis'a*. Some of the men from these villages are now vaqueros.

"But there are not many people left in these valleys now. In the old days there were many more. People here, when they visited the mission, carried back horrible diseases the Spanish had brought with them. Sickness spread among the people like grassfire and many of them died. Later, the Spanish came up here and convinced some of those who remained to go to the mission to work and be fed. Only those who refused are still here. They and their children. They do not visit the mission much any more. They are afraid to go there."

The two rode through the long valley, crossing several small streams along the way. An avian choir sang to them from the brush and trees as they passed. As they neared the steep hillside at the far end they came upon a wide, grassy field. It was surprisingly empty of livestock. "We should stop here," said Inigua. "Just for a little while, to rest the animals and let them graze. They have a hard climb ahead of them. Let us hobble them and leave them. The village of Huyawit is not far from here. We can stretch our legs and visit it. I want to talk to a man there."

When the animals were secured, Pablo waited while Inigua took some things from Chico's back and packed them in a blanket. While he was waiting, Pablo scanned the land around him. He saw movement some distance away to the north and east across the valley.

"I see something over there," he said.

"What is it?"

"It looks like an animal. It is big and brown. I think it might be a bear."

Inigua stood up and looked where Pablo was pointing. "That is a Grizzly," he said, seeing the hunched ball of fur that was its back. "That place over there is the killing and skinning ground here in the lower valley. It is called Calaveras, the place of the skulls. That bear is probably feeding on beef left behind from the burning."

"What burning is that?"

"As you surely know, when the vaqueros slaughter cattle it is not for the meat, but for the skins and the tallow. They take the hides away from that place and stake them out to dry. They render the tallow in a whaling pot and cart it to the mission. The carcasses are of no use. They are dragged by yoked oxen into a convenient pile. A fire is built in their midst and they are burned. But often not all of the bodies are consumed by the fire. That is one of the reason there are so many bears, cougars, bobcats and coyotes around here. They come and feed on the remains. They have an easy life because of it, and they multiply like rabbits.

"Come, let us go now. It is getting late."

"But what about our horses and the mule? With the hobbles they cannot run away if the Grizzly comes after them."

"That bear will not bother these animals. Why should he? He has all he can eat where he is with no effort."

Inigua gathered up the corners of the blanket and slung it over his shoulder. Then he led Pablo to the south through a grove of oak trees that reached down from the mountains behind. They followed a shaded foot path for about a half a mile until they came upon a clearing. There they found a cluster of eight or ten Indian houses made of tule. Dogs came running forth to challenge them, barking raucously, alternately advancing and retreating while looking over their shoulders at the houses.

Men and women, followed timidly by naked children, came forth to see what had stirred the dogs. They saw the old man and the boy approaching and called the dogs off. Several young men wearing taparrabos, came forward to meet the strangers. Some of them had decorated their bodies and faces with curving lines of black and white paint.

Inigua called out a greeting, "Haku, sons of Huyawit."

"Haku, grandfather and young one," came the reply.

"We come as friends," said Inigua. "I would speak with a man called Qupe."

A young man stepped forward and said, "Qupe is my uncle. He is in the family 'ap. I will take you to him."

They were led to one of the larger houses in the village. The young man called to his uncle and announced their arrival. A man's voice from within told them to enter. Pablo followed Inigua's lead and removed his boots, and then stooped through the doorway. Inside, the circular walls of the house curved up over their heads to form the roof, in the center of which a halo of light entered through the smoke hole. When his eyes became accustomed to the dimness, Pablo saw a man whose face was painted in black and white lines. He was sitting cross-legged just beyond a small fire burning in the pit. Of middle age, he wore a taparrabo and had a short deerskin cape draped over his shoulders. Pablo did as Inigua, and sat down immediately near the fire. Little heat came from the fire as it had been allowed to burn down to glowing remains.

The man put aside the strands of milkweed stems he had been braiding into a cord. "Welcome to Huyawit," the man said. "I am the one called Qupe. You honor us with your visit."

"Thank you, Qupe. My name is Inigua. I am a son of Shisholop on the coast, and this is my young friend Pablo from the mission. We bring word from your niece, Encarnacíon."

"Oh? I hope she is well."

"Yes. She sends her love, and also these gifts of food." Inigua opened the blanket to reveal cloth bags filled with beans, grain, seeds, and dried fruit. In addition there were several bowls and a large wooden spoon from the kitchen. "You can keep the blanket as well," added Inigua.

"I am thankful," the man said looking at the parcels. "Encarnacíon is a good niece. She remembers her family. These gifts are welcome. It has been a hard winter up here, very wet and cold. At times we have been reduced to fighting with the beasts over scorched meat left on the killing ground. But we fare better than many people living around here. Our village is on the high ground at least. We have had no flooding."

He then spoke over his shoulder. "'Akiwo, take these things to your grandmother. Tell her we have two guests for dinner tonight." A young girl rose from the shadows at back of the house. Pablo hadn't noticed her before. She came forward and gathered up the blanket. As she did so she glanced at Pablo and smiled. Pablo noted that she was a year or two older than he. He also noted that she was very pretty. She wore a deerskin skirt and a little vest of the same material. Pablo blushed and tried not to look after her as she carried the things outside.

"What brings you here?" asked Qupe. "Surely you did not come all this way on our account. There are many others who are in greater need."

"We have other business up this way," said Inigua. "We are on our way to see Señor Tico in the upper valley. We were sent by Padre Uria from the mission.

"And although I thank you for inviting us to eat with you, we cannot accept. We want to meet with the mayordomo before nightfall."

"It is getting late in the day," Qupe answered. "I do not think you can reach him before sundown. By the time you get there he will be eating his evening meal. Since you are not gente de razón, he will not be interrupted to see you. He is a man of very regular habits. And he runs a strict household. He retires early, and is up before dawn. And besides, there is no guarantee that he would feed you or provide you with a place to stay. He is not a generous man, at least not with Indians."

"Hmm. Perhaps you are right. We should have left the mission at dawn."

"You can spend the night here," said Qupe. "There is plenty of room in this house, and we will have a warm fire. Where are your horses?"

"In the field before the grove."

"Bring them here. They will be safer because of the dogs. Tether them behind the 'ap."

After some further conversation and the sharing of news, Inigua and Pablo returned to the valley to retrieve their mounts. On the way, Pablo said, "Who is that man Qupe?"

"He is an antap. He is only one of many different kinds of shaman. He is one who studies the sky and keeps track of the seasons."

"And who was that girl?" asked Pablo casually.

"She cannot be his daughter. She is too young. She is probably a granddaughter. Why do you ask? Do you like her?"

"I...well...what is there not to like about her?"

"You cannot speak the Chumash tongue very well, can you, Pablo?"

"I know some Ventureño Chumash, but this is different. Some words are the same, but many are not."

"That is understandable. There are many different dialects. And I do not think she speaks much Spanish. That makes it hard for you to talk to her, eh? But you know her name do you not?"

"Sí, señor," said Pablo looking off in the distance. "Her name is 'Akiwo."

"Oh. 'Akiwo means 'Star.' It is a lovely name, eh, Pablo?"

His face reddened. He shrugged. His neck itched and he scratched it.

"If you like her you should give her a gift. Maybe one of those balls of ponocha candy that Encarncíon gave you. Girls like sweet things."

Pablo averted his head and gazed up at Topa Topa. "Mmm," he muttered distractedly.

By the time they had returned to the village and staked out their animals, the sun had descended behind Sulphur Mountain to the south and west. But sunlight still lit the face of Sitoptopo in the east. The sheer rock face reflected the sunlight back over the valley diffusing it in a spectacular haze of pink light

"Look at that, señor. Isn't it beautiful? Everything has turned pink, even your face."

"Sí, Pablo. That happens here sometimes. It is a magical time. But it only lasts for a moment or two before the sun goes down. Perhaps this pink moment is an omen."

The winter sky above was cloudless. Because there was no wind, the heat rose rapidly from the valley. A cool breeze blew down the slope and through the oak grove.

"I am feeling chilled," said Inigua. "It will be cold tonight. We had better unpack our *frazadas*." They slung their heavy woolen blankets over their shoulders, and gathered a few other items from the packs. Then they made their way around to the front of Qupe's house.

They were welcomed by Qupe and his family, and given a place of honor near the fire. Qupe sat next to his wife, 'Alapay. Six other members of

101

the extended family, including their granddaughter, 'Akiwo, arrayed themselves about the fire. They dined on acorn soup, venison, dried elderberries, and fry bread made from the flour Encarnacíon had sent from the mission.

All the conversations took place in Mountain Chumash, and Pablo was lost in a fog of words. Try as he might, he could not follow what they were saying. The Chumash language had always sounded to him as if it were Spanish spoken backwards. The girl did not look at him; at least not directly. But he felt that she was watching him nonetheless.

After they had eaten 'Akiwo began gathering up the wooden plates and bowls and stacking them by the door. Qupe pulled out two steatite pipes shaped like cigars.

"Would you join me in a smoke, elder one? I have some good Indian tobacco."

Inigua nodded, "Yes, I would join you. And I have something here that you might find interesting." He withdrew the small ceramic flask that held the pear brandy. "This will help ward off the chill of the night," he said, winking.

They filled their pipes and lit them with burning twigs from the fire. They passed the flask back and forth across the fire, taking dainty, exploratory sips.

Pablo watched the girl toss the leftovers out the doorway to the family dogs. Then she collected the dishes and left the house. He gazed after her.

After a minute had passed, Pablo tapped Inigua on the knee and said, "I have to go. Where is it that one pees around here?"

"Go to the creek behind the village and follow it downstream. But do not go too far, and beware of the dogs when you return. If they come after you, do not run. Bend over and pick up a stone. If there are no stones handy, pretend you have one and are prepared to throw it. Village dogs know what it is to be stoned. They will be afraid and leave you alone."

Pablo made his way through the failing light to the creek side. He found 'Akiwo squatting there washing the plates and bowls. She turned her head and looked at him, raising one eyebrow. She smiled at his obvious shyness. She returned to her work. Pablo could think of nothing to say that she might understand.

Presently, 'Akiwo finished the dishes and stood up, looking over at him questioningly. He held out his open palm. It held a ball of ponocha candy.

"For you," he attempted in Chumash.

She looked at it, puzzled. Pablo realized that it looked like a dirt clod. "It is something to eat," he said, pantomiming. "It is sweet." He held it out. She studied it for a moment, and then took it.

Pablo felt like a fool. He turned abruptly and walked downstream to do his business. When he returned she was gone. He arrived back at the 'ap, to find her there. She was sharing her prize with other members of the family. Her dark eyes sparkled as they followed him to his place next to Inigua.

The two men sat up talking and laughing and telling stories for another hour or so. One by one the family members made their way to their elevated sleeping platforms. The girl disappeared towards the back of the house. Pablo caught himself nodding off several times. It had been a long, tiring day. Eventually, Qupe and Inigua went out together to make water and then retired. Pablo and Inigua settled down on mats spread on either side of the fire.

"Sleep well, Pablo," said Inigua. "We leave early in the morning."

"Sí, señor."

Before long the only sound in the 'ap was the deep breathing of its sleeping inhabitants.

*   *   *   *   *

Sometime after midnight Pablo awoke to find someone standing over him. From the dim red glow emanating from the fire pit, he could make out a pair of bare legs. He raised himself onto one elbow and looked up. The figure above him lifted Pablo's blanket and quickly scooted in beside him. It was 'Akiwo, and she was shivering.

"*Frio*," she whispered. "*Muy frio.*"

Pablo thought it was no wonder she was cold. She had no clothes on. She snuggled her back up against the curve of his warm body. Pablo adjusted the blanket to cover them both. His heart was pounding. Nervously, he looked around the dark interior. He could see no movement, and he heard nothing but even breathing, and a snoring coming from the back of the house. In the dim glow he saw the curve of Inigua's blanketed back on the other side of the fire pit. The steady rise and fall of the old man's back told Pablo he was sound asleep.

Pablo put his arm over the girl, drawing her closer to him. She was really quite cold. He wanted to say something, but was too afraid to make a sound. He didn't want to waken anyone. He lay there wide awake, tense and expectant.

The girl eventually stopped shivering and lay very still. He knew she was not sleeping though. After awhile she stretched her limbs, and then rolled over to face him. Her arm moved carelessly across his side, her hand coming to rest in the small of his back. "Haku," she whispered. She raised her head and nuzzled his boyish face with her nose. She inhaled. It seemed to Pablo that she was testing his scent, like an animal. She moved her head to

103

the side and placed her lips against his ear. He could feel her warm breath as she exhaled.

A tingling thrill swept through Pablo's body, but he was too terrified to act, or even to move. He felt a stirring between his legs, and a growing hardness down there. The girl's hand moved to his waist, and then wandered over his hips and his rounded buttocks. Pablo was reminded that he was only wearing his sleeping shirt and that he was naked from the waist down. He buried his face in girl's dark, smoky hair, and clutched her trim body to his chest. The girl's hand found what it had apparently been searching for all along. She clasped it, and Pablo gasped audibly.

On the other side of the fire pit, Inigua smiled into the darkness.

16

MAYORDOMO

Gray light gleamed through the smoke hole in the early dawn. Pablo awoke with a start when he heard movement behind him. Much to his relief, he found the place beside him vacant. He turned to see Inigua pulling on his pants.

"Buenos días," Inigua said in a low tone. "Are you ready to ride?"

"Sí, senor," said Pablo. Although he would like to see the girl before he left, he was also eager to put this place behind him. He dressed quickly. The two gathered up their belongings and exited the 'ap.

As they moved behind the house to their horses, they saw two villagers armed with bows climbing the slope behind the village. "They go to hunt deer," said Inigua. "Deer graze in the valley at night and then retreat to cover in the hills as day comes."

The man and boy took a bag of oats from Chico's pack and divided it among their animals. While the horses fed, Inigua took two handfuls of jerky from the pack. He handed one to Pablo and said, "Eat this when you get hungry." Inigua stuffed his own jerky in his side pocket. He took two cups of dried beans from the food pack and put them in a leather bag. He filled the bag with water, drew the drawstrings closed, and then hung it over one of the short posts on Chico's pack frame. "We will cook these tonight," he said.

They saddled the animals and led them down to the stream. When the horses had had their fill, the two riders tightened their girth straps and mounted up.

At that moment 'Akiwo came running from the family 'ap.

"Pablo," she said, shyly, as she approached the side of the boy's pony. She hesitated, looked behind her, and then raised her hand to him. "Kiwa'nan, Pablo," she said.

Pablo looked down at her, embarrassed and perplexed. He took her hand.

"She is saying 'good-bye' to you," said Inigua.

Pablo looked at Inigua, and then down at the girl. "*Adiós*, 'Akiwo," he said. His throat caught. The girl spoke again, blurting out something in Chumash. Pablo looked questioningly at Inigua.

"She wants you to come back… sometime," he said.

"Sí, sí," said Pablo, earnestly, and then bit his tongue. He was mortified at having Inigua witness this exchange. "Adiós. *Hasta otro día*," he said.

After an uncomfortable pause, Inigua said, "We must go now." He turned Tobaco down the path leading from the village. Pablo reluctantly released the girl's hand and followed. He looked back to see her standing forlornly by the stream. She raised her hand in farewell. Pablo waved and then hurried to catch up with his mentor.

They rode down through the oak grove and emerged onto the level valley floor once more. Although the sun had just risen, it was still below the high land, and the eastern end of the Ojai Valley lay in deep shadow. Pablo took his place between Inigua and the mule.

Inigua looked over at the boy. "You seem to have made quite an impression on 'Akiwo," he said, innocuously. "What did you do to win her heart?"

Pablo flushed. "I didn't do anything."

"You must have done something. Was it the candy you gave her?"

"It wasn't the candy. She just likes me, that's all."

"I think you like her too."

"I don't want to talk about it, señor."

Pablo's feelings were muddled. He was distressed at leaving 'Akiwo behind, but thrilled with his new discovery. He finally knew what it meant to love someone. The experience had been exhilarating, and it had felt so good, so right. He had never felt anything like it before. As he rode along he thought about 'Akiwo, and savored every moment he had spent with her.

But despite his feelings for the girl, Pablo was glad to be gone from the primitive village and her watchful family. He was also glad to be free of the mission and the constant restraint it imposed. He had not realized till now how oppressive it was. Pablo's reverie withered when he thought of Padre Uria, however. The boy felt a sudden twinge of guilt. The holy father would surely have been shocked by what he had done. The priest would no doubt consider it sinful. But Pablo rejected that idea. He could not imagine loving 'Akiwo to be a sin. No one had ever made him feel so alive before.

The riders rejoined the main trail and turned towards the steep hills at the east end of the valley. As the prospect of this new day's adventures grew, his thoughts of the girl dissipated altogether. It was another cloudless winter day, the first day of March, a day full of promise and sunshine and growing warmth. Pablo felt a surge of excitement. Out here in this wonderful land of sweeping vistas, glorious mountains and mysterious shadowy glens, Pablo felt a sense of freedom, and of a joy so pure he wanted to shout 'Hola!' to the mountaintops. But, of course, he dare not. It would be a childish thing to do, and he wanted to be thought of as a man. If he had been alone he might have put Rojo into a gallop and raced through the crisp, clean morning air, waving his hat as he went. But instead he put a sober look on his face and dutifully led the fully-packed mule by its tether.

They rode on in silence, munching jerky as they went. After about a mile they came to a grove of oak trees which climbed into the hills on either

106

side of the trail. The man and boy rode abreast along the trail as it rose up into the hills. The horses and mule began to labor as it steepened. The trail zigzagged through chaparral as it ascended above the valley. Rounding a sharp curve they heard a clatter of hooves off to the left, and the crash of brush. Then branches at the trailside parted violently and a deer, in full flight, flashed across the trail before plunging into the undergrowth on the opposite side.

Inigua reigned in and called, "Whoa."

Not ten paces behind the deer raced a mountain lion in headlong pursuit. The lion entered the open space of the trail directly in front of them, and, when it saw the riders, its claws dug into the damp clay, bringing it to an abrupt halt. The big cat froze and arched its back, its yellow eyes wild with surprise, malice, and fear. Tobaco screamed and reared, flailing its front legs high in the air. Caught by surprise, Inigua grabbed leather and just barely managed to stay in the saddle while keeping his horse from tumbling over backwards. The cougar panicked at the sight and shot back the way it had come. It crashed into the brush and disappeared.

Rojo screamed too, and whirled in preparation of fleeing down the trail. Its shoulder slammed into Chico, however, throwing the hapless, top-heavy mule off its feet and down on its side. Pablo dragged on the romal, desperately trying to keep Rojo in check. He jerked the pony's head hard to the left so that it had no recourse but to run in tight circles. Tobaco dropped to all fours, and Inigua somehow managed to keep him from bolting. Both riders spoke earnestly to their animals, trying to calm and reassure them. Chico's legs thrashed uselessly, unable to gain purchase and rise under the heavy pack. It could only scream, "Hee-haw, hee-haw."

After an interminable passage of prancing confusion the riders finally gained control of their animals. Pablo's heart was pounding so hard he thought it might burst his ribs.

Anticipating Pablo's next move, Inigua called out, "Do not dismount. If the horse still wants to run, you will never be able to stop him from the ground. Follow me up the trail. Leave the mule. We will come back for him."

They rode the skittish horses up the steep path a hundred yards or so until they had left the scent of the big cat behind. Their mounts began to relax and regain their composure.

Inigua said, "Do you have Rojo's tether?"

"Sí, señor. It is on my saddle horn, as you instructed me."

"Good. Slip it over his head. Then secure him high and tight to that scrub oak there. Do not use the reins to tie him; use the tether. I will do the same. Then we will go get Chico."

When this was done, they hurried down the trail on foot to the still-recumbent mule. Chico's eyes rolled in fear and his flanks quivered as their footsteps approached. Inigua spoke reassuringly to him as they unhitched the pack and urged him to his feet. They talked soothingly and ran their hands over his shivering sides. When he was calm again, they hoisted the pack rack onto his back and fastened it in place. They lashed the packs to the racks and then led him up the hill.

Inigua said, "You did well, Pablo. That was good horsemanship back there. You may have the makings of a vaquero after all."

"Gracias, señor." Pablo said, sincerely. He felt proud to be praised by this man.

Chico seemed heartened by the sight of the two horses. Soon the riders were advancing up the steep incline once more. About midway up they stopped at an overlook. They dismounted and gave their mounts a chance to catch their breath. Pablo sat on a boulder and gazed out on a sweeping vista of the Ojai Valley. He now knew what it must be like to be a bird soaring high in the sky and looking down on the land below. The view was beautiful from up here, and he could see for miles and miles across the verdant valley towards the river.

Soon they continued the climb, and as they neared the top of the steep ascent the sun embraced them in its golden warmth. They gave the animals another blow, and looked across the long, narrow upper valley. Topa Topa showed itself in the north now, looking even more massive and majestic. To Pablo, the upper valley looked like an oversized irrigation ditch carved between two massive berms. Long-horned cattle dotted the U-shaped valley. They were handsome beasts: leggy and slim-bodied with long curving horns and sloping hind quarters. They were big too, weighing six to eight hundred pounds, very strong and agile, and as wild and feckless as deer. Most were brown, but others were red, black, white, or tan. Some cattle had mixed black and white hair that actually made them look blue.

Inigua said, "In another month the vaqueros around here will begin rounding up the cattle, both here and in the lower valley. It will be the same at Rancho Piru. They will brand the calves and the strays with the *hierro* of San Buenaventura – which is an 'AB' married together into one letter. They will also notch their ears with the *señal*, or earmark, of this rancho.

Then, in mid-June, La Matanza will begin. The killing time will last for three months. If you ever become a vaquero you will both love and hate La Matanza. You will find yourself living in your saddle from dawn until dark. You will change horses several times a day to maintain a fresh mount. You will chase, you will herd, you will lazo till your arm is ready to fall off. That is, unless the mayordomo does not like you, and so orders you to work on the ground for the killing and slaughtering. Or for the skinning, scraping and staking of hides. Or the jerking and drying of beef. It is back-breaking work no matter what you do. But it is a man's work; have no doubt. It is exciting and even fun, unless of course you are hurt or get killed. And when it is over, you will have earned your rest, my friend. The rest of the year is spent working horses and driving the weekly allotment of cattle to the mission."

As they rode into the upper valley, Pablo said, "Where is Señor Tico's house?"

"I do not know. I have not been here since he came down from Santa Barbara a year or two ago. Do not worry, boy. We will find him.

"Oh, and by the way, Pablo, you had better not call him 'señor.' He may well be offended. He probably expects to be called 'Don Tico.' He sees himself as an important man. And indeed, mayordomos on these ranchos are nothing if not kings. They have the power of life or death over people and animals. They can do whatever they want. When we find him, let me do the talking."

They rode on until they saw a faint spiral of smoke rising from the edge of the valley on their right. They altered their course and headed that way, threading their way through scattered oak trees.

Pablo said, "What is that?" looking ahead at a low building with a peaked roof.

"It appears to be a wooden house."

"But who would build a wooden house? I have never heard of such a thing."

"It is strange, eh? Maybe there is no adobe around here with which to build a proper Spanish house."

"I think this place will burn down one day, señor."

As they drew closer, a house and a small barn came into view in a clearing among the trees. Directly behind the house was a corral holding a score of cow ponies. In a second corral they saw an Indian vaquero holding a reata as a young horse paced in a wide circle around him. About a half-mile beyond the corral stood a collection of 'aps where Indians could be seen moving about.

"That is Aw'hai village," said Inigua following Pablo's gaze. "Most of the men there work on the rancho. They are either vaqueros or skinners. The women render tallow during La Matanza."

Flanking the wooden house were several arbors, with roofs covered with brush. Under one stood an outdoor kitchen with raised cooking platforms and a stone oven. Two other arbors were furnished with long plank tables and wooden benches along the side.

As they came on they saw a man with a walrus mustache standing casually on the front porch of the house. He was watching them. The man looked lean and strong, with a slim waist and broad shoulders. He wore a sombrero and a short-waisted *chaqueta*. The tan-colored jacket was trimmed with bright embroidery and braided around the seams and cuffs. The man's matching pants, stuffed into fine leather boots, had silver buttons running down the side. He held a coiled bull whip in his right hand, and his left thumb was hooked behind his silver belt buckle.

Inigua called out, "Buenos días, Don Tico."

The man on the porch gave an almost imperceptible nod. "What do you want?" he said.

"We want a steer," said Inigua.

"And I want to be governor of Alta California. Just because you want something does not mean you will get it."

'My name is Inigua. I come from the mission with a voucher from Padre Uria. We need a steer to make a reata for this boy, Pablo."

Don Tico looked from the old Indian to the boy. He studied the youngster, and the pony on which he sat. Then he turned his head and spat off the porch.

"What does this whelp need with a reata?"

"He would be a vaquero one day. I am here to teach him."

"Who are you to teach him?"

"My name is Inigua."

"You said that already. One moment. Inigua. Inigua? I know that name. I have heard them talk about you around here. Here and at the mission."

Inigua said nothing.

Don Tico studied him. "They say you are a *manaña*, an old master. They also say that you are no stranger to the whipping post." He let the coils of the bull whip uncoil to the wooden floor. He flicked his wrist and it came alive. The tip snapped, like a small, nasty dog. Tico's dark eyes looked into Inigua's.

"Why are you so fond of the whip, old man?"

"I am not fond of it."

"Then why did you visit the post so many times?"

"I did not choose to go there. The post visited me."

"Why?"

"When I was younger, I thought I could change what could not be changed. But that is all in the past. I am here now on a harmless errand for Padre Uria. See this." He held up the voucher with the wax seal. "This is a note giving me permission to take one steer."

Don Tico drew his arm back and then brought it forward with a flick of his wrist. There was a 'pop,' and the paper disappeared from Inigua's hand. It fluttered to the ground between them. Inigua lowered his hand and placed it on top of the other which rested on the saddle horn.

"Pick it up," said Don Tico. Inigua sat on his horse, and made no move to do so. He looked at the man on the porch with a steady, expressionless gaze.

"I will get it," said Pablo, and started to dismount.

"No," commanded the Don. Pablo froze. "You get it, old man."

Inigua did not move.

110

Just then a little girl in a long dress with puffy short sleeves opened the door of the house. "What are you doing, Papa?" she said, skipping over to his side.

"I am talking to these drifters," he said. "Go back in the house, honey."

"What's that?" she said, spying the paper on the ground. Before he could stop her, she scampered down the steps and picked up the paper. "There's writing on it, Papa, and a red thing." She hopped back up on the porch and presented it to her father. "What does it say?" she asked.

The door of the house opened. A woman, dressed very much like the little girl, poked her head out. "Come inside, Juana," she said. The woman stepped out on the porch and took the little girl by the hand and led her inside. The woman looked back anxiously, and quickly closed the door behind her.

Don Tico held the note in his left hand, but continued staring at Inigua. He saw no fear there. But he saw no defiance either, and no lack of respect. Just an unblinking, inscrutable expression that gave him no clue of what was going on inside.

The Don's eyes shifted downward. He read the note. When he was done he slipped it into his side pocket. He thought about Padre Uria. He wondered if that fat priest might cause him trouble if he refused his request. He mulled it over and came to a judicious decision.

"This is a fortunate day for you, Inigua," he said. "I have decided to grant you permission to take one steer. We have been culling out all the old animals up here. You will find a herd of them tended by a vaquero several miles to the east. Go there and tell the vaquero I said you could take one of them. And then get out of my valley, old man. I do not want to see your face around here any more."

Inigua raised his hand and touched it to the brim of his hat. "Gracias, señor," he said, "You are most kind. Adios." He turned his horse, and Pablo followed.

17

THE STEER

Inigua was silent as they rode back to the main trail. He had a curious expression on his face. To Pablo it seemed somewhere between a grin and a grimace.

The boy said, "Ay, Dios mio, señor. You were playing with a rattlesnake back there."

"Yes, a snake."

"I cannot believe what you did. And after what you told me. You said not to call him 'señor,' that it would be disrespectful."

"I know, but I did not like that man, Tico. He does not deserve the respect he demands. He reminds me of other Spaniards I have known. Two in particular: José Camacho and Pablo Cota. All three were hatched in the same vile nest. Their souls are dark and their spirits twisted. They are the vermin that came here hidden in filthy Spanish hair. There is only one way to deal with men like that."

Pablo was aghast. "What do you mean, señor?"

"Perhaps I will demonstrate it for you one day. But right now we have two other problems to consider. One is that we must take our steer and go. I had thought we would skin it up here, but I think you will agree it would be unwise to linger in this valley. The other problem is the dampness of the ground. Look at it. It is not truly muddy, but it is still damp from the rains. That is not good for drying the hide. A steer hide must dry quickly. If it does not, the skin begins to decay and weaken. The resulting leather will not be strong. It is of utmost importance that you have a reata you can trust."

"So what do we do, señor?"

"We will claim our steer first, and then continue east. We can leave the valley by following Sis'a Creek around Sulphur Mountain. Then we shall see what we find."

They rode on through the upper valley. A couple of miles further on, as they neared the end, they came upon a small herd of grazing cattle. The herd stood in the middle of an open field to the north of the trail. A lone vaquero sat astride his horse on the far side, positioned between the herd and the hills.

Inigua and Pablo left the trail and approached. They circled slowly around one side of the herd, inspecting the animals as they went.

Pablo said, "Ay, señor, these animals look bad. They are indeed old. They are scrawny and look half-dead."

"Sí, Pablo, but that is not a problem. The best reatas are made from beasts such as these. Although they seem to be just dwindling away, their hides are tough and strong. A young steer's skin is too supple, too soft and flexible. A reata made from a young steer will stretch too much when you lasso a big animal, like a bull, or a bear." Pablo's head swiveled towards Inigua.

The vaquero in the distance put his horse in motion and rode forward to meet them.

When he drew close, Inigua raised his hand in greeting, and called, "Haku, *caballero*."

"Haku, grandfather. I am Jesús." He was a young Chumash in a big floppy hat held in place by a chin strap. He sported a wispy mustache and goatee, and wore a *serapé* against the morning chill. A red sash was wrapped about his waist, and his tight pants descended into leather leggings that came up over the knees.

"My name is Inigua, and this is Pablo. How are you, vaquero?"

"I am well. But it was a cold night last night out here in the open. I slept on the ground next to a fire. Don Tico has ordered me to stay here and keep this *mañada* together until the others come to slaughter them."

"For your sake I hope they come soon," said Inigua. "We are here to relieve you of one of your charges. Don Tico has given us permission to take one steer. With it we will make a reata for this vaquerito."

Pablo blushed. He knew he did not yet deserve this appellation.

"Oh? You have permission to take a steer? Are you sure of that, grandfather?"

"I am sure. I would not lie to you, Jesús."

"I hope not. The mayordomo would surely flay my back if I let you take a steer without his knowing."

"He told us to order you to give us one. Do not worry, amigo. I am telling the truth."

"That is good to hear, grandfather. I will trust you in this. But be aware that if you are lying Don Tico will come after you. He will not stop until he finds you. And then both you and I, and perhaps the boy, will be flogged. But if your words are true, take whatever steer you want."

"Graciás, Jesús. By now you probably know these cattle well enough. Which one do you think would make a good reata?"

"I think that red one over there would be good, grandfather. The one with the blaze on its forehead. His skin is unblemished, and his brand is low down on the flank. His hide will make a fine reata. He is also a calm animal. All the fight has gone out of him. He is just waiting around to die."

"Gracias, Jesús. We will take him, and we will help him down that road we all must travel."

"Allow me to cut him out of the mañada for you, grandfather."

"Gracias, señor."

113

The vaquero removed the reata from his saddle horn and loosened the noose. Holding it down at his side next to the horse, he rode slowly forward to the edge of the herd. Pablo watched him go and from behind he could see a sheathed knife strapped to the back of his right calf. He also saw a pair of rusty spurs strapped to his bare ankles above a pair of worn-out shoes.

The cattle raised their heads and looked warily at the vaquero as he approached. He kept the reata out of their view till the last moment. Then he raised his arm and made one quick turn of the loop to open it. He then sent it flying with a flick of his wrist. The noose flew thirty feet through the air and settled neatly over the head and horns of the chosen steer. Pablo was duly impressed.

The herd had seen the reata fly, and now moved away at a plodding, geriatric pace. The captured steer tried to follow, but Jesús had by then drawn the loop closed, pulled the reata taut, and dallied the near end around his pommel. His pony set his feet and braced for the pull. The red steer bawled after the departing herd, and strained at the reata. But after a few half-hearted tugs it gave up and looked back dejectedly at the vaquero. The steer was sullen, but resigned to its fate. It waited patiently for whatever might come.

"Bueno, Jesús," said Inigua. "That was a pretty throw."

Though it was apparent the vaquero took great pride in his feat, he muttered, "It was a lucky throw. What do you do with him now, grandfather? I can move the herd if you want to kill him here."

"No, gracias. We will take him with us. We cannot linger here."

"Do you want to drive him? Or you might try a tether. He has no fight left in him."

"We will drive him. It will be good practice for the boy."

Pablo noticed that Tobaco had assumed an aggressive stance as it eyed the lassoed steer. The horse had what all good steer ponies have: a healthy distain for lesser beasts. Meanwhile, Rojo merely looked on with a juvenile curiosity, while Chico simply could not have cared less.

Jesús said to Inigua, "I see you have a reata. Can you heel him?"

"Sí, compadre. Then you can retrieve your reata, eh?"

Jesús nodded, and then waited until Inigua had prepared his reata. He then rode forward to relieve the tension on his reata. Inigua followed. The steer began ambling after the slowly departing herd. Jesús pursued him and yelled, 'hi, hi,' which put the steer into a trot. It was then that Inigua let fly with his reata, the lasso of which somehow twirled into a figure-eight and caught both of its trailing legs. He snubbed the reata to the saddle horn, and reined in Tobaco. Jesús drew his mount to a halt too, and when the two reatas twanged taut, they jerked the lumbering steer to the ground. It lay there disgusted, and didn't even bother to attempt to rise.

"Hold steady, my friend," said Inigua to the vaquero. "The boy will remove our ropes."

Inigua nodded to Pablo, and the boy sprang from his pony and sprinted over to the recumbent animal.

"Approach him from behind," warned Inigua. "And beware of the horns."

When Pablo was in position, Jesús moved his mount two steps forward to relieve the tension on the reata. Pablo quickly removed the lasso from around the horns and stepped back. Jesús reeled in his reata.

"Bueno," said Inigua to the boy. "Now get mine loose. Then get out of there and remount."

As the steer got to its feet, the three riders moved ahead of him, cutting him off from the herd.

"Gracias, Jesús," said Inigua, as he coiled his reata.

"De nada, grandfather. I go now to round the mañada. Adios."

"Adios, muchacho."

The vaquero rode after the herd, waving farewell as he went. The steer looked at the two riders and vainly moved to go around them.

"Cut him off," said Inigua. The boy urged Rojo forward into the path of the steer. It stopped, and gave a sigh of resignation.

"Now we move towards him," said Inigua. "Drive him back to the trail." Pablo removed his hat and waved it over his head. "Hi, hi," he called. The steer turned and trotted to the south.

When they got to the trail, Inigua rode ahead, and angled the steer towards the east. Then the two riders settled in behind him on either flank. The steer looked back a few times, but then resigned itself to being driven, and settled into a comfortable gait.

As they rode along, Pablo said, "I want to learn to throw the reata like you and Jesús. That was magnificent back there. How did you make that throw, and how do I learn to do it?"

"That throw I made is called the *mangana de cabra*. It is one of many specialty throws. The only way to learn is to practice," said Inigua. "I can show you a few basic things to get started, but practice is what brings success, that and the guidance of someone knowledgeable. Begin with the simple throw. Just lasso something. First practice by standing on the ground. Lasso anything and everything you can: brush, tree stumps, rocks, dogs, whatever. Then do the same from a standing horse. Lasso everything. Then do it from a walking horse, and then a running horse. Accuracy will come in time. Then you can learn more difficult throws."

As they rode along, the valley began to narrow, and they could see the mountains to the south and the hills to the north joining together. Trees sprang up in the gap where the foothills merged. The land began to slope downwards. Soon they found themselves in a narrow cleft whose steep sides descended into a tumbling stream: Sis'a Creek. The trail ran alongside the narrow streambed which sang with the fullness of winter.

Trees filled the slopes on either side of the stream: sycamore and oak, and lower down cottonwoods and willow. When they got among the trees, Pablo smelled dampness in the air, and the scent of moss growing on rocks in the shadows.

Presently, Pablo detected another scent, one that grew stronger as they progressed. He curled his nose at it and said, "Ay, señor, what is that bad smell? It is like rotten eggs."

"That is sulfur, boy. It is a kind of yellow stone that smells strong. It comes from the mountain here on our right. Look there. Do you see that black stuff seeping from the rocks? It is oil and pitch. The Indians come here to gather the sticky stuff. We use it to glue things, and also to seal our water baskets and canoes. Some people like to chew on the tar."

They followed the stream for several miles as it rumbled down the barranca between steep rising hills. The shade from the dense growth along the banks created a chilly, dim tunnel through which they rode. The steer showed no inclination of leaving the trail for the spooky shadows.

"We are lucky it is still winter," said Inigua. "In summertime, when the berries are ripe, we would no doubt encounter bears feeding here along the stream."

They came to a place where Sis'a Creek merged with another stream. "From this point on this water is called Santa Paula Creek," said Inigua. "If we follow it far enough it empties into the Santa Clara River."

"The sulfur smell is even stronger here," observed Pablo.

"Sí, but soon we will leave it behind."

Before long, the canyon began to widen and the hills to fall away on either side. The stream bent its path to the south, following an ever-widening basin. The travelers emerged from the trees and welcomed the warmth of the sun as it fell upon them. By now it was early afternoon. The sky remained clear, with no sign of weather on the horizon.

They rounded a curve in the stream and came upon two Indian men standing nonchalantly by a blazing domed hut. Great billows of smoke rose above the inferno. The steer drew to a halt and looked at the startling scene. It turned its head to the two riders behind him to see what their reaction was. The riders had stopped also.

"Haku," Inigua called to the two men. "Stay here, Pablo. I will see what this is about." He gave the steer a wide berth and rode forward. Pablo watched as he conferred with the two men. After several minutes of conversation, Pablo saw the two men nod their heads and say their farewells. Then they set off on foot downstream. Inigua returned. The steer stood motionless, watching him. It was tired of this endless walking.

"That hut was a hunting and fishing lodge," said Inigua. "The people from down around Santa Paula use it. Those men spent the night here, but they said the place was full of fleas. That is why they burned it."

"Fleas?"

"Sí, Pablo. This is a common problem with our Indian houses. After a few years of use they become infested with fleas. The fleas come from the animals we hunt, and from dogs. They get into everything: the tule walls and thatch, the beds, your hair, your clothes, everything. The only way to get rid of them is to burn the house. That kills all the fleas. Then you build a new house in its place. It is not difficult if you know how, and have a family to help."

The two riders sat and watched the fire burn. Inigua looked around him. The burning house stood on a rise not far from the creek. It was protected from the wind to the north and south by trees, and to the east and west by hills. And yet it stood in a sunny clearing under the open sky.

"This is a good spot to camp," he said to the boy. "We are out of Don Tico's valley, and there is water close by. And you see that burning hut? The ground under it will be dry, since it was protected from the rain. It will be even dryer after the fire has baked it. Tomorrow we can stake this steer's hide within the area of that house."

"But what about the fleas, and the ashes?"

"The fleas will be dead, and you can sweep the ashes aside with a branch. The ashes would not hurt the hide anyway. In fact, some vaqueros use a mixture of water and ash to dehair the leather thongs."

"Shall we kill the steer now?" asked Pablo.

"No. It is too late in the day. We can do it in the morning if the weather is fine. The hide needs to dry in the sun all day. Besides, we are not ready. There are many preparations we must make. Let us set up camp."

They tethered the steer to a nearby tree, and hobbled the other animals. They unpacked their provisions and then removed their saddles and Chico's pack rack. Inigua handed Pablo the hatchet and directed him to cut poles and supports for the length of canvas that would be their tent. Inigua gathered firewood and started a fire with a brand from the burning lodge.

By mid afternoon they had everything arranged to their liking. Inigua put the beans on to boil in the tin pot, adding wild onion, salt, dried chili peppers, and bits of beef jerky. The two went to the stream and bathed in the bitterly cold water, then returned to the fire to warm themselves.

"We will need some stakes for the hide. Take the hatchet and find some strong, straight branches about this big around." He made a circle with his thumb and forefinger. "Bring them here, and tonight we will cut them to length and sharpen one end. We also need more firewood. It will be a cold night. I will take the horses and mule up onto that slope to the west. There is good forage there. I will hobble them and leave them overnight."

Pablo asked, "Shouldn't we feed the steer too?"

"No. His eating days are over. It will be better for us if he has an empty stomach tomorrow. But give him all the water he wants. Fill the bucket at the creek and put it where he can reach it."

117

Pablo was returning to the camp when he noticed Inigua looking south down the trail. He followed the old man's gaze and saw an Indian, dressed only in a breech cloth, running up the trail towards them. The Indian was covered in sweat, but his breathing was even and strong. When he drew near, Inigua raised his hand and said, "Haku, *ksen*."

The Indian slowed, scanned the improvised camp and the animals, and drew to a halt.

"Haku, *nono*," he replied.

Inigua said, "You are a messenger?"

"Yes. I carry word from the wots of the Santa Clara villages to those of the interior. We are planning a Spring gathering. When the people assemble, we will have a great rabbit drive, and then a feast and a festival."

"Bueno," said Inigua. "Carry a message for me too, if you will. Tell the people in the high lands that tomorrow this boy and I will kill a steer on this spot. If they want some beef, tell them to come and take what they want. We cannot use it all, and it would be a pity to leave it to the scavengers."

"I will tell them, nono. And now I must go. The day is short. Kiwa'nan." The man continued on his strong, steady run upstream.

Pablo took the hatchet and went searching along the creek for wood for the stakes and for firewood. He repeatedly returned to camp with heavy armloads. By five o'clock the sun had sunk behind the high hills to the west, and their campsite was left in shadow. The lodge had been reduced to a smoking ruin. The man and boy arranged their bedding within the tent in preparation for nightfall. The tent was close by the fire to benefit from its warmth. One end of the tent faced the fire while the other was closed off by a spare blanket draped over the opening.

When they were done, Inigua sat by the fire and surveyed the camp. "It is good to be out in the world again," he said. "I have missed it. Although it was only ten days ago that I lived at the mouth of the river, it seems a lifetime ago. Being out here in the real world reminds me of the days before the Spanish came. They changed everything, you know. The world they created... it is not my world. The mission is a world made by outsiders, a world fabricated by those who wished to change that which should remain eternal. It is a travesty. When Islay and I...When we..." His voice quavered. "Islay..." he said, and then his voice trailed off into nothing. He bowed his head.

Pablo knew not what to do or say. He had forgotten that Inigua was still mourning his wife. He could only guess at the depth of his friend's feeling, but when he looked at Inigua, it seemed to have no bottom. The old man appeared to have folded in upon himself, and shrunk to half his normal size.

Pablo looked away. He realized that Inigua had no desire for further talk. The old Indian just sat there by the fire staring blankly into the flames. From time to time he gave the beans a desultory stir with the wooden spoon.

He is probably just tired, thought Pablo. I should leave him alone. The boy rose and picked up the leaf-strewn branch he had cut earlier. "I go to sweep the ashes from the circle," he said.

"Sweep the ashes?" said Inigua, raising his eyebrows. "From the circle? Ah yes, sweep the ashes from the circle. That is good. You are wise beyond your years, Pablo."

"Huh?"

"Never mind, boy." Inigua rose from the fire. He seemed remarkably revived. "Hurry and be done with it," he said. "It will be dark soon."

While Pablo energetically worked at clearing the area where the lodge had stood, Inigua took up the old reata and walked down towards the creek. Pablo watched him go. He noticed that the old man still walked strong, though his visage was deeply lined with age. His body was lean and leathery-tough. Pablo noticed too that Inigua's legs were bowed from having been a horseman for so many years. The boy watched his mentor furtively as he swept the ashes.

The Indian inspected several large trees. He seemed to find one to his liking. He tossed the coils of the reata up and over a high horizontal limb, while retaining his grip on the lower end. The reata uncoiled as it sailed over the limb and fell down on the other side. Inigua reached out and grabbed the swaying noose.

Pablo stopped sweeping. He could not keep himself from calling, "*Qué pasa*, señor?"

Inigua turned with a grin. "Not what you think, boy. This is to raise our food beyond the reach of foraging animals in the night."

119

18

SPANIARDS

They dined on beans and tortillas that night. Pablo was ravenous, having eaten nothing during the day but a little beef jerky and dried apricots. He ate with gusto, even though Encarnacion's tortillas were a bit stale. His spoon was a mere blur of movement in the firelight. When he was done, he wiped his bowl clean with the last of his tortilla and ate that too. Then he rubbed his belly and said, "Those beans were excelente, señor. How did you learn to cook like that?"

"I am glad you liked them, Pablo. I learned to cook when I was very young. Chumash men did most of the cooking, you know. We fished and hunted, and then we cleaned and cooked whatever we caught. The women were occupied with other things. They gathered, pounded, and leached acorns, and then they boiled them in water to make porridge or soup. They gathered seeds and berries and many other foodstuffs. They wove beautiful baskets. They made jewelry and clothing and other things. They also took care of the children. They had plenty to do without cooking.

"But enough of that. We need to think about our own preparations now. It is time to make the stakes for stretching the hide. Make them this long," he said, holding his two palms about a foot and a half apart. "Start by cutting them to length with the hatchet. Hold them on that log when you chop. Then sharpen one end of each stake with a knife. But before you begin, take the dishes down to the stream and wash them, por favor. We must keep the camp free of food smells."

While Pablo was occupied with this task, Inigua took the leftover beans in their lidded pot and placed it in the center of a blanket spread on the ground. He piled the other food stores around the pot. He gathered up the corners and tied them in a knot. He carried the bundle to the suspended reata and drew the noose tight just below the knot. He then hauled the bundle twenty feet up into the darkness and tied the end of the reata to the tree trunk.

Pablo and Inigua emerged from the darkness and came together at the fire. Pablo settled down behind a log and began sorting the branches. As he did so, Inigua retrieved several items from the packs: the bota of wine, a rectangular sharpening stone, and the three knives that the blacksmith Albino had made. He unwrapped the knives from their cloth and noted that Albino had put a nice one-quarter inch bevel on all the blades. He picked them up one at a time by their wooden handles and inspected them in the firelight. He explained to Pablo that the first was a sticking knife, used for cutting the throat. Its point was sharpened on both sides for ease of entry. It was also useful for other purposes. The second was a skinning knife. Its curved blade was about eight inches long and designed to glide easily between flesh and hide. The last was a butcher knife. It was longer and wider than the others, and used for cutting meat from the carcass.

Inigua dribbled a little olive oil over the rectangular stone and smoothed it out with his forefinger. He picked up the butcher knife and began to meticulously hone it. Pablo watched with great interest.

Inigua said, "Listen, boy, and remember well. After a horse and a reata, a knife is the vaquero's most important tool. He carries it with him at all times. He does not carry a special knife like these, but one that can be used for any purpose. He keeps it sharp. A vaquero uses it every day in his work, and it is also there for his personal protection. I will speak more of this later.

"There are three steps in sharpening a knife. First: a bevel is ground on its cutting edge, either by hand using a file or by running it back and forth across a turning wheel. Albino has already done this. Second: the bevel is then honed. This is done with a fine-grained stone such as this, using oil or grease or water as a lubricant. Third: the cutting edge is brought to its sharpest by steeling it. This is done by drawing the edge up and down along a special steeling rod. We do not have such a rod, so instead we will strop each blade with a strip of leather. I have freed one from the mission shop for that purpose."

Inigua raised the bota of wine and squirted some into his mouth. "Ahh," he said with satisfaction. "San Gabriel." He wiped his mouth with the back of his hand and continued his instructions.

"When skinning an animal, you must always keep your blade at its sharpest. You must hone or strop it as often as needed. In this way you will not make mistakes and cut where you do not intend. I will show you tomorrow."

Pablo said, "I have heard that the Indians were ignorant of metal before the Spanish came. How did you skin animals before you had knives?"

"Good question. But I must tell you we were not entirely ignorant of metal. A few people on the coast had pieces of knives and swords that had been around for generations. I do not know where they came from. They might have been traded with Spanish ships that carried the first explorers. But this would have been long, long ago. Because the blades were old and rare and had grown smaller over time, we only used them to open fish and cut meat.

"Most people did not have them. They used sharpened stones to skin animals, mainly small pieces of flint and obsidian. These stones are both hard and brittle. You strike them on the side towards the edge with another stone and this knocks off flakes which leave sharp edges on the mother stone. These edges are as sharp as any knife."

By now Pablo had accumulated a considerable pile of stakes. Inigua asked, "How many do you have there?"

The boy's lips moved as he counted them. "Twenty," he said.

"That should be plenty," said Inigua. He handed the boy the honed butcher knife and said, "Now use this to give each stake a sharp point on one end. We will re-sharpen the knife later." Pablo held the hefty knife up to the firelight and admired it.

He said, "You have often told me how the Spanish changed everything when they came here, señor. And that you think the changes were bad. But it seems to me that they brought many wonderful things. Things like horses, and this knife. Things that make life easier."

Inigua looked at him in dismay. "First of all, the Spanish did not make our lives easier. Of that there can be no doubt. Second, I would say that although they brought some useful things with them, they carried more bad things than good. What they did bring decimated our people and changed our way of life forever. I would give back all the good things they ever brought in exchange for what we have lost."

Pablo furrowed his brow and said, "But the Chumash at the mission seem to be doing just fine. They are good Christians. They eat well, and have learned many useful occupations."

Inigua sighed. "The Chumash you see now are only the survivors, the ones who bowed down and accepted everything that came. You perhaps are not aware that there were many more Chumash living outside the mission than in. We numbered perhaps fifteen thousand before the Spanish came. But now there is only one of us standing where six had stood before. And what happened to the others? Most were carried off by diseases brought here by the Spanish. Others died from being over-worked, or from eating food that did not agree with their Indian stomachs. Some killed themselves with drink, or poison, or in other ways too numerous to mention."

The old man looked solemnly across the fire at the boy. He saw Pablo busily shaving slivers from the stakes and playfully sending them somersaulting into the flames.

Inigua gazed into the fire. After a time, he said, "I remember the day the Spaniards first came here. It is a day I will never forget." Then he raised the bota above his head and squeezed himself a drink.

Inigua picked up the sticking knife and held it out in front of him in the firelight. After studying it, he lowered it to the stone and began to hone.

"What did you think when you first saw them?" asked Pablo. "You must have been surprised, eh, señor?"

"Surprised, yes. I was young then, about your age. I did not know what to think when I first saw them, nor did anybody else. We thought they were just worn-out travelers passing through. So we were hospitable to them, which is our way. We did not realize then what their intentions were. I was at home when they came, in our village – *Shisholop*."

"Shisholop?" said Pablo. "That's a funny name. What does it mean?"

Inigua rolled his eyes. "I see now what Francisco meant about your habit of asking questions. I will answer this one, boy, but if I am to tell this story I must ask you not to keep interrupting me with questions. A story is best told from beginning to end without interruption. There is plenty of time for questions when it is done.

"But to answer you: Shisholop has various meanings. Some of our neighbors thought it meant 'in the mud' because at certain times of year they had to wade through a muddy estuary to reach our village. But we who lived there did not subscribe to that meaning. We were people of the sea, and proud of it. We had many canoes, and made our living by fishing and trading. To us, Shisholop means 'port on the coast.'"

"That sounds a lot better," said Pablo as he continued to whittle.

"I will tell you my story now if you are ready."

"Oh, yes, señor, tell me. I will be silent."

"The Spanish appeared here a few days after a very strong earthquake. We called it *Shup Istukun*. We used to name earthquakes because there are so many of them. Without names it was hard to keep them straight when talking about them later. Shup Istukun means 'earth knee,' because that particular earthquake was so strong it brought many people to their knees. If we had been wiser we would have known it was a bad omen."

"Excuse me, señor," said Pablo. "Just one question, please."

Inigua looked at him irritably. "What?"

"I would like to know what causes earthquakes? I felt one once when I was little."

Inigua sighed. "We Chumash believe that there are three worlds, one on top of another. The one we live in is the middle world, and it is a large island. It is held up by two large serpents that live in the world below us. When the snakes get tired they move, and that causes earthquakes. The lower world is also the home of fearful creatures called Nunasis. Sometimes at night they climb up into the middle world and do evil things."

Pablo glanced over his shoulder at the darkness. He swallowed and then asked, "And what is the third world?"

Inigua sighed again. "The third world is the one above us. It is held up by the great Eagle, who causes the phases of the moon by stretching its wings. This upper world is the home of the sky people: the old widower – the Sun; the single woman who lives nearby – the Moon; and also Sky Coyote, who is our father. There are other people up there too."

Pablo nodded thoughtfully.

"May I continue now?" said Inigua. Pablo pressed his lips tightly together and nodded.

"Shup Istukun took place in the month now known as August, in the year 1769. Indian messengers had brought us word that some strange beings were headed our way. Those beings arrived at midday, and I hurried to the

123

edge of the village to watch them come. I saw a group of men advancing in a long procession across the coastal plain. There were perhaps sixty-five of them in all, coming from the southeast. As they drew closer I could see that they were mounted on animals. It was an unbelievable sight. The animals looked a little like female elk to me. They were in fact horses, an animal we had never seen before.

In front of the main group walked six or seven Indians. We determined later that these were Yuman Indians from the far south. They were Christians. These Yumans carried long knives and hatchets and other implements for clearing the trail. They hacked at the brush near the edges of the narrow Indian path, widening it before the advancing column.

"At the head of the procession rode the leader, a noble-looking white man of middle age. He and the others of his kind had hair growing on their faces, and dark leather helmets on their heads. They wore dusty blue uniforms trimmed in red, and with shiny brass buttons down the front and at their cuffs. The leader, as my people would learn, was El Capitan Gaspar de Portola. He was followed closely by his officers, many of whom wore sleeveless leather jackets over their uniforms. These jackets were made up of six or seven layers of tanned deerskin and were thick enough to stop an arrow. From the pommels of their saddles were attached leather aprons that hung down, covering their thighs and legs, protecting them from thorns and nettles.

"After the officers rode a group of six soldiers, also in leather jackets and helmets, and with hair on their faces. But on the left arms of these soldiers hung shields made of two thicknesses of bull hide, and in their right hands, pointed to the sky, stood long lances. From the soldiers hips hung iron broadswords, and slung across their backs were short, flintlock muskets.

"Following them came a pack train divided into four groups with muleteers and soldiers for escort with each group. From the sides of the mules were slung packets of supplies.

"Then came the rear guard made up of more troops and Indians who drove an unruly herd of horses and another of mules. These were used to relieve the other beasts when they tired. Dust from their passing rose in the dry summer air and formed a dirty brown cloud that drifted across the coastal plain.

"What a sight! Never before had my people seen such creatures and men. The people of Shisholop came swarming out of their homes and running from all directions to behold the marvelous sight. They cheered and danced and sang songs of welcome to the strangers."

Inigua paused and looked over at Pablo. The boy still had his lips pressed tightly together and was busy cutting points on the stakes. Inigua took a swig of wine, and then picked up the skinning knife. He held it up to the light, and then began to hone it.

124

"Most of the strangers were soldiers, but some of the men with them were only there to take care of the animals. The animals were wonderful, and my people thought these strangers must have very powerful magic to have mastered them so. We realized how much easier travel would be riding rather than walking. Some of our hunters wondered if those animals were good to eat too, like deer and elk."

"These strangers were very odd. They seemed shocked that our men and boys wore no clothes at all, although some of the hunters and fishermen did wear belts of netting around their waist in which they carried tools they needed in their work. Most of our people wore body paint distinctly applied in two colors: red and white. The fishermen in particular used a good deal of paint on their faces, arms, and shoulders. This not only identified them at sea as coming from Shisholop, but also protected their skin from the sun. Some of our people, both men and women had the septum of their noses pierced and had decorated them with carved shells or pointed sticks. Others had pierced earlobes in which they wore hollow wooden rods filled with Indian tobacco.

"When our leaders presented themselves, clad in ceremonial capes or shawls which were open in the front, the strangers were confused. They did not at first realize that these capes indicated their rank.

"The leaders of the Spaniards seemed relieved that our women were better attired. Our women wore skirts of animal skins and covered their breasts with shawls or their own long hair. Most of the women wore bracelets and necklaces made of shells or beautiful stones. The strangers had no females with them, but they seemed very interested in our own. Of this there is more to tell.

"Accompanying the strangers were two very friendly men who smiled continually at my people. They were dressed in gray robes with white cords around their waists, and strings of beads with crossed sticks at the end. We would learn more than we wanted about them later.

"One of the Yumans from the south knew some of our words and sign language. He acted as translator. He told us the strangers were called Spaniards, and that they were headed north. He also told us that the Spaniards knew that we were Chumash. We of the village looked at one another, for that was not what we called ourselves. But we all felt it was better to let them think what they liked. It is our belief that it is better that strangers do not know your true name. That way they cannot cast spells or curses on you. Our names are sacred to us. So we said nothing, and just let them call us Chumash."

"Why did they call you that?" asked Pablo, and then clapped his hand over his mouth, realizing his blunder.

Inigua looked at him with a tired expression. "You cannot help being yourself, can you?" He sighed, "It comes from our word '*Mi'chumash*' which means 'people who make shell bead money.' It is what we called the people who lived on Santa Cruz Island. In fact, Chumash is one name for that island. The Spanish were confused on this point, as they often were. They must have gotten the name from one of their early sailors.

"But enough of this. Do you have any other questions, boy?"

"No, señor. *Perdon*."

Inigua raised his hand over his mouth to cover a grin. The fire crackled and sparked in the wasteland of darkness. A cold wind moaned down the canyon stirring the treetops. Inigua took up the bota and squeezed himself another swig with practiced hands. Then he continued.

"The Yumans told us what Capitan Portola said when he spoke. He expressed his admiration for our village and asked if he and some of his officers might visit there and see what they might see. Our *wot*, or chief, a man named Silkiset, agreed. Portola gave orders for most of his party to proceed to the river and to make camp. He and some of his officers along with half a dozen soldiers and the two gray robes descended from their mounts and prepared to follow us.

"Silkiset told our people to return to the village and prepare food and make themselves ready for a celebration in honor of the strangers. I made myself as inconspicuous as possible and stayed behind. When the visitors and most of our people had dispersed, Silkiset and some of his paha assistants then led our guests on foot towards the village.

"Silkiset was a tall and handsome man, with big arms and shoulders from rowing. His ceremonial cape was made from sea otter pelts. He wore a net woven of sea grass about his long hair, and from it hung little seashells and interesting seedpods and bits of wood.

"Silkiset pointed to the smooth, level area of packed earth with a low woven fence around it that lay just inland from our village. He explained that this was the village playground. Here we played such games as shinny, kick ball, bear tag, and the hoop-and-pole game. The *pahas* looked rather undignified demonstrating these games in pantomime.

"Silkiset pointed to the west of the playground to our ceremonial dance ground. In the middle of this area was located our *siliyik*, our sacred enclosure. The siliyik was a large circle surrounded by a high fence of woven mats. It was within this enclosure that our holy men conducted religious rituals. These rituals often took place at night in conjunction with certain phases of the moon or the appearance of seasonal stars. The audience sat outside the enclosure around campfires, sheltered by a windbreak made of matting lashed to tall poles. There we used to sing and play music and dance in connection with the sacred rituals.

"When these things were explained to the Spaniards, the faces of the gray-robed padres took on a look of distain, and they hurried from that place. This was taken as an insult by some of our 'antap shaman. But in the spirit of good hosts, they decided to overlook the rudeness of these Spaniards, who, perhaps due to poor upbringing, knew no better.

126

"Before we entered the village, our pahas pointed out our cemetery, which lies to the east of the ceremonial dance ground, and downwind from the village. The graves of our dead are marked with painted poles, or in the case of wots, by wooden plaques. On the graves or hanging from the poles are various objects that belonged to the deceased in life. For example, a fisherman might have a net, or hooks and a line, or maybe a paddle from his canoe. A hunter might have bows and arrows laid over his grave, or maybe a skull of a bear he helped kill. Women will have beautiful baskets or jewelry, and so on."

Pablo finished sharpening the last stake, and announced proudly, "I am done, señor."

Inigua stretched his seventy-five year-old limbs and yawned. "I am done too," he said. "I am tired, and would sleep now."

"But what about your story, señor? I want to know what happened next."

Inigua said, "I am too tired. I will finish it another time."

Pablo was indignant. "But you said a story is best told from beginning to end with no interruption."

"Oh? I said that? Hmm. You have a good memory, boy. Well, I better finish my story then. Hand me that butcher knife, Pablo, and we will sharpen it together."

19

SHISHOLOP

"Never hand a knife to a man like that, boy," said Inigua. "Do not point the tip at him unless you mean him harm. Hold the blade and offer him the handle. It is safer that way, and offers neither threat nor insult."

"'Sorry, señor." Pablo turned the knife around and offered the handle.

Inigua took the knife. "Some vaqueros take offense easily," he said. "You must be courteous and give them the utmost respect. When you are grown, you should expect the same from them. One small misstep, like offering a knife like that, could be taken as a slight, which can lead to trouble. I have seen just such thoughtless acts lead to bloodshed, and even death. Vaqueros have a great deal of pride, you know, perhaps too much. They will defend their honor if they feel they have been insulted."

"Sí, señor. I will not do it again."

Inigua held the butcher knife up to the light and inspected it. "Come over here, my friend. I want to show you something." He smiled and patted a place beside him. "Come, and let us turn around this way." He scooted around on his haunches and turned his back to the fire.

Pablo moved next to him and sat cross-legged on the ground. Inigua held the cutting edge up in front of him so that it faced back towards the flames.

"Look at the cutting edge," he said. "See how the firelight reflects off of it? You can see the reflection all along the edge, like a bright line. That tells you this knife is dull."

Inigua reached behind him with his other hand and picked up the skinning knife. He held it up and turned the edge towards the light. "Look here," he said. "You see no reflection, do you? That is because this edge is sharp. You do not even need to test the sharpness with your thumb. Just look at the cutting edge. If you see a reflection of light you know it needs sharpening. Comprende?"

"Sí, señor."

"Bueno. The fire feels good on the back, no? But let us turn around so I can teach you how to sharpen a blade." Inigua scooted back around to face the fire. He spread more olive oil on the stone and then demonstrated the angle at which to hold the knife, and how to move the blade across it. Then he handed the butcher knife to the boy and set him to practice, only correcting him with his hands when needed.

"Now I will finish my story," he announced.

128

"We entered the village of Shisholop from the east and the Spanish marveled at the many neatly-built domed houses – more than thirty in all. There were also numerous smaller structures. Some were visitor's huts, others sheltered work areas, still others food storage bins and cages for live animals. These bins and cages were mounted on stilts. There were also many tall drying racks for fish and game.

"More than four hundred people lived in Shisholop, and we had frequent visitors coming to trade. It was a very old village, and had seen many changes. My people had been living in Shisholop for thirty generations before the Spanish came.

"Our houses were arranged in rows bordering the seashore. Between the rows ran clearly defined avenues that provided access to the river and the beach. Placed somewhere adjacent to the entrance of each was a cooking pit.

"The houses themselves were quite large, some being as much as fifty feet in diameter and capable of sheltering four or five families. They were constructed of willow poles set into the ground in a circle. The poles were bent towards the center to form a dome, and then bound together at the top. All the houses had doorways that usually faced east, and some had a second door to the west and windows along the sides. Some of the finer houses had doorways framed by arching whalebones set into the ground at the large end and lashed together at the top. All the houses had an opening at the top for ventilation and a fire pit in the center that was used for heat or for cooking in bad weather. But because the weather is usually mild there on the coast, we did most of our cooking outside. Two mats, one outside and one inside, were used to cover the doorways during cold or rainy weather."

Pablo cleared his throat, and held up the butcher knife.

Inigua sighed. "What is it, boy?"

"I think I am finished sharpening."

Inigua took it from him and held it to the side, checking the edge against the light. Then he gingerly ran his thumb across the cutting edge. "Bueno," he said. "You put a nice edge on it. Now roll the knives up in that cloth. See to it that they do not touch each other. We will strop them tomorrow."

The boy did so with great care.

Inigua took a drink of wine. "The Spanish seemed fascinated by our houses. So Silkiset invited them to inspect the interior of his own house, the largest in Shisholop's. Whalebones framed both doors, and the floor of the interior had been repeatedly wetted and tamped to make a hard surface that was easy to sweep clean. The house was divided into four spacious apartments by walls of woven mats attached to upright poles. The apartments were occupied by Silkiset, his two wives, his five children and his many relatives and supporters. In all, twenty people lived under this one roof.

"When the gray-clad padres were apprised of the fact that Silkiset had two wives, they were visibly upset. They demanded to know if this was the case with all our men. They were told that only wots were allowed more than one wife. The padres were somewhat, but not completely, mollified by this.

"Each apartment of Silkiset's 'ap was subdivided into living and sleeping rooms. The sleeping rooms were equipped with beds laid on platforms raised several feet off the floor. Mats or loose bulrushes served as mattresses, rolled mats served as pillows, and blankets were made of woven strips of rabbit fur. Silkiset's own blanket was made from the skin of a sea lion. The household also owned several blankets of woven cotton that had been acquired in trade from the Mojaves. (Those Mojave live hundreds of miles away to the southeast, but they were always great travelers.) Adults slept on the platforms while their children had sleeping arrangements on the floor beneath.

"Two hallways neatly divided the apartments. One led from the east door to the west door, and the other across the middle running sideways. Where the two crossed was laid a large fire pit, with a smoke hole directly above it. Windows at the ends of the lateral hallway provided both light and cross-ventilation. Weapons, fishing gear, tools and storage baskets hung from the rafters and poles and dividing walls, keeping them up out of the way. The visitors were much taken with the beautiful carved and inlaid wooden plates and bowls they saw inside.

"The Spaniards emerged from the 'ap well impressed, and continued on their tour of the village. Meanwhile, an old man of the Siliyik began to spin a bullroarer over his head. A group of our musicians gathered and began to play their whistles, flutes, and rattles. The enchanting sounds and rhythms they made twisted and mixed with the sea breeze and filled our people with a festive mood. They stood in front of their houses and darted curious, but polite glances at the Spaniards. They did not stare, however, for that would have been impolite."

Pablo started to speak, but Inigua held up his hand for silence.

"As our group wandered towards the beach, the Spaniards let out a cry of surprise and wonder, for they had spied a number of our *tomols*, or canoes, lined up there above the high-water mark. The Spaniards pressed forward eagerly to examine them.

"We natives of the south coast are famous for these canoes. They are light, fast, maneuverable, and very sea-worthy. We used them for fishing and trading along the coast, and often paddled them out to the islands beyond the wide channel.

"The makers of these tomols were very important and respected men in all coastal Chumash villages. Without these boats we would have been as poor and hungry as those primitive tribes of the interior. The art of making these fine canoes was a closely guarded secret, kept so by the Brotherhood of Canoemakers of which Silkiset and my father were members.

"Our tomols were made of pine and sometimes redwood planks. The planks were formed by splitting logs with antler or bone wedges. The planks were then shaped by bending and staking them on the ground when wet. When dry, flint knives, shell scrapers, and sharkskin sandpaper were used to smooth them. Carefully fitted, the planks were then bound together with stout milkweed cords that pass through drilled holes. The seams and holes are caulked with tar and pine sap pitch. The hull was painted with a red ocher sealer, and sometimes decorated with inlaid mother-of-pearl. Our marvelous tomols ranged in size from a mere ten feet to as large as thirty feet in length.

"As the Spanish stood inspecting them, the red tomol of one of our fishermen was just then returning from the sea. It was splendid to see how rapidly it flew across the water, powered by four men wielding long, double-bladed paddles. When the tomol got in close, its experienced boatmen timed their strokes so that they caught a wave as tall as a man and rode it all the way to the beach. The Spanish seemed much pleased at this, smiling and clapping their hands together."

Pablo raised his hand like he used to do at the mission school. Inigua ignored him.

"We continued on our way, and it soon became clear that the displeasure and disgust the padres had experienced earlier was not yet complete. For right then we came to the House of the *Aqis*."

Pablo looked a question at him.

"Aqi is our word for transvestite, boy. Do you know what a transvestite is?"

Pablo nodded uncertainly.

"This house was the headquarters of Shishilop's society of homosexuals back then. Many of the aqi lived in this gaily-decorated house which was towards the river-end of the village. There were a dozen or more of them. Some of these men, or joyas, as the Spaniards call them, wear the twin skirts of women and cut their hair in bangs. They also bejewel and paint themselves in an extravagant style. The visitors saw some of the joyas holding hands with other men, men that looked like men, and sharing other signs of affection with one another. Some of the Spaniards drew back in horror at what they saw, while others were visibly angered. Still others turned red in embarrassment or laughed behind their hands.

"The Spaniard's reaction seemed strange to us. We Chumash think nothing of these aqi practices. We are used to them. While some of our men and boys occasionally lie down with aqi, it is just for the moment's pleasure, and nothing more. It has no great meaning. To others of us, these antics are merely a source of jokes and funny stories. We never had any big problem with the aqi, other than sometimes they had loud parties that disturbed our sleep. We never felt threatened by aqis. We considered them men who are like women. They were no different than some of our women who looked and lived like men. These people were interesting because of their difference

131

from us. And these people frequently displayed great powers of imagination and creativity. And since there have been homosexuals since time began, we accepted them as part of the natural world. Life would not be the same without them."

Pablo could not contain himself. "Please, excuse me, señor..." he said.

"Somehow I knew you had to ask a question here," said Inigua. He took a swig of wine.

"I am sorry, señor. I really was trying to be quiet. But there is something I must know."

Inigua sighed, "What, boy?"

"Why do some men like men instead of women? I have seen this thing myself at the mission. And why do some women like women instead of men?"

"And why do you bother me with these questions, boy? I do not know the answer. I have thought much about it, but I still do not know. If you ever find out, you tell me. The only thing I can say is this – Do you remember when you first saw that girl 'Akiwo?"

Pablo blinked, and said, "Sí, señor."

"Do you remember how you felt when you saw her?" Pablo eyes glazed, and he nodded. "Well, that is what some men feel when they see another man they like. It is the same for women who like women. I do not know why. They are just different, that is all. May I finish my story now?"

"'Sorry. Of course, señor."

"The group of Spaniards, with the padres in the lead, forged rapidly ahead towards the river, leaving the house of the aqi behind. At the far end of the east-west avenues, near the riverside, ran a cross-street. Along this stood a row of earth-covered mounds. The Spanish were puzzled at first as to the purpose of the structures. Our pahas explained that these were sweathouses.

"Unlike sweathouses we had heard about in the lands far to the east, we did not heat stones nor use water to make steam. The fire alone was enough for us. We entered the sweathouses by climbing up footholds on the outside of the mounds, and then down a slanting, notched pole that protruded through the smoke hole from its source in the floor. The person entering would bring some wood with him to feed the fire. It took good balance to get into that smoky place carrying an armload of firewood.

"Sometimes, during the winter when the wood was wet, it got so smoky inside that we had to lie on the floor in order to breathe. Sometimes we had contests to see who could take the most heat. The sweathouses were located near the river so that when you came out of those hot places dripping with perspiration, you could immediately jump into the cool river.

"This practice invigorated us and kept us clean and healthy. Our hunters also used the sweathouses to remove all trace of human scent from their bodies. That made it easier to get close to game.

"Different sweathouses catered to different guilds or associations in our village. Each person goes regularly to the same lodge. The pahas invited the Spaniards to enter the sweathouse of the village council, but they drew back with obvious misgivings. They seemed wary for reasons we could not fathom. They did not want to go into the cold water of the river either.

"I overheard one paha saying to Silkiset that perhaps the strangers did not want to take off their clothes. He said maybe they were ashamed of themselves. Another paha suggested that perhaps the Spanish power lived in their clothes, and if they took them off they would lose it. I knew there was power in those clothes all right… and it had a powerful smell.

"My people were disappointed that the Spaniards did not want to cleanse themselves. We could understand them being dirty and sweaty from their travels, but we could not understand their refusal to alter their state. We were offended by their smell. Not only did they smell bad, but many of them were sick. Quite a few had missing teeth, and they bled from their gums. Their breath smelled bad, and some were emaciated and looked unhealthy.

"Having completed their tour of the village, the Spaniards began to walk upriver to join their comrades who were camping further upstream. They made it clear to us that they were hungry. Word of this was sent back to the village, and before long many people came to their encampment bearing baskets of sardines and other, larger, fish. We brought so much fish that the Spanish could not eat it all.

"They camped by the river that night. Some of our enterprising craftsmen brought forth carved wooden bowls and plates, which the Spanish had seen and much admired in our village. There was much bartering among the Spanish officers, and the craftsmen made advantageous sales. The Spaniards paid handsomely with beautiful red glass beads. This made our woodworkers very happy because they had never seen such wonderful things. They were thrilled to own something of theirs, even if it was only a handful of red beads."

Here, Inigua took another swig from the bota.

"Many people came from Shisholop painted and decorated with feathers. They began to entertain their visitors by playing reed whistles, rattles, and clapping sticks. They also danced and sang songs of welcome. Between entertainments, the 'antaps gave speeches pledging our friendship and inviting the strangers to stay for awhile and rest. Our leaders wanted time to learn more about the magic these strangers possessed.

"But our people were not able to learn anything about the strangers that night except that they not only smelled bad, but had bad manners and foul tempers as well. Their captain and some of his officers and soldiers came forward and heatedly told us to be quiet and go home. He said he and his men would be leaving early the next morning and wanted only to sleep. He told us if we continued to disturb them they would no longer be our friends and that they would offer us harm if we continued. This hurt our

133

feelings and embarrassed us and we fell silent. Some of our young men began to grumble. Their leader, El Capitan, had his men distribute red glass beads to us to make us feel better. Although we liked the beads, our feelings where still hurt. Finally, we decided to do as they asked and went home.

"At dawn the next day the strangers packed up their belongings and headed west along the coast. Some of our people accompanied them for a ways. Others ran ahead to announce their coming to our friends at Shuku, Mishopshno, and Helo villages. While on the trail, my cousin, Stuk, liberated a knife from one of the muleteers. It was much newer than the ones we had. After several days, the last of our people came back and we did not see the strangers again for four months. Now I am finished with my story, boy."

20

THE KILLING

Pablo did not sleep well that night. He had much to think about. Images of those first Spaniards riding into Shisholop played before his eyes in the dark, just as the old man had described them. He wished he could have been there to see it. And the village seemed so lively, so interesting. He wondered what it would have been like to be born and raised and live one's whole life in such a place. And it must have been wonderful to go out fishing in the sea in those splendid canoes, and to visit the islands that could be plainly seen from the mainland. All his life Pablo had looked out on those islands and wondered what they were like. He would like to visit them one day. He was beginning to understand why Inigua felt so resentful about the Spaniards coming and changing everything.

Pablo set aside these ruminations when he became aware of animals out there in the dark. First he heard the dreary, rhythmic hoot of an owl slowly repeating itself over and over from high in an unseen tree. A little while later he heard the lonesome call of a coyote way off in the distance. Then he heard the splash and hiss of raccoons squabbling over something in the creek, and still later came the ominous swish of foliage as something big pushed its way through the underbrush. Several times Pablo heard the steer whimper in fear and blow air through blubbering lips as it stood tethered under the tree. As the night lengthened, the boy grew chilled. Several times he forced himself to crawl out of the canvas tent to feed the fire. Returning quickly to his blankets, he felt warmer and safer in the light of the flames. Inigua had told him that wild animals feared the fire and would stay away as long as it burned.

The boy's mind continued to churn, now coursing over his memories of the girl, 'Akiwo. He wished that she were here now, lying next to him. They could keep each other warm, and perhaps do the thing they had done before. Pablo felt himself grow hard just thinking of it, and of her: her smooth tan skin next to his, her budding breasts, the roundness of her hips, her full and eager lips. Despite the cold and his fear of animals, the boy was driven from his bed once more. He hastily relieved himself in the darkness behind the tent. Then he hurried back to the safety and warmth of his blankets.

He felt calmer then. But he still could not sleep. Guilt over what he had done began to gnaw at him. Padre Uria would no doubt condemn him as a sinner for what he had done. Pablo dreaded the thought of having to confess to him. Perhaps he could wait until Padre Cuculla was hearing

Confession to tell it. Only then could he receive Holy Communion again. The thought of being once more in a state of Grace comforted him. He was finally able to relax a little, and then weariness carried him off to sleep.

But it seemed only moments later that Inigua woke him by shaking his shoulder and saying, "'Time to get moving, boy. There is much to do."

Pablo groaned, and looked out at the first shadowy outlines of a gray dawn. He had no idea how long he slept, but he knew it was not long enough. He sat up groggily and mumbled, "Sí, señor." Perhaps this was part of his penance.

Inigua emerged from the tent fully clothed and wearing his frazada against the early morning chill. He went into the bushes to make water, and then shuffled back to the fire. The boy had added more wood in his absence, and the old man stood before it warming his hands.

"I will make food," he said, as he rubbed his stiff, gnarled claws above the smoky heat. "You better go up the hill and fetch the horses and the mule. Bring them down here and water them at the creek. I want them close-by today in case we need them. Give them oats, and then stake them out downstream so they can graze. But see they are far enough away that they do not smell the blood when it comes."

Pablo walked through the tall, dew-covered grass to the base of the hills to the west. He whistled, and the animals raised their heads. He heard Rojo whinny a grateful hello. It had been a long night for him too. Pablo released each of them from their hobbles and mounted Rojo bareback. He led the others down to the creek. As he rode, he gazed ahead at a layer of low clouds suspended above the hills to the east, their soft underbellies bathed in pink and orange light from a sun that was just now rising. He descended into the valley of shadow. After tending to and staking out the animals, Pablo made his way back to camp. He found Inigua seated cross-legged by the fire. Propped on rocks above the fire, the pot of leftover beans was beginning to bubble. Next to it was perched a steaming pot of tea.

"Come and eat, boy. Here are the beans, and there are a few tortillas left. Come. Sit."

Inigua ladled some beans into a bowl and handed it to Pablo. He took up a steaming cup of tea, and asked, "How did you sleep, joven?"

Pablo picked up a dry tortilla. "Not so well, señor. I was thinking about the story you told me last night… and of other things." Using the tortilla like a spoon, he scooped up some beans and began to eat.

"And how did you sleep, señor?"

"I slept like an old man who has traveled far and missed his siesta two days running. I did not wake in the night as I usually do. To tell you the truth, it was the first good night's sleep I have had since Islay…" His voice trailed off.

Pablo looked away. The two were silent for a time.

Inigua sipped tea. "So, tell me, Pablo, what was it about my story that kept you awake?"

"Oh, I don't know, señor," Pablo said. "But I liked it very much. It made me see things that I did not see before. I can see things more from your point of view now, but I still have many questions."

"I thought you might. Would you like some tea? This is what they call Mexican tea." He offered the pot. "I do not know why they call it 'Mexican tea.' We Indians were drinking it long before they came here."

Pablo nodded and took the pot. He looked into it and saw many stems floating in green water. He poured some in a cup and sipped. "Mmm, that's good. Well, señor, while I have many questions about your story, I am most curious about what happened next – when the Spaniards came back to your village. You said they were gone for four months."

Inigua nodded and ladled some beans into his bowl. "Yes, they had been to a place in the north called Monterey," he said, "and had visited the San Francisco Bay. Those hairy-faced foreigners looked even worse than before. They were filthy, and exhausted, and hungry. Their faces were gaunt and their clothes were worn and tattered. They smelt even worse than before. And they had fewer mules and pack horses. We learned they had been eating them on the way back. They had run out of food and did not know how else to feed themselves. That showed us how ignorant they were.

"Although we were less happy to see them this second time, we felt sorry for them. But we had less food ourselves because the good fishing time had passed. It was by then the beginning of the season of sea storms, December. But we gave them what fish we could spare, and made trade with them for some of our dried food. Seeing their need brought out the trading instinct in us. We got many more red beads in exchange for food, and even some articles of clothing in barter. These latter items were much sought after. Some people thought the strangers' power lived in their clothes.

"The Spaniards did not linger, but headed south the next day. They were returning to a place they called San Diego. That was their first mission in Alta California. We were happy to see them go. We hoped that they would not come back. They looked sick, and we did not want their illness amongst us. We found out later they had something called scurvy."

Wiping his mouth with the back of his hand, Pablo said, "But they did come back, eh, señor?"

"Yes, in the springtime of the following year. This time Portola had only half as many men as before. We wondered if the others had died. But they had not. Some were left behind because of some trouble at San Diego. Others traveled north from San Diego by ship, including the leader of the priests, Junípero Serra. Again the land travelers did not linger at Shisholop, but rode north to Monterey. There they met the ones who traveled by ship and carried supplies. Together they founded the second mission: Mission San

137

Carlos Borromeo de Carmelo. They also built a fortress for their soldiers. It was the Presidio of Monterey.

"After that we did not see them for awhile, at least not in large groups. Every once in awhile a few of them would pass by on horseback. Some came from the north, others from the south. They were soldiers and couriers. Sometimes there were pack trains of supplies.

"Meanwhile, life went on for us Chumash as it had before. Looking back on it, those were precious times – the last of the good times we would know. But they did not last long, for soon the soldiers and couriers began to cause trouble for us."

"What trouble, señor?"

"Some of them were evil men, especially the soldiers. Since they had no commanding officers to watch over them, they felt they could do as they pleased. And they were dangerous because they were always heavily armed.

"But this tale must wait for another time. You need to know what is going to happen today. After we eat we will pack all our things in readiness for departure. We are going to kill the steer this morning, skin it, and stake out its hide. Killing any living thing is a momentous event, boy, and is not to be taken lightly. We are taking something sacred from that which holds it. But as you will learn, this is a harsh world in which we live. Animals and men kill one another at will. You and I have need of what this beast possesses. And we will take it. But not before apologizing to him and asking his permission. It is the only decent thing to do. And I have never known a cow or steer or bull to have refused this permission once requested.

"But you must know that once we have taken its life, the body of this poor beast will present a problem for us in return. Its death will attract many things, both animal and human. The animals will smell it, and they will come to feed. If scavengers like birds or bobcats or coyotes or foxes come, it will not be too difficult to keep them at bay. Bears and cougars are a different matter. We can only try to frighten them off. But if they are truly hungry there is nothing we can do. At that time we must leave. That is why I had you bring the horses down.

"Humans will come too. I have sent word both to the north and south that there will be a killing today. The Indians will come, either sooner or later. They will bring something with them, but they will expect something too: fresh meat. Of that we have more than we need or can use. They are welcome to it. The meat of this steer will not be much good anyway. Since he is old, his flesh will be tough and somewhat tasteless. The best meat comes from yearlings, but the best hides come from old cattle.

"Even though the meat will not be much good, we Chumash are not like those Spanish and Mexicans who think nothing of leaving a carcass to rot. We believe that to do that would be what they call a sin. It is a sin and it is wasteful. We believe everything should be used. To do otherwise goes against all that Hutash teaches us."

"Hutash?" asked Pablo.

"Hutash is our mother. Think of her as the earth-mother if you like. We will take what we need from this steer and give the rest away. At any rate, we may not be spending another night here. It may be too dangerous, for the smell of what remains could bring many scavengers."

The old man and the boy finished their breakfast, and Inigua scanned the sky.

"It looks like a good day. There should be plenty of sun this afternoon to dry the hide. Come. Let us make ready."

They took down the tent and collected their belongings into one spot. Then they gathered the cooking implements and took them down to the creek to wash. The tethered steer mooed to them as they passed. The old animal tugged at the rawhide tether that ran from the base of its horns to the tree trunk. The two noticed it had kicked over the water bucket during the night.

Inigua spoke to it, saying, "You are lonely, eh, Señor Vaca? And hungry too. But do not worry about it, my friend, for soon you will be neither."

When the implements were clean, Inigua turned to the boy and said, "Take these back to the camp, boy. Bring the stone, and the knives and the leather strop. I will water the beast, and then we will begin."

The sun shone down from its place above the hills and began to dispel the morning chill. Pablo felt excited and nervous as he returned to camp in the speckled light under the trees. He gave the steer a wide berth and only a sideways glance as it turned to watch him go. He did not want to look it in the eye. He had become oddly attached to the docile animal, and he dreaded the thought of what was to come. He quickly gathered up what was requested and returned. He found Inigua and the steer on the slope that led down to the creek. Using the water bucket as a lure, Inigua had maneuvered the steer so that it stood on the slope facing downwards, its tether stretched to its limit.

Inigua left the steer where it was, and walked to a nearby sapling. He motioned Pablo to him. He took the strop and tied the attached thongs around the trunk of the sapling. Then he took up the sticking knife and began to strop it. Pablo felt the anxious thumping of his own heart curiously synchronized with the strokes across the leather. He began to feel a strange numbness, and a growing sense of unreality about everything around him. It was as though he was not truly there, but looking down on it as in a dream.

He heard Inigua say, "Go down to the creek and gather a handful of that deer grass growing there. When you bring it back, conceal it behind you. When I tell you, approach the steer from the front, but do not get too close to him."

As Pablo was gathering the succulent grass he heard Inigua speaking to the beast: "I am sorry we must take you life, Señor Vaca. But you should think of it this way: you have roamed free for all of your days. These hills

139

have fed you well during all that time. The streams hereabout have given you your fill of refreshing water. You have slept under the moon and stars, and then stood contentedly as the sun warmed you each morning. You have been blessed with as good a life as one such as you could have hoped for."

The old steer gazed placidly into his face as he spoke.

"But now, with all due respect, I must ask you to give it up to me. We have need of your body parts. I trust you will not deny them to us, now that you know our need. We thank you. You honor us with this generous gift."

Pablo climbed up the bank of the stream to just below where the animal stood. Inigua stood aside and said, "All right, now show him the grass, Pablo. Hold it out to him, but just far enough away that he cannot reach it. Talk to him as you do it."

Pablo held out the grass and said, "Here, Señor Vaca. Are you hungry? Here is something for you." The steer saw the grass and stepped down the slope, straining at the tether that held him. Inigua approached him from the side, the sticking knife held behind him in his right hand. The steer's attention was now riveted on the boy and the tuft of grass.

"You remember my story about the coming of the Spanish, don't you, boy?"

"Si, señor," said Pablo nervously. He hoped that the tether held, and that the steer would not turn on Inigua.

The steer did glance at the old Indian when he spoke, but then returned its attention to the proffered food. He stretched its neck and drew back its muzzle to try to nibble the grass.

"Watch closely, boy. This is what we should have done to the Spaniards the first day they showed us their ugly faces." Inigua took a quick, fluid step forward and stooped under the broad horn. In one graceful movement he swung his right hand up in an arc under the opposite side of the neck. He placed the tip of the blade just under the ear, and then, stepping back as he did so, plunged the knife into the neck and pulled with all his might. Pablo heard a sickening rip as the blade slit through the throat, cutting it cleanly from ear to ear.

The steer's head rolled to one side, nearly decapitated, as Inigua danced nimbly away. Reflexively, the beast tried to swipe at him with its horns, but its head just flopped. The animal swayed briefly, eyes bulging, tongue lolling from the open mouth. Then the legs gave way, sending six hundred pounds of dying flesh thudding to the leaf-strewn ground. As the body rolled onto its side, the hot, red, misty blast of its last breath sprayed out of the gaping hole in its neck.

Pablo was stunned into a wide-eyed, statue-like immobility. He held the deer grass in both hands now, like a bouquet of flowers. He stood with his mouth open, watching great fountains of bright red blood arching from the yawning throat. He saw the steer's body jerking spasmodically, and its legs kicking forward and back in a pathetic parody of running. Pablo eyes were drawn to the steer's lifeless, dilated eye. It stared back at him with what Pablo was sure was a look of reproach.

"Aieee," cried Inigua. "That was a good kill. Remember this boy: it is much more difficult and dangerous to kill a standing animal. You will rarely do it this way. During La Matanza we lasso and heel them so that they fall to the ground first. It is easier to cut the throat when they are lying down. Do you remember how you took Jesús' lasso off this steer up in the valley? That is when you cut the throat too, Pablo."

Hearing no reply, Inigua looked over at the boy. Pablo's expressionless face was the color of a flour tortilla. "Pablo?" said Inigua. "Pablo? Are you all right?"

The boy turned away and stumbled down the embankment. When he reached the bottom he bent over and vomited his breakfast into the stream.

Inigua stood by the fallen steer watching him. After awhile he said, "When you are done there, boy, I need you back up here."

21

SKINNING

Now for the first time Pablo had seen how swiftly and profoundly Death could be made to visit the living. What he just witnessed had been cunning, brutal, savage, and the sight of it had revolted him. He had always been sheltered from such things. It was Padre Uria's wish that this orphan boy would one day grow up to enter the clergy. He had groomed the boy for it, and had done his best to shelter the future priest from the unpleasantness of life. He had done this so as to encourage the boy to spend his time contemplating beatific images of an ecclesiastic nature. It was Padre Uria's opinion that a young mind should acquire an appreciation for the purity and goodness of the Almighty before learning the facts of an oftentimes sordid world.

When Pablo had finished retching, he knelt down and raised water from the creek with cupped palms. It tasted sweet and clean. He swished it around in his mouth and spat it out. Then he took up more water and swallowed it. It had a biting coolness, and it soothed his raw throat. Furtively, he glanced up the slope, fully expecting to see his mentor looking down at him with disdain. But instead he observed the old man, seemingly uninterested, standing with spread legs over the fallen steer. Inigua's spread feet pinioning the lower front and back legs of the beast to the ground. He held the upper legs in separate hands, and was vigorously thrusting them up and down. With each swing of the legs a fresh arch of blood gushed from the open wound. The steer seemed like some giant bovine bellows, and Inigua, some fiendish blacksmith pumping thick streams of molten blood into the morning air.

The blacksmith spoke: "I am bleeding the steer, Pablo. Moving his legs like this helps pump it all out. Notice too that I have the steer's head facing downhill. This helps empty him as well. In the future, try to arrange it this way if you can. Hillsides are good places to bleed an animal. But remember this: if you are only going to skin him and not use the meat, there is no need to waste time bleeding him. Come up here and take over, boy."

The boy felt a little better now, and although he was embarrassed at having been sick, he gamely climbed the slope.

"Stand on his lower legs, Pablo, so he does not kick you while you pump." Inigua took the sticking knife and rinsed it in the water bucket, then dried the blade on his pant leg. He set it down and took up the skinning knife. He began to strop it.

142

Inigua spoke again. "Those pompous Spaniards thought they were teaching us something new when they showed us how to slaughter cattle by slitting their throats. But we Chumash have always known this method of killing.

"Did you know there is a way of hunting deer with only a knife, boy? It is true. A hunter lies in wait by a game trail with nothing more than a flint knife in his hand. The best trails are those that lead to water, and that are thickly lined on either side by chaparral. When a deer comes along the hunter lets it pass, and then springs after it, running as fast as he can. By the time the deer sees or hears him it is too late. It tries to run away, but the hunter is already running at full speed. The deer is hemmed in by the thick brush and can only go straight ahead. The hunter catches up to it on the dead run and slits its throat with his flint knife. The deer rarely takes more than a few steps after that."

Pablo was glad Inigua was talking. It took his mind off what he was doing and kept him from feeling sick again.

As he continued to pump, Pablo asked, "But what if there is no brush nearby?"

"Then it takes two hunters. They conceal themselves in brush along an open game trail. When a deer passed between them, they begin running after it, one on either side to make the deer go straight. If you get a good head start you can often catch them. But even though it is good sport, we do not need to hunt that way. Our hunters usually go after deer with bows and arrows. But first they fashion a headdress out of the severed heads and necks of past kills. They clean and dry and stuff them with dried grass and wear them on their heads. They also drape deer hides over their shoulders and walk bent over. Our hunters are very clever at mimicking the movements of deer. They can approach a grazing herd from downwind and get right up close to them. The deer think they are other deer coming to join them. Our hunters rarely come home empty handed."

"Eh, señor, I think there is no more blood in this steer. There is only a trickle now."

"Good," said Inigua, as he held the skinning knife up to the light. "Now go get a couple of big rocks from down there by the creek, boy. Make two trips and bring the largest ones you can carry. Put one on either side of Señor Vaca."

While the boy went about this, Inigua untied the tether from the tree and removed the loop from around the base of the steer's horns. He coiled the tether and put it aside. When all was in place, Inigua directed Pablo to take hold of the rear legs while he took the front. Together they rolled the animal over onto its back. Inigua held it up while Pablo scooted the rocks over against its sides to hold it in place.

"We must work fast," said Inigua as he took up the skinning knife. "It is important to get the hide off and staked out while the heat is still in it.

143

"Stand over here, Pablo. Here, behind me. Watch me closely. There are many ways to skin a steer or any other animal. I will show you the way they do it on the ranchos. You will do this yourself many times when you are a vaquero. I will give you some practice as we go along." The boy took a deep breath and steeled himself with a silent prayer.

He watched Inigua circumscribe each hind leg with a cut just at the knee joint. Then Inigua cut down the back of one leg, across the groin area, just in front of the anus, and up the back of the other leg. Pablo was amazed at how easily the skin parted under the slight pressure from the razor-sharp blade. He was also surprised that there was no bleeding.

"Be careful when you are skinning," said Inigua. "Keep your blade sharp at all times. Keep stropping as you go along. If it needs it, both hone and strop it. A dull knife can cause you to slip and cut too deep, or worse, slice through the hide."

Pulling at the hide with his free hand while cutting underneath with the other, he skinned the thighs of both hind legs. Pablo heard a sucking, popping sound as the skin separated from the flesh. Inigua stropped the knife again, and then, almost viciously, thought Pablo, cut off the penis and threw it far into the brush.

"That is what I call the Catalonian cut," said the old Indian with a grim chuckle. "Now we do the front legs. Here. You give it a try. First, cut the hide around the knee, but this time cut down the front of the legs."

Pablo moved to the front of the steer. With somewhat unsteady hands he made the circular cuts, and then drew a line down the front of the forelegs. It was easy, like cutting butter.

"Good," said Inigua. "Now cut a line from the base of your cuts up the chest to just under the ear where the neck is severed. Good. Now skin the legs like I did. If you ever feel yourself working too hard, your knife is not sharp enough." Pablo cut and peeled the skin from the forelegs, guided by the old man.

When the legs were bare down to the shoulder, Pablo stepped back in disgust at the spectacle of exposed flesh, sinews, and leg-bone. Inigua said, "Good job, boy. Now, we should strop the knife again. Come, you try it this time."

Pablo methodically stropped the skinning knife. His movements were not as fast nor as adept as Inigua's, but he made a reasonable job of it. Inigua took the knife and studied the edge.

"Bueno," he said. "Now we do the belly. This is the most delicate part. If you cut too deep you may puncture the guts. You do not want that. You must cut from the inside out, like this."

Inigua stropped the knife, and then carefully inserted the point midway along the neck cut. The cutting edge was turned up and the tip pointed towards the tail of the animal. He began to slit the hide, slowly moving down towards the belly. He stopped long enough to step around to the side, and then continued cutting down until he met the anus. He cut a circle around the anus and then continued all the way down the underside of the tail to its very tip. He stopped again to strop the skinning knife.

"Now we are ready to do the siding. We must be careful here. There must be no nicks in the hide. One slip can ruin it for making a reata."

He inserted the tip of the knife sideways under the corner where the belly cut met the groin cut and peeled back the corner. Taking this corner in his free hand, he began cutting under the hide with the curved blade, freeing it from the underlying flesh. He held the hide aside with his free hand. As the work progressed, Pablo saw steam beginning to rise from the exposed flesh. He smelled the strong scent of raw meat. Inigua worked fast, but ever so carefully, and he stopped repeatedly to strop the knife. Before long he had the hide peeled almost down to the rock that propped the beast on its back.

Pablo gazed down at the exposed flesh and was surprised at how dark it looked. It had almost a maroon color. The dry, yellow-white fat looked sticky and revolting.

"Why is the meat so dark?" asked the boy.

Inigua shrugged, "The older the animal, the darker the meat." Inigua pointed at the stone on the opposite side from where he was working and said, "*Por favor*, joven, move that rock away from there."

Struggling and grunting, Pablo dragged it away. Then Inigua pushed on the upraised legs, and the steer rolled away from him onto its side. Inigua continued skinning all the way down to the spine and a little beyond. Pablo watched him closely. He noticed he kept the loose skin pulled away and stretched tightly as he swept the curved blade under it. Pablo could tell from Inigua's practiced, almost effortless movements, that he had done this many times before.

When the old man was done he sliced a final line across the back of the head from one end of the throat-cut to the other, and skinned that portion of hide below the cut. Then Inigua spread the loose skin over the rock on his side and out flat on the ground. He folded the skin over onto itself with the loose end of it nestled under the beast's back. He had Pablo help him roll the now grotesque carcass back onto it by lifting on the supine legs. Pablo then scooted the rock back in place to hold the carcass in place, its two grizzly half-skinned legs standing in the air.

Inigua said, "Now it is your turn, boy. You skin the other half. Strop the knife first."

When Pablo was ready to begin skinning, Inigua told him, "Just be careful. You must not nick the hide. That membrane under it is what gives it all its strength. If you want a strong reata, cut with care."

Pablo dreaded the thought of ruining the hide. It did not help that Inigua was standing over him watching every move. But the boy was determined to do it correctly. Having watched Inigua carefully he felt confident he knew how. Regardless of that confidence, Pablo began to sweat

145

profusely from the tension and the intense concentration that it demanded. As the sun drew higher in the sky he was grateful for the shade under the trees along the creek.

While the boy worked on the siding, Inigua took up the butcher knife and cut through the flesh of the neck until he exposed the back bone. He insinuated the tip of the knife between two vertebrae and jabbed down hard, severing the spinal cord. Then he severed the remaining flesh circling the neck, effectively decapitating the beast. Inigua grasped a horn and hauled the heavy head aside. He then went to the rear of the animal and coaxed the tail out of its skin.

It took Pablo twice as long as his mentor, but he managed to skin his side of the steer without damaging it. Inigua moved the other rock away so Pablo could roll the animal on its side to work down the back. When the boy was finally done and the hide lay on the ground in a soggy mess, he straightened his stiff back and stood up straight. He looked down at his soiled hands. Flies were beginning to gather about his perspiring face and he waved them away with greasy hands. He had a desperate thirst, and felt totally spent.

Inigua looked down at the skin and smiled. He said, "Good work, joven. Now we must hurry. We must not let the hide cool. Quick, roll up your side of the hide up onto itself. Roll it tight with the fleshy side inside. Roll it right up to the back of the steer."

When this was done, Inigua said, "Now, this is the tricky part, just the two of us getting the carcass off the skin. On the rancho we hitch two oxen to the beast and drag it off. But do not worry, I know how to do it without help. Here, you and I each take hold of a hind leg. Bueno. Now, leave him on his side, but help me scoot his rump around so that all four feet are pointing uphill."

When this was accomplished Inigua directed the boy to go down the slope. "Make sure that rolled-up hide is tucked in under his back, Pablo. I will stay up here and keep him from sliding down." The boy tucked it in as far as he could, and then rejoined Inigua. Lifting both bottom legs with one hand, while holding the folded hide in place with the other, together they rolled the steer over. Gravity did the rest. The meaty carcass thumped ingloriously onto its opposite side sending up a puff of dust and dried leaves as it did. It then slid several feet down the slope, leaving the hide behind.

"Aiee," said Inigua. "That is how you take a skin from a steer. Or any other large animal. Now roll up the hide and bring it along." As the boy knelt to the ground, Inigua began stropping the sticking knife again. Pablo grimaced when he hoisted the warm, heavy hide onto his shoulder and trailed Inigua to the burned-out hunting lodge. They left the sad remains of the steer behind. It lay alone and at peace under the speckled sunlight.

The freshly-swept lodge-ground lay in full sunlight now as the morning sun continued to climb. The two unrolled the hide, flesh side up, and spread it out on the dry ground. Inigua sat down next to it and took up the sticking knife. "We begin by making small slits around the edges. I will start here at the neck section." He stuck the two-edged tip through the skin near the edge.

"The slit need not be long, just long enough to accept the stake without ripping. Cut the slit parallel to the edge, about two fingers widths from the edge. The slits should be about two feet apart, like this." He began cutting additional slits, scooting along on the ground as he did. Pablo watched him closely as he progressed down one side. When he reached the rump he paused to hone the knife tip.

"Now continue along the outer edge," he said. "Notice as you go along that the thickness of the hide varies from place to place. The belly part is thinner than the rest. Cut your slits a little further from the edge there."

While Pablo worked on his side of the hide, Inigua went over to their pile of belongings and returned with the stakes. He set the stakes down one at a time around the circumference of the hide. He left again and returned with two stones about the size of a child's head.

When the slits were all cut, the two sat down on opposite sides of the hide. Under Inigua's direction, they each took hold of the edge of the hide and pulled in opposite directions, stretching it as far as they could. They then stuck a stake through the opposing holes and hammered them home with the stones. They moved ninety degrees around the hide and repeated this action. Then, always working opposite each other, they staked all the holes around the sides until the entire hide was stretched out tight and smooth.

By now it was late morning, and the sun shown down on the two sweating humans with a growing heat. Steam rose from the pinioned, purple skin. To Pablo, the hide looked like a great raw sore on the face of the otherwise unblemished earth.

The boy sighed. At last, he thought, we are done. He got to his feet to have a better look at their handiwork, and then he staggered. He caught his balance, but stood swaying. His vision blurred and his legs felt weak and rubbery. He struggled mightily to stay on his feet, for he did not want to embarrass himself again.

Inigua immediately rose and went to him. He put his arm around the boy's shoulders and said, "Come with me, son." He led him over to the shade of a nearby tree. He lay Pablo down in the grass. "Just lie here and relax," Inigua told him. The old man stood looking down at the boy, and then went to their packs and returned with a bota of water and a handful of jerky and dried fruit. "Here," he said, "you need something in your stomach."

While Pablo ate and drank, Inigua went over to the staked hide and studied it closely. With his back to the boy he looked off into the sky, and, after a time, murmured something. Pablo, still feeling ill, wondered what he was saying, and to whom. Inigua turned and walked back towards the boy. Midway, his attention was drawn by two ravens gliding down out of the sky

147

and landing atop an elm tree near the creek. It was the same tree where the steer had been tethered. The ravens cocked their heads and studied the slope below, and then raised them to the heavens, cawing raucously.

22

BUTCHERING

Inigua stuck Pablo's hat on the boy's head, and said, "You had better wear this. The sun is strong today, even though it is only March. How are you feeling, Pablo?"

"Much better, señor. I don't know what happened to me. I just felt dizzy all of a sudden. I am sorry for my weakness."

"You are not weak, boy. You felt that way because you lost your breakfast. Then you worked hard all morning and stood up too fast under the bright sun. But now you have eaten. If you are feeling well enough, we still have more to do."

Pablo swallowed and said, "I am ready, señor."

"Bueno. Then you had better change into your taparrabo. This might get messy."

Pablo swallowed again. What he had already seen was bad enough, but he knew it would get worse. They were about to butcher the steer.

When they had both changed into their loincloths, Inigua led the boy back down to the carcass. They carried with them all that was needed, including one of the cooking pots.

Inigua had Pablo refill the wooden water bucket and bring it up the slope. Together they swung the steer around so that its hind legs were pointing downhill, and propped it on its back. As Inigua stropped the sticking knife, he said, "We are going to open the carcass down the middle. You want to start up here by the breastbone. I will show you."

Inigua made an incision just below the breastbone and cut a slit long enough to fit his hand. Holding the knife, he inserted his fist into the hole. The blade was pointing upward on the outside, his hand and the handle inside.

"This is the best way to open the abdomen, Pablo. See how the blade is standing up and is pointing towards the hindquarters? This way I can cut and not puncture the paunch or intestines. You can put your other hand inside too, like this, to protect the guts by holding them down."

Inigua methodically slit the abdomen open from the breastbone to the cod. He then cut through the muscle midway between the hind legs, exposing the pelvic bone. This he split with a swift blow from the hatchet. Pablo winced when the blow was struck. Looking down between the splayed legs, he felt dizzy again.

"See all that fat between the legs, Pablo? That is called the caul fat. We need that to make tallow for your reata. I will cut it out now. Bring that

149

cooking pot over here." He carefully removed the fat and tossed it into the pot.

Inigua then returned to the forequarters, and cut through the brisket with his knife, exposing the breastbone. Swinging the hatchet parallel to the bone, he carefully chopped through the breastbone and opened the chest. He handed Pablo a short piece of heavy twine. At the boy's questioning look, he said, "Tie this when I tell you.

With the knife he loosened the windpipe and gullet. "Wrap that twine around this, and then tie it tight." When this was done, Inigua cut the gullet above the knot. He stropped his knife and returned to the ruined hind quarters. He handed Pablo another short piece of twine.

Inigua bent over and cut around the rectum to loosen it. He pulled on it, exposing several inches of lower intestine, and said, "Now, boy, do the same thing here." Grimacing, Pablo complied. When he was done, Inigua worked the rectum loose from the backbone.

"Now we cut out the liver, boy. There it is, there. You have to be careful. You do not want to break open that little thing there. That is the gall bladder. If it breaks it will foul the liver." After Inigua had cut the liver free, he grasped the gall bladder connective tissue with his fingers and pulled the bladder loose. "This part is no good," he said as he threw it into the bushes.

Inigua held out the liver. "Here, take this boy. Wash it off in the bucket." Pablo looked at the steaming glob, and a new wave of revulsion swept over him. He reluctantly took the moist purple heap in his hands. The heat of it startled him. Looking down he saw wisps of steam rising from it, even here in the pool of sunlight in which he stood. He carried it to the bucket and swished it around in the cold water.

As he looked up at his mentor he was startled to see the old man bent over with his arms buried up to the elbows in the maw of the steer's gaping midsection. He seemed to be embracing the intestines. It was a sight Pablo would just as soon have not seen. Grunting and struggling, the old man jerked and pulled the entrails from the carcass. The mottled mass spilled out on the ground about his feet. The sight of the surprisingly pale intestines repulsed Pablo. They were the color of pus, all but for the spleen, which was hideously speckled in red, yellow and blue. Standing above the whitish heap, with the tendrils splayed around his ankles, Inigua smiled and said, "You can leave that liver in the bucket for now, boy. Help me drag these guts into the shade, will you? We will leave them there for now. When the people come they might want to make tripe." Cringing all the while, Pablo helped the old man drag the repulsive reptilian cords, replete with their two balloon-like stomachs, into the shade.

"Thank you, boy. They are heavy, are they not?" Pablo looked around for a place to wipe his hands. "Use the bucket," said Inigua.

They both rinsed their hands. Then Inigua returned to the carcass and bent down over it. He cut through the diaphragm and reached up inside, explaining what he was doing. He cut out and removed the heart, lungs and gullet. These he tossed them over with the entrails.

"Oh, look, Pablo," he said, "look there at the steer's head. Ha-ha. I did not notice it before. You see what happened in the short time we were away? Ravens came down and plucked out its eyes. That just shows you that you cannot leave bodies lying around here very long without something getting at them. Indeed, it is a hungry world in which we live."

"I am not hungry," mumbled Pablo.

Inigua grinned. "Losing the eyes is unfortunate," he said. "I was thinking of roasting that head. Now it will lose some of the moisture through the eye-holes. Here, help me turn it over anyway."

Together they rolled the head face down on a bed of leaves. Inigua bent over it with the sticking knife and cut along both sides of the jawbone. He pulled the jaw wide, and said, "Grab the tip of the tongue, Pablo, and pull on it. Yes. Like that. Now hold it."

Inigua picked up the hatchet and chopped through the bones at the base of the tongue. Then he made a cut under the tongue with the sticking knife, and Pablo pulled it free.

Inigua said, "Thanks, boy. Now hand it over, and I will show you what you do."

The old man washed the tongue off in the bucket and then scraped it with the knife from tip to base, leaving the fat in place. He rinsed it again in the bucket. Then he walked over to a nearby tree. Using the sticking knife, he cut off a low-hanging branch near where it joined a larger branch. He left a sharp point at the tip of the stub near the juncture. He then skewered the tip of the tongue onto it and left it there to drain and cool. He cut another branch in a similar manner, and skewered the liver.

Inigua turned and said, "Now, there is one more thing we need to do. We need to collect a little more fat for tallow. Come. I will show you."

Inigua led the boy back to the carcass and stropped the sticking knife. He bent over and spread the long cut along the abdomen, exposing the nearly empty insides of the steer. "Look here," he said, pointing with the knife. "Do you see that big glob of fat there? That fat surrounds the kidney. We can use that fat. So you cut around it like this. And this. Just so."

Inigua removed the large glob of fat from the carcass, sliced it open, and removed the kidney. He tossed the fat into the pot, and the kidney over by the intestines. With a sure hand he then cut the fatty meat from around the abdomen – the flank, short plate and brisket – and added them to the pot. He looked into the pot and said, "Bueno. That should be enough for our purposes."

"Aieee," he said, standing up and arching his back. "My back is hurting me now. That is enough of this business. But at least you know the main things. The butchering part can wait till another time. Besides, I could not help noticing, boy, your face is looking a little green."

151

"I do not like this business," said Pablo. "I want to be a vaquero, not a butcher."

Inigua laughed. "I understand, Pablo. I truly do. But do not take too seriously the disgust you feel at handling this poor creature's organs. It is normal to feel that way the first time. But after awhile you get used to it, and think less of it. Do not look with disdain at these poor remains here. This dead animal, and all those like him that meet the knife, are the end-result of every vaquero's work. There is no need to dwell on this part, Pablo. You will spend most of your time in the saddle, but you need to know what I have shown you. From time to time you will be called upon to do this. Do not dwell on the unpleasant parts of being a vaquero. Rather, think of the riding and roping and the wild adventure of it. Think, too, of all the life that goes into such a death as this."

"Sí, señor. I will try."

"I hope so. Now I go to wash myself. Will you join me, Pablo?"

"Gladly, señor."

When they finished washing themselves with soap weed and had rinsed themselves in the icy water of the stream, Inigua said, "Do you feel well enough to collect some firewood, Pablo? We need to render the fat. And we should cook something. We will be hungry soon."

"I may not ever be hungry again," said Pablo.

"Nonsense. You will be hungry soon enough. I think I will cook the tongue first."

"The tongue?"

"Sí, joven."

"Uh, señor, I do not think I want to eat tongue."

"Oh? You might like it. But if not, what piece would you like? How about the liver? That is always nice."

"Uh, señor, when I am ready to eat again I think I would just like a regular piece of meat."

"A regular piece?"

"Sí, señor."

"All right boy," Inigua said looking over at the carcass. "I think that we can find you a regular piece of meat."

23

VISITORS

Pablo returned to the pit laden with an armload of firewood. He found Inigua in the act of pounding the pointed ends of two forked branches into the ground on either side of the fire. He noticed too that the steer's tongue was skewered on a stick and propped up to smoke over the fire.

"Hola, joven," said the old man. "Add a little wood to the fire, will you? Then you can help me put the tallow on to boil."

Pablo used the hatchet to chop the wood, and then fed the fire. As he worked he glanced over at Inigua and saw him reaching into the water bucket. Out of the corner of his eye he watched the old man pull out the raw liver, examine it, and take an exploratory bite. "Mmm," he said, chewing, "Not bad." He caught Pablo's look, and shrugged, "Perhaps it is an acquired taste." Pablo mimicked gagging, and then grinned. He was feeling better now.

When the fire was burning well, Inigua said, "Now we add the pot." The old man took up a stout, four-foot-long branch and threaded it through the half-circle of the pot's hinged handle. "Take the other end, boy, and lift."

Together they raised the branch and set both ends in the upright forks so that the pot hung over the fire. "Bueno," said Inigua. "Now we are getting somewhere. Soon we will have tallow to go with our rawhide. We need it to lubricate, soften and preserve the leather. You will see."

A short while later, as they stood looking down at the fat melting in the pot, they both heard a strange sound in the distance. It was a buzzing sound, an eerie whirring that insinuated itself into the stillness of midday. Inigua cocked his ear. He looked at Pablo's face, which held a look of puzzlement and concern. Perhaps the boy thought a swarm of bees was heading their way.

Inigua smiled an answer, "'Our guests from Santa Paula, the Mupu people. Quick, before they show themselves, let us gather up all our belongings – the knives, the ax, the strop, the bucket, everything that is lying around. Put them all here with the rest of our things. We must, uh, present a tidy camp."

They hurriedly secured everything under the tent canvas. They returned to the fireplace just in time to see the approaching natives round a bend about a quarter of a mile down the trail. In the lead was a handsome Chumash man, his body painted in red ochre. He whirled a wooden bull-roarer on a six-foot tether above his head. About two dozen Mupu walked behind him dressed scantily in the skins of deer. They seemed of all ages, from gray-haired elders to young children skipping along beside their parents. Mothers carried infants in reed cradles slung on their backs. Everyone in the advancing party bore a burden, whether it be a woven basket, a wrapped bundle, or a carrying net slung from their forehead and down their back. Men carried rolled matting, wooden staffs, bows and arrows, lances, or musical instruments. Three or four in the group carried feathered banners on long poles pointed to the sky. Some of the women wore feathered skirts and men sported feathers in their hair. As they drew closer, Pablo could see that most of the people's faces and bodies were painted in red ochre: circles and dots on their torsos and red stripes about their limbs.

When the Mupu spied Inigua and Pablo standing by the smoking fire they let out a joyous whoop. The man in the lead drew in his bull-roarer, and at a sign from him, the party broke into song, accompanied by the playing of bone flutes and reed whistles, and the shaking of shell rattles.

"Here we come," they sang. "See us walking. We are the people of the eastern river. We walk moving our brilliance and feathers. See us walking. Listen to the sound of our music. Here we come, singing our greetings and friendship. See us walking in our brilliance and feathers."

Inigua said, "Wave to them, boy, and smile. Let us show them they are welcome." The man and the boy did so in unison.

Pablo stood spellbound by the sight of the approaching column, for it seemed a most bizarre, primitive, and exotic pageant. The procession of heathens walked in a rhythmic cadence with an eager bounce to their steps, and smiles lighting their faces. Above them golden eagle feathers fluttered in the breeze from their long poles, as the whistles and rattles sounded.

Pablo and Inigua were distracted from the spectacle by a loud cheer coming from behind them. They turned and looked up the sloping trail to see another group of Indians approaching from above. These, no doubt, were from the village of Sis'a. There were perhaps twenty of them. They too had their faces and bodies painted, though theirs were done in wavering stripes of black and white. They too had banners and poles, but these were decorated with black feathers, feathers of the condor and raven. They had seen Inigua and Pablo standing by the fire, and the approaching villagers from below. At a sign from their leader the Sis'a people began their own rhythmic song accompanied by the outlandish clatter of clapping sticks, and the shrill tones of flute and whistle.

They sang, "Haku, to you before us. See us walking. We hail from the high place, from the home of the condor. We are the sons of the Grizzly and the daughters of Cougar. We sing greetings to our friends and our kinfolk. Greetings from the children of Sis'a. Greetings from the shadow of Sitoptopo."

Inigua and Pablo waved at them in the distance, while the Mupu cheered from below.

When the two groups had finally drawn up on either side of the encampment, they stood quietly and expectantly awaiting the necessary formalities. Inigua raised his hand first to one group and then the other. He cleared his throat and said, "Haku, my countrymen. We welcome you. I am the one called Inigua, and this is my great-grandson, Pablo. We invite you to join us in this our temporary dwelling place, and we invite you to share in the bounty of our good fortune."

Pablo recognized that he was speaking not in the dialect of the coast, but of the interior.

Inigua continued, "Down that slope, there by the running water, is a newly slain steer. We killed him this morning with the permission of Padre Uria and of Don Tico. We have taken the beast's hide for our own use, the one you see stretched here before you. We have taken some fat for the making of tallow. The rest we gladly offer to you. We invite you to feast with us. Eat all you want, and take with you all that remains. Please make yourself at home around here.

"You who came from below, you may have seen our horses and mule staked out down downstream. The use of them was granted to us by the padre-superior of the mission. This boy and I will be camping down there tonight. You are free to make use of this place. Perhaps you would like to stay for awhile? Why not set up camp along the creek. We will have a great feast. Taney, taney. Thank you for coming."

The combined groups were cheered by this speech and gave loud acclaim. Then the leaders of each party gave a short speech in return – speeches of greeting and of gratitude. When the formalities were complete the people of Mupu and Sisa began to intermingle, for there were many who had friends or were related by marriage to members of the other clan. A cacophony of voices and laughter surrounded Pablo and Inigua as they watched old acquaintances and relatives embrace and slap each other on the back. A fine cloud of dust rose above the campground from the many moving feet.

Inigua noticed that a few of the older men hung back, eyeing members of the other group warily. It dawned on him that there might be old feuds between some members, feuds that remained unsettled. He hoped nothing would come of them at this meeting place.

Pablo noticed there were a few boys of his own age among the visitors. They seemed friendly enough, but they were reserved, eyeing him furtively, measuring him. Pablo was certain they knew he was not like them. He took off his hat. Pablo also noticed there were several young girls standing shyly around the edge of the milling crowd. They glanced at him, but quickly looked away. None of them, however, was she who he longed to see: 'Akiwo. He had hoped the people of Huyawit would come. He looked up the trail, but it was empty.

After awhile the groups began to separate, orders were given by the wots, and the older folk and children set out in all directions in search of firewood. It was decided that the people of Sis'a would set up camp over on the eastern side of the creek, and the Mupu would take up residence here on the west side. Women began setting up the respective camps. They unrolled matting, propped up impromptu lean-tos on poles carried here for that purpose, and gathered stones for the fire circles.

The men followed Inigua down to the carcass where a great deal of haggling and laughing went into deciding how to divide up the meat. They insisted Inigua choose the first piece. He deftly cut a three-pound section of sirloin from the carcass with his butcher knife.

He stepped back, holding it in one hand, and said, "Thank you, friends. The rest is yours."

The men gave a hearty cheer. Flint blades and a few well-worn mission knives were produced, and the cutting up of the carcass began. One sharp-eyed old man picked up the kidney Inigua had tossed aside earlier and bit into to it. He walked away smiling and gnawing at it. Inigua returned to the fireplace and joined Pablo, who had been left to watch their kit.

Pablo saw the hunk of beef in his hand and said, "I thought you were going to take the head, Inigua?"

Inigua shook his head. "Although it is true I like a nice roasted cabeza de vaca… I decided it was too much trouble and takes too long. We might have to leave here quickly if there is trouble."

"Trouble? Why would there be trouble?"

"I guess you did not notice because of the excitement and general feeling of good will, but there seems to be some bad blood between some of the people here. It is not an uncommon thing. We Chumash often quarrel with one another. Sometimes a man might have sex with a woman from another village without her consent. Sometimes a man might steal another man's wife. Sometimes things get stolen, or one group trespasses on another's gathering or hunting or fishing ground. These offenses are not forgotten and do not go unpunished. If someone does something against us, we Chumash take matters into our own hands. We seek justice and extract revenge. This is the way it has always been. Unfortunately, sometimes when vengeance is taken it is over-done. Innocent people get hurt. It is then that vendettas are born.

"I could tell you a tale or two about these things. But this is not the time." Inigua handed the sirloin roast to Pablo. "Here is your 'regular' piece of meat. You can roast it here at the fire."

By mid-afternoon a peaceful calm replaced the initial hum of activity on both sides of Santa Paula Creek. Old folks and children napped in the warmth of the afternoon, mothers boiled acorn soup, and men tended fires where large chunks of meat slowly roasted. It seemed as though the Chumash were catching their breath for the fiesta to come – a fiesta to be written in the annals of a vanishing race.

24

DANCING

"I think we should move our camp," said Inigua. "Even though it is quiet here now, I do not think it will remain so. I am tired and I need my rest. Can you go get the mule, Pablo?"

"Of course, señor. What about the horses?"

"No. Just bring Chico. We will load most everything on him and find a good place to spend the night."

"And the steer hide, señor?"

"Let us have a look."

Having lain under the bright sun for several hours, the hide's crimson flush had paled. It looked less raw, less fleshy than before, and Pablo could see that it had shrunk considerably. It was now stretched as tight as a drumhead between the stakes. Inigua squatted down and grasped the skin between his fingers, testing for moistness. He then ran his hand over the fleshy side.

"It is drying well," he said, "but it needs more time." He scanned the sky. "We will leave it for now. There are still a couple of good hours of sun left."

When Pablo returned with Chico, he found Inigua stirring the pot of melted fat with a wooden spoon. From time to time he scooped out bits of meat and gristle that rose to the surface and ate them. "The tallow is coming along nicely," he said. "But it needs to simmer for a little while yet to fully render. The heat will help preserve it too. Care must be taken that it does not scorch, however. Burnt tallow is weak and gives your reata a funny smell.

"When it is done we will leave it in the pot to cool and harden. In former times we used to dig a hole in the ground and pour the hot tallow into it. We would put a wooden stake in the hole along with it. The next morning when the tallow was hard, we just pulled up on the stake and the tallow lifted out of the hole."

Inigua reached down and picked something up from the opposite side of the fire. "Here, Pablo," he said, "try this." He handed the boy a small rectangular wafer of what appeared to be thinly sliced, cooked meat.

Pablo looked at it suspiciously. He glanced at Inigua's innocuous expression, and took an exploratory bite. "Mmm," he said. "It's good." He popped the rest of the wafer in his mouth and chewed. "Is this the regular meat?"

"Uh, well, not exactly."

Pablo stopped chewing. "What is it then?"

"Oh, just a little slice of roast tongue."

Pablo's eyes bulged. His face took on a deep, thoughtful look, and then he forced himself to swallow. The boy shook his head and said, "I have to admit it doesn't taste bad. But next time, could you please tell me what I'm eating beforehand?"

"I think it is more fun this way," said Inigua. "Besides, you would not try it if I told you beforehand, and then you would not know what you are missing. I have something else for you to try, boy."

"If it is the raw liver, forget it," said Pablo.

"See, I told you you would not try it."

Together they hoisted the pack rack on Chico's back and fastened it in place. They quickly lashed most of their belongings onto the rack, including the canvas tent. They walked downstream about a hundred yards and picked out a new campsite, one screened from the Chumash camp by a thicket of trees and shrubs. Inigua returned to tend the pot, taking Chico with him. He left Pablo to set up the tent and gather wood for a new fire.

By four in the afternoon the shadows from the high hills to the west had crept nearly as far as Santa Paula Creek. The hide was by now as dry as it would get, and the tallow was clear and clean. The man and boy removed the pot from the fire and set it aside to cool.

They pulled up the stakes that bound the hide to the ground. The hide was quite stiff. To ensure there would be no decay, Inigua powdered the fleshy side with a layer of salt, and together they folded the hide onto itself.

"This is all that one does with hides out on the ranchos. Most of them are taken to the mission for trade," said Inigua. "We stack them up, and ox-drawn carretas carry them to the mission warehouse where they are stored until a Yankee ship comes. They are then traded for manufactured goods, and sometimes gold coins.

"Some hides are kept for use at the mission. They are taken to the tannery. There they are placed in large stone-lined pits in the ground. Perhaps you have seen them. The pits are filled with brine, salt and oak bark. They soak there for several days, being shuffled occasionally like playing cards. This process is what they call tanning the hides. The hides are then re-stretched, dried, cut into thongs or other shapes depending on their intended use. After de-hairing, the leather is rubbed down with tallow.

"There are any number of ways to tan hides. One is to smear a paste of the animal's brains all over the fleshy side of the hide. That is the way we Chumash used to tan the hides of rabbit, deer, bear, seal, or any other animal. I am thinking of another way that is being used more often these days. It is an easy way to clean and cure the hide."

"How is that, señor?"

"You take it down to the ocean and stake it out in the shallows at low tide. The rising and falling of the tide washes and cleans the hide. After a couple of days you stretch and dry it again. It is then ready to work."

Pablo thought this over, and then said, "But isn't there a danger the waves will carry it away? It seems like they could. I don't want to loose my hide."

"You just have to pick the right place to stake it," said Inigua, "a place where the waves and current are not too strong. I know several places like that. One is over there by the village of *Hueneme*. It is only a mile or so east of the mouth of the Santa Clara River. I have done it there before."

"Tomorrow we can follow this creek to where it joins the Santa Clara, and hence down to the shore. If we get an early start we could be in Hueneme by afternoon. Tomorrow is Saturday. If you want to go visit the padre on Sunday it is not too far from there."

"That sounds like a good plan, señor. I think you know what is best."

"Bueno. Now let us go to our camp, for I am very tired. Put the hide and the other things on Chico's back. You and I will carry the pot of tallow. We have to be careful it does not spill."

When they got to their new campground, Inigua went into the tent and lay down. Before he dozed off, he said, "If you want your regular piece of meat, Pablo, get the fire going and put it on a spit. You might want to add some salt and other spices. It is not the best cut of meat."

Pablo cooked his simple meal amid the fading, late-afternoon light. He sat by the fire eating and watching clouds gathering to the south, clouds that turn from white to yellow to orange to pink. The forgotten sun, out there somewhere beyond the western hills, closed its eye behind a wind-blown sea. The homeless clouds turned red as a purple light descended on the valley.

Pablo felt tired, and suddenly quite lonely. His mentor was no company, for he was fast asleep in the tent. The boy thought of Padre Uria. He missed the jolly old friar and the comfort and safety of his home in the quadrangle. But when he considered once more the strict routines of the mission, dictated by the omniscient bells, he was glad he was here rather than there. He much preferred being out here in the country with Inigua where they were free. He also felt excited and eager that work would soon begin on the reata.

Pablo gathered up all the food, as he had seen Inigua do the evening before. He noted that the tongue was nowhere to be seen. Inigua must have eaten it. Pablo hurried, for the light was failing rapidly. He placed it all in a bundle and hauled it into a tree beyond the reach of scavengers.

Returning to the fire, Pablo heard a single flute begin to play in the distance. The sound came drifting to him from upstream. He listened to the slow, sinuous melody, a formless thing that floated through the air as if on darkened wings. It seemed a beckoning plea, a plea that languorously drifted through the mist that was just beginning to rise from the creek bed. Its haunting strains intermingled with the liquid murmur of the stream.

Soon, a second flute joined the first, followed by a third and a fourth. A rhythmic clicking of sticks ensued, followed by a low rattle. Human voices began to chant a strange litany that sent a shiver up Pablo's spine.

The boy found himself walking towards the sound, picking his way carefully through the darkened woods. As he drew closer to the sounds, the flicker of firelight appeared between clumps of low brush, and a golden glow lit the surrounding trees. As he neared the source of the light he could make out shadowy figures moving to and fro before the bonfire. Pablo circled around towards the creek, concealing himself in the protective darkness amid the brush.

He chose a spot where he had a clear view of the Chumash encampment. There was a large bonfire laid in the center of a spacious, open circle. He saw the dusky backs of the Mupu people sitting in a crescent around one side. On the opposite side sat the Sis'a. Sitting between the two groups, and on opposite sides of the open area, musicians sat facing each other.

A willowy Indian woman stood to one side of the fire, swaying as the music played. Ever so slowly, she moved around the fire, swaying all the while. She was naked except for her dancing skirt of black feathers. The skirt, though short and scant, had a long, thin train of feathers behind. She also wore a woven belt from which dangled red abalone shell ornaments cut into the shapes of stars and half-moons. On her head perched a feathered corona in white and black. Her face was painted a dark red, dotted with numerous spots of black and white. Her hair cascaded down behind her as she raised and lowered her body swaying in time with the music.

Three men knelt on one knee along one edge of the dance ground. They were her singers. They used no instruments, but merely placed their left hands over their eyes as they sang, and slapped their thighs with their right hands. Pablo could not understand all the words of the song, for they were in a dialect he did not know. But he knew one word, a word oft repeated – the word 'seaweed.'

Pablo guessed that this woman must be from the Channel Islands, or from some distant place along the coast. There was no question that this dance mimicked the swaying of seaweed or kelp in the ocean currents. And the woman did it so effectively that Pablo could almost feel the currents himself. The firelight shimmered on her body as she twisted and turned.

Pablo quietly climbed into the low-lying branches of a nearby tree so that he could get a better view. He could not take his eyes off the woman's full, bare breasts. This was a new experience for him and he found it fascinating and not a little disturbing. He was quite sure it was a sin to ogle this woman. But he could not help himself. Well, he thought, here is another sin I will have to confess.

Sooner than he would have liked, the dance ended, and the beautiful Chumash lady disappeared into the shadows. A man took her place on the dance ground. Pablo recognized him as one of the Sis'a people.

"Haku, friends and kinfolk and little children," said the man. "I have come to warn you – a bear shaman is coming to dance at this place. He brings with him all the character of the bears of the wild. He brings with him the fierceness of the wild too, so be careful. If anyone even makes a small noise, the bear may pounce on him and bite him."

The people sitting around the dance ground grew very quiet. A tense rattling sound came from the musicians. The spectators waited expectantly. Children snuggled close to their parents. And when the suspense was at its high point, the bear shaman came bounding out of the nearby bushes. He was a large man with a barrel chest. He wore a kilt of brown feathers and matching headdress. His face was painted in brown clay, and about his broad shoulders was pinned a much-traveled bearskin. On his hands and forearms he wore what at first looked like a pair of over-sized gloves. They were in fact real bear paws, replete with claws. Three new singers lined up on the edge of the arena. The dancer circled the open ground, swinging his arms, mimicking a bear looking for something to eat. He made hungry animal sounds.

The singers chanted: "Listen to what we are about to sing. Listen to the bear breathing on high. Listen to his stamping. He tears up the ground. Listen to his groaning."

The bent-over dancer stalked around the bonfire groaning and swinging his paws before him. He grunted and looked about with a menacing air.

"Look! Listen!" cried the singers. "He grunts on high. The ground shakes. In the night he makes a noise like a terrible thing. *I yaka mi ha mi.* Clear the way! Clear away when he steps forth with pride. Here is a creature of power. He stands and begins walking to the mountain tops, to every corner of the world. He is a creature of power."

The bear dancer stood up at full height, threw back his head and gave a fearful growl.

Pablo was so delighted with the spectacle that he forgot himself and giggled out loud. The bear dancer grunted in anger and looked towards the sound. The boy held one hand over his mouth and froze. The bear dancer very deliberately raised his two paws while opening and closing his fists. He then gave an enraged growl and rushed towards Pablo's tree. He leaped up, swiping with his claws at the boy cowering in the tree. One of the paws nearly caught him. Pablo quickly stood up on the limb and climbed higher, whining in terror. The entire crowd burst out laughing.

Fear was replaced by embarrassment as Pablo's face blushed crimson in the firelight. The laughter seemed to go on and on at the sight of him hugging the tree. Pablo glanced down and saw that the dancer had begun to laugh too. The big man gave one more menacing growl and disappeared into the darkness. The crowd cheered and laughed again. They called out to Pablo, insisting he come down and join them.

Feeling very much the fool, Pablo complied. When he came forward he endured many friendly jibes and insults to his courage. Men slapped him jovially on the back before he finally found a place to sit at the edge of the Mupu people.

The next dance began soon afterwards. It was the Blackbird Dance. There were three dancers. They wore feathered kilts and their upper bodies were painted black. Their faces were blackened too, with tiny dots of red, yellow and white. On their shoulders and extending a little ways down their arms were large red ovals, like those of the red-winged blackbird. The musicians skillfully blew on bone whistles, imitating the sound of the birds. The dancers mimicked making a rumpus in the trees. Then they waved their outstretched arms and jumped to indicate leaving the trees. Tilting their arms they flew in circles around the central bonfire, soaring effortlessly until they thumped their feet and landed. They scraped at the ground with their feet and jumped back like a chicken does when it is scratching for something to eat. Later, the dancers demonstrated the birds bathing, and then they flapped their arms up and down and flew away into the darkness. The crowd cheered and slapped their thighs in appreciation. Pablo was amazed at the realism of their portrayal.

This was soon followed by another dance: the Rabbit Dance. Two Chumash, a man and a woman, wore feathered kilts, and each had two bundles of feathers in their headbands shaped to look like rabbit ears. There were no singers, only the soft slap of clap sticks. They danced separately for a while, hopping around the bonfire, seemingly unaware of one another. They nibbled imaginary food. From time to time, a rattle sounded, and they would stop and look to this side and that – as the rabbit does when a predator is close-by. Near the end of the dance the two rabbits discovered one another. They hopped around each other, sniffing and nuzzling and rubbing their bodies up against one another. Then the man clasped the woman from behind and mounted her, as Pablo had seen animals do. The dancers smiled and ground their hips, mimicking sexual union. In the dim light it was hard for Pablo to be sure they were only mimicking. The crowd cheered and laughed as the two hopped into the shadows still joined. Pablo was shocked. This dance, with its blatant sexuality, would no doubt be deemed sinful at the mission. He puzzled over the fact that the Chumash thought nothing of it. To them it was just a joke.

While this caused a good deal of merriment, it was by no means the end of the festivities. Preparations were made for the next dance. This one was called the Devil Dance. Pablo was feeling quite tired and uncomfortable now. He'd had enough shocks and surprises for one day, and he wasn't sure he wanted any more. But he could find no way to gracefully extricate himself from the crowd.

There were two performers in the Devil Dance. The Devil wore a black wooden mask with feathers sticking straight out around the edges. The mask had holes for the eyes and nose. The Devil wore a netted cloak across his shoulders and a loin cloth. The other dancer was the legendary Coyote. Coyote the prankster, Coyote the lecher, Coyote the sage. His body, girded in a loin cloth, was painted in the mottled colors of a coyote. He wore a crown of feathers and carried a bow and arrow. In this dance Coyote was hunting the Devil. The Devil led him a leisurely chase, zigzagging, treading, circling the fire, and giving a hoarse whistle every once in awhile to lead him on. Coyote followed behind cautiously, his bow at the ready. Pablo's nerves were again on edge. He wasn't sure if Coyote intended to let his arrow fly or not. That could be dangerous. Pablo prepared himself to dodge or duck if necessary.

Near the end of the dance, the Devil surprised everyone by taking off his loin cloth and lifting up his network cloak from behind. He bent forward and leaned his hands on his knees. Coyote, who had been cautiously stalking the Devil all the while, was overcome with curiosity. He danced up behind the Devil and bent forward to investigate. As he gazed up at the Devil's bare bottom, the Devil gave a great blast and spewed a liquid blob of defecation in his face. The crowd screamed, and then howled in laughter as Coyote danced away pawing at his face and shaking his head and sneezing. Pablo was thoroughly disgusted at this. But he seemed to be the only one. Everyone else had fallen down laughing, holding their sides.

This performance was soon followed by the Rattlesnake Dance. An old man in a loin cloth came forward. His body was painted in brown diamond patterns which continued along his spindly arms and legs. He lay down and made hissing sounds while gyrating his body. He slithered over to a netted bag from which he withdrew a live rattlesnake. Sitting on his haunches he held it up for all to see. He then allowed the snake to wind up his arm as he slowly got to his feet and began to dance. People close to the dance ground recoiled in fear and scooted back, crowding those behind. The dancer removed the snake from his arm and wrapped it around his forehead like a crown. Pablo could hear the snake's rattle buzz. The snake did not like being handled so roughly. The dancer raised his arms out to the side as if balancing on a beam. Then Pablo saw a sudden blur of movement, and in an instant the snake had struck the old man on the shoulder. The man gasped and fell over backwards grasping the area of the bite. People screamed as the snake slithered across the dance floor towards the shadows. One of the hunters rushed forward and clubbed the rattler with a branch of firewood. Members of the dancer's family hurried forward and carried the old man off. The crowd grew silent, looking at one another in confusion and concern.

Pablo had seen enough. He could not stay here for another minute. As inconspicuously as possible he slunk off into the darkness.

25

TO THE COAST

The sun was already up by the time Pablo awoke. He heard the crackle of the fire and the sizzle of something frying. Whatever it was, it smelled delicious. He looked out of the open tent flaps and saw Inigua squatted by the fire holding the frying pan and looking over at him with a bemused grin.

"Buenos dias, joven. You slept well, I hope."

"No, not so well. And you, señor?"

"Mine was a good sleep. You were up late last night, boy."

"Sí. And what a night it was. You should have seen it, señor…oh, the dancing!"

"I am no stranger to those dances. Did you know that the old man died last night?"

"No." Pablo got on his knees and crawled out of the tent. He was still wearing his clothes from the day before. "The man who was bitten?"

"Sí. A woman told me this morning. That viejo had been drinking bush brew before the dance and it made him careless. They will bury him today. I want to leave this place soon. I do not like funerals. I have had my fill of them."

"I want to leave too. But I am starving, señor. What are you cooking?"

"I was out picking wild onions earlier. I am frying them with liver in some tallow. The woman who told me about the old man gave me some acorn mush too. It is here. Eat, and then we will go."

While they ate, Inigua said in a casual manner, "So, tell me about the dances last night, Pablo. I heard you had a good view from up in a tree."

The boy blushed. He bent over his wooden plate and cut into the fried liver. "The dances were amazing, señor. They each told a little story. They were very good. But some of them made me feel sick too: the Rattlesnake Dance and the Devil Dance."

"The Devil Dance?"

"Sí. Coyote was in it. He was chasing the Devil, and then the Devil shit in his face."

"Ah, that Coyote. There are many dances about Coyote, and they are mostly dirty. The padres never let the people put on a dance about him at the mission. This Devil Dance must be something new. Usually it is Coyote who does the shitting. Down along the coast and out on the islands the dancer who plays Coyote drinks sea water in the morning. That makes him able to shit

164

anytime he wants. Up here they probably drink tea made from *Chili-cojote* or *Rosa de Castilla.*

"In some dances Coyote has sex with someone. Sometimes he even tries to get people in the crowd to lick his penis. If they refuse, he licks it himself."

"Please, señor. That is disgusting. I am trying to eat." Pablo did not seem to lose his appetite, however. He wolfed down the liver and acorn mush.

"Did you notice that some of the people were drinking bush brew, Pablo?"

"Sí, now that you mention it. But I did not know what they were drinking."

"It was probably fermented cherry juice." Inigua paused, and his expression fell.

Pablo said, "That would explain why some of them were acting so funny. They seemed overly happy, and they laughed at everything."

"I am glad they had a good time," said Inigua, "and that there was no trouble between the two groups. I was afraid they might quarrel.

"Do you know about the wild cherry plant, Pablo? It is quite common around here. It is called… Islay." This last word caught in his throat. He disguised it by saying, "There is one over there by the creek."

Pablo looked where he indicated and saw a bushy shrub which stood about ten feet high. It was covered in dark shiny leaves that curled and had sharp points at their tips, like holly. He saw small white flowers coming into bloom all over the bush.

"There is no fruit now," said Inigua," but later in the year that plant will bear dark red cherries that eventually turn black. The cherries have large pits. The people grind up the meat of the pits and make it into balls. They are quite delicious. You can eat the fruit of the cherries too, or crush them up and add water to make juice. Some people sweeten it with honey. If you leave the cherry juice long enough it ferments. Then it contains alcohol, like wine."

Pablo thought about this, and said, "I don't like alcohol, señor. It tastes bad. Why do people drink it?"

"*Quién sabe*? Who knows? But I think they do it to be happy again, like the way they were when they were children. Sometimes, when people get older, life brings sadness to them, so they drink to become happy again."

"And does it make them happy?"

Inigua looked away. "Only for a time."

The man and boy set about breaking camp. They watered their mounts, and loaded their belongings onto Chico's back. Lastly, they lashed the hide on top of the load.

Just as they were preparing to depart they were paid a visit by a delegation of Mupus and Sis'as. Their spokesman, Qaq [Raven], the leader of the Mupus, gave a short speech of thanks for the outstanding feast. It would be long remembered, he said, although sadly by the friends and relatives of the snake dancer. The Mupu leader then offered them a parting gift, a gift symbolic of their friendship. It was the bull-roarer that Inigua and Pablo had heard upon the Mupu's arrival.

"Give it to the boy," said Inigua. "It is to him that we owe this beneficence."

Pablo took it gratefully, and offered a convoluted thanks in Ventureño Chumash. He stepped back, and, holding the bull-roarer by its cord, swung it in a tight circle about his head. His face beamed at the sound, and he let the cord slip through his fingers widening the ark of the spinning wooden stick. Inigua ducked when it came dangerously close to his head. This caused the delegation to laugh.

"Sorry, señor," said Pablo with a wide grin. He gathered in his new toy and placed it in the saddle bag behind Rojo's saddle.

Final farewells were exchanged, and then Inigua and Pablo mounted up and headed south along Santa Paula Creek. The watercourse wound down through the narrow valley, its banks bounded by a ribbon of dense foliage. Birds sang at the richness of the morning and raced busily from ground to branch and back again, building their spring nests. The ascending hillsides were alive with fresh grass and great swaths of blooming wildflowers. The riders felt a lively breeze spring up from the south. It blew the freshness of a new day into their nostrils. Inigua noticed a vast cavalcade of clouds gathering in the direction of the sea.

They rode down the trail for five miles until they came to the nearly deserted village of Mupu. A host of mongrel dogs came forth to challenge them. Inigua and Pablo reined in and waited while several old people came out and called them off. Mupu was a miserable little village of perhaps ten domed huts, a mere shadow of its former self. It was, however nicely situated on a rise above the confluence of the creek and the Santa Clara River. The riders did not tarry, but rode on to the river. They found the channel running full freshet, fed as it was by Santa Paula Creek and numerous streams upriver. The main river, like its cousin to the west, the Ventura, was only a part-time river. As impressive as it looked now, by mid-summer it would dwindle down to a timid trickle.

The river bore off to the southwest, and the riders followed the trail that hugged its bank, looking for a place to cross. The river valley began to slowly widen as it opened onto the coastal plain. When the riders left the cover of the hills they were buffeted by a strong, swirling wind. The clouds had thickened, and the sun winked dim and bright as they streamed across its face.

Scanning the sky, Inigua said, "I think we may be in for rain. We had best hurry to the coast."

As they rounded a bend in the river they looked down and saw where a high bank on the far side had been eaten away by recent flooding. Tree

166

roots dangled from its sheer face amid the bright faces of newly unearthed river rock. Just then the two heard the rumble of approaching hoof beats. They looked behind them and saw three horsemen galloping down the trail. The smallest of the riders, the one in the lead, was Fernando Tico. Inigua and Pablo urged their mounts off the trail to let them pass.

As the three drew abreast of them, Don Tico raised his right hand to call a halt and reined in. The mayordomo ordered his two companions to wait on the trail, and rode slowly over to Inigua and Pablo. He wore a fine sombrero and was dressed in dark leathers. An impressive bone-handled knife hung in its scabbard from his belt. There was a reata dangling from one side of his pommel, and his notorious whip from the other. Tico casually surveyed their belongings. His eyes fell on the hide lashed across the mule's back. He hocked up a gob of phlegm and spat.

"I see you have skinned your steer, viejo. Take good care of it. You will not be getting another one from me. And that goes for the Indians I passed coming down the trail too."

"Whatever you say, señor," said Inigua. Tico's eyes flared into sizzling black orbs.

"Listen, old man. If you wish to address me, the correct title is 'Don' Tico. I overlooked your insolence once before, but I will not do so again. Do you understand?"

"Ah, but of course, Don Tico. I did not mean any undue disrespect. You must forgive me. I am only an ignorant heathen. And to put your mind at rest, we have no need for another steer. This small, insignificant animal whose hide you see here is all we require. We are not greedy like some people. We even shared the meat with those Indians you passed."

Don Tico scowled. "I do not appreciate your generosity, old man. I don't want those Indians getting a taste for free beef. It might give them bad ideas – ideas that they would later regret."

"You seem to be riding awfully hard this morning, señor, er, Don Tico," said Inigua. "Where are you going in such a hurry, if I might ask?

"I always ride hard. And where I am going is none of your business, cabrone. But I will tell you any way, for it might be instructive for you to know. There has been trouble at the mission."

"Trouble at the mission?" blurted Pablo.

Tico looked at him with distain. "Yes. Trouble. At the request of the padre-superior I go to teach a harsh lesson to those who think they are free to do as they please. Some neophytes visiting from other missions caused a disturbance the other night. I will give the backs of those who were caught a good hiding tomorrow. I will send them home with a painful and lasting reminder of their visit to Mission San Buenaventura.

"Come and watch tomorrow afternoon if you like. In fact, I insist that you come. I want you to see my handiwork, and what is in store for those who think they can ignore the rules of civilization. I will look for you

167

both. Adios." With that, Don Tico turned and spurred his horse down the trail. The two vaqueros rode after him. Inigua and Pablo watched them go.

Pablo shook his head. "Why do you do that, Inigua? You are like that man who performed the snake dance last night."

"You know why I do it. But I am sorry I did, for now we must both go to the mission. I was hoping to avoid that."

"I want to go," said the boy. "I am worried about Padre Uria. I hope he is all right."

"Come, boy, let us ride. We will go to Hueneme and stake the hide in the sea. It is only about ten miles from here. We can spend the night there."

Inigua lapsed into silence after that. As they rode along he answered Pablo's occasional questions in monosyllables or mere grunts. He seemed preoccupied, as if in deep thought. At midday they stopped to rest at the invitation of friendly villagers at Sa'aqtik'oy, the place the Spaniards named Saticoy. They were given food, and then traveled on. Inigua had been civil to their hosts, but had said very little.

Just downriver from Saticoy they found a place where the river widened and the water grew shallow. They crossed over there to the eastern side. The broad coastal plain, alive in lush new growth, spread for miles in every direction. Other than a few isolated grassy knolls, the land was flat and featureless. It sloped ever so gradually towards the Pacific shore, divided here and there by seasonal watercourses. The riders could see evidence that much of the plain had been burned the previous fall. The blackened and twisted remains of stalks and branches stood out in sharp contrast to the verdant green all around.

As they rode, Pablo puzzled over Inigua's sudden reticence. It was unlike him to have so little to say. The boy tried to think of some way to break the silence. Finally an idea came to him. He said, "When would you like your next 'reading and writing' lesson, señor? I have been neglecting my teaching duties."

"I do not think it will be necessary to continue with the lessons," replied Inigua.

"But why, señor? We are making a trade. You teach me how to make a reata, and I teach you how to read and write."

"I release you from the bargain."

"But why?"

"I am thinking I must do something about Señor Tico tomorrow. What I do will no doubt cause trouble. I may not be available for lessons."

Pablo looked at him in alarm. "No, señor. Please don't do anything. What are you thinking? What are you planning?"

"I have not decided yet."

"Please don't do anything, señor. I beg you, for your own sake, and for mine. If you do something bad they will hurt you, or put you back in the curatel. They might even..." Tears formed in the boy's eyes, and his voice

168

cracked when he said, "I don't want anything to happen to you, señor. If anything happens, how am I to learn how to make the reata?"

"I am sure the padre can find someone else to teach you, boy."

"But I don't want anyone else. I want you. Only you must teach me, señor."

They rode in silence for awhile. Finally Inigua sighed and said, "I suppose I can wait a little while to settle with Señor Tico. At least until the reata is finished. But then he must be made to suffer."

"Suffer? Why must he suffer, señor? He hasn't done anything to you?"

"It is not about me. It is about him, and others like him. People like Camacho and Cota. I fixed them, and I will fix Tico too."

"What do you mean you fixed them?"

"Do you remember the other night when I told you about the Spanish coming to Shisholop the second time, and about the trouble we had afterwards?"

"Sí, señor."

"For years before the founding of Mission San Buenaventura couriers and soldiers passing to and fro preyed upon our women. They bullied our men when we tried to intervene, and threatened us with their weapons. Our women took to running and hiding whenever horses came into view. Sometimes the soldiers chased them down and lassoed them. The worst of the Spaniards was a man named Camacho. He was truly evil, and voracious. He brutalized many women, including my sister. He gave her a horrible sickness between her legs. For that I made him disappear."

"You made him disappear? What do you mean?"

"I followed him late one afternoon after he crossed the river on his way north. Because he had stopped to fulfill his lust he had fallen behind his companions. He was a careless and impulsive man. I followed him at a distance, along the beach, until he came to those steep hills on the way to Santa Barbara. You know the ones, do you not? The ones that fall straight down to the shore. By then the sun had set and the tide was coming in, blocking his path. He must have been unwilling to climb up and down those many steep hillsides in the dark. He must have decided to wait for low tide. I came upon him sleeping by the trail there at Pitas Point. There used to be an old Chumash shrine there. I was only nineteen, but I knew what to do."

"What did you do?"

Inigua rubbed his chin. "If I tell you, you must promise not to repeat it to anyone. What I say is just between you and me – *mano o mano*. Comprende?"

"Yes, of course. I promise not to tell. What did you do?"

"I broke his head with a rock."

"No! Señor! You broke his head? You mean you killed him?"

"It was a big rock. It must have weighed forty pounds. I raised it over my head and brought it down on his head with all the strength I possessed. Yes, I am quite sure I killed him."

"I don't know what to say. You... you are a murderer."

Inigua shrugged. "He was a bad man. He raped my sister. He deserved to die."

"But... but what happened? Didn't the Spaniards come looking for him? Didn't they know he was murdered?"

"His companions came back looking for him the following day. They found his horse grazing on a hillside above the beach. They never found him. They assumed rightfully that the sea had taken him."

Pablo was appalled. He had never known a murderer before. He was shaken too. He realized now that Inigua was capable of anything. While he didn't fear the old man, he wondered what else Inigua had done, what else he was capable of.

"Who was that other man you mentioned, señor? The one you called Cota?"

"Oh, yes. Sergeant Pablo Antonio Cota."

"I think I have heard that name before. Did you kill him too, Inigua?"

"No, but not for a lack of trying. He was another one of those who could not keep his *i'ikpik* in his pants. He was one who considered our women his personal property. In some ways he was worse than Camacho because he was in a position of authority. He was the commander of the guards at Mission San Buenaventura when it was first founded. He used his rank to silence everyone about what he was doing. He would gain access to the women by threatening to harm their families. In this way he made them do what he wanted. My intent was to cut off his *huevos*, but he was too careful, too sly for me. He was a hard man too, and he intimidated everyone. Everyone but me.

"I set a trap for him using Islay as bait. I arranged that the padre-superior, Vicente de Santa Maria, should know the when and the where of it. Cota was discovered, and as a consequence he was removed from the mission. Unfortunately, they did not punish him, but only demoted him transferred him to the presidio at Santa Barbara. But at least he was gone from our midst."

Pablo realized now that Inigua was fully capable of 'fixing' Don Tico too. This gave him much to think about. Now, it was Pablo's turn to lapse into silence. They continued to ride.

By late afternoon they were in sight of the coast and could hear the deep rumble of breakers pounding the beach. The blustering wind brought with it the sharp sweet tang of ocean brine.

170

26

HUENEME

Inigua and Pablo rode up to the outskirts of *Wene'me* village. Though much smaller than in pre-mission times, the settlement called 'Hueneme' by the Spanish still clung to the high ground at the edge of a salt marsh. A meandering stream to one side emptied into a nearby lagoon and provided potable water. Adjacent to the stream stood the village's most prominent structure: an earthen sweat lodge. There were perhaps ten tule houses scattered about, none of them of any great size. The riders saw a smoky fire burning down on the beach where five men were busy caulking the hulls of two sea-going canoes.

The by now familiar village dogs came out barking as the riders approached. This drew a dozen or more people from their huts to see who was coming. The men on the beach left their work and mounted the slope to the village.

Inigua startled Pablo by throwing back his head and crying in a loud falsetto, "Cree, cree, cree, cree." To Pablo it sounded like an excited seagull. The boy's surprise was compounded when the men from the beach replied in kind. The resulting chorus reminded him of a flock of gulls squabbling over a tasty morsel.

When the calls subsided, Inigua turned to Pablo and said, "That is the way of these Hueneme people. My greeting shows them we know their customs, that we are friends and mean no harm. By answering my call they show we are welcome. Those who live here have always been wary of strangers on horseback."

A middle-aged man with an upper body of great bulk separated himself from the group and came forward. His spindly legs seemed hardly capable of supporting his over-sized torso. The man's face and shoulders were painted white. Wavy black lines ran horizontally across this pale background. He greeted them by calling, "Haku, horsemen." He took a closer look at the riders and said, "Ah. I recognize you, old one. You are the one called Inigua. It has been a long time since we saw you last." He turned to the villagers and said, "Here is the father of Xaua." On hearing this, their faces broke into smiles and they made exclamations of welcome.

Taken aback, Inigua said, "Haku, Malak. You and your people are looking well. How is the fishing?"

"Taney, Inigua. The fishing is regrettable. Too many storms, too much rain this winter. So we only fish close to shore when the weather clears

171

and the sea calms down. But we still have plenty of shellfish to eat and are doing as well as can be expected."

Pablo was able to follow most of this exchange as it took place in the Ventureño dialect.

"What brings you here, Inigua?" asked Malak.

"We have come to stake a hide down there by the cove, this boy Pablo and I."

"Ah, you have a hide. Good for you. But you had better hurry. The tide has fallen."

"Taney, Malak. We will go now and stake it out, and then pay you a visit if it is acceptable."

"But of course, Inigua."

"Do you have any *tok* you can spare?" asked Inigua.

Malak motioned to a young man behind him who hurried into one of the huts and emerged with a coil of braided milkweed fiber. He handed it up to Inigua.

"Taney. It will be returned."

"Don't bother," said Malak, "we have plenty."

Inigua led Pablo beyond the village to the beach and headed east. The leaden skies had turned the sea a murky olivine. At odds with itself, the choppy waters of the channel hurled confused waves against the shoreline.

Pablo looked over his shoulder at the two canoes resting on their sides in the sand. He could see that they were constructed of curved wooden planks sewn together, caulked and painted over. They were the color of dried blood. Pablo's eyes were drawn to the two half-round wooden disks mounted on either side of both bows and sterns. He wondered what they were for, or what they represented. They looked a little like cupped hands. He saw tiny sparks of light reflecting from the gunwales where they had been inlaid in mother of pearl. Pablo found the smooth, sweeping lines of the canoes very pleasing. They bespoke of both function and beauty. He wondered what it might be like to ride in one of these magnificent crafts. He had never been in a boat before.

Inigua led them along a crescent of sand which brought them to a rocky point jutting out into the sea. The riders cut across the small promontory to the far side and came upon a relatively calm body of water.

"This is the spot," said Inigua. "The current does not draw here, and the waves are thwarted by the rocks. See how they break out there on the point. Come, let us hurry."

They dismounted and removed the hide and stakes from Chico's back. They took off their clothes and waded out into the chilly gray water. Pablo shouldered the hide while Inigua carried two round beach stones and the coil of tok.

Inigua said, "Even though the tide is out, we should stake the hide underwater so that the next low tide will not leave it exposed."

172

They found an area of sandy bottom in about a foot of water, and Inigua directed Pablo to spread the hide out on the surface, flesh side up. They pushed it down into the water with their feet and then stepped on top of it. The cold water surged and swirled about their calves.

Inigua set the two rocks down on the hide and said, "I will stay here with the hide. Bring the stakes, Pablo." While the boy went ashore, Inigua took hold of the steer's tail and tied the end of the braided cord to it. He rotated the hide so that the tail pointed towards shore.

Bending over in the frigid, foam-laced water, the man and boy stretched the hide out once more, and, inserting the stakes into the holes previously cut in the edges, drove them into the sand with the rocks. Inigua directed Pablo to pound the stakes at an angle so there was no chance the hide could lift off of them. The splashes from their hammering drenched them both and stung their eyes. When they were done and satisfied that all was secure, Inigua took up the braided coil of tok and waded ashore playing out the cord. They drove one final stake deep into the sandy beach above the high water mark and tied the cord to it, thereby anchoring the hide to dry land.

"That should hold it," said Inigua. "And this tok will make it easier to find the hide if we come for it at high tide. If all goes well it will be ready in a couple of days."

The two stood wet and shivering on the wind-swept beach scanning the immediate area to get their bearings so as to be sure to find the spot again. Pablo's gaze wandered along the shore to the east. About five miles away he saw where the Santa Monica Mountains tumbled down out of the clouds and fell into the sea. A great, jagged rock at the mountain's edge cut into the sea like the bow of some colossal ship.

Inigua saw where the boy was looking and said, "That place is called *Muwu*, which simply means 'beach.' The Spanish called it Mugu. See that lagoon just on this side of that rocky point? There is a village there, at the mouth of the lagoon. There used to be a lot of fine fishermen and traders living there, and here in Wene'me too. Most are gone now.

"If you went around that rocky point there you would find that the coast begins to bend a little to the south. There are many more mountains all along there, and they come right down to the shore. There is great fishing in the kelp beds offshore. If you were to keep going you would come to another rocky point. That one is called Point Dume. It is named after Padre Dumetz who was at Mission San Buenaventura in the early days. After Point Dume the coast curves back to the east again and into Santa Monica Bay. There used to be a village down there called *Humaliwu*, which means 'the surf sounds loudly.' The Spaniards called it Malibu. It was the last village in Chumash territory. If you continued on you would find yourself in the land of the Gabrielaños."

"Haku, travelers," came a voice behind them. They turned to see a young man approaching across the strand.

"I am Liyam, son of Malak. My father invites you to the village sweat lodge. A fire has been lit, and you are welcome to partake of its warmth."

"Taney, Liyam," said Inigua. "Gladly."

The intense heat inside the domed lodge was more than welcome, and it warmed them quickly. Before long they were sweating profusely and wiping themselves clean with rib bones claimed from a sea lion. With them in the sweat lodge was Malak, one of the last living makers of canoes, and the long-time wot of Wene'me village. His two sons were with him, Liyam and Shup.

After a time, Malak said, "We have not seen you for many years, Inigua. I did not know you were still working on the rancho."

"I am not working there any more."

Malak arched one eyebrow. "Then how did you come by that hide? You didn't steal it did you? We don't want any trouble here."

"Of course not. We had permission from the padre and the mayordomo to take one steer for the making of a reata. This boy Pablo is going to be a vaquero one day."

"Vaquero? You want to be a vaquero, Pablo?"

"Yes," replied the boy, wiping sweat from his arm.

"But why? That is such a hard and dirty life, dangerous too."

"I don't mind a little dirt. I think it will be fun," said Pablo. "And I love riding horses."

"If you want fun, you should consider fishing. Not only is it fun, it is clean. I can think of nothing I would rather do."

"But I don't know anything about fishing."

"We can fix that. Isn't that right, boys?"

Liyam and Shup smiled and nodded. The oldest son, Liyam, a youthful replica of his father, said, "There is nothing as fun as fishing, Pablo. And there is nothing like being out in the ocean in a good canoe. Out there you are free, and far away from the dirt and smell of the shore. Why don't you join us one day? We can always use an extra pair of hands."

"I would like that, but I don't think it will be soon. Tomorrow we must go to the mission, and then we must make the reata."

Shup, the younger brother who was shorter and stouter than the others of his family said, "Why must you go to the mission? Why not stay here with us? You can fish with us. Or we can go diving and get some shellfish. If you think riding a horse is fun, you should try riding the ocean swells in a canoe."

"Unfortunately, we cannot. The mayordomo of Rancho Ojai, Don Tico, has ordered us to go to the mission. He wants us to watch him punish some Indians."

174

Malak said, "Why should he care whether you watched him or not?"

Pablo looked to Inigua. The latter said, "We go to the mission because I have unfinished business with Señor Tico."

But for the crackle of the fire, there was a silence in the sweat lodge. Pablo stared at Inigua with a thoughtful expression.

Malak finally spoke. "I am sorry I do not know you better, Inigua. I only know what I have heard about you over the years, and what I heard often disturbed me. I don't know anything about your business with Don Tico or the mission, and perhaps it would be well that it remain so."

After their sweat bath they plunged into the nearby stream. When they were dry and clothed again, the visitors went to tend their horses. They unpacked the load from Chico's back and staked their mounts out in a grassy area on the far side of the stream. They had just finished erecting their tent there when Malak approached them.

"'No need to set up a shelter," he said. "You can stay in my family's 'ap tonight. It will be warmer and drier there. Come now and be fed."

"Taney, Malak. But we want the tent up anyway, if it is alright with you. It will keep the ground under it dry so we can stake the hide here in a day or two."

"Smart," said Malak. "I think it will rain soon."

Inigua turned to Pablo. "I wish to speak with Malak for a moment. Can you put our saddles and other things in the tent so they do not get wet? Then come along to the 'ap. It is that one, the one closest to the sea." Then Inigua picked up his bota of wine and his blanket, and walked off towards the 'ap with Malak.

When Pablo eventually arrived at Malak's hut he was introduced to his wife, Luhui. She was a handsome woman of middle years from the island of Mi'chumash. Luhui looked very kindly upon Pablo. Her eyes grew soft and loving, the eyes of a true mother. She reached up to smooth his hair away, and then tenderly ran her hand down the side of his face. "Poor boy," she murmured, "poor boy."

Pablo wondered why she said that. Inigua must have told them he was an orphan. While he didn't like being pitied, her kindly gesture and her heart-felt concern made him feel suddenly very sorry for himself. Although he welcomed the comfort she intended, he found Luhui's affection embarrassing in front of the men.

"Come, sit by the fire, Pablo," she said. "You must be hungry."

They all gathered around the fire as sheets of rain began to fall along the coast. Inigua produced his bota of wine, and it was passed from hand to hand as they talked and ate.

"These abalone are delicious," said Inigua, "and the lemon juice is a nice addition."

"Taney," said Malak. "We learned that from the Mexicans. There is an abundance of abalone in these waters now, here and over beyond Muwu.

175

It has been so for ten or more years now, ever since the sea otters were hunted out."

"The Aleuts," said Inigua, grimly.

Malak nodded. "They and their Russian masters. They shot all the otters for their furs, the greedy *putas*, and now there are no more to feed on the shellfish. Those Aleuts were hard on the Islanders too. They killed anyone who tried to interfere with the slaughter. They terrorized and burned many isolated villages out there. And, as you no doubt know, that is the excuse the Padres used to bring all the surviving Islanders to the missions – for their own safety."

Inigua nodded.

No one spoke for a while. Pablo became aware of the waves pounding out there in the darkness. He listened to them heave and sigh, plunge and withdraw under the overlay of falling rain.

Malak sighed. "Ah, well, that is all ancient history. We live in a different world now. But I am happy to say that we in Wene'me still fish and gather food from the sea as we always have done. We trade the excess to inland Chumash, and to the mission and the pueblo that is growing up around it. I think the only reason the padres have left us alone is that we continue to provide them with seafood for their Friday meals. For this we are grateful."

When they were finished eating, the plates and utensils were set aside and everyone in the family found some work to perform. Malak set himself to attaching a barb just below the head of a harpoon with a detachable fore-shaft. His wife Luhui took up her basket-work and began to weave. Liyam worked grinding a curved hook from an abalone shell, while Shup took to repairing a gill net fashioned out of milkweed.

Malak cleared his throat and said, "You no doubt heard me mention your son when you first arrived, Inigua. The reason I did so is that your boy, Xaua, has always held a special place in our family's heart. Because of this, I will tell you now, grandfather, that if you ever find yourself in trouble and need our help, we will do whatever we can for you."

Inigua was surprised and embarrassed. "Taney, Malak. But, why?"

"Because your son saved the life of my own son. This one here." He pointed to Liyam, who blushed and smiled sheepishly.

Inigua said, "Oh? I did not know that. Xaua never told me."

"Your son was not one to boast. We knew Xaua many years ago, when he was a fisherman at Shisholop. They still had canoes in those days before the earthquake and the big ocean wave that followed destroyed them all. We encountered him often out in the channel, either fishing or on his way to or from the islands. He was always with several cousins and shipmates. This must have been over twenty years ago. My son, Liyam, was just a little boy then. We only took him along to bail the canoe, for he was still too small to paddle.

"It was in early fall that year, and we were out fishing for tuna. A sudden wind storm came up. It was one of those hot, dry, east winds that blow out of a clear sky. All the other fishing tomols raced towards the nearest shelter. Unfortunately, we were far out in the channel when it hit. There was no land close by. We tried to paddle back to Wenc'me, but we could make no headway. As sea-worthy as our canoes are, they are no match for a strong head wind.

"I decided to bring our canoe about, hoping to make it to the lee side of *Anyapakh* [Anacapa Island], which was downwind and the closest landfall. As we were coming about a big swell picked us up and exposed us to a sudden gust of wind. It hit us broadside and we capsized. It was all my fault. I was still young and inexperienced.

"The crew surfaced on both sides of the overturned canoe. We had lost our paddles and were distracted by trying to retrieve them. We were only able to catch one of them. After that we hung onto the gunwales and stayed with the canoe because we were so many miles from land. In the confusion we didn't notice that Liyam had been carried away by the wind and current. By the time we discovered he was missing, he had drifted far from the canoe. No one dared swim after him. In fact, I ordered them not to. It would have meant certain death. Anyone swimming after him would not be able to make it back to the tomol against the wind and current. I resigned myself to the fact that I had lost my first born.

"That is when Xaua came along in his own canoe. The swells were very large out there and he must have seen us when we rose up on them. Because his tomol was heavily laden with steatite from Catalina, the wind did not affect it so much. He was heading towards us when he sighted Liyam. He went straight to him and plucked him from the water. Then he and his crew retrieved our lost paddles and carried them to us. They helped us right our tomol. It took a long time to bail it out. Xaua stayed with us until well after dark when the wind finally subsided. Then he escorted us home. For this we will always be in Xaua's debt.

"We were sorry to hear that he died some years back. The cholera, wasn't it?"

"Yes," said Inigua, staring into the fire. His eyes glazed over and he was silent for a long while. Finally, he said, "He was a good son. In fact, all of my children turned out well. It does not seem right that I am still here, and they are gone."

Pablo was disturbed and saddened by this. He only remembered Inigua talking about his wife, Islay. He hadn't thought to ask about Inigua's other loved ones. He silently chastised himself for not showing more interest in the old man's life, in his family, or in how he filled the many years he had lived. Pablo went to bed that night determined to know his mentor better.

177

27

THE WHIPPING

Pablo awoke to the sharp crack of a wave shattering the morning stillness. He listened as it rumbled ashore. The wave paused momentarily, and then withdrew amid a clatter of pebbles. Pablo was not accustomed to dwelling this close to the perpetual sounding sea. He found its restlessness unsettling, though not in an altogether unpleasant way. The sounds of the sea stimulated him, inspiring a curious mixture of excitement and expectation, and, in the intermittent silences, a sense of the lonely emptiness of the ages. The sound of it stirred something deep within him, something primeval, something for which he had no name.

He glanced around the dim interior of the hut and found it deserted. He quickly dressed and went outside. The sun was up, but had not yet emerged from behind the Santa Monica Mountains. There was not a cloud in the sky, and not a breath of wind. Pablo marveled that it could be so after the previous night's rain. The sea was as smooth as a mirror, but for the long-lined swells that surged relentlessly towards shore.

Pablo joined Inigua and the family of Malak on the beach for a breakfast of steamed mussels and tender pieces of raw seaweed. It was the strangest meal Pablo had ever had, but it left him satisfied. The two travelers then saddled their horses, said their farewells, and rode west along the coast. The mouth of the Santa Clara River proved impassable, so they rode upriver for a mile or so until they found a place where they could cross. They continued west across the broad, coastal plain and watched as it gradually narrowed between the green hills to the north and the blue sea to the south. It was a fine, sunny morning and they made good progress along El Camino Real. Pablo tried to engage Inigua in conversation, but the old man had no inclination to talk.

By late morning the arrowhead-shaped plain had narrowed considerably. Near the point where the hills met the sea, the bell tower hove into view. Pablo could sense Rojo's excitement at the prospect of home. By noon they were at the outskirts of the pueblo surrounding the mission. There was a noticeable lack of activity, it being Sunday, the day of rest.

Inigua reigned in as they neared the curatel. He turned to Pablo and said, "Take the animals to the corral, boy. I want to stop here and have a word with the prisoners."

"Sí, señor. You aren't going to do anything, are you?"

"No. Just talk. I will see you later. Go to the kitchen and get yourself something to eat."

178

Pablo rode on, leading Tabaco and the mule. He unsaddled the animals and turned them loose in the corral. He spoke briefly with José Sabino as he stored their gear in an empty stable. He told the old vaquero about their trip and informed him they would be staying the night and departing sometime tomorrow.

The boy entered the quadrangle to find most of the neophytes settling down to their siesta. Padre Uria's door was closed, and the boy supposed that the good father was probably napping too. He decided to postpone his visit. Pablo went to the kitchen in search of Encarnación.

Meanwhile, Inigua approached two men secured in stocks just south of the curatel. Their bodies were bent forward at the waist, their hands and feet protruding from holes cut in the rough timbers. Dressed only in taparrabos, they looked hot, cramped and weary. It was obvious they had spent many hours confined here under the bright sun.

"Hola, compadres," said Inigua. "Qué tal?"

One of the men, a portly Indian who was sweating profusely, raised his head to the stranger and said, "*Mierda*! How does it look from where you stand, viejo?"

"Not good. What did you do to be punished so?"

"Nothing much. We were only trying to have a little fun. We held a little fiesta down by the beach the other night. Much drinking and dancing. Even a little love-making. When the soldiers came and tried to break it up, we fought with them. They beat us with wooden clubs. A few of us unlucky ones were captured and brought here. We have been taking turns in the stocks. Those bastards will whip us today after their siesta."

"That is regrettable. I am called Inigua. What is your name, amigo?"

"My name is Bernardo. I came all the way from San Fernando to help out here, and this is the thanks I get. This miserable one next to me is Domingo. He hails from San Gabriel."

"Where are the others?"

"There are two more men in the curatel. They are sleeping now. They were out here in the stocks all night in the rain. There is a woman there too. Carmen. She is in a cell of her own. She was caught coupling with Domingo."

Domingo managed a tired smile.

"When will they come for you?" asked Inigua.

"In a few hours. Why? Do you want to watch them mutilate us?"

"No. I would like to help you."

"How? They have iron locks on these stocks and on the doors of the curatel. There is no escape for us."

"How would it be if I gave you some Indian herbs, something that would dull the pain?"

"*Conyo*! That would be very acceptable to me. How about you, Domingo?"

179

"Ah, yes, por favor. Any relief would be a blessing. I am going half mad thinking about the whip biting into my back. I hear this man Tico is a bad hombre."

"I will return in a little while with something for all of you. Do not mention this to anyone."

Inigua headed towards the mission. He went first to the corral and found José Sabino. When the stable master saw him he smiled and said, "Buenos dias, 'Anakuwin. Welcome back. I saw that boy Pablo a little while ago. He told me you had a good trip."

"Sí, José. It is good to see you. 'Sorry, I cannot talk just now. I am in a big hurry. Where did the boy put our things?"

"Over there in that covered stable on the end. Can I help you, 'Anakuwin?"

"No, gracias. I will speak with you later."

Inigua retrieved a large leather pouch, the wooden bucket, and a tin cup from their packs. He carried them to the kitchen and found Encarnacion curled up on a pallet in the corner.

"Haku, Encarnacion," he said. "'Sorry to disturb your siesta. I bring greetings from your family in Aw'hai."

"Oh! Haku, Inigua. How are they?"

"They are all well. Your aunt and uncle send their love and thank you for your gifts. They sent you some things too. 'Alapay sent this necklace made from the seeds of wild cucumber, and this dog tooth bracelet. Qupe sent a packet of herbs."

"Oh? That's nice. I fed Pablo a little while ago. Are you hungry, Inigua?"

"I have no time. Can you give me some hot water? A bucket full? And then I must go."

"Certainly, Inigua." She dipped a large pot in the barrel of water and put it on the fire. "I will make you a little burrito while we wait. So, what is the news from the valley?"

"They have had a lean winter up there, but are doing all right. I could not help noticing your great-niece, 'Akiwo. She took quite a liking to Pablo."

"Oh? She must be all grown up now. I have not seen her for some years. She was such a pretty little girl."

"She is still pretty, but she is a young woman now."

"Hmm. And does Pablo like her too?"

"My guess is that he is in love with her."

Encarnacion laughed in delight. "Oh, that is wonderful. Maybe Pablo will join our family one day."

"Who can say?"

"What do you need all this hot water for, Inigua? Are you going to take a bath?"

"No. I want to make some tea. A lot of tea."

180

"What do you have there?" she said, eyeing the pouch.

"Herbs. Some are for you from Qupe. Others are for my own use. I am making a blend of Momoy, Yerba Santa, and Willow bark."

"Oh, my goodness. Are you having trouble sleeping, Inigua? Are you in pain? And why do you need so much? You can't possibly drink a whole bucket. It would kill you."

"It is not for me. It is for the prisoners, those who are to be flogged."

"Aiee, Inigua! Are you *loco*? What you intend will cause big trouble."

"Maybe not. At least not for you. If anyone asks, you never saw me."

When the water had boiled, Inigua poured it into the bucket and added the herbs. He then covered it with a lid and let it steep. Encarnacion retreated to her pallet and sat down, studying the old man as he munched on his burrito.

"I do not understand you, Inigua. What are these prisoners to you? Are they relatives?"

"No. I do not know them. But I have been in their position before. They are waiting to be scourged. That is almost as bad as the beating itself. This tea will help them. My wife secretly provided it to me a couple of times."

After the tea had steeped Inigua prepared to depart. "You can have the pouch," he said.

"No, Inigua. You keep it. You may need it more than me before you're through."

"Thank you, Encarnacion. And thank you for your help. Adios."

"Vaya con Dios, Inigua."

As had been prearranged, at three o'clock the De Profundis bell began to chime, summoning the neophytes to the place of punishment. Amid its melancholy tolling, the residents sleepily donned their cotons and straw hats and dutifully filed out of their quarters. As they made their way through the various lanes of the pueblo, a carnival-like atmosphere enveloped them. Enterprising vendors along the way proffered roasted pine nuts, ponocha, and tiny bone whistles. Children skipped and giggled alongside their parents. The murmur of animated conversation and laughter rose among the adults as they approached the curatel. It was commonly agreed that this would be almost as entertaining as a bull and bear fight. Since only one of those to be punished was from Mission San Buenaventura, the harlot Carmen, it made the event all the more festive.

The mayordomo, Corporal Sanchez, and the six members of the mission guards were arrayed in a wide circle around the whipping post, which stood just to the north of the curatel. The alcalde, Luis, and two regidores stood waiting by the door of the curatel. The padres Uria and Cuccula, wearing their wide-brimmed hats, their hands tucked into opposite sleeves, sat on oaken stools some thirty feet from the post. The boy, Pablo, stood next to the padre-superior and scanned the crowd for his mentor.

When the six hundred or so neophytes had finally assembled themselves around the circle of guards, Corporal Sanchez stepped forward and in a loud voice commanded, "*Silencio!*

"You in the front rows, sit down on the ground. Those of you behind them, kneel. Those in the back remain standing. In this way you can all see."

When this was accomplished and the crowd had settled down, Corporal Sanchez continued, "We are gathered here today under the eyes of the Almighty and in the presence of his messengers, the holy padres of Mission San Buenaventura. We are bidden here by both God's laws and those of the noble Republic of Mexico, to deliver a just punishment to those who have trespassed against us. Those who are about to undergo this corporal punishment are not only sinners, but criminals, and are justly deserving of the chastisement they are about to receive. Let you who bear witness today take heed, and learn the hard lesson of delinquency through their suffering. And here, to deliver this hard lesson is the mayordomo of Rancho Ojai, Don Ferrrnaaando Tiiico!"

A forced cheer went up as Tico emerged from behind the curatel flicking his whip. He strode forward, bare-chested and hatless, wearing only tight-fitting leather pants tucked into tall boots. His pale torso, well-muscled and slathered with olive oil, glistened in the afternoon sun. A female murmur of appreciation rose from the crowd, for though short of stature, Don Tico was a fine figure of a man. He twirled the tips of his moustache in response to his admirers.

"Bring out the first prisoner," called Corporal Sanchez.

The chubby one, Bernardo, was led from the curatel. His hands were bound in front of him with a thick leather thong. Studying him, Pablo was struck by how peculiar he looked. The man seemed dazed, and curiously serene. He wore the expression of a simpleton with a broad smile on his face. He looked as if he found the whole proceedings rather amusing. In fact, he looked more like a man on his way home from the cantina than one about to meet the lash.

Bernardo stumbled slightly on his way to the post, and giggled at his own clumsiness. The regidore, Felipe, stood on a wooden barrel next to the post waiting for him. He had a stout rope in his hands which he tied between Bernardo's bound wrists. He then threaded the free end through an iron ring fixed high up on the post. Felipe leaned back and put his weight on the rope, drawing Bernardo up onto his tiptoes. The regidore then secured the rope to the ring. It was then that Pablo noticed Inigua standing in a cluster of neophytes behind the post. His mentor had a sober, serious expression on his face.

Don Tico, impatient to begin, stretched his muscles and swung his shoulders in a semi-circle, limbering himself for the work ahead. When all was ready, he smoothed his walrus moustache one last time, and took up his freshly oiled whip.

The leather snake whipped through the air and made a vicious snapping sound as it struck Bernardo across his bare back. His body jerked, but he did not scream. The blow did, however, elicit a gasp from the crowd, and a raw, red line across Bernardo's torso.

"One," called Corporal Sanchez.

Tico paused, surprised at the prisoner's lack of response. He knew better than anyone that it had been a good blow. The mayordomo's face took on a studied look as he drew his arm back again. The second stroke fell harder than the first, and again the body jerked. But still no sound.

"Two," called Sanchez.

Don Tico seemed puzzled. He let fly another blow, even harsher than the one before. All it gained was a short grunt from the prisoner.

"Three."

Don Tico's face took on a look of determination as he settled into his work. Methodically, he laid on three more heavy blows with military precision. But still there were no sound. No screams, no wails, no whimpering.

"Six."

"Damn this man!" mumbled Tico. He felt a growing frustration, and the beginning simmer of anger. He set his feet and began delivering blow after evenly spaced blow, each stroke accompanied by a whoosh, a snap, and the sharp crack of leather on bare flesh. A steady rhythm of blows sounding on the metronome of pain. Only there seemed to be no pain. Bernardo's back was bleeding freely now, and each time Don Tico drew back his whip he sent droplets of blood flying into the faces of those behind him.

"Twelve."

Like many of those around him, Pablo flinched each time a blow was struck. He heard several children crying at the sight and sound of it. He looked across the open circle at Inigua on the opposite side. He saw the old man's eyes glancing from Bernardo's face to that of Don Tico, and back again. Pablo could not be sure, but he thought he saw Inigua nod with satisfaction.

Tico was sweating now. He aimed his blows carefully, ensuring the man's back was striped from shoulders to waist. Tico's face was red, not so much from exertion, but from his growing anger. The final few blows were savage, delivered with all his strength.

"Twenty-five," said Corporal Sanchez. "Finito! Take this man down. Bring out the next prisoner."

When Bernardo's arms were lowered, he turned slowly towards Don Tico, and astounded the crowd by smiling at the man. He was then led back to the curatel, staggering as he walked, his back awash in blood.

Don Tico shook his head. He was clearly perplexed and disappointed. He muttered to himself as he wiped his whip clean with a cloth.

Domingo was led out next. His hands were bound before him as had Bernardo's. Pablo was puzzled at this man's appearance too. His hair was in disarray and he seemed half asleep, as if he just awoke from his siesta. He seemed unaware of the crowd, or the reason for their gathering. When he was secured to the post, Don Tico went to work on him in a very professional manner. His strokes were masterpieces of power, accuracy, and timing. The snap of the whip came just as it should – the merest instant before contact with the flesh. Domingo's body jerked from the force of the blows, but incredibly, no sound issued from the prisoner.

Pablo sensed Don Tico's growing distress. He could tell that the mayordomo was working hard, putting every ounce of strength and concentration into each blow. It was obvious that Tico yearned for the yelp, for the scream, for the plea for mercy. But they did not come. He was not getting what he wanted and could not understand why. He was becoming more and more incensed. His accuracy began to fade and his timing to falter. His only reward was the blood that he saw flowing down Domingo's back.

"Twenty-five," called Sanchez. "Enough. Release him."

Murmurs began passing through the crowd, punctuated by the occasional snicker. Tico stood bathed in sweat, coiling his whip and pretending not to hear. He face had taken on a scarlet hue.

The next two prisoners were a recurring nightmare of those which came before. In fact, they were worse. Both prisoners seemed to lose consciousness early on in their whipping. How then could they feel the pain? Try as he might, Don Tico could not elicit any sound other than the occasional grunt from his victims. Laughter was now circling the crowd, timid at first, then gradually growing louder and more open. Bored spectators at the rear of the crowd began drifting off and heading back towards the pueblo.

The Don's eyes stung from his own sweat. He felt like weeping, but of course he could not. Sweat drenched his leather pants around the waist. Someone in the crowd commented that it looked like he had peed his pants. Laughter ensued, and Tico looked about angrily, but could not determine who had spoken.

His spirits lifted when they brought out the last prisoner – the local woman, Carmen the Fornicator. Here at last Don Tico knew he would hear the sounds of suffering that he so yearned to hear. When Carmen was secured to the post, but before Tico had begun, she turned her head and said saucily, "Hey, maricón. Come on and give it to me, if you are able."

This, of course, enraged Don Tico and amused the crowd. He laid the lash upon her buttocks unmercifully. Carmen writhed under it, as though performing some erotic dance. Midway through she began humping the post like a dog. But still no sound. Only the crack of the whip and Sanchez's infuriating numbering of the strokes. That, and the growing derision of the crowd. Tico became so distracted that halfway through the beating his whip slipped from his grasp and flew from his hand. He was forced to chase after it and pick it up out of the dust. The crowd howled with laughter.

"Silencio!" shouted Corporal Sanchez.

Don Tico was near collapse by the time the twenty-fifth blow was struck. Carmen slowly turned towards him with a look of distain, a sneer curling her Indian lip.

28

GRUNION RUN

Padre Uria insisted that Pablo and Inigua join him for supper that night. Although he was feeling rather ill, the padre-superior was delighted at having the boy back, and wanted to spend time with him. They gathered around the table in the sitting room alongside the padre's four immense blue Maltese cats. A candelabrum on the tabletop lit the assembled faces and dispelled the growing darkness around them. After grace, Inigua did the honors and poured the wine.

"Your cats are looking fat and happy," he said. The cats, sitting two to a chair, ate contentedly from plates resting on the table. "But I cannot say the same for you, Francisco. You do not look well."

"Don't call me Francisco. Call me Padre. I am in a lot of pain. They tell me I have Piedra de Variga. I feel bloated and have a strong pain in my stomach. You probably noticed I have a problem with gas too."

"I was not going to mention it, but, yes," said Inigua, "it is quite evident. I notice too that your ankles are quite swollen. And your color is not good. You look a little yellow."

"Thank you for pointing it out, old friend. I know I look bad. My body is betraying me. And just when I need it most. I wish I were done with all this. I truly do. The responsibilities of the mission are too much with me now. And that debacle this afternoon – how awful."

"Yes, awful," said Inigua with a wry smile. "Señor Tico seemed very upset. Things did not turn out as he expected."

"His title is Don Tico," said the padre, emphatically. "Why can't you call people by their proper names? The poor man left immediately after delivering the punishment. He was beside himself, and refused to stay at the mission any longer. I'm afraid he has a long ride home tonight."

"That is too bad," said Inigua. "But I feel worse for the prisoners. They did not seem to suffer much today, but they will tomorrow, and in the days to come."

Padre Uria took an angry swig of wine and said, "I hate that whipping business. It is an abominable practice, although sometimes necessary. And it nearly got me killed when I was at Mission Santa Inez. Corporal Cota, the mayordomo up there, he used to have a whip with a metal tip on it. One day he almost killed a visiting alcalde from La Purisima with it. The neophytes at Santa Inez became enraged when they witnessed it."

"Who can blame them?" said Inigua.

186

The padre ignored this comment. "They had been grumbling about their own mistreatment at the hands of the soldiers long before this even happened. But when they saw this particularly brutal whipping it pushed them over the edge. They went absolutely mad, and attacked the soldiers. The whole mission broke out in revolt. What a terrible day that was."

"And you did not see it coming?" asked Inigua.

Again the padre ignored him. "Luckily, the neophytes did not blame me. In fact, they adored me, as I had always loved them. But still they held me hostage, along with the families of the mission guard. The neophytes made war all day against the soldiers and set fire to the mission. Only when it threatened the church itself did they stop and help put out the fire. That was eight years ago, in 1824. In the days that followed, the rebellion spread to La Purisima and Santa Barbara as well. You remember don't you, Inigua?"

Inigua nodded as he tore a leg bone from the duck Encarncíon had roasted for them.

The padre continued, "The whole episode was dreadful. Tragic, in fact. Soldiers from the Presidio of Santa Barbara came to put down the uprising. Many of our neophytes fled to La Purisima. The soldiers followed, and severe fighting took place there. Many people died. Some of the Indians escaped and never came back. They are over there in the San Joaquin Valley even to this day."

"I have been there," said Inigua. "They seem to be doing fine."

Padre Uria waved his hand in dismissal. "And the whole sad episode ended with me being held responsible for the stupidity of the military. But you both must surely understand that it was not my fault. I tried to stop them, but the soldiers ignored me whenever I said anything. They justified their cruelty by saying it was necessary to maintain order and discipline. But I know the real reason. The soldiers were angry at not being paid their back wages. After the revolution in Mexico there was no money to pay them. The soldiers were frustrated and took it out on the neophytes. But it was me who took the blame for everything. After sixteen years of loyal service and endless toil at Santa Inez, this was the thanks I got – the padre-presidente transferred me to Mission Soledad. I spent four years in that wretched place, and that is what ruined my health."

Inigua took a drink of wine. "I think you have worked too hard for too long, Francisco," he said. "And for what?"

The padre's eyes flamed. "If you don't know the answer to that, then you have learned nothing in the last fifty years, you scoundrel."

"I think I learned a lesson you Spaniards did not intend to teach," said Inigua.

Pablo looked on in distress as the two men he had grown to love glared at one another. He didn't want any trouble between them, but felt it was not his place to interrupt.

187

Inigua glanced at Pablo, and then leaned back in his chair. He said in a more reasonable tone, "I think maybe we should not talk about politics and religion any more, old friend. We already know our differences. I am just saying I think you need a nice long rest. Maybe then you would recover your health. In the meantime, I may be of some help to you. I have some herbs that might ease your pain and settle your stomach. Yerba Buena might help. I cannot cure you, but I can make you more comfortable. I wish I knew more. If Islay were here she might have been able to cure you."

"I don't think there is a cure for me," said the padre, glumly. "I am an egg with a broken shell. I cannot be fixed."

He took a sip of wine and said, "But let's not talk about me anymore. I want to know about you two. Tell me about your plans, yours and Pablo's. The boy told me what you have accomplished so far. It sounds like you have made good progress."

"Sí, Francisco," said Inigua, "good progress. Tomorrow we will return to Hueneme and retrieve the hide from the sea. When it has dried we will begin the reata. But in the meantime we need more food, and another bota of wine. I drank the last of it last night."

Padre Uria raised an eyebrow. He considered addressing the wine request, but decided against it. He was too tired to wrangle. He sighed and said, "Remind me to write you some new vouchers. I will be leaving in the morning to work on the dam. We have decided the only way to survive is to rebuild it. The repair of the canal is nearly complete. The roadwork is progressing, and the fields will be ready for planting in a couple of weeks.

"Tell me, Inigua, where do you intend to stay while you make the reata?"

"I have been thinking about that..."

"Why don't you come back here?" said the padre. "You can have your old room back, you and my little Pablito. I want him near me."

Shaking his head, Inigua said, "We discussed this before. There is too much noise and confusion around here. It is better that we stay out on the land. And look at Pablo. Does he not look better than when he left? He has color in his cheeks now, and he looks stronger, does he not? He may even be a little wiser than when he left. The outdoors is good for him.

"But I understand you wanting him back, Francisco. Perhaps we can move over this way for a little while. Maybe down there by the mouth of the Ventura River. We could camp out there, and Pablo can visit you if he wishes."

"This sounds like a very good plan to me," said the padre, rubbing his ample stomach and letting out a long satisfying fart. Inigua and Pablo grimaced. The cats froze and cocked their heads at the sound.

"Perdon," said the padre, grinning and blushing. "I cannot help myself."

"But we can help ourselves," said Pablo. He took up a lit candle and waved it in front of the padre. They all laughed as the candle flared and fluttered in the gaseous air. Pablo was happy now, and relieved. Not with the padre's flatulence, but with the plan, and with the peace that had returned to the two men.

Inigua and Pablo spent much of the next day gathering provisions. Everywhere they went they heard people talking about the whipping. It seemed as though Don Tico had become a laughingstock. People were saying that he must have lost his touch.

By mid-afternoon Inigua and Pablo were ready to depart. They carried everything to the corral and loaded it onto Chico's back. As they were saddling their horses, José Sabino came close and drew Inigua aside.

In a confidential tone the stable-master said, "I heard something I think you should know about, 'Anakuwin. This morning there were two vaqueros here at the corral getting ready to ride to Rancho Ojai. One of them was telling the other that old Vicente told him he was up in the bell tower yesterday afternoon and saw you coming from the curatel just before the whipping. Old Vicente told the vaquero you were carrying a bucket and a tin cup. He thinks you gave the prisoners some medicine. I am thinking that old Vicente's words will reach Fernando Tico before too long."

"Oh?" said Inigua. "That is unfortunate. But it is good to know. Thank you for telling me, José."

"Is it true, 'Anakuwin?"

"Sometimes it is better not to know the truth, José."

"I understand, 'Anakuwin."

"I have a favor to ask, my friend. The boy and I are going to Hueneme for a few days, and then moving to the mouth of the Ventura River to camp out. If you hear anything more I should know, can you send word to me?"

"Sí, 'Anakuwin. I will send my youngest son, Paco."

Inigua and Pablo said their farewells and retraced their steps across the treeless plain. They followed El Camino Real under a cloudless sky towards the Santa Clara River. A chill wind blew in off the Santa Barbara Channel, scouring the wildflowers, and whirling gusts that fluttered the hats and cotons of the riders. The lowering sun painted the distant Santa Monica Mountains in the vivid tones of early spring.

Pablo was happy to be back in the saddle. His youthful enthusiasm bubbled up and flowed out of his mouth. "It is good to be away, eh, señor? What are we going to do now?"

"We are doing it. By the time we get to Hueneme it will be almost dark. We will make camp where we left the tent, and sleep there tonight. That is if we get any sleep."

"Why wouldn't we get any sleep?"

"Did you notice the moon the other night, boy?"

189

"No, señor."

"It was a full moon. Do you know what that means?"

"No, señor."

"Since this is the month of March, it means the grunion will be running for the next few nights."

"What is a grunion, and where are they running? Can we lazo them with a reata, señor?"

Inigua laughed heartily. Pablo was delighted to hear it. Laughter coming from Inigua was a rare thing.

"You are joking, of course," said Inigua.

"I am not joking, señor."

"Well then, you had better start practicing your lassoing right away. Those grunion are hard to catch." He undid the worn-out, old reata from his pommel and handed it over to the boy. "See if you can catch that boulder up ahead."

For the rest of the ride, Pablo tried to lasso everything they passed: rocks, brush, burnt stumps, rabbits, and even birds perching on branches. He caught no animals, but on those occasions when he was successful with stones or branches he had to stop, dismount, and undo the lasso. Then he had to put Rojo into a trot in order catch up with Inigua.

The sun was settling down in the sea by the time they arrived at Hueneme. They found the village bustling with activity. There had obviously been an influx of visitors in their absence. People from all over the coastal plain had come – from Mugu, Saticoy, and even as far away as Mupu. They gathered here on this, the second evening after a full spring moon, for the first grunion run of the season. Smoke from numerous cooking fires wafted above the village as excited children ran to and fro. Dogs wandered around in confused circles trying to keep up with all the activity. Malak waved a greeting to the riders from the midst of a gathering of men down by the beached canoes. Inigua and Pablo went directly to their tent and unpacked their gear.

The wind died down rapidly in the twilight. While Pablo gathered wood for a fire, Inigua walked down to the beach to check on the hide. He found the tok line still attached to its stake in the failing light. He tugged lightly on the line that ran from the stake down into the water, and found it still taut. He returned to camp to find Pablo scrunched down over some kindling making sparks with small pieces of flint and steel.

"The hide is still there," announced Inigua. "We will bring it ashore in the morning."

"And what about the running grunion, señor?" A spark caught on the tinder, and Pablo bent over and blew life into the fire.

Inigua laughed. "The tide is coming in now. Soon it will be high. In a few hours we may see the running grunion, if indeed they show themselves."

"But, señor, I still don't know what a grunion is. What do they look like?"

"You are truly an ignorant boy. Everyone knows that grunion are little fish. They are about this long." He held his hands about six inches apart.

Pablo's face fell. "I cannot lazo such a thing," he said, looking at Inigua accusingly.

Inigua chuckled and said, "It has never been tried before. People usually catch them with their bare hands."

Inigua looked up at the sky, at the waning gibbous moon that shone down on the sea.

A puzzled look came over Pablo's face in the luminous light. "But, señor," he said, "how can people catch these grunion in the water with their bare hands? In fact, how can they even see them in the dark?"

"They do not catch them in the water, you funny boy. The grunion ride the waves up onto the beach. You will see. You will know them because these grunion have a bluish green back, and silver sides and belly. Some people call them Silversides. Grunion is a Spanish word. It means grunter. They are called that because the fish make little squeaking noises while they spawn."

"Spawn?"

Inigua rolled his eyes. "Is there no end to your questions? The grunion come up onto the sand to make babies. The females burrow down tail first into the wet sand. They actually twist around and drill themselves in. They go down till over half their body length is buried. If there are male fishes around, the females lay their eggs in the sand. Then a male fish comes along and curls around the female. He gets excited and lets his milt out around her."

"His milt?"

"Must I explain everything? You know that stuff that comes out of your i'ikpik when it is hard. That stuff."

"Oh," said Pablo, blushing. He was glad it was dark enough to hide his embarrassment.

"When the male and female are done, they wriggle back to the sea. In about ten days the eggs are ready to hatch. Then another nighttime high tide comes along and the eggs hatch. The baby fish swim out into the waves and out to sea."

"Ah, I understand now," said Pablo. "So what do we do when these grunion are running?"

"We hunt them. When we find them we catch them."

"Why do we want to catch them, señor?"

"To eat them, of course. What do you think? After all, they are free food delivered to our doorstep by Hutash, the earth-mother. It would be ill-mannered of us to refuse her offering."

191

"All right, señor. I am ready for her offering. I will catch many of these grunion, for I am very hungry."

"We shall see," said Inigua.

"How do we catch them, señor?"

"Why, you run after them and grab them in your hands. You put them in a basket or something until you have enough of them. Then you scale and clean them and fry them up. They are delicious."

"I will catch all the grunion, señor."

"I do not think so. You would not want to anyway, for then there would be none left for the next time. The Russians and Aleuts made that mistake with the sea otter. They took them all, and now there are none for the rest of us. At any rate, do not set your hopes too high. You might not catch any tonight. You had better eat some beef jerky right now just in case."

By nine o'clock the tide began to fall. People started gathering along the beach. They spread out, staking out patches of shoreline for their own. Children were told to hush up and stop running around, that they would scare the grunion away. Parents gathered them onto mats under the silver moon and talked to them in hushed tones, telling them stories of long ago. Young couples wandered off down the beach seeking privacy. Several enterprising fishermen unfurled a finely-knit seine net in the event the run was a heavy one.

Inigua and Pablo came down to the beach and found their own likely spot. Pablo carried his hopeful bucket, and Inigua his fresh bota of wine. They sat in the sand and waited. It wasn't long before they began to see little flashes of silver begin to appear behind each receding wave.

"Look, señor, they are running. The grunion are running!"

"Sí, joven. They are just beginning. There will be more and more as time goes on. Why not go down there and see if you can catch some?"

Pablo stood up eagerly and, carrying his bucket, sprinted down to the shoreline. Inigua watched him running this way and that along the wet sand, stooping as he tried to catch the slippery fish. Before long, Pablo joined a group of other boys his age as they roamed along the beach. Inigua could hear their excited hoots and laughter as they failed or succeeded in their hunt. He leaned back under the light of the moon and took a swig of wine. He felt the first hint of contentment since the day of the flood.

29

THE WHALE

The communal fish fry went on till well after midnight. The whole village slept in the following morning, including Inigua and Pablo. The two finally awoke when their tent was set aglow by the sun emerging from behind the Santa Monica Mountains.

Inigua led the still heavy-lidded Pablo down to the shoreline. Wading out into the frothy surf, they pulled up the stakes that pinned the hide underwater. Together they dragged the dark, sodden mass up to the beach. It took their combined strength to carry it to their campsite. They plopped it down in the shade of a stand of young cottonwoods by the stream.

Arching and rubbing his back, Inigua said, "There are any number of ways to finish a hide. Now that the hair has 'slipped,' we have several options. One is to stretch and dry the hide, and then cut the spiral. We could then shave the hair off the strip. It is easier that way. But I think we should shave the hair now while the hide is still wet."

"Why is that, señor?"

"Because I think we should smoke the hide. It is better to smoke it with the hair removed."

"Why should we smoke it?"

"There are several reasons. If you are working cattle around water, or if it rains when you are out in the open, your reata will undoubtedly get wet. When it dries it will be stiff. Smoking the rawhide does something to it. It protects it. When your reata gets wet, it dries out soft and pliable. Smoking also gives the leather a nice color and smell, and prolongs the life of your reata. Usually, a working reata will last about five or six years. If you smoke it beforehand it may last ten years, if you take care of it. This is your first reata. It is special. You should try to preserve it as long as possible."

"Sí, señor. I agree. Let's smoke it"

"Bueno. The first thing we must do is shave it. Those two days and nights in the sea will have made the hair slip. That is what they say when it has loosened. Go get the skinning knife and strop, Pablo, and I will show you how." While the boy was rummaging through their packs, Inigua scouted along the stream until he found a large driftwood log with smooth sides. He had Pablo help him roll it up into the shade next to the hide. While Inigua stropped the knife, he directed the boy to drape the wet hide over the log, hair-side up. When the blade was razor sharp, Inigua straddled the soggy skin and showed Pablo how to shave off the hair, taking special care not to cut the hide. When he finished one section, he stood up and pulled a fresh portion of hide over the log. Then he stropped the knife and handed it to the boy.

While Pablo worked on the hide, Inigua dismantled the tent and moved it aside. He then picked up the butcher knife and disappeared into the brush. In his absence, Pablo worked carefully at his task. It reminded him a little of shaving the padre, only with a ten-day old beard. Nearly an hour passed before Inigua reappeared carrying an armload of freshly cut green sage. The sage was bundled and tied with a short length of tok. Pablo watched Inigua take it down to the bend in the stream and drop it into the water. The old man then weighed it down with a stone to keep it underwater.

"Are you hungry, boy?" he called when he returned.

"Sí, señor. But I wasn't going to say anything. I can wait until you are hungry."

"I could eat now. But let us wait until we stake the hide. Are you finished with the shaving?"

"Sí, señor, just now."

Inigua inspected the hide carefully. "Good job, boy," he said. "It is as smooth as a plucked chicken. Now we will stake it out over there where the tent was before. The ground is dry there."

They laid the hide out flesh-side up in the sun. Pulling on opposite sides as before, they pounded the stakes into the holes they had cut around the edges. A light steam began to rise from the stretched skin.

"You need to use the knife to clean off those last bits of clinging flesh and fat," said Inigua. "You must do it before it gets too dry. But we have a little time. We should eat now. What would you like?"

"I am getting a taste for seafood, señor. I have been thinking about those grunion last night. They were so good. I especially liked the ones made by that one family who fried them in cornmeal batter. I think they put mustard seed in it. Do we have any grunion?"

"No. Every last fish was eaten."

"Will there be more tonight?

"It is possible. Grunion usually run for two or three nights in a row. Then they stop. They may run again in a couple of weeks with the high tides of the new moon."

They settled for beef jerky and dried fruit. When they were done eating Pablo knelt down over the hide and began scraping it clean with the skinning knife. Meanwhile, Inigua went down along the stream and gathered some driftwood poles and sticks. He brought them back and began to trim them using the hatchet and butcher knife.

"What are you making there, señor?"

"A frame for smoking the hide. You will see. When you are done there, I need someone to dig some holes."

"Sí, señor."

By early afternoon the hide was clean and drying nicely in the bright sunshine. Pablo had dug three holes in a row in the soft ground near the bank of the stream. Inigua had marked the spots where he should dig and supplied him with a digging-stick fashioned out of driftwood. Now they planted long poles in two of the holes about six feet apart, and then tamped earth around the bases. Together they lashed a third pole spanning the two uprights about eight feet off the ground. The third hole Pablo dug was aligned midway between the two uprights.

Standing back and appraising their handiwork, Inigua said, "Bueno. Now let us turn the hide over and dry the other side. Then I want my siesta. I am not used to all this activity. I must be getting old."

"I must be getting old too, señor, for I am also very tired."

They reassembled the tent and lay down in its shade to rest. But Pablo found that he was so energized by their progress that he could not sleep. He turned his head and looked at Inigua. The old Indian was lying on his back with his eyes closed.

"Are you sleeping, señor?"

"Not yet."

"Can you tell me a story?"

"A story? What kind of story? We Chumash tell three different kinds. One is told to instruct young ones on our beliefs and the nature of the world. A second is told strictly for entertainment, to pass the time. The third kind consists of stories about true things that happened in real life."

"Tell me the third kind. Tell me about your life."

"I do not think that is a good idea."

"Why not, señor?

"Because I am an angry man. You do not want to hear angry stories, do you?"

"I don't think so. But why must you tell angry stories? Why not tell me a happy one?"

"That would be difficult. Though it is true I had many happy times. But when I think about the good times and the way they turned out it always makes me angry. I try to put the anger behind me, but people like Tico and the Padre always bring it back."

There was a long pause, and Pablo thought perhaps Inigua had fallen asleep. But then the old man said, "I will try to think of a happy story." Another pause followed, and then, "Ah, I know. Since you have developed such a fancy for seafood, how would it be if I told you a fish story?

"Is it a happy story?"

"I guess it depends on how you look at it. At least it is not an angry story. Do you want to hear it?"

"Sí, señor."

Inigua laced his fingers behind his head and fixed his gaze on the canvas roof. "All right," he said, "this story took place in the fall of my fourteenth year. The Spanish had already come and gone twice, and their soldiers and couriers had not yet begun to bother us. At that time my older brother Toma and I went on a journey together."

"You had a brother?"

"That is what I said. You aren't going to keep interrupting me, are you?"

"No, señor. 'Sorry."

"Our father, Hew, which means 'Pelican,' had just finished building a new tomol. He gave us permission to take his old canoe and travel to Shuku village."

"Shuku? Where's that?"

"Hold your tongue, boy. All will be explained. We went to *Shuku* to visit our uncle and his family. My uncle was a well-known ksen, and a respected member of the Siliyik society." Inigua ignored the boy's questioning look.

"My father wanted me to get to know my uncle better because I showed some promise as a ksen myself. I was a strong runner with good lungs and a knack for learning languages. My father had decided that Toma would follow in his own footsteps as a canoe-maker. He thought I would be more useful to the family as a messenger and translator.

"My older brother, Toma, was very good with his hands. He helped my father build plank canoes and was a fine fisherman and seaman as well. That must be why my father had him come along with me, to see that I got to Shuku and back without any trouble. At that time our home village of Shisholop was having a feud with a village to the west of us along the coast. It was called *Chwayuk*. A girl from our village had run away with a boy from that place. Or maybe she had been taken. Since Chwayuk lay between us and Shuku, my father thought it safer to travel by sea.

"Shuku was located on a point of land the Spaniards named *El Rincon*, the corner. There is a small cove at Shuku and next to it a stream by the village. The people of Shuku were fisherman and traders like us in Shisholop. But we were more prosperous because we had the Ventura River valley from which to gather food and game. We also did a lot of trading with the Indians of the interior. But there are only dry hills behind Shuku, and although they have chia and other seeds, they had only a few oak trees.

"Our visit to our uncle in Shuku was very enlightening. My uncle, whose name means 'High-Step,' told me all about what it was like being a ksen. These ksen served a vital function in our lives back then. They kept everyone informed about what was going on elsewhere. They carried messages regarding meetings, trading fairs, wars, and important religious observances. They also carried gossip. In this way everyone knew what was going on. Sometimes ksen even acted as spies for the 'antaps. These ksens were great runners and could speak the many dialects of our language. They also knew how to communicate in sign language.

"High-Step was very fond of his profession. He loved to visit the many different villages along the coast and the ones inland as well. He told

196

wonderful stories of the adventures he had had in his travels and of the interesting people he had met.

"I think one of the reasons my uncle liked being a messenger was that it enabled him to get away from my aunty, who was something of a nag. High-Step looked forward to being sent away on business by the wots and the 'antaps. He was often gone for days at a time. I got the impression that although he loved the mother of his children, he also loved other women as well. He knew the names of quite a few in the different villages.

"I learned that not only was he a very handsome and knowledgeable man, but that he was a great dancer as well. He was the best dancer in Shuku village, and for that matter, in all this part of Chumash territory. He had danced so often to the accompaniment of musicians and singers from Shuku that they knew what each other were going to do ahead of time, and had worked out some marvelous rhythms and dance routines. I was deeply impressed and decided at that time to become a ksen, just like my uncle.

"I would have liked to stay longer in Shuku, but we had to leave after six days. Our father wanted Toma home on a certain day so that he could go with him on a trading voyage out to the islands. So before we left home father had given Toma a short, thick cord onto which he had tied seven knots. Toma was instructed to untie one knot every morning when he woke up. The day the last knot was untied was the day we were to return to Shisholop.

"On the day of 'one-knot,' the day before we were to return home, the weather turned very hot, and a strong east wind began to blow. This made the sea very rough. Since these east winds often blow for days at a time, we decided to travel that night when the wind died down.

"We waited till the night was half gone before we took our leave. By the time we had said our goodbyes, a full moon had risen above the coastal hills. Not a breath of wind ruffled the water as we followed the shining path of the moon towards Shisholop. I knelt in front, my brother to the rear where he could steer. Our long, double-bladed paddles made little swallowing sounds as they dug into the still sea.

"We synchronized our swallows and sang a paddling song to the rhythm we made. In the background we could hear sleepy waves peeling along the shore. We stayed near the beach, following the curve of the coast.

"We made good time and enjoyed the coolness of the evening under the bright light of the moon. Every once in awhile we would hear the flutter of sardines rippling and skittering along the surface, and sometimes we heard the tail-slap of the larger fish that hunted them. We were still some distance from Shisholop when we came upon a very powerful fishy odor. Then, up ahead in the moonlight, we caught sight of a massive, shadowy form lying in the shallows near the shore. My brother let out a whoop of delight, for we realized that it was a stranded whale, a gray whale.

"That big fellow had beached himself on a barren stretch of coast just west of Pitas Point. It was a joyful discovery for us, for our people were always on the lookout for these rare beachings. Much free food could be had, with little labor. As we drew closer to the whale we could make out the agitated zigzagging of shark fins in the shallows. The tide was out just then and the water was not deep enough for them to get at the carcass. They milled back and forth, swishing their tails impatiently as they waited for the tide to change.

"We came in very close because my brother wanted to inspect the whale to see if it was rotten. When we felt the bottom of the canoe scraping the sand, we prepared to go ashore. I had one foot in the water, with the other still in the canoe, when we heard a vicious ripping sound. I froze. There was something alive on the land-side of the whale.

"I quickly stepped back into the canoe. Silently, my brother and I stuck our paddles into the sand and pushed off. We backed away into deeper water and turned the canoe seaward into the gentle waves that lapped along the shore. Toma shouted a greeting to whatever was there.

"We heard a shuffling splash behind the whale, and then the sound of a great throat-full of food being regurgitated. In the next instant we saw two huge grizzly bears come galloping out from behind the whale. When they caught sight of us out there in the surf they stood up on their hind legs and roared in a most threatening way. We could see their fangs flashing white in the moonlight, and their long, dripping claws pawing the air. The fur of their faces and arms glistened with oil, and here and there on their bodies hung gobs of blubber and whale gore. Their eyes looked fierce in the cold fire of the moon. We had intruded on their feast, and they did not like it.

"My brother shouted an apology to them. But they did not accept it. The biggest one, undoubtedly a male, roared at us again and came charging into the water as if to attack us. We quickly paddled into deeper water, looking back fearfully over our shoulders as we went. But the grizzly, startled by the sudden flash and swirl of shark fins, retreated to the shore.

"My brother shouted again, telling the bears and the sharks to feed well tonight, because tomorrow our people would come and take their turn at feasting.

"We arrived back at our own village in the early hours of the morning. We excitedly told our father of our discovery. By mid-morning, most of our village had packed up their blades and bowls and cooking pots and departed for the whale.

"And that is the end of my story. I would sleep now. Kiwa'nan."
Within moments Pablo heard Inigua softly snoring.

30

SMOKING

By the time they awoke from their siesta it was mid-afternoon. Inigua directed Pablo to build and light a fire in the hole beneath the smoking frame. While the boy went about it, Inigua tested the hide between his fingers. Satisfied that it was dry, he walked around the outside pulling up the stakes. He turned the hide over and then folded it onto itself along the spine. The hide thus formed a rough half-circle, with the neck portion on top and the tail at the bottom. He retrieved the sticking knife and began making small perforations around the curved outside edges of the skin, piercing both the top and bottom layers. He spaced the holes several inches apart. When Pablo had the fire started, he rejoined Inigua.

"What are you doing, señor?"

"Making holes. We are going to sew the edges of the hide together where the stomach and legs used to be. This will form a kind of bag, which will be open at the top and bottom. Bring the tok over here, Pablo, and those bone fids I freed from the mission leather shop."

Pablo went over to the pack that held their tools and implements. Fids, he thought disconcertedly. What in God's name is a fid? He nervously rummaged through the gear. Ah, this must be them. He picked up two six-inch long pieces of white bone. They looked like they might have been fashioned from the leg of a sheep. One end had a knob like a knee joint. From the knob, the bone tapered down to a pointed tip at the opposite end, curving slightly as it did so. He carried what he hoped were fids, along with the coil of braided milkweed fiber, to his mentor.

Together they sewed the sides together, pushing the cord through the holes with the pointed end of the fids. Inigua cut additional holes in the neck section and threaded several foot-long strands of tok through them. "These are for hanging the hide from that crossbar up there," he said. "The open bottom will be secured to the ground around the fire. But first we have to wait till the fire burns down so only coals remain. We must be careful not to burn the hide."

Inigua and Pablo sat down in front of the tent to wait.

"How long will it take to smoke the hide, señor?"

"Oh, not too long. Maybe an hour or so."

"I have been thinking about the story you told me earlier, señor."

"That is gratifying."

"I was wondering if you ever became a ksen like your uncle High-Step."

"Why, yes, I did. When I was about sixteen. Good ksens only last ten years or fifteen years. It is too strenuous for an older man. When one of the ksens of our village got to the age where he had to give it up, there was an opening in the guild. That is when I had my first opportunity.

"Being a good ksen required one to be very fit. That is because we ran everywhere we went. It was not always necessary for us to run, but it was a matter of pride with our particular guild. You had to have strong legs, tough feet, and good wind to be a ksen. Here is an example: I often ran from Shisholop to the Aw'hai valley with messages. It is about fifteen miles. I usually left Shisholop in the morning when it was cool. I would deliver my message, and then return on the same day carrying the reply."

"Thirty miles, señor? In one day?"

"Sí. And the first half was mostly uphill. Although running downhill is harder than you might expect. But for a ksen, running was the easy part, once you got used to it. The hard part was remembering the message. When the wots or 'antaps gave us a message to deliver, it was expected that we memorize it word for word. When I first started they used to test me before I was allowed to leave. When I arrived at the other end I had to recite it verbatim. If the message involved something that was to happen in the future, I would deliver a knotted cord so they could count the days by untying the knots."

"Did you carry such messages often, señor?"

"Oh, it all depended on the time of year. We ksens were more active in the summer and fall. That is the time when trading fairs were arranged. But we could be called upon at any time of year. If someone found a beached whale, like we did in my story, a ksen would be sent to inform our friends and neighbors. Or if someone died and had relatives in another village, ksens carried the sad news to them. The Siliyik cult, our high council of priests, would also send ksens to announce the dates of sacred ceremonies or astronomical observances.

"Another challenging part of being a ksen was that you had to be able to communicate with all kinds of people. The Chumash lived over a vast area: from well beyond *Lompoc* in the west to Malibu in the east, from the Channel Islands in the south to *Cuyama* in the north. Our people spoke seven different dialects and many sub-dialects, some of them incomprehensible to the others. We ksen had to learn those dialects so we could translate the messages. Sometimes we had to resort to sign language.

"And sometimes we were required to go beyond Chumash territory. We visited the lands of the Tatavians and Yokuts to the north, the Luiseños and Gabrielaños to the east and south, and the Coastanoans to the northwest. On rare occasions we ranged even farther."

Pablo nodded in appreciation. He sat and thought for awhile, and then asked, "Did you like being a ksen, señor?"

200

"I liked it very much, even though it was demanding, and risky. You always had to be alert for danger. You never knew when you would come upon a rattlesnake or a bear in your path. One time a mountain lion stalked me for several miles up in Matilija Canyon. Another time a hunter mistook me for an animal and shot at me with an arrow. I was lucky his aim was off.

"But I loved how running made me feel. My body was as lean and hard as a mountain deer. Sometimes when I was running I felt like a soaring bird, my legs were my wings and they propelled me effortlessly through the air. I never felt so alive, so free.

"But one thing I liked in particular was that I was frequently sent to the villages in the Aw'hai valley. It gave me a chance to visit Islay up there in Matilija. I courted her for several years that way. Because ksens were rewarded by both the senders and receivers of messages, I was able to put together her 'bride price' by the time I was eighteen. Then she became my wife." Inigua stopped here and looked away. "Go check the fire," he said.

Pablo got up and went to the pit. "I think it is ready, señor. You'd better come see."

Inigua looked down into the pit and saw that the fire had been reduced to a layer of coals dusted in ash. "Bueno," he said. "Now we bring the hide."

Standing on the overturned bucket, Inigua tied the strands of tok attached to the neck portion to the crossbar. Pablo held the tail section away from the fire pit. Inigua then went down to the stream and retrieved the submerged bundle of sage. He divided the soggy mass in half, shook one of them free of water, and dropped it onto the coals. A hissing sound ensued, and then a cloud of steam rose from the pit. This was followed by a fragrant plume of smoke.

Pablo sniffed and said, "Ah, señor, I like that. It is a very nice smell."

"Yes, and sage is said by some to contain sacred properties. But you should know that some people prefer to use wood when they smoke hides. They like to use hickory, but just about any wood will do as long as it is rotten, wet, or green."

Inigua waited to be sure the bundle of sage did not catch fire, and then he and Pablo spread the open tail section of the hide in a circle around the pit. The hide now formed a cigar-shaped chimney. They placed stones around the edges at the bottom to seal it. A lazy column of smoke began to rise from the top.

Inigua turned to his apprentice and said, "Go fill the bucket with water, will you, boy? Bring it back quickly. We must be vigilant. If the sage catches fire we must douse it immediately, lest it scorch the hide."

They hovered around the three-foot wide leathern column as it smoked. From time to time Inigua placed his hand on the outside to gauge the heat. Every five minutes or so they lifted up the tail section and peeked inside. After a half hour had passed, Inigua lifted up the underside of the hide and inspected it.

"Come look, boy. See how the hide has darkened? It is a nice dark brown color, as it should be. This was the hair side of the hide. It will be on the outside of your reata. For esthetic and practical reasons it should be darker than the flesh side. Now we can take it down."

Once the hide was on the ground and had cooled somewhat, Inigua stuck his arm up inside from the tail end. He gathered in the leather until he could reach the neck portion. With Pablo's help, he managed to turn the hide inside out like an oversized glove. Then they reattached the neck portion to the crossbar. The old man added more wet sage to the pit, and the two secured the bottom as before.

"This side should not be as dark. That is why you leave it till last. The coals are cooler now. The leather on this side will be inside your reata."

While they were waiting for the second side to smoke, Pablo said, "So, señor, I want to know more about the time you were a ksen. How long did you do that?"

"I continued to run until the Spanish came and established their ninth mission in Alta California: Mission San Buenaventura. They founded it on Easter Sunday, 1782. On that day everything began to change for us. My last official act as a ksen was to carry word of it to the people of the interior."

"But why did you stop being a ksen, señor?"

"That is a long story; a story best kept for another time. But I probably would have stopped soon anyway. I was twenty-six by then, and had been running for ten years. I was beginning to feel it in my bones."

When the inside of the hide had taken on a nice sienna tone, they brought it down. With the sticking knife they cut through the tok line that sewed it together, and removed the twine at the neck. Then Inigua rolled the hide tightly up onto itself, and secured it with tok.

"I am pleased," he said as he stood. "Now the hide is cured and smoked. We will let it set overnight. Tomorrow we will carry it with us to the Ventura River. Most of the hard work is done now, boy. Soon we will begin making your reata."

"I am very happy, señor. Thank you for teaching me. I can hardly wait to begin."

Inigua looked around the immediate area and said, "We should clean up our camp. It will be dark in a few hours. Help me take down the smoking rack, and then we must stow everything away. I like to keep a tidy campsite. And we must think about what we will eat tonight."

They took down the rack and returned the poles to the streambed. Inigua walked over to the log they had used for the shaving, and considered whether they should leave it or not.

Pablo came up next to him and said, "What about all that hair down there on the ground, señor, and all those little bits of flesh from the hide?"

"We could use them, if you want to try something new."

"What new thing, señor?"

"Well, actually it is a very old thing. Some of the Indian vaqueros used to make a kind of soup from the hair and scrapped flesh."

"A kind of soup? Hair soup? Uh, no thank you, señor."

"I thought not. But still, we have to decide what to eat tonight. We should have a nice meal to celebrate."

Just then they heard a commotion coming from the beach. Inigua and Pablo walked down to the bluff overlooking the shore. An orange sun hung over Santa Cruz Island, its rays glazing the sides of white caps out in the Channel. Inigua and Pablo saw Malak's wife, Luhui, and several members of the extended family standing by a fire circle on the beach. They were talking excitedly and gesturing out to sea. Following the direction of their gaze, they spied Malak and his two sons, Liyam and Shup, riding in a tomol just beyond the breakers. Malak and Liyam were manning the paddles, while Shup stood hunched over the gunwale amid-ship. In his grasp was a thick fishing line that bucked and jerked in his meaty hands. Shup set his feet and began drawing it in, his powerful arms and shoulders alternately extending and flexing. His muscles bulged as he pulled the line aboard.

Shup gathered line until an ugly dark head emerged from the water. Below the head, a wide, flat body thrashed and slapped against the side of the tomol. The back of the monster was a glistening murk, the belly a ghostly white. Liyam shipped his paddle and came to his brother's aid. He bent over and bludgeoned the ugly dark head with a club until the body hung still. Shup let out a victorious yelp. "Heat the pan," he yelled towards shore. "We caught a good one."

His mother and relatives cheered. They hoisted a large, rectangular slab of stone and placed it directly over the flames of the bonfire. It was propped up on either end and made level by rocks that circled the pit.

"What is that dark stone?" asked Pablo. "I saw them using it last night."

Inigua replied, "That is a frying pan made of *steatite*. They probably got it in trade from Catalina Island. Steatite is found in abundance there. It is a very useful stone. It is dense and heavy, yet soft and easy to carve. You can make many useful things from it: cooking bowls, frying pans, pipes, and arrow shaft straighteners. You can even make little charm stones, effigies, or beads. The best thing about it is that it does not crack or break when exposed to high heat."

Malak and Liyam guided the tomol so that it caught a small wave which they rode victoriously in to the beach. The paddlers beamed widely as it came to rest on the tomol's flat bottom.

As the fishermen dragged their catch ashore, Pablo turned to Inigua, and said, "That is a funny-looking fish, señor. I have never seen one like that before."

"That is a halibut, boy. It lives on the sea floor. That is why it is flat. It likes to feed in shallow water near the shore. Just look at the size of it. It must weigh forty or fifty pounds. I think the question of what we are to eat tonight has been answered. Come, let us go congratulate the fishermen."

31

TO THE RIVER

They broke camp early the next morning and headed west towards the Santa Clara River. They rode upriver and then crossed over onto El Camino Real. The sixty-year old road was a well-trodden dirt track that followed the easiest and most logical route up and down the coast. It was just wide enough for two carretas to pass abreast, or for vaqueros to drive a small herd. Judging from the animal droppings, normal travel had resumed along El Camino Real after the floods had brought it to a standstill a fortnight before. A tangle of mustard, just now coming into bloom, formed a dense hedgerow on either side.

Tabaco and Rojo seemed to know they were headed for home. Given their heads, the horses undertook a lively pace. Trailing behind, the heavily-laden Chico struggled to keep up.

"A horse is a wonderful beast, is it not?" said Inigua. "They are simple in thought, and yet pure of heart, and possessed of a wonderful instinct. If you understand him and treat him well he will come to love you. Once a horse does that, he will be as true and faithful a friend as you will ever know. A good horse will sense what you want of him and try his best to please you. I did not get to know horses until after Mission San Buenaventura was built. Only the soldiers rode horses before de Anza came to California."

"De Anza?" said Pablo. "I have heard that name."

"Yes. Don Juan Bautista de Anza. He was a Spanish soldier from Sonora, in Mexico. He was a famous Indian fighter over there, like his father and grandfather before him. They fought with the Apaches. He came through here twice, about midway between the arrival of de Portola and the founding of Mission San Buenaventura. I remember seeing him then."

"What was he like?"

"Oh, he was quite a man. He was handsome in his uniform, and he had dark, piercing dark eyes like those of an eagle. One glance from them was enough to halt you in mid-step. He was a leader of men, that de Anza. He was the one who blazed the trail through the desert from Sonora to Alta California. The first time I saw him was in the spring of 1774. He had a couple of padres with him and twenty or so soldiers when he arrived in San Gabriel. He had some cattle with him and thirty-five pack mules of supplies. He brought a mañada of 140 horses too. He went up north to Monterey and then returned to Mexico.

"De Anza came back the following year. This time he had thirty soldiers, three padres, and many more people. There were about 240 of them in all. Some of them were women. It was the first time I had seen females of that foreign race. They were a hard-looking bunch. I suppose because the journey was difficult they all had to be pretty tough. They came with their husbands, who were craftsmen and herders and farmers. They settled around various missions and taught the Indians how to work. Over the years other groups followed de Anza's trail from Sonora. They started families here. Their children and grandchildren are what we now call gente de razón.

"I remember de Anza brought some beautiful horses that second time. A few of them were Palominos. Though they are handsome beasts, they did not make very good cow ponies. But the others were good. We were surprised at the number, which, along with mules, numbered 700. The travelers brought a lot of cattle too, about 350 head, and they left them at different missions along El Camino Real. That is when the herds really began to grow."

"Have you traveled the King's Road, señor?"

"Not all the way. I have been as far as Mission San Diego in the south, and to Paso Robles in the north. But the road goes very much farther, to a place called Sonoma. It links all twenty-one missions. The Spanish take credit for the road, but in fact it only follows Indian trails that have been there for untold centuries. All the Spaniards did was widen it."

"When did you become a vaquero, señor?"

"Oh, not for some years after the Mission San Buenaventura started up in 1782. That was fifty years ago. I spent the first few years working on the zanja and dam, and later the mission buildings. I was such a fool back then. I let my curiosity get the better of me. I wanted to learn the secret to what I thought was Spanish magic. After awhile I found out it was not magic at all, but only the logical application of knowledge.

"When the cattle started multiplying, the padres realized that the mission needed help in herding them. They wanted to teach some of us how to ride. But the military was against it, of course. They were afraid we might cause trouble. They thought if we had mobility we might rise up against them or run away. But in the end the padres had their way. The only way to control the cattle was by sharing the knowledge of horsemanship with us. I was one of the first vaqueros."

"And yet you did not rise up, señor. Why not?"

Inigua glared crossly at the impish boy. The old man's jaw muscles tightened into hard cords. With an effort of will he pushed down his anger and shame. Seeing him struggle so, Pablo swallowed and looked away.

The old man took a deep breath and exhaled slowly. "We used to talk about rising up. We had heard about the attack in San Diego, and the killing of Padre Jaime. We also heard about the trouble at San Juan Capistrano a few years later. But both of those incidents happened years

206

before the Spaniards started Mission San Buenaventura. We did not know what the fighting was all about. But now I wish we had done something in the very beginning when we had the chance."

"I still don't understand why you hate the Spanish and Mexicans so much?"

"That is because you do not listen to me. But that does not surprise me. You were raised as one of them."

"But I am not one of them, señor. I am half Chumash."

"One could not tell," said Inigua petulantly. "How would you like it, for example, if the *Americanos* came to Alta California and claimed it for themselves? What if they took over and changed everything? What if they did not give a damn for what was here before and just made it the way they liked it?"

"I cannot imagine that, señor. And besides, the Americanos could never do such a thing. There are too few of them."

"There were only a few Spaniards here in the beginning. None of us knew how many of them were to follow. And it is the same with the Yankees. There is only a handful here now, but more and more come each year. I hear they are a vast nation of white people, and that they have a lust for land. How would you like it if they came and took over one of these days?"

Shaking his head, Pablo said, "There is no way that could happen, señor. The church and the Mexican soldiers would never allow it."

"Ha. We shall see, oh smart one. You should understand that it only takes one strong leader to change everything. The Spanish had de Portola and Junipero Serra. And then de Anza came along. He showed the way for the others to follow. The Mexicans, in their revolt against Spain, had Hidalgo, and the others who came after when he was executed. I wonder who the Americanos will send."

"Do you know any of these Americanos, señor?"

"I know only a few. I know that man Joseph Chapman who was once a Bouchard pirate. After he was captured by the Spaniards, he went to work for Padre Uria up there at Mission Santa Inez. He is a very talented man. He can make things with his hands like no other person I know. He married one of the Ortega girls and now lives in Santa Barbara.

"I also met that man Pattie who came through here inoculating everyone for measles. And I know the gringo physician that Padre Uria goes to see in Santa Barbara – Doctor Anderson. I have also met many sailors who come here on ships from a place called New England. All the Americanos I have met have been strong and brave, although extreme in their beliefs. I am sure there must be weak and cowardly ones, but I have not met any. I think if they decide to take California, no one will be able to stop them."

Pablo said, "If we had another Junipero Serra we could stop them."

"Maybe. I have to admit that he was a remarkable leader."

"Did you know him, señor?"

"I do not think anyone really knew him other than his childhood friend, Padre Palou. But Palou worshipped the man, and his opinions cannot be trusted. Although Serra was a remarkable leader, he was also a very strange man in my opinion. Half the time he seemed to be living in another world, a world of his own making."

"I don't know what you mean, señor."

"One of the things about Serra that puzzled me was that he was always so deathly serious. There was no humor in the man at all. I never saw him laugh once, or even smile. He cared nothing for good food or conversation or any of the other human pleasures. He only sipped wine during mass because it was part of the ceremony. Why, he could not even gaze directly at a woman. He always looked away.

"And he seemed to consider it a duty to inflict pain upon himself. One time I heard him give a sermon. This was in the first days of the mission. The sermon was about the necessity of doing penance for your sins. Near the end of his talk he dropped his habit below his shoulders and began beating himself across the back with a chain. He did this in front of everyone. And I have been told he often whipped himself in private until he bled."

"Dios mio, señor."

"There is more. Serra had this heavy shirt he used to wear sometimes. It had sharp barbed wires woven into it. He would wear it all day sometimes. Other times he would burn his own chest with a candle, or beat it with a stone.

"And I cannot fail to mention that terrible sore he had on his leg. It was a sore that never quite healed. I was told he got it from a scorpion's sting many years before, when he was living in Mexico. He walked all over California with that sore oozing down his leg. He seemed not to care whether it healed or not. But he was a great walker, that Serra, which is surprising because he had a bad case of asthma.

"I guess he liked suffering. Strange, is it not? It was he who condoned, nay, even encouraged the beatings we Indians got if we disobeyed the rules. Serra thought of us as his children, and he thought a father should punish his sons with blows.

"I think it is a shame that Fernando Tico and Junipero Serra lived at different times. They might have gotten along well together. One likes to dish it out and the other liked to take it."

"That is a terrible thing to say, señor."

"Why? It is true. Serra and Tico were made for one another."

"Oh, that reminds me, señor – last night I heard you talking to Malak about Don Tico. It was after that delicious halibut we ate. I did not hear all that you said because Shup was talking to me at the time, but I heard you repeat Tico's name several times. What were you saying?"

"I was telling Malak that I think Señor Tico might be coming after me one of these days. Malak offered to help me. It was a brave offer."

"Come after you? Why would Don Tico come after you?"

"He may think I did something wrong."

Pablo scratched his head. "But what did you do, señor?"

"Oh, I gave something to the prisoners before they were whipped the other day, something to ease their pain."

"No, señor, you didn't!"

"One does what one feels is right."

"But if Don Tico comes after you, he will harm you, señor. What will you do?"

Inigua tilted his head. "I think it might be a good idea to disappear for awhile."

"But where will we go? There is no place that he cannot find us. He will ride us down wherever we go."

"What do you mean, we? I was thinking about maybe going out to the islands. As far as I know, his horse cannot walk on water."

"The islands?" Pablo looked across the coastal plain, and beyond to the glowering Santa Barbara Channel. It was a hazy day and the three islets of Anacapa were only vague silhouettes before the horizon. To their right, the great purple mass of Santa Cruz stretched for miles across the choppy water.

"Do you know those islands, señor?"

"Of course. When I was young I visited them many times on fishing and trading expeditions. Later, as a ksen I delivered messages to all the northern Channel Islands. Several thousand people used to live out there."

"What are they like, señor, the islands? I have often yearned to go there."

"They are a lot like the mainland, only they have less of everything out there. And they have none of some things. There are no deer, no bear or mountain lions. No coyotes. And water is scarce. There are fewer trees and not as many useful plants. The land is silent, but for the perpetual wind. It is a place of deep thought, and it is the homeland of all Chumash. Perhaps you will visit it one day. But I do not think that will be soon."

"Why?"

"Because if I have to go, it would be better for you if you stayed behind."

"No, señor. I want to stay with you."

"If Tico finds out you have run away with me you may never have a chance to become a vaquero. I have no doubt he is a man who holds a grudge."

Pablo could think of nothing to say in reply. They rode along in silence as Pablo digested what he had been told. The boy's gaze shifted back and forth between Rojo's bobbing head and the enigmatic islands lying mute some twenty miles out to sea.

Finally, the boy spoke up. "Don Tico does not own the world, señor. He only runs one rancho, and punishes wrong-doers at the mission. There are many other ranchos. He can't stop me from being a vaquero."

"That is true," said Inigua. "But he could make it difficult for you."

"I don't care. I haven't done anything wrong. I can go somewhere else. To Rancho Piru, or that one up in the Conejo Valley, or to Santa Barbara or Santa Inez."

"You surprise me, boy. You are becoming a stubborn young man."

Pablo smiled and shrugged.

By mid-morning Inigua and Pablo were nearing the mission. They could see neophytes in the distance fields plowing with teams of oxen. Inigua veered off the King's Road and headed for the beach. The two riders had to be firm with the horses, which wanted to head straight to the stables. Following the sandy shore below the clay bluff, they reached the mouth of the Ventura River. Inigua reined in. He sat astride Tabaco and surveyed the shore and the surging springtime sea. He sat for several minutes, erect and alert, gazing out over the water as if in deep thought. He seemed to be searching for something out there, and was oblivious to all else.

A nicker from Tabaco brought him back. He turned the horse upriver and crossed the drifting sandbank that had reformed at the river mouth. The sandbank dammed the river and channeled the flow into a narrow, swift-flowing ravine. Pablo followed his mentor, leading Chico. Behind the sandy berm at the mouth, a kidney-shaped lake had formed. It was perhaps a hundred feet across and twice as long.

Inigua reined in near its upper end. "This looks like a good spot," he said. "It is level here, and those trees along the bank will screen us from the mission. We will make camp here."

After they had set up their temporary home and lunched on jerked abalone, Inigua said matter-of-factly, "Shall we begin your reata now, Pablo?"

The boy's head snapped to attention. "Oh, yes, señor. Let's start right now. What do we do first?"

"Let's have a look at the hide." When it was unrolled and spread out on the hard-packed shore, Inigua picked up the edge and felt it with his fingers. He then bent the hide, testing its pliability.

"It is a little stiff," he said. "That indicates it is too dry. When you are working with rawhide you must always pay attention to how moist and pliable it is. To cut easily, leather must be neither too wet nor too dry. You will learn with experience how to control the moisture."

"So what do we do, señor?"

"I say we should do this…" Inigua picked up the hide, and, with a great heave, hurled it into the river.

210

32

SPIRAL

"Señor!" cried Pablo. "What are you doing?" Without waiting for an answer, the boy jumped into the river and waded after the hide.

Inigua chuckled and called after him, "That is called moisture control, boy! Yes, that's good, bring it back in now."

Pablo dragged the hide ashore, grumbling and shaking his head. Inigua helped him hold it up until the excess water had drained off. They then draped it over Chico's wooden pack rack to dry out a little more. After about a half-hour Inigua tested its pliability again.

"That feels about right," he said. He had Pablo feel it too, and then they spread the hide out on the ground nearby.

"Go ahead and sit down on it, Pablo. That's right, cross-legged, only sit closer to the edge. Bueno. I hope you are comfortable, for that hide will be your home for awhile. Notice that you are sitting on the smooth side, the shaved hair side. Notice too that it rests on hard ground that is flat, dry, and level. That is the way it should be.

"Now we will begin making the reata. The first thing you need to do is trim the edge of the hide so as to leave yourself sitting on a large oval. Once this is done, you will begin cutting a long, continuous strand of rawhide out of the hide. You will start at the outer edge and cut around in a circle, or rather, a spiral. The spiral will grow smaller and smaller as it travels towards the middle. Cutting in this manner will leave you with a long strip of rawhide. Comprende?"

The boy smiled broadly. "Sí, señor."

"This is the sticking knife, boy. I have already honed and stropped it. You will begin by cutting off those parts that stick out from the edge: the tail, leg, and neck sections. I will save the scraps for later use. As you go around the edge, trim it wherever needed to form a nice smooth line around the outside of the oval."

"I will do it, señor."

"Before you begin I must tell you that you should not cut straight up and down. You need to bevel the cut. Doing so keeps the hair side from curling up on the finished braid. I will start the cut to show you. Then you do the rest."

Inigua stepped over to the hide and sat down. He held the knife at an angle, the handle of the blade tilted towards the center. He cut along the outside edge for about a foot. "This is the way," he said. "Do you see?"

211

"I understand, señor."

The boy took the knife earnestly and began to cut. He removed the tail section first. It was easy with the razor-sharp knife. Pablo then scooted on his haunches a little way to his right. Trimming along in an even line as he had been instructed, he then cut off one of the hind leg sections. He continued in this manner around the hide until he came to the last leathery projection: the other hind leg.

"Stop there a moment," said Inigua, "I want to show you something." He took the knife and removed the last section himself. He did so in a manner that left an L-shaped notch on the outer edge of the hide. "This is where the spiral will begin," he said.

"There are several things you need to know before you begin cutting the spiral: First, make the strand about as wide as my thumb." Pablo watched him place his thumb on the notch and press down. The space covered was about an inch wide. "Second, take your time and work carefully. If you accidentally slice into the strand, or cut it too narrow, it will create a weak spot in the finished reata. Third, the hide is thinner where the stomach sections are, so you need to cut the strand a little wider there. I will show you when you get there. Later, when we soak and stretch the strand it will all even out. The last thing you need to remember is to keep your blade sharp at all times. Keep honing and stropping as you go along. In fact, you had better strop it now before you begin."

Pablo stuck his big toe through the loop at one end of the strop and pulled it taut with his left hand. With his right he stropped the knife until its edge was as keen as before. Then he picked up the spiral and began to cut at the L-shaped notch. Working carefully, he sliced along the first two feet of the strand, making sure it was of a consistent width.

"Bueno," said Inigua." "Go slow and concentrate on what you are doing."

Inigua sat in the shade and watched the boy work. When Pablo reached the stomach section, the old man showed him how to gradually widen the strand by a quarter of an inch, and then after several feet, to taper back to one inch. Pablo took the knife then and worked on.

When the boy's back was to him, Inigua broke the silence by saying, "Do you mind if I talk, Pablo?"

"No, señor."

It will not distract you?"

"No, señor. I can listen and work at the same time. Talk."

"Bueno. I was just going to say I think I owe you an apology."

Pablo paused, but resisted the urge to glance over his shoulder. "For what, señor?"

"For what I said earlier, about your upbringing. I said you did not listen to me and were raised as one of them. I was wrong to say that. You do listen to me, and you cannot help how you were raised. I cannot blame you for believing what the Hispanics have taught you. I am sorry if I offended you, or if I hurt your pride."

"You did not, señor. Besides, I am used to people saying things like that. It is because I am mestizo."

"That does not mean I was right. I was only trying to impress on you how we Chumash felt at the time the Spaniards came here, and explain why we did not rise up. I feel ashamed about that."

"You should not, señor.

"Yes, I should. I wish I could tell you how it was for us."

"Go ahead, señor, tell me."

"All right." Inigua fixed his gaze in the distance. "When Junipero Serra came here to found the mission in the spring of 1782, there were many soldiers with him. There were about seventy in all. They were heavily armed and under the command of Lieutenant José Ortega. Many of the soldiers brought their families with them. Muleteers drove dozens of pack animals bearing utensils for house, field and church. Vaqueros drove a herd of cattle which the party used for food. There were some neophytes from Mission San Gabriel accompanying them too, to help with translation and construction.

"All the visitors were very friendly, and we were equally hospitable, as is our way. At first we did not know why they had come. We assumed they were just traveling through like de Anza and so many others had done. But no. They were here to stay. They referred to our homeland as *La Asunción de Nuestra Señora.*

"I did not know what that meant, for I only knew a few words of Spanish at that time. I remember hearing Lieutenant Ortega speaking to his soldiers that first day. I could not understand what he was saying, but he seemed to be admonishing them. Whatever he said must have impressed them, for there was no trouble and they continued to be friendly – a little too friendly if you ask me.

"As to who was the overall leader of the expedition there was no doubt, it was Junipero Serra. He ordered his companions to begin building brush shelters and a wooden cross. The next day was the Christian day of Easter, March 31st. That was fifty years ago this month. It was on Easter Sunday when Serra raised the cross and held high mass along with his fellow priest Padre Pedro Cambón. We Chumash stood around and watched. We could tell whatever they were doing was some kind of ritual so we were quiet and polite."

Pablo had completed one complete circuit of the spiral by now. He paused when Inigua stood up to inspect it.

"Bueno," said Inigua. "Now just continue on around, keeping the line straight and the width the same as the first spiral. Just leave the loose coils lying where they are. Then they will not become tangled." Inigua sat back down in the shade and continued his story.

"In the days that followed, Serra and Cambon, using Indian interpreters, tried to explain to us the purpose of the mission which they named San Buenaventura. They tried to convince us to get baptized and join their religion. But no one wanted to. We did enjoy watching them, however. There was always something interesting or amusing to see. They were very industrious, and some of our people even helped them build a few shelters and a stockade. The Spaniards had chosen a spot about half way between Shisholop and *Mitsqanaqa'n*, which was a village a few hundred yards west of where the present mission now stands. Mitsqanaqa'n means 'place of the jaw.' It is named so because the hills on either side of the river reminded us of the shape of a coyote's jaws.

"Junipero Serra stayed three weeks. In that time his people began building a place of worship, the place that would become known as San Miguel Chapel. When Serra finally left he was somewhat disappointed. He had convinced none of us to join them or be baptized. He took most of the soldiers with him, leaving only fourteen here. Serra and the others went up and established the Presidio of Santa Barbara then. He tried to start a mission up there too, but was frustrated in his attempt. It would be four years before that mission was founded. By then Serra was dead.

"Padre Cambón was left in charge of Mission San Buenaventura. But he was only here a few months, long enough to design the mission water system. During the summer he was replaced by the padres Francisco Dumetz and Vincente de Santa Maria. I got to know them well in the years that followed.

"After awhile we grew bored watching the Spaniards. We hoped they might get bored too and leave. But this was not to be. We tried to ignore them, but they would not leave us alone. They kept coming around and trying to talk to us. At the time, we were busy getting ready for the fishing season. They wanted us to stop that and come help them construct a water system and build houses. They offered us food and glass beads for our help. Some of our people agreed. Eventually, I joined them too."

"Why did you agree to help them, señor? I thought you hated the Spaniards."

"I had not learned to hate them yet, even though that man Camacho had raped my sister some years before. But since I had crushed his head, I figured we were even. Besides, I knew that there are bad men in all tribes, even my own. The Spaniards had done no harm to me directly. Even though they were sometimes a nuisance, I wanted to see what they were up to. And, to tell you the truth, I felt a little sorry for them. They obviously did not know the first thing about living off the land."

Pablo finished the second spiral and began the third under the watchful eyes of his mentor.

Inigua said, "By then I was nearly recovered from my snake bite."

"Snake bite, señor? What snake bite?"

214

"Oh, I did not tell you? I mentioned before that my last act as a ksen was to deliver the news of the Spaniards' arrival to the outlying villages. I went up the river to the Aw'hai valley, and on to Sitoptopo, Sis'a, and Mupu. I then went all over the Lulapin country with the news. On the way back I was running near some brush and did not see a rattlesnake coiled up in the shade by the side of the trail. I must have startled it, for it did not even have time to sound its rattle before it struck. I only saw the movement, and felt the fangs sink into my right ankle."

"Dios mio, señor. What did you do?"

"What could I do? I went a little way down the trail to get away from the snake. I was starting to feel a lot of pain. I lay down then and prepared myself for death. I knew that if I continued to walk or run I would be dead very fast. I wanted some time to think before I went. My ankle and foot began to swell and turn an angry blue color."

Pablo glanced over at Inigua's right ankle. There was a mottled scar there he hadn't noticed before.

"I lay there for some time, just thinking about my life and about Islay, and my son Xaua and my little daughter 'Alahtin. I was sad about leaving them on their own. I began to feel very tired and must have dozed off. I awoke when I heard someone coming down the trail. It was a group of villagers from Mupu. They were on their way to the beach at Shisholop to have a look at the Spaniards. I was surprised to find myself still alive. By now my lower leg and foot were very swollen and painful, but I realized that the snake must not have given me all his poison. It was not a 'dry bite,' but one with little poison. If it had been otherwise I would be dead by now.

"The men of Mupu took turns carrying me on their backs and brought me home. The bite was very painful. It got infected later, but Islay kept it clean and covered it with poultices. I could not walk for many days. After that I could only get around by using a long branch of driftwood as a crutch. The wound took a couple of months to heal. I spent that time just sitting around and watching the Spaniards. I started talking with some of them and getting to know them. It was during this time that I began learning their language. I picked it up pretty fast."

Pablo had completed another spiral. He paused to hone and strop the knife.

"You have cut through all of the thin stomach section now, boy. From here on just cut the strand thumb-width."

"Sí, señor. Tell me, what were your people thinking at this time, señor? Didn't they want to get rid of those outsiders?"

"Some did. Especially the young men. The only thing that stopped them was the fear of the soldiers' muskets, and their swords and armor. On horseback, the soldiers were formidable opponents. The older men, the village council, met often in those first weeks and months. They spent many hours discussing what was to be done. Some felt the Spaniards had

215

overstayed their welcome. It was pointed out that we did not invite them here. They invited themselves. But some of the 'antaps, and the wot, Silkiset, wanted to study them for a while longer. They felt that once we learned the source of their magic we could then easily overpower and expel them. This, in hindsight, was a grievous mistake."

"So what happened?"

"Some of our people began to work with the outsiders. Those that did were mostly from the lower classes. They were the layabouts, the beggars, the drifters, and the drinkers. Most of them were without permanent homes or families. They were the castoffs of Chumash society. They joined the Spaniards because they were offered food for their services. They had no other place to go, and nothing else to do, so they followed where the food led them. After awhile, they did whatever was commanded of them, including getting baptized and joining the church. They did not know that once they were baptized they belonged to the church. The church would own them body and soul.

"I was lucky to be a member of a successful and respected family of fishermen, traders, and boat-builders. My family had plenty to eat. As for myself, I knew my days as a ksen were over. I was tired of running, and my ankle continued to give me pain. I had a choice: either return to the sea, or join in with the Spaniards. I knew all about fishing and trading already. The Spaniards were something new, something I found intriguing. I decided to spend some time with them to see what they were about. I thought that if I decided I did not like them, I could always go back to the sea. Islay was curious too. Since she knew so much about medicinal plants and herbs, she was curious about what kinds of medicine they had. She wanted to get to know the white women too."

The spiral was beginning to close in on Pablo now. He found himself sitting on an ever diminishing raft of rawhide, the circling strands like ripples of muddy water lapping about him. He stopped to sharpen the knife.

"So, what was the first thing you did with the Spaniards, señor?"

"Well, in the beginning I still could not walk very well. So, being a former ksen, it was only natural that I spent my time learning Spanish. One day after the new padres had arrived they came to me, and, with the help of an interpreter, asked me if I would help them build a dam and a canal to carry the water. I knew what a dam was. We Chumash used to use rocks to dam creeks and rivers to form ponds for fishing and bathing. But I did not understand why the Spaniards needed so much water. They told me they needed it to grow things. I still did not understand. Rain was all that the earth-mother, Hutash, needed to grow things.

"Because my ankle was still weak, they knew that I could not carry stones yet. But they knew I could speak a little Spanish. So they asked me to be a translator, and to help supervise the Indian workers. They offered to give me all the food I and my family could eat. Much to my later regret, I agreed.

216

"That summer we moved up to San Antonio Creek, to the place where it empties into the Ventura River. Islay and 'Alahtin came with me, while Xaua continued to learn the ways of the sea under the tutelage of my father and uncles and cousins.

"There was already a large group of people camping out upriver. They were Chumash and Christianized Gabrielaños, along with a number of Spaniards. Padre Dumetz was in a big hurry to build the dam before the winter rains came. He always had his nose in this large book that told him how to do it. He and his mayordomo, Sergeant Cota, drove the workers hard all summer and into the fall.

"Meanwhile, Padre Santa Maria and a corporal of the guard led a group that was building the canal that followed the curve of the hills in the river valley. Some of the Indians were put to work making something called Roman Cement. Others carried rock from the river. Still others were set to digging in the ground, not with our traditional digging sticks, but with wondrous metal-tipped tools provided by the Spaniards.

"The Indians had to work hard that first year because there were not too many of them. They began questioning the wisdom of their choice. Most of the other Chumash had decided to ignore the Spaniards and go about their own business."

Pablo had reached the point where the spiral had closed in to his feet. "What do I do now, señor?"

"Get up and sit on the strands. Keep cutting towards the middle until you reach the end.

"We did not finish the dam until the following year. It was a fairly dry winter, so we kept on working right through. Sometimes we had to stop until the next batch of lime for the cement was ready. During these times we went back home, or went hunting and gathering as we always had done. When winter came, more and more Indians came down out of the hills to join us. They wanted the free food. Life in wintertime is often hard up there in the high country.

"I remember spending a lot of time with Padre Santa Maria. He wanted to learn to speak our language, so I taught him. He was a good student. He might have made a good ksen. But he irritated me too. He was always pestering me about getting baptized. I could see no reason for it, for I did not have a strong religious nature. I was a simple man. I was not even convinced of the truthfulness of some of my own people's beliefs. I thought many of them just made good stories to tell children when you wanted them to sleep, rather than revealing any eternal truths. I thought the stories were probably just things people made up to pass the time.

"It was Islay who first decided to get baptized. She had gotten to know some of the wives of the soldiers and muleteers. She liked them, and she wanted to be like them. She wanted to wear clothes like them. All our people were fascinated by the clothes and ornamentation of the Spaniards.

Those things came to represent a kind of status that we did not possess. Islay had by now traded many of her beautifully-made baskets in exchange for red glass beads. She wore the beads proudly on strings around her neck and on her wrists and ankles.

"Islay wanted our daughter 'Alahtin to be baptized too. I resisted for a couple of years, but in the end we all got baptized together. I thought, what difference does it make? It will not change me, and it will make others happy. Oh, my dear boy, I was so wrong. I had no idea what I was letting myself in for."

Just then Pablo reached the end of the spiral. "I am finished, señor!" he announced proudly. "And look, I did not make one mistake."

Inigua sighed. He stood up and studied the boy's work. "Good job, Pablo. It looks fine."

Then the old man's gaze drifted off in the distance. His eyes climbed into the afternoon sky and beheld the crimson sun suspended above the shimmering sea like one of those infernal glass beads of yore.

33

STRETCHING

From the cover of the trees by the riverbank they heard the Angelus bell begin to chime. It rang to summon the neophytes to evening devotions. The old Indian and the boy glanced at one another.

"Go on, if you want," said Inigua.

"No, gracias, señor. Not tonight." Pablo looked down at the spiral. "What must we do now?"

"We need to gather the strand into a coil and soak it overnight. Stand over here and I will show you."

Inigua stepped into the middle of the spiral and took the end of the strand in his right hand. He raised his arm and bent his elbow up at a right angle. With his left hand he began to wind the strand around his open palm and the back of his arm. As the strand rose to the coil, Inigua turned slowly in a circle to gather it in. When he reached the opposite end he removed the loops from his arm. He wound several courses sideways around the loops to bind them together, and tucked the end into the courses.

"We need a stake," he said, "a long one. Take the hatchet and see if you can find a piece of driftwood or something. Bring one that is straight and strong, about four feet long. You might as well gather some firewood while you are at it. It might be cold night."

When the boy returned, Inigua approved the chosen stake. He had the boy sharpen one end using the hatchet. They then waded knee-deep into the fresh-water cove alongside their campsite. Pablo held the stake while Inigua pounded it into the sandy bottom with a heavy stone. The top of the stake protruded a foot or so above the surface. One end of the loop was then threaded over the top of the stake and dropped in the water. Finally, the pounding stone was placed on top of the coil to weigh it down.

"Bueno," said Inigua. "Tomorrow morning we will stretch it."

"Why must we stretch it, señor?"

"It must be stretched now so that the finished reata does not stretch too much when you lasso a large animal. Too much stretching then would loosen the braid. Doing it now eliminates that, and evens out the width so as to ensure a smooth braid. You will see."

"I am getting hungry, señor."

"We have food here, or you can go to the mission and eat there if you want."

"Will you come with me, señor?"

Inigua shook his head. "I do not think that is a good idea. Now that I think about it, it may not be wise for you to go either. Everyone knows you are with me. It would be better if no one knows where we are."

"I understand, señor. But it will be dark soon. I want to visit Padre Uria."

"Ah, well, you may go if you wish. I can look after myself. I have food and wine here."

"I could bring you some atole. I will get some from Encarnacíon."

Inigua shrugged. "It is of no consequence."

The sun disappeared behind Santa Cruz Island as the boy helped Inigua set up the tent and ready the camp for nightfall. As they were watering the horses at the river they heard the St. Mary of Sapopa's bell begin to chime, calling the mission Indians to supper.

"It is less than a mile to the mission," said Inigua. "If you are determined to go, I think it would be better if you walked. Riding in on horseback would announce your arrival to all who have ears. Travel through the fields. Wear your hat and coton, and, when you get there, stay out of the light. Speak to as few people as possible."

"Do not worry, señor. I will be careful. And I will take a small pot to carry back some atole. I will visit with Padre Uria, and return by the time the De Profundis bell rings."

"Bueno," said Inigua, as he set about constructing a fire circle between the tent and the river's edge. "Carry my greetings to Francisco. Tell him I will visit him one of these days. Hasta luego."

A waning three-quarter moon stood high in the sky as Pablo climbed up out of the river bottom and onto the coastal plain. He could see the white-washed walls of the mission church in the distance. He came upon the carreta trail that bisected the wheat fields, and turned onto it. His sandals slapped softly along the rutted track. To his left the newly plowed fields were dark and pungent with the smell of fresh-turned earth. To his right, the as yet unplowed portion stretched flat and expectant in the moonlight. In the quiet of this early March evening he could hear the soft murmur of surf along the beach. Pablo was happy to be by himself for a change, and was looking forward to his visit with Padre Uria. His stomach growled in anticipation of the flavorful and familiar atole. The boy's eyes scanned the moon-washed mission complex, and, though he could not be certain, he thought he saw a shadow move in the bell tower.

Back at the river, Inigua got the fire going and settled back with his bota of wine. He leaned against a fallen tree trunk. He drank, and listened to the sounds of the night. He tried not to think about the flood that had ravaged this river so recently, the same flood that took his wife and the last vestiges of his past from him. But his eyes could not help seeking out the accursed tree that had they had climbed together. He saw it glowing there in the ghostly moonlight, mocking him for his failure.

He did not want to think about Islay's spirit roaming aimlessly out there somewhere in the Santa Barbara Channel, but he could not help it. He could only hope that the ancient belief was mistaken, as he had found so many others to be.

The flood seemed to have happened such a long time ago, but in fact it had only been two weeks. He marveled at how much his life had changed since that day. He was grateful to have the boy. The young fellow had helped him get back on his feet again. If it hadn't been for Pablo, he knew he would not have been able to go on.

In many ways, the boy reminded him of his own son, Xaua, at that age. They both had the same simple purity, the same innate humility and respect, and the same inexplicable ambition to accomplish great deeds. Inigua supposed that he himself had been like that once. But those days were long gone. Too much had happened in his life to twist and pervert him. All that was normal had been wrung from his life. If it weren't for the making of the reata, he could think of no good reason to continue with the charade that was his life.

The old man drank. In time, his chin slowly lowered to his chest. Before long he was sound asleep. He awoke with a start an hour later when he heard the curfew bell ringing in the bell tower. He noticed that the fire had burned down to coals. He looked about him, and then behind him into the dim interior of the tent. Pablo was nowhere to be seen. Inigua felt a sudden uneasiness, and considered what he should do. Before he could decide, he was relieved to hear the soft pad of approaching footsteps.

A voice came out of the darkness. "Hola, señor. It is I."

"Ah, Pablo, I was wondering where you were."

"I brought you some atole, señor. And I have much news. Here. You must be hungry."

Inigua eyed the tin pot. He rummaged through their gear, feeling for a spoon. "What news have you?" he asked.

"A new priest has arrived at the mission, señor. His name is Padre Blas Ordaz. He hails from Mission Santa Inez. He has come to replace Padre Uria, who is very ill."

"Francisco is worse than before?"

"Sí, señor, much worse. He has been confined to his bed since we last saw him. His ankles are too swollen and painful to support him, and he is sick all the time. I was able to talk to him for only a short while. He looked bad, señor, but he seemed happy to see me. After we talked for awhile he told me he is leaving the mission soon."

Inigua's spoon paused in mid-air. "Where will he go?"

"He said he is going to Santa Barbara to be treated by Doctor Anderson. Then he will wait for a ship to take him home to Spain. He says he wants to die in the land of his birth. He will be staying at the house of Captain de la Guerra at the Presidio until the ship comes."

221

"That is sad news. Although I loathe Franciscans as a rule, I am fond of Francisco."

"I know he is fond you too," said Pablo. "He asked after you, and said to send you his regards."

"Did he say anything about what happened on the day of the whipping?"

Pablo scratched his head, trying to remember. "N-n-no. And I did not mention it."

"Bueno. Did anyone else see you, or talk to you?"

"Only Encarnacíon, señor. All the neophytes had already eaten by the time I went to the kitchen. I kept my hat pulled down over my face. Encarnacíon fed me. As I was eating she inquired if you were safe and well. She said to send her love, and she gave me some ponocha candy. I did not tell her where we were."

"Bueno."

Pablo put fresh wood on the fire as Inigua finished his meal. Then they retired to the shelter of the tent for the night. In the darkness Pablo heard Inigua tossing and turning in his blankets, and, later, mumbling in his sleep. The old man was obviously upset. The boy's heart went out to him, and to Padre Uria. It must be hard getting old, he thought. He felt suddenly very small and lonely lying there in the dark. He was saddened by the fact that Padre Uria would be leaving soon. The prospect of life without the jolly friar was too distressing to imagine. And if anything should ever happen to Inigua, he would be left all alone in the world. He dreaded the thought of being abandoned again. What was to become of him? The only thing he had to look forward to was finishing the reata, and then, hopefully, learning all he needed to know about becoming a vaquero.

The long night passed slowly for Pablo, but he finally managed to get some sleep before dawn. They both awoke to the sound of the Angelus bell ringing at sunrise. They looked out and saw early morning fog clinging to the coast and extending a chilly gray finger up the Ventura River valley. Pablo got up and fed the fire. They squatted by the welcome heat and ate leftover atole for breakfast.

"I want some herba buena tea," said Inigua. "My bones ache this morning, and my joints are stiff." He went down to the river and rinsed and filled the empty pot with water. His splashing startled a flock of geese gliding on the still waters of the river. They squawked in alarm, and flapped their wings as they ran along the surface. Before long they were wheeling up into the foggy air and turning north. Inigua watched them go. He then checked to make sure the staked coil was still in place.

When he returned to the fire, Pablo said, "What do we do now, señor?'

"We will stretch the strand of rawhide. It will not take long. Then there is nothing in particular to do until it dries."

222

"How long will that take?"

"A couple of days. Maybe three. It depends on the weather."

After Inigua had his tea and they had both visited the bushes, they went down to the river and retrieved the coil. The water was very cold, and the darkened coil came out soggy and limp.

Inigua said, "We need to find two trees with strong, low-hanging limbs. Let us try those up along the riverbank."

The boy followed him up the bank to a stand of cottonwood, willow and alder on the rim of the river. Inigua paused next to the line of trees and unwound the courses that joined the coils. He handed one end of the strand to Pablo.

"Take this and walk over that way," he said, indicating a leaf-strewn path along the base of the trees. Pablo held the damp end and carried it down the path as Inigua fed line from the coil. When the boy had gone perhaps eighty feet the line was all fed out.

"All right, boy," called Inigua, "hold on tight."

"Sí, señor."

Inigua, holding firmly to his end, began to walk backwards. Pablo felt the pull and gripped tighter, holding on with both hands. Inigua kept walking and the strand began to stretch. He stopped when he could go no further without losing his grip.

"Do you see?" he said. "See how it stretches?"

"Sí, señor. It is amazing. What do we do now?"

"Why, we stand here for two or three days until it dries."

"Ha ha, señor. You make a joke."

"Sí, Pablo. Now bring your end back here towards me."

The man and boy walked towards each other and met in the middle. Inigua tied the two ends of the strand together. "This makes a large loop, eh, boy? Now go back the way you came and pick up the end of the loop. I will do the same on this end."

The boy did as he was instructed.

When they were both in place Inigua called to him, "We must find two trees a little farther apart than us."

They followed one another along the path until they found two cottonwoods that were five or six feet further apart than themselves and had horizontal limbs extending from their trunks.

Inigua said, "These might do. Put your end around that limb, boy. Sí, that strong one up above your head. Now, move the loop a little way down along the limb." When it was in place, Inigua pulled on his end. The limb bent towards him to accommodate the pull. "Bueno. Now come over here, boy."

When Pablo was at his side, the two pulled on the loop and walked backwards as far as they could, the twin bands of rawhide stretched tight.

"Let's see if we can get it around this limb. This one here." Inigua reached behind him with one hand. He grasped the limb and pulled it towards them as far as he could. With some difficulty they managed to thread the limb through the end of the loop. Inigua adjusted the loop along the limb, and then they gingerly released it. The tree limb swung back towards its original position. The two limbs, pulling in opposite directions, held the loop stretched tightly between them. Inigua tested one of the bands by plucking it. It gave a low hum.

"Bueno," he said. "That is about right. Notice the strand is well up from the ground. That will keep it out of reach for any animals and bugs that might nibble on it."

Pablo tested the tension of the strand so that he might know how tight it should be. It seemed to him as tight as a fiddle string.

"Now what do we do, señor?"

"Now we wait. The strand is in the shade here. That is how it should be in the beginning. It will dry slowly. It will shrink as it does so. Someone will have to watch over it to see that it does not become too tight and snap. We have to watch out for coyotes too. If they smell it, they might try to pull it down and eat it. Coyotes will eat almost anything."

"So, what can I do now, señor?"

"Do? Why, do whatever you want."

"Whatever I want?"

"That is what I said. It only takes one of us to watch over the reata. I can do that. You can do as you please. But I do not want you going to the mission in the daylight. Comprende?"

"Sí, señor. But I don't know what to do with myself."

"Well then, go get some firewood and think about it."

Pablo took the hatchet and walked upriver. He was not accustomed to having a choice in the matter of his time. He was only used to obeying the orders of others. As he gathered wood he thought long and hard, and came up with what he thought was a brilliant plan. He went back to the campsite and dropped the armload of driftwood by the fire.

"I have decided what I want to do, señor."

Inigua stopped sorting dried pinto beans and dropping them into a pot of water. "What?"

"I would like to ride up to Ojai."

"Ojai. And what would you do in Ojai?"

"I... I would...I would visit the family of Qupe."

"Oh? I did not know you were so attached to that family."

"Well, I... I..."

"Is it the family you wish to see, or is it 'Akiwo?"

Pablo started to stammer, and then blushed and looked away.

"It is a long ride to Ojai," said Inigua. "I do not know that it would be wise for you to go alone. It can be dangerous. There are wild animals, not

224

the least of them long-horned cattle."

"But I know the way, señor. And I would be careful. You have taught me what to look out for."

Inigua rubbed his chin. In some ways it might be a good excursion for the boy to take alone. If all went well, Pablo would come back with more confidence in himself. And it might not be a bad thing for him to forge an alliance with Qupe's family. Although there was a risk in letting a thirteen year-old travel by himself, he knew the boy was too timid to do anything rash. Inigua realized, of course, that Padre Uria would never approve. It was this more than anything else that decided him to allow it.

"I will let you go on two conditions," he said. "First, you must be very careful. Keep yourself and Rojo clear of any danger. Second, you must return here before sunset tomorrow."

"I will do both, señor. Muchas gracias."

"Take some jerky and dried fruit for yourself, and some oats for Rojo. Follow the river bottom until you get to the dam site. Then go around it and stay out of sight of the men working there. If anyone questions you, tell them you are on an errand for Padre Uria."

"Sí, señor." Pablo felt such a surge of excitement that his legs quaked. He could not wait to begin his journey. Within a half hour he was packed and saddled and ready to go.

Inigua sat by the fire and watched the boy's preparations. He was proud of how far the boy had come since they'd met. But one could not see pride in his expression, for it was grave. When Pablo presented himself, and had said his cheerful, bright-eyed goodbyes, Inigua stood up and replied, "*Hasta mañana*, grandson." He took Pablo in his arms and hugged him. "Please do not make me regret letting you go."

"I will not, señor. I will return tomorrow afternoon. Don't worry, grandfather. I'm only going on a small journey."

"I could not but worry," said the old man. And then he released him.

34

SEPARATION

It seemed very quiet along the river after Pablo had gone. Inigua finished sorting the beans and set them aside to soak. At least he would have food while the boy was gone. He wished he had the kind he preferred: seafood, acorn mush, venison, or a nice roast duck. But those things required much labor, and the efforts of a whole family.

Inigua was reminded of what a great burden it was to have no family at this time in his life. There was not even a village that he could call his own. He could not help feeling disheartened about how things had turned out for him. He felt too the surge of that old familiar undercurrent of resentment. It rose and fell like the mid-ocean swells that endlessly lift and drop a canoe.

If it hadn't been for the Spaniards, he would be living in Shisholop still, surrounded by his loving family, by his relatives and friends. He would be esteemed for his age, and valued as one of the wise ones. He would be kept safe and sheltered, and have his meals provided to him. In return he would dispense knowledge and advice, and tell stories that both entertained and instructed.

Considering these things brought home to Inigua the weight of the years, and the true extent of his loss. He knew he could not so readily muster the energy he'd had once in such abundance. In truth, he felt a tiredness that reached down into his very bones. He could no longer rise to the effort required for gathering, hunting or fishing. It was easier just to boil a pot of beans. Acknowledging this made Inigua feel even glummer.

He looked forlornly about him. The sun had by now burned off the morning fog. He gazed across the river valley and saw a flock of sheep grazing on the green hills to the northwest. There was a boy and a dog trailing along with them. Inigua wouldn't mind a nice leg of lamb to go with his beans. But he knew that was not to be.

He turned his eyes in the direction Pablo had gone, to the north, towards the hazy blue mountains of the interior. His gaze then wandered to the east, across the steep coastal hills, and finally to the line of trees that screened the mission from view. He saw the two bent limbs that held the rawhide loop. He was disconcerted that he couldn't see the loop. He rubbed his eyes. Had they gotten that bad? Inigua stood up and climbed the slope. When he got close he was relieved to see that the loop was still intact, and all was well.

It was then that he heard voices calling to one another from beyond the trees. He crouched down, and, keeping well concealed, crept quietly through the fringing grove. Peeking through the foliage he looked out on the coastal plain. Again he was relieved. It was only a handful of neophytes attending teams of oxen. They had just begun to plow on the near side of the carreta path. On the far side, between the path and the mission, he saw children scampering barefoot over the planted field. They squealed and waved their arms. These young ones had no doubt been set to scaring the birds that would otherwise settle and feed on the new-sown grain.

Inigua's eyes wandered over to the right, to the edge of the bluff above the beach. It was there that Shisholop had once stood. But he could not now see any evidence that it ever existed. He reconstructed the village in his mind, the way it used to be. He recalled the day when all his people had been ordered to move out. They had been told to build new quarters close to the church that was then being constructed at the base of the hills. Within a few months, everyone was gone. He remembered watching the soldiers set fire to the 'aps, and seeing his and his neighbor's homes burn to the ground. Within days, the site which his ancestors had occupied for eight hundred years had been plowed under and planted with wheat. Even the burial ground had not been spared the indignity of cultivation.

He recalled all the useless curses called forth by the 'antaps and aimed at the newcomers during the month's leading up to the village's demise. He remembered all the charms they carved from soapstone and then crushed into dust, all the cave paintings that implored 'Alishaw, the merciless sun, to descend and consume the Spaniards. He remembered the secret ceremonies in the Siliyik where the powers of the unknown were called upon to expel the outsiders. He remembered the calls for war which were ignored by timorous and already seduced leaders. All had come to naught. The powers of the shamans had proved counterfeit, their beliefs meaningless and irrelevant in the face of the new religion, the new way of living. Not even those Chumash living far from the mission, in the recesses of the hinterlands, had avoided their insidious influence.

Inigua remembered being taught the tenets of the new religion. He remembered feeling dismayed and disappointed when he discovered how preposterous they were. Who could believe such nonsense? Who could believe, for example, in the immaculate conception of a child? Or a dead man rising up from the grave and ascending into the sky? Who could believe in an almighty and merciful God who took credit when things went well, but who turned his back when things went wrong? And who could believe that by simply confessing your misdeeds to a priest, you were absolved of guilt no matter how loathsome and unforgivable the act?

What was left if his own people's beliefs had proven to be devoid of truth, and yet the new religion was even more far-fetched and ridiculous? Back when this question had first arisen, it had seemed to Inigua that only a great vacuum remained. Life seemed then to have no meaning. It was at that time that he had come to the conclusion that only his own actions defined

227

reality and gave it meaning. There was no redemption, no heaven, no hell. He soon became what the missionaries called a 'Bad Indian,' the emblem of his title inscribed in scarlet lines across his back.

Inigua turned away now from the coastal plain and retreated to the shadow of the trees. He felt dirty, and in want of a sweat bath.

*   *   *   *   *

Pablo had put Rojo into a canter as soon as he got out of sight and hearing of Inigua, and made good time up the river valley. He was happy and expectant, and grateful for the opportunity of seeing 'Akiwo again. But as he neared the Gatekeeper tree, the giant Sycamore at the bend in the river, he began to have second thoughts. How would he explain to her family his sudden appearance, and the absence of Inigua? They would no doubt ask questions, and wonder why he was there. Would they not guess that Pablo had come to see the girl? And then he remembered he had neglected to bring a gift. Would they consider him uncouth to arrive without a gift? He eased Rojo into a walk.

Pablo began to reconsider the wisdom of his journey. He tried to think of some excuse to tell the family. Maybe he could tell them he was on his way to upper Ojai, to visit the rancho. He could pretend that he was just a tired traveler hoping for a night's lodging. But would he not then be telling a lie? And wasn't lying a sin? But, then again, it was not as big a sin as fornication, a sin he had already committed with their daughter. He was sorry now he had found neither the time nor the courage to confess it to the padre. He wondered if he would go to hell if he should to die on this journey.

As Pablo rounded the curve where the two hills pinched the bending river, he reined in. Maybe he should consider turning back. But what then? he wondered. Wouldn't Inigua be disappointed in him? Wouldn't he assume that he was too afraid to make the trip alone? And if Inigua thought of him as a coward now, he would never have faith in him becoming a vaquero later. No, Pablo decided. I cannot go back. He clucked to Rojo and continued on. He felt better about it when he remembered secreting the ponocha that Encarnacíon had given him. It was in his saddle bag. He could offer that as a gift to the family.

But as the miles passed one behind the other the boy began to feel wary. Trees and undergrowth were closing in on the river now, and he could not see for any great distance ahead. His eyes and ears became alert for danger. Wanting to avoid seeing anyone coming to or from the dam, he stayed clear of the trail and picked his way along the river's edge. He stopped often to listen.

Pablo wondered what Inigua would do in his position, say if he were going to see Islay. After considering it, he decided that the old man would not tell a lie. He would either say nothing, or he would tell the truth. He would merely pay the family a friendly visit, and if they asked him why he was there, he would confess his interest in their granddaughter. Pablo decided he would do the same. The family might not ask him anyway. But if they did, and he told them, would they be angry? If so, what would they do? Well, they probably wouldn't kill him. But they might beat him, or maybe just run him off.

But so what? He would be no worse off than before. The boy decided it was worth the risk. Nonetheless, he began to sweat. It must be the heat, he thought. It seemed so much warmer up here than down on the coast. He stopped to change out of his long pants and coton, and to don his taparrabo. Then he continued on. When he got to the place where San Antonio Creek emptied into the river he paused in the shade of a tree. He could hear voices upstream, and the sound of pounding and digging. He dismounted and peered around the foliage in the direction of the sounds. A hundred yards upstream, where two ridges came together at the stream, he saw a group of neophytes working. They were all very busy at their appointed tasks. When he felt the time was right, he led Rojo across the rushing stream and into the shrubbery beyond. He watched closely as he crossed, and was thankful no heads turned in his direction.

He remounted and rode up the river to Mira Monte, to the place where he and Inigua had watered their horses before. And there, much to his surprise, he came upon 'Akiwo's family, along with several other Chumash, camped out by the riverside. He saw Qupe and three men standing knee-deep in the middle of the river. They were building a low dam out of river rock. There were a couple of makeshift brush shelters on the shore, and a small fire burning there. Five women, one of them 'Akiwo, looked up at the sound of Rojo's hooves clattering among the river rock. 'Akiwo's eyes found his. She gave a small exclamation of joy. "Pablo!" she called, and came scampering towards him.

The men in the river stopped their work and looked at him. "Haku!" Pablo called, raising his hand to them. He felt cold sweat trickle down his armpit as he reined in.

When the girl was at his side, he looked down at the beautiful girl who had tormented his dreams and said in faltering Ventureño Chumash, "What you doing here?"

"We are making the fishing," she said, smiling. "See." She pointed to the women on the bank. "We weave the long-handled nets. The hard-headed fish, they are traveling upriver now. The men, they catch them in the nets as they jump over the dam.

"And why are you here, Pablo?" she asked, placing her hand on his calf and looking up at him.

Pablo blushed. "I was just out riding my horse. I was lucky to find you. I am happy."

'Akiwo smiled.

The men in the river were still standing motionless, watching him.

"I can help you," he called to them.

Qupe nodded without changing his pensive expression.

Minutes later Pablo was standing knee-deep in the frigid water piling rocks on the dam.

*   *   *   *   *

A single candle burned by the bedside. Inigua hardly recognized the bloated and blanketed figure that lay before him. The room smelled sour. The fetid scent of sickness was thinly masked by the acrid odor of burnt hemp.

"It's good to see you," said Padre Uria. "I was hoping you'd come. Where is Pablo?"

"He is not here. We are stretching the rawhide for making his reata. Someone must keep an eye on it."

"Oh, too bad. I was hoping to see him once more. I am leaving in the morning. A carreta has been arranged to carry me to Santa Barbara."

"Pablo told me you are going home."

"Sí, to Spain. You can understand my desire to see my homeland once more, old friend. I only hope I live long enough to see it."

"I hope you do, even though I will never see mine again."

"I know. I'm sorry. Please, pour yourself a goblet of wine. It is out there in the sitting room. But none for me, thanks. It makes me want to pee, which gives me great discomfort."

When Inigua returned he said, "Are you in pain, Francisco? I could bring you some herb tea or something."

"Do not bother. I have been smoking *mota*. It distracts me from the pain, and doesn't make me want to pee."

Inigua drank from the goblet. He looked over at the padre. "I am sorry to see you in such a condition, and more sorry to see you go."

"It is my time. Are you still at the river mouth?"

"Sí. But I do not wish anyone else to know it."

"I understand. That was a clever trick you pulled last Sunday."

Inigua glanced sharply at him. "You know about that?"

"I know you. After awhile I figured out what happened."

"Have you heard from Señor Tico?"

"I have heard nothing from Don Tico. But this matter is no longer my concern. It is Padre Blas Ordaz's concern now. But I fear you are in trouble once again, my friend. Very deep trouble. Don Tico is not the kind of man you should trifle with."

"Tico is not any kind of man in my opinion. He is a devil, right out of your bible."

Padre Uria inhaled deeply and held it. Then he gave a long sigh. "What is to become of you, Inigua? While I wish you the best in your final years, I can see no good ending for you."

"I will take care of my own ending."

"Fine. I don't give a damn about your ending. But I am worried about Pablo. You were supposed to take care of him."

"I am taking care of him."

"How will you take care of him when Don Tico comes to extract his pound of flesh from your mangy hide?"

"My hide is not so mangy. Do not worry, Francisco. I will take care of Señor Tico when the time comes."

"How can you do that? You are not half the man you once were."

"I am man enough. I know what to do."

"What do you mean?"

"What I mean is of no importance. Only know this – I will see no harm comes to the boy."

"You had better not."

A silence descended on the sick room. Inigua took another sip of wine. "Do you have any family left in Spain?"

"Yes. I hope so anyway. I have a brother and two sisters, but I have not seen them since I boarded the ship in Cádiz thirty-six years ago. There are probably nieces and nephews I have never seen. My parents died years ago."

Again there was a silence.

"I wish there was something I could say to you, Francisco, to make you feel better. But you know better than to expect me to congratulate you on your life's work. I have already expressed to you all that you need know about the way I feel. Except for this: I will truly miss you. I will miss talking with you and joking around. I will miss the arguments and the laughter. And I will miss drinking your wine."

"Ha. Still the scoundrel. But thank you nonetheless, my friend. I will miss you too. I only regret I was not able to convert you."

"Ha. Not a chance."

"Damn. You are a hard man, Inigua. But I want to tell you something before you go. I have known you now for how many years, twenty-five?" The old Indian nodded. "I have seen you grow harder and harder as the years passed. You know, when things become too hard, my friend, they break. Can't you soften your heart just a little in your old age? Can't you open it up and let the boy in? I would feel so much better knowing that he was in good hands, and that he was loved."

Inigua swallowed and said huskily, "There is no need to worry about the boy, Francisco. He is loved. I will look after him until he no longer needs me."

Padre Uria's tears glistened in the candlelight. "Muchas gracias, compadre."

Pablo returned to the river mouth late the following afternoon. He found Inigua sitting by the dead campfire with a knife in his hand. He was carving a shallow slot across the top of a thick, squared post.

"Haku, Inigua. *Me'peshumawish?*"

"Haku, Pablo. *Shumawish*. Thank you for asking. You look older somehow. And I see you have learned some new words of our language."

"Sí, señor. What is that you are cutting?"

"A jig. The rawhide strip is dry now. I am making this jig for splitting it in two. It will be easier this way."

"Where did you get that wood?" Pablo asked, looking down at the three-foot long post.

"I freed it from the stack behind the carpenter's shop. I went to the mission last night."

"Oh? Did you see the padre?"

"Sí. He is gone now."

Pablo's jaw dropped. "Gone? What do you mean gone?"

"He left this morning for Santa Barbara."

"Oh, no! I wanted to see him again before he left."

"I am sorry; you are too late. How was your journey to Ojai?"

"Oh…well… muy bueno, señor. I will tell you about it. But first let me take care of Rojo."

When the boy returned from watering and staking out his pony, he told Inigua all about the journey and of meeting the family and fishing at the river. He told him everything except the part about his moonlit walk with 'Akiwo.

Inigua finished carving the one-inch wide slot. He said, "There. The jig is ready. We will use it to slice the rawhide strip right down the middle. There is still plenty of light to work."

"Why are we cutting it in two, señor?"

"Because the strip, as it is now, is too wide for braiding a reata. It only needs to be half as wide. So we will cut it down the middle. Then we will grease the strings. Only then will we begin to braid.

"I will retrieve the strip, boy. Meanwhile, you take that digging stick there and dig a hole right here. Make it just big enough around to plant this post. Make the hole just round enough for the post, and only deep enough so that half its length is buried in the ground."

As Pablo was digging he saw Inigua take down the rawhide strip. The old man untied the knot and smoothed out the ends, then coiled the strip around his arm as before. The boy had finished digging and testing the hole by the time Inigua returned. Together they rammed the post into the hole and tamped earth firmly around the base. Then Inigua honed and stropped the sticking knife. He directed Pablo to hold the end of the strip while he carefully cut down the middle of it for about six inches. Then he had the boy brace the post as he stuck the tip of the knife into the center of the groove, with the blade parallel to the sides. He stuck it in firmly, at a sloping angle.

"The blade is slanted to one side so as to bevel the cut," explained Inigua. "Now we begin. Sit down on that side of the post. I will be on this side. Take the end of the strip that I have divided and guide them through the slot on either side of the blade. Now, brace the post with your foot and begin pulling. Pull slowly, and be sure the blade cuts down the center of the strip. You want each half to be the same width. I will brace the post from this side with my feet, and help guide the strip past the knife."

Pablo began to pull, and as he did, he marveled at the deceptive ease of separation.

35

FLIGHT

It did not take long to divide the strip, despite the care that it took. Now they had two rawhide strings, each over a hundred feet long and about a quarter of an inch wide. Inigua showed the boy how to coil them so they did not become tangled.

"I thought we needed four strings, señor," said Pablo, as he wrapped one of them about his arm.

"We do. But we will double these two upon themselves, making four. You will see. There is still some light left, boy. If you are not too tired, you could begin rubbing down the strings with tallow."

"I will do it."

"Use your fingers. Afterwards, use a little scrap of rawhide to wipe it down. Here is one here. Here also is the pot of tallow we took from Señor Vaca. I will show you how to begin."

Inigua dipped his fingers into the gray, solidified mass of rendered fat and scooped up a dollop. He spread it between his thumb and fingers, and demonstrated how to apply it to the string. He started at one end and worked meticulously, greasing both sides thoroughly by rubbing his fingers and thumb together with the string in between. He took care to coat the edges as well. Pablo watched the rawhide change from a light tan color to a deep, rich brown, and take on a soft, lustrous sheen. He saw the treated string dangling, soft and pliable, as it emerged from Inigua's hands, and felt a sudden thrill at the transformation.

"Do not be afraid of using too much tallow," said Inigua. "The string will soak in what it needs. Just wipe off any excess with the scrap of leather. When you finish this string, go on to the next. Later, we may find they both need a second greasing." He placed the string in Pablo's eager hands.

"Now I will go get some wood and start a fire. We are having leftover beans. They are always better the second day anyway. I have tortillas too."

Inigua made his way upriver in search of firewood. As he walked along he heard the prayer bell begin to chime. He turned his head towards the mission and spied a likely looking pile of driftwood up on the river bank. He climbed the slope and began collecting. His eyes were drawn to a movement in the distance, at the base of the eastern hills. It was a lone horseman coming downriver. Inigua could not make out who it was, but he saw that he rode a fine Palomino. The rider was dressed in leather and wore a dark sombrero. The man was just now rounding the bend and heading towards the mission.

234

Inigua had no doubt that it was Fernando Tico.

So, he has come at last, he thought. *He will probably go to evening church services and then have his supper. And then what? Tomorrow is Sunday: a good day for a whipping. He will make enquiries regarding our whereabouts. Someone may have seen us, or seen our campfire. Old Vicente could probably see the glow from the bell tower. Perhaps Señor Tico will come tonight. Yes, if I were him, I would come tonight.*

Inigua finished collecting wood and returned to camp. Pablo had just completed the first string, and started the second. Inigua did not speak to the boy, but built a fire and prepared their simple meal.

Pablo wolfed his food, for he was eager to get back to work. Even though it was getting dark, he meant to finish the second string. He could work by firelight if necessary. But he relished the beans nonetheless. They were richly flavored with comino, peppers, beef jerky, and wild onions.

"Eat well," said Inigua, "for it may be a long night. We need to pack up and get out of here."

Pablo looked up in surprise. "But why, señor? What's the hurry?"

"The only reason we came here was to be close to the padre. He is gone now."

"But still, what's the hurry? Can't we wait till tomorrow?"

"Tomorrow may be too late. Señor Tico has arrived at the mission."

"No, por Dios! That is not good. But he doesn't know we are here, does he?"

"There are not many secrets at the mission."

They heard St. Mary of Sapopa's bell announcing supper, and looked at one another.

"He will eat now, along with the others," said Inigua. "We have some time. Why don't you finish the second string, and then start packing. I will take some oats and feed the animals. Then I will bring the mule."

Pablo's hands trembled as he went about greasing the second string. It took all his concentration to do a thorough job. He could not help thinking of the consequences if Don Tico found them. He wished Padre Uria was still here. Without him they had no protection. When the boy was done, he re-coiled both strings.

Inigua returned with Chico. He harnessed the pack racks on his back by the light of the fire. Then he washed the eating and cooking implements in the river. Together they took down the tent and began packing.

"You finish up here," said Inigua. "I will go saddle the horses." He turned and walked into the darkness. The horses were tethered fifty yards upriver. Their saddles and tack lay under an old blanket on the high ground. As Inigua was saddling Tabaco, he heard the soft pad of approaching hooves. They came from the direction of the carreta path. Inigua froze.

A dark figure on horseback appeared on the river's rim, silhouetted against the night sky. The white mane of the Palomino shone in the moonlight. The rider scanned the river bottom but failed to see Inigua who was concealed by the shadow of nearby brush. The rider turned towards the light of the fire and urged his mount down the embankment.

Pablo heard the horse approaching and assumed it was Inigua. He continued gathering their belongings and loading them onto the mule.

A voice came from behind him. "Where do you think you are you going, vaquerito?"

Pablo flinched, and turned to face the voice. "D…D…Don Tico. What are you doing here?"

"Answer my question. Where are you going?"

"I'm…I'm going to the mission."

"Don't lie to me, boy. Where's the old man?"

"What old man?"

Don Tico untied the whip that hung from his pommel. He grasped the handle and flicked it so that it uncoiled. "I'm not going to ask you again."

Pablo felt the strength drain from his legs, and an urgent need to void himself. "You mean Inigua? He…he is not here."

Tico drew back the leather snake and whipped it forward. It whizzed through the firelight, its nether end curling over the boy's shoulder. There was a snap followed by a loud pop. Pablo gave an involuntary yelp and staggered forward. A searing pain erupted along his back. It grew hotter as the moments passed.

"Speak now, boy. Or I will strip your back and feed the pieces to the gulls."

Pablo gritted his teeth and glared defiantly at the dark figure towering above him. Through clenched jaws he said, "He is not here."

Don Tico's eyes blazed, and he drew back his arm once more. Pablo heard a whirring sound and closed his eyes, bracing himself for the next blow. But it did not come. Instead, he heard a strangled gasp and the clatter of horse's hooves. He opened his eyes to see Don Tico, his whip arm suspended in mid-air above his head, his left hand clawing at his neck. Pablo glimpsed a braided rope encircling the man's neck and trailing under his upraised arm. In the next instant, the man tumbled backwards off the startled Palomino. His sombrero and whip went flying. Pablo looked beyond Tico and saw Inigua rapidly backing Tabaco away, with the end of the old reata wound round the pommel. Inigua turned his horse and yelled, "Heeya." Tabaco bolted off into the darkness with Tico gagging, tumbling and twisting along behind. Pablo heard the clatter of rocks as the man was dragged over the rough terrain of the river bottom.

Racing beyond the grove of trees, Inigua guided the horse up the riverbank. At the top, Tabaco leaped over the rim and hurdled forward, gaining speed with each stride. But then the horse reared and almost went down as a sudden jerk yanked at the reata. Tico had snagged momentarily on the rim, before somersaulting over. Somehow one leg got tangled up in the reata. Inigua urged Tabaco forward again and galloped along the carreta path towards the mission, pulling the flailing body behind him. Tico's body was pounded by the uneven wheel ruts, and slammed into rocks and other flood refuse gleaned from the plowed fields. Inigua finally reined in a hundred yards shy of the tree-lined lane that ran from the mission to the sea.

The old man's face felt flushed and his heart pounded wildly in his chest. He had not felt so alive in years. He ordered Tabaco to hold, and dismounted. He walked through a cloud of settling dust to the motionless form of Don Tico. He bent down and rolled him over. Tico gave a weak groan. Inigua saw that one of the man's legs was twisted at an odd angle. He removed his reata and stood in the moonlight, coiling it.

"You should not have come looking for me, pendejo, he said. "And you should never raise your hand against a child. My curse is upon you."

Don Tico's voice gurgled as he said, "Mierda. You have killed me."

Inigua looked down, studying him. "I think you will live. But I would have someone sew your ear back on. It is only hanging by a thread. And the skin of your nose and face will probably grow back all right. However, I do not like the look of your leg."

"Dios mio!"

Inigua paused, and spat. "*Me cago en Dios*. Try to be brave, *ese*. It is not very far to the mission. If you crawl fast enough you will be there before the De Profundis bell rings. You would not want to be out after curfew, would you, eh, maricón?"

"I will find you, *culero*."

"No, you will not find me. But you should worry about me finding you again. I will not be so kind next time. Adios." Inigua remounted and galloped back the way he had come. He descended to the river bottom and went directly to the fire. He found Pablo standing next to an already saddled Rojo and a fully loaded Chico. The Palomino was there too, looking confused and frightened.

Inigua dismounted and said, "Are you all right, boy?"

"Sí, señor."

"Let me see your back." He turned the boy around and lifted his coton. He ran his finger gently down the welt. "It is not bad. The skin is not broken. Your coton saved you."

"No, you saved me, señor. Muchas gracias. Where is Don Tico? Is he still alive?"

"He is alive, but injured. I took him close to the mission. He will be found soon enough, and then the soldiers will come here looking for us. We must go now."

Just then, the two heard the sound of hoof beats coming from upriver. Inigua quickly kicked dirt onto the fire, snuffing it out. He whispered, "Help me lead the animals up the slope and into the shadows." They moved away from the river and waited.

A horseman rode into the clearing and sat gazing down at the smoking fire circle. He looked around him, and then spoke, "H...Hola. Is anyone here? I have a message for Señor Inigua, por favor. It is I, Paco, the stable master's son."

Inigua said, "I am the one you seek. What is your message, boy?"

Paco's head jerked towards the sound. "M...m...my father told me to tell you that Don Tico is at the mission. He intends to come here. You must flee."

Inigua chuckled mirthlessly. "You are too late, boy. He has already been here. But thank you for coming anyway. Tell your father we are safe, and that we are going away now. Tell him we will send the horses and mule back to the stable one of these days. Now go home. By the way, which way did you come?

"I rode El Camino Real to the river, and then down along its bank."

"Good. I want you to go back the same way. Do not go through the wheat fields. Comprende?

"Sí, señor. Adios."

When he had gone, Inigua asked Pablo, "Where is the whip?"

"It is there somewhere on the ground."

After a quick search they located it, sprawled in the dust like some nocturnal snake. Inigua took the skinning knife and cut it into a dozen pieces, arranging them end to end in a circle around the fire pit. Then they mounted up

"What about the Palomino, señor?"

"Leave him here. I tied his reins to a branch. The soldiers will find him."

Inigua led the way downriver. When they got to the beach, he turned right, saying, "This way." He guided Tabaco across the shallows where the river fanned out across the sand. It was low tide, and he continued along the sandy beach, riding well above the high water mark.

"Where are we going, señor?"

"We are leaving a false trail. We will go a little further, and then ride down to the water. Then we turn around and head east. We will stay in the shallows till we are beyond the mission. From there we can ride at the edge of the sea. In a few hours the tide will rise and cover our tracks, but not these here. When the soldiers come they will see them and think we are traveling west. But we are not. We are going to Hueneme."

They rode along the shoreline under a three-quarter moon which by now was encircled by a halo of misty light. A dense fog was beginning to form over the sea. As they rode past the mission, Pablo glanced over his shoulder. He was beginning to realize the repercussions of what had occurred. He was now a fugitive. He would be considered as guilty as Inigua – at least in the eyes of Don Tico and the mission guard. He gazed wistfully across the wheat fields, at the bell tower gleaming white against the dark hills.

Pablo knew now that his life had changed forever. The mission, which had been the only home he had ever known, was now lost to him. It was now only a place to be feared and avoided. If he showed his face there again he knew he would certainly be thrown in the curatel, and then given a sound whipping at the post. There was nothing for him there any longer. His parents were gone, his aunt and uncle, and now even Padre Uria. There was nothing for him there at all, nothing but his memories, and a shaken faith.

The gentle murmur of shore break did little to comfort him. It only magnified his sense of loneliness and abandonment. The rhythm of the surf blended with the sand-softened hoof beats and the creak of leather. They formed a muted cadence to the desolation of his flight.

They rode for several hours in silence. By midnight, the gray mantle of fog had crept in off the sea and engulfed them in its chill embrace. Pablo felt Rojo shiver beneath him. Eventually, the domed huts of Hueneme emerged from the fog looking haunted and unearthly. After much confusion and the barking of dogs, the two refugees were admitted to the house of Malak. The sleepy and tousle-haired family welcomed the unexpected visitors in the darkened interior.

Malak sat before the dim embers of the fire and fed it twigs until a welcome flicker of flame lit the interior. He looked across the circle of light at his exhausted guests. "You look like trouble," he said. "What has happened?"

Inigua explained, and then added, "But do not worry, Malak. No one knows we have come here. We left no trail. We are here to respectfully request the help that you once so generously offered. We would like to go out to the islands. It is the only place they cannot find us. We will be safe there. If you could lend us a tomol, or take us there, we would be forever grateful. By doing this you will have repaid the debt, the debt you incurred when my son saved your son's life."

"You know that I cannot refuse you, Inigua. But I do not want to bring trouble to my family, or my village. I will lend you an old canoe. It is not large, and it is not the best. But it is seaworthy. We only recently re-caulked it. If the authorities come here looking for you, and notice it is missing, we will tell them you must have stolen it in the night. Is this acceptable?"

"Perfectly."

"And what about your horses, and that mule? They cannot remain here."

Inigua rubbed his chin. "Perhaps someone can take them back to the mission. If you take them at night, no one will know."

"That sounds dangerous. If one of us is seen with them, all is lost."

"I agree. What if you take them to Mupu? We have a friend there. His name is Qaq. He is the wot of Mupu village." Malak nodded. He knew Qaq. Inigua continued, "If the situation is explained to Qaq, he should be willing to help. I shared a steer with his people. If he agrees to take the animals back to the mission, tell him it should be done at night. He would not even have to take them all the way. Once they see they are close to home, they will go there on their own."

"This sounds acceptable to me," said Malak. He turned to his eldest son. "Liyam, can you take these animals to Mupu?"

"Of course, father."

"Good. Then you should leave immediately. I want you to do it while it is still dark. Take some food with you, and a gift for Qaq. Be sure to warn him of the danger. He should keep the animals out of sight until tomorrow night."

"I am happy to go, father, for I too owe a debt to this man who is the sire of Xaua."

Malak turned to Inigua. "Do you have food and supplies to take with you?"

"Yes. They are all loaded on the mule."

Malak turned to his other son, Shup. "Unload the mule and stow everything on the beach near 'Sopo.' Include some fishing gear. Leave the saddles and tack on the animals."

"Yes, sir."

Malak turned to Inigua. "I am loaning you some fishing gear. You may need it. Who knows how long you will be out there."

"Taney, Malak. We will stay in the islands long enough to finish making the reata. By then the soldiers will have given up looking for us. We will return the canoe to you one day, and then find some other place to go where it is safe."

"Good. I know you will take good care of my tomol. You were once in the Brotherhood-of-the-Canoe. But now, I think you two had better get some rest. You should start at first light."

240

36

THE CROSSING

Dawn came early for the weary fugitives. Malak knelt close to them and spoke softly. "It is time now." Inigua grunted, and cast his blankets aside. Pablo opened his eyes, but did not move. He could have slept till noon if left alone.

Malak's wife, Luhui, fed her guests a quick meal of acorn mush and dried fish. Then the leader of the clan led them down to the beach. In the early light, they beheld a dense layer of fog covering the sea and blanketing the coastal plain. Through the mist they saw Shup standing at the shoreline next to the red tomol named 'Sopo' [Charmstone]. The vagabonds' gear was piled on the beach above the high water mark and covered with mats. Two long, bladed paddles were balanced atop the pile.

The wot of Hueneme village studied the two would-be voyagers. One was a tired seventy-five year old man, the other, an equally tired thirteen-year old boy who had never been in a canoe in his life. Malak sighed and rubbed his forehead. "I don't know," he said. "Do you think you two can do this? It is a difficult journey."

"We can make it," said Inigua.

"I'm not so sure," said Malak. "How long has it been since you manned a tomol?"

"Many years.

"It is plain to see you are in no condition for paddling. I would hate to lose you – either one of you – not to mention a valuable canoe."

"The sea is calm," said Inigua. "There is no wind."

"But it is still a long paddle. Although Hueneme is the closest point on the coast to the islands, it is still twelve miles. And that is just to *Anyapakh* [Anacapa]. You say you want to go to *Mi'chumash* [Santa Cruz]. Add another eight miles at least. You and Pablo don't look like you could paddle two miles, much less twenty. And in this fog, you cannot even see your destination."

"Do not worry, Malak. I have done this before. We can make it."

"I cannot agree. You forget how challenging the crossing is, even in good weather. I believe the only way you can make it is with help. I want to send Shup with you. He is the strongest paddler in the village, and he knows the waters."

Inigua looked at Shup, then at Pablo, then back to Malak. He sighed. "You may be right. I would not want to lose your tomol in the attempt."

"It will be better anyway," said Malak. "Shup can bring 'Sopo' back in a day or two. Then the soldiers will not be suspicious of its absence."

"But how will we get off the island if he goes? We cannot stay there forever."

"We will come for you as soon as they have stopped looking for you, weather permitting, of course." Malak folded his arms.

The gear was divided and rearranged into two bundles. The three men and the boy then lifted the tomol and carried it into the water. Curious seagulls circled above the canoe, tilting their heads, searching in vain for tidbits. Pablo and Inigua held the tomol steady in the shore break while Shup and Malak stowed the two bundles in the canoe, leaving an open space between. Inigua had seen to it that the reata strings were well wrapped and covered. A third paddle was produced, and Malak steadied 'Sopo' as the voyagers prepared to board. Pablo was directed to climb in first.

Malak said, "Don't sit on that board there in the middle, Pablo. It is not a seat. It is the spreader. It helps the tomol keep its shape. Kneel on the floor in front of it."

Pablo knelt down amidship, between the two bundles. He was glad to be out of the cold water. Inigua got in next, and knelt near the bow. Shup handed them each a paddle, and then climbed into the stern position with his own paddle.

Malak steadied the craft as it floated in the shallows. He bowed his head and uttered a short prayer: "Travelers upon the sea – may you reach your destination safely, with the aid and guidance of the earth mother, Hutash. But if she is sleeping, or busy elsewhere, let Saint Christopher keep you safe and lead you to calm harbors." Pablo looked up, surprised and puzzled. Malak concluded, "May the sea be gentle, the winds calm, the fish kind and willing, and the afternoon sun warm upon you."

Farewells were said, and then Malak retired to the beach, where he stood looking on with Luhui by his side. Shup steadied the canoe with one blade of his paddle pressed against the sandy bottom. He gazed beyond the craft, studying the incoming swells.

"Which is your strong arm?" he asked his shipmates. Inigua and Pablo both raised their right arms. "Good," said Shup. "On the way out I will call that your west arm. Soon we begin. Be ready to paddle – your west arm first."

Inigua and Pablo sat at the ready, holding their long, double-bladed paddles near the middle between the gunwales. Pablo shivered with cold excitement.

When Shup spied a lull in the incoming waves, he gave a shout and began to chant:

Give me a WEST arm pull
Now an EAST arm pull
Now a WEST arm pull

Then an EAST arm pull

Stroke HARD my friends
Dig DEEP 'til the end
Use your BACKS my friends
Scoop the WATER on end

The three paddled in unison, their buoyant craft plunging forcefully into the incoming waves, and then rising up and over them. Before long they were out beyond the surf and gaining momentum. Shup continued to chant:

Leave the WAVES behind
Leave the SHORE behind
Leave the LAND behind
Leave your HOME behind
Give me a WEST arm pull
Now an EAST arm pull...

Soon they were making good headway, gently rising and descending over the low mounded swells in deeper water. Shup paused, and looked back at the shore. "Look behind you," he said. When they turned their heads, he pointed. "See those two tall posts back there? One is on the beach above the high water mark, and the other is further back next to the village. We want to line the canoe up with those two posts. We use them when it is foggy like this to point the way to Anacapa. It is important we start out with a good heading. Then we must try to maintain as true a course as possible."

Looking back, Pablo was surprised to see how far they had come from shore. It was difficult to judge the speed of the canoe, but it seemed to him that it traveled the pace of a trotting horse. The village looked very small. Malak and Luhui, standing alone, looked even smaller. The dark line of brush beyond the village faded into the fog. He could see nothing of the coastal plain or the hills beyond. Before long, he could only make out four horizontal lines: the gray fog, the dark brush, the tan stretch of beach, and the white line of surf. The boy looked around him at the smooth, olivine sea. He stared down over the gunwale, but could see little below the water's opaque, gleaming surface. All about him the calm sea spread until it joined with the moist, clinging grayness above. Swells drew in from the west and thrust themselves against the starboard bow.

"Look sharp, boy," said Shup. "Keep paddling. We want to make good time while the sea is calm. You must establish a steady rhythm with your paddling. You won't tire as fast that way. Listen to me, and paddle with the rhythm."

Oh, the TIDE comes in
And the TIDE goes out
The SWELLS rise up and
The SWELLS die down
Paddle HARD my friends

243

Paddle HARD

Oh, the FOG comes in
Then the FOG burns off
Oh, the WIND comes up
And the WIND dies down
Paddle HARD my friends
Paddle HARD…

Shup stopped chanting when all had settled into the rhythm. Pablo paddled easily. He enjoyed it, and was glad to be active. It helped keep him warm. As they got out into the deeper water of the Santa Barbara Channel, the sea lost its olivine cast and took on a purple-blue hue. The rise and fall of the boat reminded Pablo of the motion of a horse. The light, streamlined canoe glided almost effortlessly over the surface of the sea, bobbing from side to side as it rose and fell with the angled swells. After paddling for some time, Pablo glanced behind him. He was not altogether surprised to see nothing but fog. All about him, to the front, to the sides, and now behind, there was nothing but fog – fog merging with the sea until they became one. The only sound was the rhythmic slap and scoop of their blades on the water. The eerie seascape made Pablo feel infinitely small, and more than a little frightened. He had never been out of sight of land before.

Over his shoulder he asked, "Shup, how can you tell if we are still headed in the right direction?"

"Look there, boy – see the swells? They are coming out of the west. Our heading is southwest. I keep the swells coming in at the same angle off our bow. I do it by occasionally using my paddle as a tiller. It is a matter of experience."

As time passed, Pablo became aware of sea life around him. First he saw a flock of brown pelicans gliding low over the water, heading towards some unknown destination to the east. Then he noticed a pod of dolphins rising and plunging among the distant swells, their dark dorsa glistening in the gray light. The dolphins spied the tomol and swam over to investigate. They swam effortlessly alongside the canoe, breeching occasionally as they peered at the paddlers. Their small, black eyes gleamed above mouths that turned up at the corners making them look as if they were smiling. The dolphins seemed friendly and playful as they accompanied the voyagers. Then they spied a patch of fluttering water in the distance – a school of fish. The dolphins left the canoe then and went loping off in its direction. A little later, Pablo watched as a large circling sea bird, a cormorant, dove straight down out of the sky and plunged into the sea. Seconds later it emerged with a small fish dangling from its beak. The dark-headed bird threw back its head, tossed the fish in the air, opened its mouth wide, and then deftly caught it and swallowed it whole.

As the morning lengthened, the fog began to lift, and the wind and swells to freshen. Several times the bow struck low down on the moving swells, sending jets of spray into the faces of the paddlers. Occasionally, water splashed over the high gunwales, and sloshed about the bottom of the canoe.

"Pablo," said Shup, "see that wooden scoop behind you, under the spreader? It is a bailer. Use it to scoop up the water. Throw it overboard. No, not on that side – downwind!"

Up until now, Inigua had knelt in the bow looking straight ahead, paddling steadily, but now his arms and shoulders were beginning to tire. He was strict with himself, however, and refused to acknowledge his body's growing discomfort. He now begrudgingly accepted the wisdom of Malak's decision to send Shup with them. He had resented it at first, but now he knew it was the right thing. He also knew that before long he would have to rest. He didn't think he could keep this pace up much longer. His shoulders felt the worst. It was as though they were being prodded with hot metal rods. He felt too the old familiar ache in his knees and the painful pressure on the top of his feet.

Pablo was feeling the effects of the cramped position too, and the hard work of paddling. His arms and shoulders began to stiffen and burn with a dull fatigue. Both he and Inigua began to fall off the set rhythm of the paddling. Noticing this, Shup reached behind him and withdrew a small packet from his sealskin bag. He said, "Why don't you two rest for a little while. Go ahead, ship your blades. I will keep paddling to maintain our heading. Pablo, take this." He handed the boy the packet. "There is something to eat in there. They are little bars made from chia seeds and honey. Take one for yourself and give one to grandfather up in the bow. They will revive you and give you energy to continue. You'd best drink some water too."

As Shup continued his relentless paddling, the old man and the boy refreshed themselves. Inigua finished his crunchy, sweet bar and scooted around so he could speak to Pablo.

"How are you doing, joven?"

"I am better now. It is nice to rest a little, eh, señor? We must have paddled for a solid hour and a half. How do you feel?"

"Better too. We must be nearly half way across." He glanced over his shoulder. "Look there. You can see Anacapa up ahead."

Through the thinning fog, Pablo saw the long, low outline of a purple island floating on a sea of gray.

"It looks like one island," said Inigua, "but it is really three: East, Middle, and West Anacapa. They lie very close together."

To Pablo, Anacapa looked like some vast sea serpent basking on an imaginary sea. On the left, at the eastern-most tip, was the head. It was a large arched rock penetrated by an open hole that resembled an eye. The

245

serpent's long body extended to the west. It was flat on top for a good deal of its length, and then there were undulations as it tapered up and down to a rocky tail in the west.

Inigua and Pablo drank water from a sealskin bota and rested for a while longer. Then they took up their paddles once more. Shup set the pace.

Oh, the SUN comes up
Then the SUN goes down
And the STARS come out
While the MOON shines down
Paddle HARD my friends
Paddle HARD…

When he saw that his shipmates had settled into the rhythm, Shup took his own break from paddling. He leaned back against his sea bag, relaxing his massive, sweat-glistened shoulders and arms. The boy and his mentor paddled on as he drank water and rested. From here on, they took turns paddling and resting every half hour as the miles glided under the hull of the tomol.

The three islands of Anacapa grew before them. East Anacapa now lay dead ahead. Pablo could see its rocky cliffs clearly, a dark line running along the bottom where the waves surged, and its upper reaches whitewashed with guano. The island's tilting flat top was bursting with green growth and gaudy yellow wildflowers. The mountainous forms of Middle and West Anacapa lay off the starboard bow.

Shup said, "Inigua, do you want to stop and rest at Anacapa, or do you want to go straight on to Santa Cruz?"

Inigua glanced to his right. He could just barely make out the shadowy outline of Santa Cruz Island emerging from the thinning fog. "We will lose time if we stop," he said, "though it would be a welcome relief. If you were not with us I would certainly stop. But you paddle well, Shup, and this day seems a good one for the crossing. What do you think?"

"For this time of year it is indeed a good day. Though you never know what might happen as the day advances. Conditions can change quickly, as you well know, grandfather. But the fog lingers, and the sea is still relatively calm. If this weather holds, we could make it to Santa Cruz without much problem. Where do you want to go on Santa Cruz, Swaxil or Kaxas?"

"*Swaxil*, on the eastern end. It is the closest. Although making the crossing without stopping will be difficult for the boy and me, I think we should try. Are you feeling strong?"

"Strong enough," said Shup. "I will change course then." He brought the tomol's bow around to the west, and headed directly into the approaching swells.

An hour later, the dark mass of Santa Cruz rose prominently before them. The high volcanic spine of the interior climbed into a lifting sky. The highest peak, Picacho Diablo, scratched the underbelly of the clouds.

As they approached the strait between Anacapa and Santa Cruz, the swells grew larger, and a strong current began to swirl about the canoe. The current was confused, first pulling one way, then another. As the canoe advanced, the waters became more turbulent. High peaks and low valleys began to form, and a gusty wind skimmed the crests and filled the air with spray. Shup, who had been resting, took up his paddle again.

"Now we must work hard," he said. "This is the difficult part. Once we are in the lee of the island things will calm down. But right now, my friends, look sharp."

Summoning the last of their stamina, Inigua and Pablo paddled as though their lives depended on it. The strait was tumultuous, and the canoe repeatedly took on water over the gunwales. Several times Pablo had to stop paddling and bail. The wind swirled about them, sending Inigua's long white hair flying in all directions. Pablo had never been so frightened in his life. The massive swells, surrounding them on all sides, seemed at every moment about to overwhelm them. Their small craft, buffeted and reeling, was only saved by its buoyancy and the steady flow of its forward momentum. Shup saw to it that their bow met each swell head on.

Amid the howling wind, Pablo, cold and shivering from repeated drenching, was reduced to a state of near catatonic fear. He cowered between the bundles of cargo, convinced that he was about to die. He had never felt so helpless. And he dreaded what was to be the worst death he could ever imagine: drowning in this cold, suffocating brine, and then sinking into the dark, hideous depths as sharks tore at his flesh.

Inigua glanced back at the boy's pale face and saw the animal fear in his eyes. "Do not lose heart, boy. Pick up your paddle. We need your help." At this urging, Pablo somehow found it in himself to comply.

A quarter of an hour of unremitting struggle brought them out of the maelstrom and into relatively calm water once again. They continued to paddle, calling on their last reserves, as Santa Cruz loomed before them. The precipitous cliffs at its eastern end rose straight up out of the sea. They passed the eastern tip of the island, San Pedro Point, and followed the north coast towards the west. In the lee of the island now, the wind abated, and the swell diminished rapidly. The paddling, despite their exhaustion, was easy. As if to mark the end of their ordeal, the midday sun broke through the clouds and shone down on their weary limbs. They had been paddling now for over five hours.

They sidled along the north side of the island, coming so close they could hear the surf breaking along its rocky shore. Before long they sighted an indentation in the coast where a stream flowed out of a narrow valley surrounded by high hills.

"The Bay of Scorpions," announced Shup. "The village of Swaxil was here once, by that stream there."

They coasted into the calm waters of the bay and drew in near the mouth of the stream. Shup called a halt, and waited until there was a lull in the waves. "Now we go," he said.

They paddled in, thrust forward by swells, until they felt the tomol scrape the sandy bottom. Inigua looked back and smiled tiredly to his companions. "Congratulations, compadres. That was a fine crossing. Shup, you are man of great strength and courage, a true man of the sea."

"Taney, grandfather. Pablo, get out and steady 'Sopo' while Inigua and I unload."

The two tired men carried the cargo ashore, Inigua stumbling several times on his way to and from the beach. When the tomol was empty the three of them half carried, half dragged it up onto the cobble and sand beach. Then Pablo and Inigua fell down prostrate on the sand and lay gasping. Shup, looking like a giant, stood gazing along the beach.

"The tide is up now," he said. "I think we can safely leave 'Sopo' where she is. Shall we make camp by the stream?"

"Soon," said Inigua. "'Just a little rest first."

When the old man and the boy were somewhat recovered, the three picked up what they could carry of their belongings and proceeded inland along the stream. They chose a level spot above the beach and set their parcels down.

It was on his return to the beach to fetch more gear that Pablo noticed the bones. They were scattered over a large area along the beach and alongside the stream. Some of them glinted on the surface; others lay half-buried in the sand. They looked old, brittle, sun-bleached. They had obviously been here for a long time, picked over and scattered by seagulls and other scavengers. Pablo wondered what kind of animals they were. He was about to ask, when he noticed a human skull among the litter. He gasped, and looked closer. It was lying on its side. There was a large hole in the back of the head, and, looking closer, Pablo saw that there was something alive inside – a large hermit crab.

Pablo looked about him, and saw the white globes of other skulls scattered about, many of them broken, or with holes gaping. He began to distinguish hip bones, leg bones, rib cages. They were everywhere. Pablo looked questioningly at his two companions. They had been silently watching him. They looked back grimly.

"Murdered," said Inigua. "Men, women, children. All of them murdered."

248

37

SANTA CRUZ

"These people, the people of Swaxil, were killed fifteen years ago," said Inigua. "They were cut down with rifles, clubs, and axes. Their murderers were Aleut Indians from the far north who came here on a Russian ship. They had been carried here from Alaska to hunt sea otter. But when they arrived they found that most of the otters were already hunted out. Their Russian masters were angry and frustrated. They blamed the lack of game on the islanders.

"This assumption was false, of course. We Chumash had been hunting sea otters for centuries, taking only what we needed, and there was never a shortage. Their numbers only declined when foreigners started coming every summer and taking them by the hundreds. They took them for their pelts, which were then sold to make fur coats for rich people. The Russians, Americans, and Spaniards had only themselves to blame. But they did not see it.

"In the years leading up to this massacre, whenever the people of Swaxil saw a hunting ship sail into this bay, they would run up that valley into the hills and hide until the foreigners had departed. They had learned this lesson by hard experience. But this time the Russians were determined to eliminate them. They landed a party of armed men about five miles to the west. These ones came overland, through the interior, and lay in wait above the village. Their ship then sailed into this bay. Small boats were lowered with armed men. The people of Swaxil fled up the valley, and were ambushed there. They ran back, only to be caught between these two parties and killed, one by one. The females suffered outrage before they died."

Pablo looked about him in horror. The silence that followed was finally broken when he said, "I don't think I want to camp here, señor."

Inigua and Shup looked at one another. Inigua sighed. "I do not think we have a choice, Pablo, at least not today. I, for one, am too tired to paddle any more. What do you say, Shup?"

"If being here troubles the boy, why don't we camp back in that valley alongside the stream?" Shup saw Inigua frown. "Or we could stay near the coast but higher up, away from the beach." Pointing, he said, "There is a ridge up there on the other side of the stream."

"That sounds better to me," said Inigua. "I do not want to camp back in the valley. I want to be able to look out and see if anyone approaches from the sea. If Tico is somehow able to follow us I want to know before he gets here. We can then escape and lose ourselves on the island. It is surly big enough. What do you think, Pablo?"

"I...I..." Pablo's shoulders sagged. "Oh, all right, señor. But why is it these people were never buried?"

"Who would bury them?" asked Inigua. "Certainly not the Aleuts or their Russian masters. After this massacre all the remaining islanders were evacuated by the Spaniards and taken to live at the missions."

"Why can't we bury them?" asked Pablo.

"How?" said Inigua. "Just look – there are so many. There must be a hundred or more. It would take a long time for anyone to bury them. And we have nothing with which to dig. Come. Let us do as Shup suggests."

The three mariners hauled their gear up to the ridge above the curving bay. They found a level spot and raised the tent. As soon as it was secure, Inigua crawled inside with a bota of water and his blankets. He lay down, and said, "Forgive me, but I can do no more. I must rest now."

The afternoon wind blew along the Channel sweeping away the remains of the fog, leaving only a thin haze in its place. Pablo looked out across the waters at the vague outline of the California coast some twenty miles to the north. It seemed so distant, like another world altogether, a lost world inhabited only by memories. He gazed about him at the silent, forlorn emptiness of Santa Cruz Island and felt a fathomless melancholy.

Shup said, "Haku, Pablo. Why don't you and I go catch some fish for supper? I know a good place by those rocks to the west. We might find some abalone too."

Although exhausted from paddling, Pablo knew he could not sleep, and he could think of nothing better to do with himself. They left Inigua behind and made their way towards the rocks. Shup carried his knife, a bone wedge, fishing line and hooks, and a small harpoon.

"There are a lot of fish and shelled animals in this bay," said Shup. "That is one reason there was a large village here. It is also nicely situated as a trading center. But the main reason people lived here was to mine the deposits of chert that lie close by."

"Chert? What is chert?"

"It is a kind of stone, something like quartz. It is brittle, and chips easily. It can be worked to produce points with sharp cutting edges. The people here made tiny drill bits from it."

"Why did they do that?"

"You know about shell bead money, don't you, Pablo? The people on this island were the ones who made it. In the old days they traded it to the mainland for things they needed, things they could not get here. The people on the mainland traded it in turn with everyone else. The islanders needed tiny drills so they could make holes in the beads for stringing them together. First they would take pieces of broken Olivella shell and grind off the edges to make them round. Then they would drill holes in them and string them

250

together. Finally, they would roll the strung beads across a stone slab until they were all the same size."

"That sounds like a lot of work, Shup."

"I'm sure it was. But they were making something out of nothing – and they were making money. The strung beads served the same purpose as the coins and pesos of the Mexicans. And by making something of worth, these islanders made it easier for everyone else to trade. Imagine how hard it would have been to just barter one thing for another. Say you were a hunter and had a deer hide you wanted to trade for some fish. How many fish would you get in exchange? Well, let's say a tanned deer hide was worth a strand of beads long enough to wind two times around your hand. A large basket of fish might be worth one turn. So the fisherman would take the hide in exchange for the fish, and give one turn of beads as change."

"Ah, I see now," said Pablo. "That is clever."

"Yes. Then the deer hunter could go trade the turn of beads for something else he wanted, like obsidian from the Yokuts, or honey from the Aliklik."

Shup led him along the shoreline, pointing out where to find shellfish when the tide was low. He showed him where fish could be caught by the kelp beds close to shore. He cautioned him about being caught unawares by swells when fishing from the rocks. He pointed out to him where to find eggs from sea birds, and where seals sometimes hauled ashore.

Shup caught a small crab among the rocks. He broke it open and used its flesh to bait a V-shaped hook. Above the hook, tied to the line, was a small, grooved stone used as a sinker. Twirling the line about his head, Shup cast the jig out into open water between the rocks and a raft of kelp. They waited. After a time, Shup gathered in the line and cast it in a different spot. Pablo sat on a boulder nearby.

Shup watched Pablo out of the corner of his eye. The boy was staring out across the wind-swept Channel looking tired and listless. Shup said, "I am going home tomorrow, Pablo. And while you and I are here by ourselves, I want to ask you a favor."

"What is it, Shup?"

"I want to ask you to take good care of the old man when I'm gone." Pablo looked up at him with mild surprise. He was used to Inigua taking care of him.

Shup continued, "I could not help noticing how much he suffered in the crossing. He is not young like you and me. It was a brave thing that he did. And I think he did it for you. I know I speak for my whole family when I say that we would hate to see anything happen to Inigua. He is a great man. And it is a great shame he has no family to care for him. Can you do it, Pablo, for all of us?"

"I would be honored to take care of Inigua. He means everything to me."

251

"He will be tired for a few days, I think. Please do what you can for him – do the big things, and the little things too."

"I will do everything I can, Shup."

"One last thing, Pablo."

"Yes?"

"Don't tell him I asked you."

Just then, Shup felt a strong jerk on his line. He held on firmly and slowly drew the line in hand over hand. When his catch was close in, he saw that it was a sea bass. Once he had the flapping fish on shore he dispatched it with a blow to the head. He then showed the boy how to scale and clean it.

"This is a nice little catch," said Shup. "It is nearly ten pounds – plenty for our supper tonight. Remember this place, Pablo. It is a good fishing spot, and at low tide you can find abalone, mussel, lobster, and crab among the rocks. I will leave this bone wedge with you. It will come in handy collecting shellfish. I'm sure Inigua knows how to cook all those things.

"You might ask him to show you about kelp too. There are certain kinds that are edible. It makes good eating once you get used to it. We'd better go back now and get a fire started."

Pablo gathered an armload of driftwood on the way back to camp. The sun was lowering in the sky by the time they had the fire going. Inigua still lay sleeping in the tent. Shup showed Pablo how to de-bone the fish, and then fillet it. He seasoned it with salt and pepper and herbs from their supplies.

"One thing you need to keep in mind, Pablo: there are many hungry birds around here – seagulls, eagles, ravens, shrikes, blue jays and many more. The most troublesome are the gulls. Look at them up there, and all around us. They are always hanging around looking for something to eat. If you don't pay attention they will swoop down when your back is turned and steal your supper. There are a lot of mice and foxes around too, so you can't leave food out, especially at night. Hang any leftover food up high."

"What about snakes, Shup? Are there rattlesnakes?"

"No rattlers, only gopher snakes, racers, and a kind of night snake. None of them are poisonous though. The only things you have to look out for are scorpions. They can give you a nasty sting. But they probably won't kill you. Just be sure to check your bedding before you sleep. One good thing – you don't have to worry about big animals like mountain lion or bear – there are none."

When the fire was reduced to a bed of red coals, Shup propped a large frying pan over the circle of stones. He added some tallow, and, when it was melted, laid on the flour-dusted fillets. As the delectable smell of fresh sizzling fish began to spread, Inigua awoke and peered from the tent with surprise and delight.

They feasted sumptuously as the sun bent down behind the mountains of the island and secretly kissed the sea. Scraps from their simple meal were tossed over the ledge near their campsite, where they were immediately set upon by squabbling seagulls.

Exhaustion then claimed the weary mariners for her own. Full-bellied and content, the trio settled down in the tent and was sound asleep before darkness brought an end to twilight.

* * * * *

Pablo awoke to the silver glow of hazy sunlight shining on their canvas cocoon. He looked sleepily around the interior. Inigua was still dozing, but Shup's place was empty. Pablo got up and went out to the now lifeless fire pit. Shup was nowhere to be seen. The boy made his way to the ledge that overlooked the bay. The beach below was vacant but for the silent, glistening bones. Using his hand to shade his eyes, he gazed out across the Santa Barbara Channel. He saw the red tomol several miles offshore, bearing northeast across a calm and windless sea.

38

BRAIDING

Inigua saw 'Alahtin standing naked, high up on the edge of the cliff. He watched her look down the vertical rock face and shudder. She glanced once behind her, squared her shoulders, and stood gazing resolutely across the rugged, moonlit landscape. She took a deep breath, and then gathered herself for the leap. Inigua, standing below her in the canyon, felt himself mouthing the word, "Noooo!" But, inexplicably, no sound issued forth. It was as though he had been suddenly struck dumb. He could feel his face contorted with effort, but still, no sound came. Then 'Alahtin, in her nakedness, launched herself into the void.

Inigua jerked awake, and was finally able to scream, "Noooo!"

Within seconds Pablo appeared at the entrance of the tent, his face a troubled mask. "What is it, señor? What's wrong?"

Inigua stared wildly at him. "Oh, Pablo, it is you." His body quivered as he buried his face in his hands. When he spoke again it was with a voice twisted with anguish, "Oh, my. How dreadful."

Pablo reached out to him and said, "Qué paso, señor? Are you hurt? Are you in pain?"

Inigua lowered his hands and shook his head. Pablo watched intently as the old man slowly regained his composure. Finally, Inigua said, "Ah, boy, I am sorry to have alarmed you. It was only a bad dream."

"A dream, señor? Dios mio. You scared me half to death."

"I am sorry, Pablo. I was dreaming about my daughter. Oh, the poor, dear girl. Why did she have to do it?" Inigua began to shake involuntarily, his face a miasma of twisted fissures.

Pablo quickly entered the tent and knelt down next to him. He put his arm around the old man's shoulders. "Don't worry, señor. Everything is all right. It was only a dream."

"It was more than a dream, Pablo. It really did happen. Only I was not there. Why did this vision visit me now?"

"Come, señor. Come outside. The sun is shining. You will feel better out there." The boy helped Inigua to his feet and led him into the sunlight. Still shaken, Inigua looked around the bright island morning. Its calm beauty mocked his frailty, and made him feel ashamed of himself. Feigning normalcy, he asked, "Where is our friend, Shup?"

"He is gone, señor. Come over here by the fire pit. Sit on this blanket here. I have made you some tea. Sit. Drink."

Inigua did as he was told.

"Do you want to tell me about it, señor?"

Inigua sipped his tea. He sighed and said, "The dream was about my daughter, 'Alahtin. She was a lovely girl, a girl of just sixteen when she died."

"Ay Dios mio, señor. How did it happen?"

"I…I cannot give words to it. Not yet. Please, forgive me, Pablo. I will tell you in a little while. Just let me be for now."

Pablo went to the small grove of ironwood trees below the camp and lowered their food bundle. He removed some strips of jerky and carried them to Inigua. "Here, have something to eat. You will feel better."

Inigua tore off a piece of dried meat with his teeth, and said, "So, our friend went home?"

"Sí, señor. Early this morning."

"He is a good one, that Shup. He paddles like the men of old." Inigua ate, and drank tea.

"How are you feeling now, señor?"

"Better, but I am still tired. My muscles are stiff and sore. How about you, Pablo?"

"I am a little the same, but I feel fine. I was just going down and see if I can find some abalone among the rocks."

"You will dive?"

"Not unless I have to, señor. Shup lent me this bone wedge to pry them off the rocks."

"Bueno. Take the bucket with you. Fill it with sea water and put your catch in it. You want to keep abalone alive till you are ready to cook. But, listen, when you get back we need to start work on your reata. Where are the rawhide strings?"

"Here, señor, in this sack."

"While you are gone I will ready them for braiding. There is no reason to delay our work any longer. There have been too many interruptions already."

"Maybe you should just rest, señor."

"No. It is better that I keep busy. You go now. Be sure to ask permission from the animals before you take them."

When the boy returned two hours later he found Inigua looking calm and collected. By all appearances he was his old self again. With a glance, Pablo saw that he had finished applying a second coat of tallow to the strings.

Inigua looked up when he heard Pablo approach. He appraised the boy's blood-shot eyes, his downcast expression, and the empty wooden bucket dangling from his hand. "What happened?" he said. "No luck?"

"No luck at all, señor. The tide was too high and I could see no abalone. I dove, but I could not get any."

"Sometimes that happens no matter how hard you try. Try again when the tide goes out. How deep did you dive, boy?"

255

"I don't know. As deep as I could go. Maybe ten feet."

"Maybe you need to dive deeper, or try a different spot. I will go with you next time."

"But now we have nothing to eat, señor."

"It is of no consequence. While you were gone I decided to go on a fast."

"A fast? But why?"

"I want to take the Chumash sacrament."

"What is that?"

"Momoy."

"You mean *Toloache*?"

"They are the same."

"Why do you want to do that, señor?"

"I sense a great change coming. I want to see what it is. Momoy will show me."

"Can I take the sacrament too?"

"If you desire it. But it is no small thing. It will change you."

"You told me before about the coming-of-age ceremony, señor. You said all young people used to take the sacrament so that they might become adults. I want the same thing."

"That is your choice, Pablo. But you must realize this is not a game. It is serious business. It must be done properly in order for you to benefit from it."

"As always, señor, I will do whatever is necessary."

"We shall see, Pablo. You had better think about it before you decide. For one thing, you need to understand that to prepare properly for the sacrament it is necessary to cleanse the body, both inside and out. First comes the fast. You drink only water for several days to cleanse the inside. Then you visit the sweat lodge, and afterwards wash your body and hair in the stream. Only then are you suitable for the sacrament.

"But let us set this topic aside for now, Pablo, and talk of the reata. The strings are ready. Shall we begin braiding?"

"Sí, señor."

"All right. The first thing we need to do is to make *tamales*."

"Please, señor, do not make a joke. Do not talk of food, for we are going on a fast."

"I am not speaking of that kind of tamale, silly boy. Tamale is what vaqueros call a special coil they make for braiding. Anyone who has ever braided knows that as the work progresses, the loose ends of the strings begin to form into a braid of their own. This reverse braid must be repeatedly unraveled. Often the strings become knotted and tangled. But by first gathering the loose strings into tamales, the braider avoids the tangling. He can draw out the quantity of string needed for braiding from the center without destroying the shape of the tamale or causing it to collapse. I will show you. Right now we need to arrange a good working place. Since braiding a reata takes considerable time, we should find a place in the shade."

They discovered a sheltered area under a stand of ironwood trees nearby that suited their purpose. The ground was level, and a section of exposed root provided a sturdy place to which they could secure the strings while braiding. They staked out an old blanket on the ground before the root.

"This work surface," explained Inigua, "will keep dirt out of the braid. Come here and stand on the blanket next to me."

Inigua took up one of the coils of rawhide string, and handed the other to Pablo. He said, "First we want to find the middle of each string. Do it like this." He loosened the two ends from his string, and, holding them in one hand, dropped the coil onto the blanket. Pablo followed suit. "Now," said Inigua, "pull the two lines through your other hand until you come to the loop at the end. That will be the halfway point of the string."

When they had both accomplished this, Inigua tied his loop around a low overhanging limb. Pablo did the same. "Now for the tamales," said Inigua. "Separate the two strings hanging down, and hold one of them like this." Inigua grasped the end of the string in one hand near his waist. "Coil the dangling string in a circle about a foot in diameter, and when you bring it up to the top, wrap it around the hanging string, like this." He made half a turn around the string suspended from the limb. He shifted the coil to his other hand and let the dangling string drop down to the blanket. "Now, this time, when you bring the string up again in the coil, go around the hanging string in the opposite direction as the first. Switch the coil to your other hand, and then we just continue in this manner, first one way, then the other."

Pablo followed his example and began coiling his string onto the hanging piece. Within minutes they were both nearing the end of the first string. "Now," said Inigua, "you just make several turns around the coil with the remainder. Make the wrap tight, but not too tight. You do this to tie the tamale together so that it holds its shape. Just tuck the bitter end into wrap."

"The bitter end?"

"Yes, that one in your hand. The opposite end, the end tied to the limb, is called the standing end. It is named so because it does not move. The standing end becomes the working end when we start to braid. But right now, let us make another tamale with the second string. When we are done we will have four strings and four tamales."

They draped the first tamales over the limb and started on the second. When they were done, Inigua untied the loop from the limb and directed Pablo to do the same. Then he took Pablo's and held the two middles together. He knelt down and tied them to the exposed root.

"Bueno. Now we are ready to braid. Have you ever done this before, Pablo?"

"No, señor."

"It does not matter. It is easy. It just takes a little practice. I will show you. But first we must gather everything we will need: the bone fid, some short leather ties, and some water to quench our thirst."

When all was assembled, they sat down in front of the root to begin making the reata.

"I will start by showing you how it is done," said Inigua. "Then we will take turns braiding. It is important that you concentrate, Pablo, and that you do not rush the work. There is no need to worry about mistakes. They are easy to undo and fix. The important thing to remember is that you keep tension on all four strings while you braid."

Inigua began by tying a short string of rawhide tightly around the standing end, near the root. "This is to ensure that the braid does not loosen when we untie the standing end," he said.

Inigua took two braiding strings in his left hand and two in his right.

"Uh, señor, before you start, how does one tell the strings apart? They all look the same."

"It does not matter. The pattern is what matters. You see we have four strings. The two on the outside are the halves of one string, as are the two in the middle."

"But what will we call them?"

"We do not need to call them anything. But if you insist, call them anything you like. Go ahead, boy, name them."

"I don't know what to name them."

"Well, think of something. Call them 1, 2, 3, 4."

"No, I don't like that. You say the two strands on the outside are of the same string. Why don't we call them Inigua and Uria? You are both my mentors. Inigua on the left, Uria on the right."

"As you wish. And what about these two in the middle?"

"Why don't we call the one on the left Pablo, and the other…"

"What?"

"I don't know."

"How about 'Akiwo?" said Inigua with a twinkle in his eye.

Pablo blushed, but then broke into a grin. "Ha, ha. That is a good one, señor. Inigua and Uria, and Pablo and 'Akiwo. Ha, ha."

"You have an odd way of naming strings, boy."

"Well, señor, if you have a better idea, you name the strings. We need to call them something so I can tell them apart."

"I do not care what we call them. We will do as you suggest. Now, here is how you begin: first take Inigua and Uria, the ones on the outside, and cross them, with Inigua over the top, and place them inside the other two. Now I take up Pablo and Uria in my left hand, Inigua and 'Akiwo in my right. From here on you will always have these same strings in the same hands.

"Now to start braiding: first we begin with the outer string in my left hand, Pablo. He goes behind Uria, under 'Akiwo, over Inigua, and returns to the left hand, this time ending up to the inside of Uria. Now we do the same movement with the right hand – 'Akiwo, who is on the outside, goes behind Inigua, under Uria, and over Pablo, ending up on the inside of Inigua. We have now done the identical movement with each hand. That is called a step. You just keep repeating this step over and over. You always have the same two strings in each hand, but the strings change position from inside to outside with each step."

"Ay, this is confusing, señor."

"Only until you do it yourself. It is simpler than you think. Watch me again. Notice that I am keeping the rough side of the string, the fleshy side, on the inside of the braid. The smooth side is on the outside. That is how it should be.

"Now, before I continue, I take the tamales and untwist the strings so they do not become tangled. Now I start again: Uria, who is now on the outside, goes behind Pablo, under Inigua, over 'Akiwo, and returns, this time to the inside of Pablo. Then with the right hand, Inigua, who is outside, goes behind 'Akiwo, under Pablo, and over Uria. He returns, but to the inside of 'Akiwo. Now we have taken two steps and are back where we began."

"I am going insane, señor."

"Ha. How can you tell? I will do a few more steps. Forget about the names, Pablo. Just observe the pattern."

Pablo watched closely as the old man worked. By the time he had completed the fourth step the reata was beginning to take shape. Pablo could see a strong, rounded rope emerging from the standing end of the four strings, its surface patterned with smooth, evenly-spaced diamond shapes.

"Oooh, I like the look of that, señor. Can I try now?"

"Sí, Pablo. But first, hand me that bone fid. I need to tighten the braid."

Holding the four strings taut in his left hand, Inigua held the fid in his right. Starting at the standing end, he stuck the pointed end of the fid between each place where the strings crossed and pushed up, turning the braid as he worked to reach those on the back side. He moved down towards the working end, tightening as he went. When he reached the working end, he said, "While I hold this, Pablo, take one of those short pieces of rawhide and tie it around the bottom. That will keep the previous work tight." Pablo did so. "Now, before you try, boy, notice that we are running out of string with which to braid. When this happens we just draw some more out of the tamales, like this." Inigua took hold of one of them and pulled it away from the reata. Fresh string emerged from the top as it drew out one of the interior circles of the coil.

"Ah," said Pablo, "I see. That is most excellent, señor."

"Now you pull out the others, boy, and then start braiding."

259

Pablo's lips moved as he began braiding. He silently repeated the pattern – behind, under, over, and return inside. Behind, under, over, and return inside…

"That's right, boy. Just keep going like that, and try to keep the braid as tight as possible. When you have done a foot or so, stop and go over it with the fid. When all is tight, move the tie from where I stopped to where you stopped."

The two continued to take turns braiding, scooting backwards on the blanket as the reata lengthened. When they reached the edge of the blanket, Inigua untied the standing end, and re-tied the reata to the root near the working end. Then they continued to braid.

Midway through one of Pablo's turns he stopped and said, "Ay, señor, my hands are beginning to cramp."

"That is not unexpected. My hands are tired too. It is because we are working muscles we are not accustomed to using. Finish that step and we will give ourselves a rest."

When the boy was done, Inigua tightened the braid with the fid, and then moved the anchor tie to the end of the work. They scooted around on the blanket and gazed out across the Santa Barbara Channel as the afternoon wind whipped whitecaps up out of the blue. Pablo took turns shaking and massaging his own hands.

"I have a question, señor."

"What is your question, boy?"

"Actually, I have several questions."

Inigua sighed. "Why does that not surprise me? What do you need to know?"

"Well, among other things, I have been thinking about your daughter, the one you dreamed about this morning. Can you tell me what happened to her?"

Inigua looked off in the distance. "I will try."

39

THE DEVIL

The old man looked down at his stiffened hands. He clenched and unclenched them. "Sometimes your questions cause me pain, joven. This is one of those times."

"I'm sorry, señor. You don't have to answer if you don't want to."

"Well, no, I should probably tell someone the story of 'Alahtin before I die."

"You're not going to die, señor."

"Oh, no? That would be unique. Nevertheless, I am willing to tell you her story now. It might help you understand me better."

"I would like that, señor."

"Do you remember me telling you about the founding of Mission San Buenaventura, and about my learning Spanish and becoming a translator?"

"Sí, señor."

"My daughter was six at that time. As she grew up, so did the Mission-by-the-Sea."

"Pardon me for asking, señor, but how old were you then?"

"Already the interruptions begin. Well, I think I must have been in my mid-twenties. I had my wife Islay of course, and two young children, my son Xaua, and my daughter 'Alahtin. Anything else, boy?"

"I have never heard that Chumash word, 'Alahtin, señor. What does it mean?"

"It is our name for the full moon. We named her so because she was born by its light."

"What was she like, señor?"

"Listen, boy, I am trying to tell you a story. I will never get it told if you keep pestering me with questions. This I will tell you: she was the sweetest little girl you can imagine. She seemed always to be happy. Her giggles began at first light, like birdsong, and continued until we put her to bed at night. My daughter was beautiful, and had the most lively, sparkling eyes you ever saw. She was the light of my and Islay's lives in a time when dark changes grew up all around us."

"What changes were those, señor?"

"Please, Pablo. You asked me to tell you what happened to my daughter. I am trying.

"The changes I speak of were occurring at the mission. It grew very slowly at first. I remember that in those early years we were sometimes sent

261

away to fend for ourselves because the mission ran out of food and could not feed us. This was not a great burden for my family since we lived by the sea. It was another matter for those who had abandoned their homes elsewhere. But we were always summoned back with entreaties and promises, and with each passing year the mission grew stronger, and its grip on our lives more complete.

"As time passed, the Spaniards brought domestic animals from sister missions. These included not only horses and cattle, but sheep, goats, pigs, cats, and chickens. As these animals multiplied, my people were taught to tend them. The Spaniards brought trained craftsmen too: blacksmiths, leather workers, carpenters, candle makers, and so on. These people hailed from Mexico, mostly from Sonora and Sinaloa. They followed the route De Anza had discovered, and when they got here they set about teaching certain chosen Indians their skills.

"But in those early years we Chumash were mostly given common labor to perform. We dug irrigation ditches, plowed and sowed fields of grain, cultivated vegetable gardens, and constructed adobe walls to protect the crops from grazing animals. Later, we planted olive and grape orchards above the river. As the mission grew we were ordered to cut down untold numbers of fine old oaks and other trees to use for firewood and in construction. We built a temporary church, and dwellings for the Spaniards and the newly arrived gente de razón. We built granaries and warehouses and a tannery. We did all this under the watchful eyes of the padres and the iron hand of Sergeant Cota and the mission guard.

"From the beginning our people were beset by Spanish diseases: tuberculosis, measles, chicken pox, smallpox, and syphilis. They descended on us like buzzards from the sky. That is why the average neophyte only lived for six or seven years. They either died of disease or from the relentless work and unaccustomed food. My parents succumbed early on. As death took its toll, new recruits were rounded up in outlying villages to feed the labor needs of the growing mission."

"And what about 'Alahtin, señor?"

"Stop, Pablo. This is not an easy story for me to tell. You have to let me do it in my own way."

"'Sorry, señor."

"'Alahtin was oblivious to most of what was going on. She was just a child playing around and having fun in the world as she found it. That is what children do.

"While we adults stood in wonder at the transformation taking place in our land, a transformation initiated by the Spaniards but purchased with our own sweat, we could not but yearn for the easy life we once had. You have to understand, Pablo, that we Chumash had long enjoyed our leisure. This does not mean we were lazy. In the old days, when work was required, we went about it gladly, and with unbounded energy. And we took great

262

satisfaction in the success of our endeavors. We earned our leisure by applying our knowledge of how to live off the land and the sea. We followed the dictates of the seasons, and worked only when it was necessary. We had learned how to live well by following the time-honored ways, and we were for the most part content. Perhaps we were innocent, child-like in that way.

"But we were now starting to realize that despite the many improvements imposed on our world, the fact was our life had become an endless cycle of forced labor, intimidation, and the humiliation of being treated as second-class citizens in our own land. We took little joy in our accomplishments."

"But, señor, what about 'Alahtin?"

Inigua cocked his eye at the boy. "I'm coming to that part. Just be patient, boy. Or would you rather we just get back to the braiding and forget about it?"

"No, no, señor. Please continue."

"Discipline grew stricter as time went on. No one was allowed to leave without permission. Whippings silenced the malcontents, and anyone who ran away was hunted down and dragged back to the mission to be publicly flogged. The unrepentant were confined in stocks or had heavy wooden clamps attached to their feet when they worked in the fields. I know this, for I was one of them.

"During the first ten years of the mission I gained a reputation as a trouble maker. I was outspoken in my criticism of the Spaniards and their religion, and of what I perceived as their enslavement of my people. Neither corporal punishment nor confinement silenced me. It was during this period that Islay and I set a trap for the philandering Sergeant Cota. After he was caught and court-martialed, he was demoted and transferred to the presidio of Santa Barbara. Because of this and other things, the padres decided they needed to get rid of me too. A new rancho had been established up in the Aw'hai valley. I was sent there to get me out of the way."

"Why did they start a rancho so far from the mission, señor?" He immediately put his hand over his own mouth.

Inigua sighed. "If you must know, they were having problems with the cattle getting into the fields and orchards. The cattle also roamed the hills all around the mission and were difficult to round up. The Spaniards chose the Ojai valley because it was only a half a day's ride away, and since it is surrounded by mountains the animals were walled in, like they would be in a corral. May I continue now?"

"Sí, señor. Sorry."

"Islay and 'Alahtin were not allowed to go with me to Aw'hai. That was part of my punishment for being incorrigible. Meanwhile my son, Xaua, who was now a young man, continued living with his uncle Toma along the coast. He was allowed to stay outside the mission because he was a fisherman. His skills were needed to help feed the people."

263

Pablo almost asked another question but stopped himself just in time.

"Now, as you know, Pablo, when girls reach the age of twelve or thirteen they are taken to live in the monjerio along with all young unmarried women. This is done to protect them from boys and men. The coupling of unmarried people has always been considered a sin by the church. When I was sent to Aw'hai, 'Alahtin and her mother were taken into the monjerio. They spent their days spinning and weaving wool into blankets and clothing. At night they were confined behind high walls and locked doors with the other single women.

"When I first arrived in Aw'hai, La Matanza was just beginning. I spent the next three or four months, during 'the killing time,' slaughtering and skinning cattle. The following winter I was taught to ride a horse and do the work of a vaquero."

Pablo almost spoke, but bit his lip instead.

"Now, I can only relate the next part of the story as it was told to me. This is because I saw little of my family during this time. Islay told me that one day 'Alahtin met a boy of her own age at one of the periodic fiestas held at the mission. By all accounts he was a good-looking young fellow. His name was *Puk*, which means 'gray owl,' and he was the son of the chief of Matilija village. Islay told me 'Alahtin fell in love with him. My daughter, who had just turned sixteen, no doubt felt the same way I did about Islay when I was young.

"Puk and 'Alahtin began to see each other secretly. It is thought that she snuck out of the monjerio from time to time in order to do so. Eventually, they could no longer accept being separated and decided to run away together. One night he scaled the walls of the monjerio and carried her away. They hurried up the river to a canyon high above Matilija where they went into hiding. I only learned of this later, of course. With the help of an expert tracker, the soldiers of the mission guard eventually followed the runaways to their trysting place.

"They came silently upon the young lovers in the evening. The two were camped by the side of a stream next to the hot springs up there. Due to the sound of the running water, they did not hear the soldiers approach. They were surrounded in the growing darkness and ordered to surrender. The couple dashed across the stream and tried to escape. Musket fire rang out, and Puk fell, mortally wounded. It is said he died in my daughter's arms. As the Spanish soldiers closed in, 'Alahtin managed to elude them in the darkness. But they continued to pursue her. She made her way up into the mountains, only to find herself trapped at the edge of a high cliff.

"I can only imagine what 'Alahtin must have been feeling then. Her heart was no doubt broken, and she must have felt frightened and utterly alone. She would have known she only had two choices: one was to surrender and be taken to the mission to be flogged and imprisoned in the monjerio again; the other was to jump to her death. My darling girl chose the latter, and joined her lover in the canyon below."

A prolonged silence followed this telling. Inigua kneaded his stiffened hands.

Finally, Pablo spoke. "I'm sorry, señor. I should not have asked you."

"Never mind, boy. Every life has its sad tale, and every story has its price. But I would be remiss if I did not tell you the ending of this one."

"There is more? I thought 'Alahtin died."

"She did die. I felt like dying too when I heard about it. But it is what I did that brings this tale to an end."

"Tell me, señor. I must know."

"When word came to me at the rancho of what had happened, I was at first overcome with sorrow and remorse. But after a time my sorrow grew into anger, and my remorse became an undeniable urge for revenge. The following Sunday, during siesta time, and unbeknownst to the others, I rode down to San Buenaventura. I spent the evening collecting materials. I waited till long after the De Profundis bell had rung that night, and then made my way to the mission church. I confess to you now that I set it ablaze."

"No, señor, you didn't."

"I knew the church was at the very heart of the mission. I treated the mission as I would a dangerous beast that I sought to kill with an arrow or a lance. I went straight for the heart. Because everyone was asleep by then, the fire went undiscovered until it was too late. As the flames lit up the night sky I made my way back towards the river valley. As I fled, the church was engulfed in fire."

"Dios mio, señor. How could you do it?"

"It seems like another time now, Pablo, another life. But back then it seemed the only thing I could do. The mission guard quickly mobilized as the fire raged. Someone had seen me heading up the river, and the soldiers gave chase. I attempted to lose them by crossing the river and heading up into a side canyon, the one now called Diablo Canyon. The soldiers somehow picked up my trail and followed me there. That is when I set a second fire. This one blocked their advance and an advantageous wind blew it down in their faces. They returned to the mission with singed eyebrows, convinced they had witnessed the work of the devil. And maybe they had."

"I don't know what to say, señor."

"Then do not say anything. I returned to the rancho that night, and was present for roll call the following morning. My deed was never discovered, although there were suspicions. I went about my work as usual and waited for the mission to collapse. But this was not to be. Although it took many years, they constructed a new church in a different location. It is the one that stands there today. To me it stands as a testament to my failure, my failure to kill the beast."

265

40

RELIGION

Inigua scooted on his haunches over to the reata and took up the four strings. He undid the holding tie and began to braid. Neither he nor Pablo spoke for some time. By now the leather rope was over ten feet long and growing steadily between Inigua's gnarled hands.

"How long will my reata be when it is done?" asked Pablo.

"Oh, I would guess about fifty feet," said Inigua. "That is what you usually get from a steer's hide. But, of course, a fifty foot reata is longer than you need for working cattle. There is a benefit here, however, for when you use a reata every day on the rancho it gets a lot of wear and tear. The lasso-end is the part that takes the punishment. Sharp horns and hooves are what usually do the damage. If the strength of the reata is ever compromised, you must cut off the damaged end and attach a new *honda*. To do otherwise endangers both you and your horse."

"A honda? What's a honda?"

"That is what they call the eye of the working end. It is a small loop through which the reata passes to form the lasso. A honda is often reinforced with a leather boot, or wear-leather, so that it can withstand the frequent passing of the reata in and out. There are various types of hondas. I think the San Juan is the best. When we are finished braiding, we will make one and attach it to the working end. We must also decide on what to do with the bitter end. We can either tie a terminal knot in the shape of a knob, or perhaps create a decorative flail. I have always been partial to the Turk's-head knot myself. It forms a handsome knob that is useful in whacking reluctant animals. But there is something to be said for a flail as well. It looks nice, and resembles a tail on your reata. Flails are good for swatting flies and can be used like a quirt to flick your horse's flanks when you need instant speed. But the shape of the bitter end is really not all that important. It is more a matter of style. It is an expression of the vaquero's personality and preferences. It is, therefore, your choice to make, Pablo."

"Gracias, señor. I will think about it."

Inigua nodded, and worked on in silence. After a time, he said, "When we stopped braiding earlier you said you had several questions of me, boy. You asked first about my daughter, 'Alahtin, and I told you her story. I am curious about what else you wanted to know?"

"Ah, thank you for reminding me, señor. There is one thing that has puzzled me ever since I heard it. Do you remember yesterday morning, over in Hueneme, when we were getting ready to paddle?"

266

"Yes. What about it?"

"Do you remember the prayer Malak said before we set out?"

"I remember."

"Malak first prayed to Hutash, and then he called upon Saint Christopher to give us a safe crossing. How can Malak pray to a Chumash god and a Catholic saint at the same time?"

"That is an interesting question, boy. I do not know precisely how to answer it. But I will say this: it is not uncommon for our people to believe in both. Just because most of us were converted to Christianity does not mean we gave up the old religion."

"But, señor, Catholicism maintains it is the one and only true religion. If you are a Catholic, you cannot follow another religion."

"Obviously, you can," answered Inigua. "Malak does. I know many others who do as well. Even my wife, Islay, believed in both."

"But how can they do that, señor? I don't understand."

"I can only say that the Chumash are by nature a very religious people. Faith permeates our lives, both privately and publicly. But our beliefs are very different from those of Christians. For one thing, we do not truly have gods. We only have powerful beings. Some of them are good, and some, bad. We do not actually worship them. We honor them, beseech them, or fear them depending on their nature. We do not have a single god that we adore and pray to like they do in Christianity. We might fear or respect our deities; we might ask them to aid us; but we do not adore them as the Christians do.

"We consider them the cause of what happens in the world: the passing of day into night and back again, the changing of the seasons, the bounty or scarcity of rain and of game. We do not consider the gods flawless or almighty, for we know that they make mistakes. We know they have weaknesses, and that they are subject to caprice. They are influenced by emotion: anger, remorse, pity, loneliness, and all the others. They are like us in that way. We honor and flatter them because they are powerful. It is our fervent wish that they look kindly upon us.

"Our traditional religious observances are utilitarian in nature. We perform rituals on all notable occasions with the hope that we might influence the outcome. The birth of a child is one such occasion, as is the naming of the child, the coming-of-age ceremony, marriage, illness, recovery, or death. We also observe seasonal ceremonies, such as when the rattlesnakes emerge from hibernation, when the seed and acorn harvest has been completed, and, of course, the summer and winter solstices.

"Catholicism, on the other hand, is a religion of dispensation. Priests mete out the sacraments – baptism, confirmation, confession, and so on. They perform rituals called masses wherein they deliver sermons, arrange choir singing, command the recitation of prayers and the Doctrina. The only private part is the silent saying of prayers, prayers its converts are forced to

267

repeat as penance... either that or to beg for something. I was never much one for penance or for begging."

"But, señor, how can you believe in both religions?"

"I did not say I believed in either one, at least not all the time. There are times when I believe in nothing at all. I think religion is a human invention. It exists as an attempt to explain our existence and give meaning to the world around us. It also fulfills a useful purpose – to try to teach us the correct way to live our lives.

"Padre Uria once told me that there are many religions in the world besides Catholicism. But he refused to describe them in any great detail. He only condemned them all as being heretical. Since I know little of them, I cannot speak about them. I can only say that from what I have heard, they all seem to hold that they are the one true religion. And I ask you, Pablo, how can this be? Tell me, boy, which one speaks the truth? Or do they all speak the truth? Or do they all preach falsehoods?"

Pablo shook his head. "I do not know, señor."

"I have come to the conclusion that all religions are suspect."

"Why do you say that, señor?"

"Let me tell you a story to illustrate what I mean. One time when I was a little boy my mother got very sick. So my father, who was an important man in the village, sent for an 'antap. This 'antap, or priest, was also a medicine man. When he arrived at our 'ap I was playing outside and he did not notice me. I saw him put a small stone in his mouth and hide it there between his cheek and gums. Only then did he announce his presence to the household. I followed him inside and watched as he burned white sage in an abalone shell and bathed my mother in its smoke. Then he massaged her all over, chanting as he did so. He called upon the powers of the Sky People to save her. He began feeling around my mother's stomach, and eventually stopped at one spot. He pulled a cane tube from his carrying net, the tip of which he applied to that spot. Then he began to suck on the other end. He made a big show of sucking very hard. Suddenly, we heard a click, and a look of surprise came over his face. He sat back with a satisfied expression, and spat out the stone. He held it up and announced that this was what was causing my mother's illness, and that having removed it, he had cured her. I knew that he was lying, and it was then that I began to question the religion he claimed to represent."

"And what happened to your mother, señor?"

"Well, after a long time she did get better. But I knew it was not because of the stone."

"But, señor, that does not mean all religions are false. It only means the 'antap was a fake."

"Perhaps. But in hindsight I think he may have just been trying to make my mother believe she was going to get well. But he was a fake, just like the Catholic priests are fakes."

Pablo furrowed his brow. "I don't think priests are fakes, señor. Some might be. But even if they are, it doesn't mean the religion is false."

"How many times have you prayed to the Catholic God for something and not gotten it, Pablo?"

"Many times. But maybe it was just because God didn't want me to have it."

"Or maybe there is no God at all, and that is why praying did you no good. Look, boy, I am a simple man. I only know of the Chumash and Catholic faiths, and a little about some of our Indian neighbors' beliefs. Although I am suspicious of religion in general, I think there is one good thing they all have in common, and that is the stories they tell. There are many fine stories in Chumash lore, and some great ones in the bible. These stories are useful and instructive."

Pablo scratched his head. "I did not mean to question your beliefs, señor. But I still don't understand how Malak, or anyone else, can believe in two religions at the same time."

"Well, Pablo, I can only explain it by saying that the two run together."

"The two run together?"

"Yes. When one fails, the other helps."

"But how can this be?"

"Let me put it this way," said Inigua. He attached a holding tie to the braid, and then held his hands in front of him. He formed them into fists, but for a knobby brown forefinger extended from each. He moved one finger ahead of the other, and then moved the second ahead of the first. He repeated this action several times. "See? It is like two horses running neck and neck, alternating in the lead position. There is your answer."

"But...but..."

"Despite my reservations about religion, I do not condemn any one of them, least of all the Chumash religion. They all have their uses. There is one final thing I would say on the subject, Pablo, and this you should remember – it is not what religion gives you that is important, but what it does not take from you."

"Ah, señor, you are speaking in riddles now. I am truly lost. These matters of religion are growing fuzzy in my mind."

"In that we are the same."

*　　　　　*　　　　　*　　　　　*　　　　　*

"Then let us talk of something else, señor. I have another question for you."

"Another question! Is there no end to them?"

Just one more, señor."

"What is it?"

"I want to know why you wanted me to teach you how to read and write."

Inigua sighed. "At the time I thought I might write a book about the Chumash people. I wanted to tell their story so that the memory of them would survive after I and the other old ones are gone. Since that day I have told you much, and yet it is only a small part of their story. There is so much more to tell. But I realize now that it will never be told. There is no time left."

"Of course there is time, señor. I can still teach you."

"No, there is no time. And I am tired of talking now. My back hurts, and my hands are beginning to cramp up again. You braid for awhile, Pablo." As he moved aside he added, "Tighten my work with the fid before you start."

Pablo took up the bone fid and began snugging the strings where they crossed one another. Inigua chose a spot in a pool of sunlight along the edge of the blanket, and lay down on his back. He laced his fingers across his chest, and lay motionless. Pablo glanced over at his companion. Inigua's long white hair was splayed about his bony head, and his gaunt face was drawn with exhaustion. He looked very old just then, and the boy was reminded again that his mentor was seventy-five years old. Inigua took a deep breath and let it out slowly. He then lay very still, so still that Pablo began to feel anxious. It didn't seem as though the old man was breathing at all. He may have just died for all Pablo knew. The boy was about to reach out to him when he heard Inigua begin to snore softly.

Pablo sighed with relief, and turned back to the reata. As he worked, his stomach began to grumble with hunger. He'd had nothing to eat but a few slices of jerky early that morning. It was now well after midday. He glanced up at their bundle of food suspended from the tree. He was tempted to lower it and find something to eat. But he chastised himself for the thought. He had told Inigua he would fast too, and he was now committed to it.

41

FASTING

As the afternoon progressed, a stiff wind began to blow out in the Santa Barbara Channel, trailing with it a mantle of fog. An hour passed, and the sun dimmed to a vague silver ball suspended in a gray sky. Eventually the sun disappeared behind a shroud. Swirls of chill air rocked the ironwood trees and set their leaves to trembling. Pablo shivered at the sudden change in weather. He went to the tent and donned his coton and trousers. He returned with a blanket, which he gently spread over the sleeping Inigua.

Another hour passed before the old man began to stir. When his eyes finally fluttered open they gazed up at a darkened sky. He looked over at Pablo, who was still bent over his work. The boy was fully dressed, and now had a blanket draped over his head and shoulders.

"Brrrr," said Inigua, sitting up and wrapping his own blanket about him. "It is cold, eh, boy? Old Man Sun has gone home early. And now I feel a great hunger growing in my belly."

"I feel it too, señor. I am so hungry I could eat dirt."

Inigua laughed. "Ah, boy, it is good to hear you make jokes."

"I'm not joking. This is serious."

"It will be easier for you if you just accept the hunger, boy. Treat it like a distant cousin who has come to visit. Make friends with him. He will only be here for a couple of days. Then he will go away. Understand, though, that it will probably be another four or five days before you eat again."

"I don't like being hungry, señor. It brings me pain. And being cold like this is awful. I can't seem to get warm. My fingers are so cold I can barely braid."

"What you are feeling is normal when you fast. You cannot do anything about the hunger, but we can try to stay warm. Why don't you get up and move around? Go collect some firewood. That would be good. We will build a fire, and I will make us some nice hot tea. In fact, you had better make several trips for wood. I think it will be a long, cold night."

As Pablo attached the holding tie in preparation for leaving, Inigua said, "This is why we usually fast and perform the coming-of-age ceremony in the summertime. You don't get so cold then."

"That is little comfort to me now," said Pablo, petulantly.

As Inigua walked to the tent to dress more warmly, he smiled to himself. The boy was getting irritable. Things were going to get interesting now.

In the fading light of late afternoon, Inigua made tea using the bark of a shrub that grew above them on the hillside. It proved to have a powerful effect on both of them. No sooner had they finished drinking it and had warmed themselves by the fire, than they both were seized by a powerful need to void themselves. For the next hour they made frequent and urgent visits to the bushes.

When Pablo returned from his final trip, he sat down at the fire holding his head in one hand and his stomach in the other. "Ay, señor, what kind of tea was that? It turned me inside out like a glove."

"It is a tea made from the bark of what the Mexicans call *Cascara Sagrada*. It comes from a bush that others call the California Coffee plant. In the old days we used to drink it when we got plugged up from eating too many acorn cakes. I made it now so that we might purge ourselves."

"Purge ourselves? Am I not miserable enough without that, señor? Here I am starving to death on a deserted island; I am shivering with cold on one side and frying with heat on the other; I have an aching in my head as I have never had before; and now you force me to empty out my bowels in the most violent way. Ah, señor, how could you do this to me? I am truly in hell."

"Oh, don't be so dramatic, Pablo. Do you think that I am not suffering right along with you? Although I must say, I do not feel as badly as you claim. You must understand that this is a vital part of the ritual. You must pass through this in order that you become something other than what you are. Be brave, my boy, things will be better tomorrow, and better still the day after that. You will feel less and less hungry as time goes on."

"I think I will die before then, señor. I feel so empty inside. I don't understand why we are doing this, and can think of no good reason to continue. I want to eat something in the most desperate way, señor, and yet I have vowed to fast with you. Now I think I would rather just crawl into a hole and die."

"Don't be silly, boy. Do you think you are the first to have felt so? I probably uttered words very much like yours when I first went through this. You must be strong, Pablo, if you are to be a man. Life is a hard thing. You must learn to be hard too in order to survive and grow old like me. And this is how you begin."

"But I am only a boy, señor, an extremely hungry boy, a boy with no family. I don't care about being a man – I just want to be fed."

"You are just feeling sorry for yourself. If you had a mother I would send you home to her to be fed. Really, Pablo, I thought you were made of sterner stuff than this."

Pablo's face grew crimson in the firelight, and he looked as if he were about to burst into tears. Inigua quickly got up and went into the bushes, even though he didn't have to go anymore. He did not want to see Pablo cry, and yet was determined to do nothing to comfort him. Although

272

his heart was with the boy, he knew he could do nothing at this point. Pablo had to find the strength within himself to go on. No one could help him.

When Inigua returned to the fire, the boy seemed calmer, although decidedly glum. He refused to meet Inigua's eyes, or even look at him.

Inigua chose a straight stick from the stack of firewood and sharpened one end with the hatchet. Then he pounded the stake into the ground five feet from the fire. Pablo winced with each blow. Inigua spread a blanket before the stake, and tied the reata to the upright. Pablo looked on sullenly.

Inigua said, "You made good progress this afternoon. The reata is nearly half done." There was no response. Inigua took up the fid and began to snug the braided strings. When he was satisfied that the full length of the reata was emerging uniformly from the standing end to the working end, he commenced braiding.

Pablo broke the silence by saying, "I hate this fire, señor."

Without looking up, Inigua said, "Why is that, boy?"

"It keeps crackling and popping. Why does it do that? Why can't fires be quiet? This constant noise is getting on my nerves. And there, down there," he said, pointing, "listen to the surf. The waves keep breaking over and over. Why are they so loud? Why can't they just be quiet for a while."

"You are just irritable because you are hungry, boy. This often happens when people fast. Little things bother you, little things that you would not otherwise notice."

Pablo scowled and said, "I'm tired of it all. I need my rest."

"If you are so tired, why don't you go into the tent and sleep? I had a nice nap today. I'm going to stay up and braid."

The boy made an exasperated guttural sound and stalked into the tent. He abruptly shut the flap without even saying 'goodnight.' Inigua sighed. He gazed off into the misty darkness beyond the circle of light.

Growing chill, Inigua fed the fire and then returned to the braiding. Nearly an hour passed before he was startled by the sound of Pablo bursting out of the tent behind him.

"I cannot sleep, señor. I cannot stop thinking about food. What am I to do with myself?"

"Come here to the fire, boy. Sit. Drink some water. That will fill the void."

Pablo picked up their bota of water and drank greedily. When he was done, he grimaced and cradled his stomach. "Ah, señor, that did not help. It feels like someone kicked me in the belly."

"Sit down. The feeling will pass."

Pablo plopped down cross-legged before the fire. He spread his hands to the flames. "Remind me again, señor, why are we doing this to ourselves?"

273

"I have my own reasons, Pablo. You are doing it as a preliminary to the coming-of-age ceremony. Despite what you said earlier, I believe you want to become a man. In order to be one you have to go through the ordeal of hunger, and then the rigors of sacramental Momoy. And make no mistake about it, boy – they will both challenge your spirit, your mind and your body. The fasting is meant to purify and strengthen you so that you are wholesome when you stand at the threshold of manhood. The Momoy will burn your childhood away, and enlighten you to the existence of other realities. If you are strong you will survive these tests. If you are not, there is the very real possibility that you might die. Some young people do."

Pablo's dark, anxious eyes searched Inigua's face.

Inigua looked up when he felt them. "Most survive, however," he said. "Those who do are considered worthy, or at least healthy enough to become parents and help the race continue. Surviving the coming-of-age ceremony will prove that you are deserving of manhood. If you are one of the gifted ones, and I think you are, you will create a whole new person for yourself in the process. Do you understand?"

"I think so, señor. I would like to understand more fully. And I am willing to accept these challenges, if you think I am ready."

"I know you are ready, boy. I knew it when I first met you. You have a good heart."

"Gracias, señor." A full minute passed before Pablo added, "I'm sorry I was so childish earlier."

"Never mind, son. It was only a passing weakness. I know you will be strong."

*   *   *   *   *

They stayed up late braiding and talking, trying to distract one another from their hunger and discomfort. During this time, Inigua introduced Pablo to all the old-time Chumash beliefs, for this was part of the ritual. He tried to explain to the boy how his people viewed the universe. He pointed out how they made no distinction between the natural and supernatural. He told him again of the three worlds of the Chumash: the Upper, Middle, and Lower. He talked of the time when animals were people. He spoke of the great flood, and how the cleverest of the first people escaped into the Upper World and became celestial beings. He tried to explain how the exigencies of life – war, sickness, power, and death – were inextricably tied to celestial events. He told him of Shimilaqsha, the land of the dead, which lay to the west of Point Conception – how it was a pleasant place, a place where the souls of the dead resided in warmth and comfort, where people had all they could eat, and entertained themselves with dancing and revelry. Only those who were evil, or had drowned, were denied entrance.

Those who were drowned turned into dolphins and it was their fate to wander the sea forever.

"But, señor, what you are speaking of is Chumash religion. I thought you distrusted all religion."

"I do. But this is all I have now. It is only you and I here alone on this empty island, alone but for the spirits of those people whose remains lie scattered along the beach. We have left all else behind. The world does not exist beyond this island. As soon as we finish the reata we will both travel to another place. We are coming to a fork in the road, boy. You will go one way, and I another."

"No, señor, I want to stay with you."

"You cannot. You are young and have your whole life ahead of you. I am old, and have only the grave before me. I may not even have that."

"Please don't talk like that, señor. I don't know what you mean when you talk like that. You and I will always be together. All we have left is our friendship."

"We have more than that, Pablo. We have our destinies to fulfill.

"One of the things you will learn when you become a man is that we are all alone in this world. We have always been alone. Do not attempt to cling to me. I am here only to guide you onto the right path. Once you are on it, you are on your own."

Tears welled up in Pablo's eyes when he heard this. His heart filled with a sublime sadness and a withering fear of the empty years stretching before him. He saw their outline in the darkness beyond the firelight.

"Can you braid now?" said Inigua. "My hands are tired."

*   *   *   *   *

They worked on till nearly midnight and then slept soundly, covered by every blanket they possessed. In the early dawn Inigua left the boy and went foraging in the brush. In his absence Pablo revived the fire from the remainder of the wood pile. The boy then sat before it holding his throbbing head in both hands. Inigua returned carrying a bouquet of leafy stems.

"I have a headache," announced the boy. "It is worse than before. And my stomach cries out for food."

Inigua held a stem out to him. "Chew a few of these leaves, Pablo. Do not swallow them, just swallow the juice. Spit out the leaves when you are done."

Pablo looked a question at him.

"They will not harm you, boy. This is Indian tobacco. The leaves will ease the hunger and make you feel alert. They might even help your headache. Here, look, I will chew some too. Since we are not swallowing the leaves, we still maintain our fast."

275

Within minutes Pablo felt better. He spat out the old leaves and inserted new ones.

Inigua looked out across the Santa Barbara Channel, and spoke around a wad of leaves.

"The fog is breaking up early, boy. It seems we will have a fine day. I think we can complete the braiding today. Then we will make the honda. We are nearing the end, Pablo. Only a few more steps remain."

"I am happy for that, señor. It seems like such a long time since we first began. And I am feeling much better too. Those leaves are good medicine."

Pablo went in search of firewood while Inigua commenced work on the reata. They took turns braiding throughout the morning. While one braided, the other foraged for wood. On one such excursion, Inigua returned with a three-foot long driftwood board. Though worn, it had been milled on all six sides, probably at Mission San Buenaventura. It may well have come from San Miguel Chapel, which had been destroyed in the flood.

"This is a good find," said Inigua. "Do not burn it, Pablo. We can use it in the final stages of making the reata."

By early afternoon they were nearing the end of the braiding. The benign sunlight cheered them, and kept their famished bodies warm. As Pablo's hands flew towards the completion of the braid, Inigua took up the driftwood board. With the sticking knife he began drilling a hole in it. When the tip of the knife pierced the back side, he turned the board over and enlarged the hole from that side. He made sure the edges of the hole were beveled and smooth. When it was large enough to poke the tip of his index finger through, he started a second hole some distance from the first.

"What are you doing, señor?"

"Making holes in this board."

"I can see that, señor. I may be ignorant, but I am not blind. Why are you doing that?"

"It is for the reata. Here are the steps we will follow: first, when the braiding is complete we will roll the reata under foot on one of those flat rock shelves over there by the drop off. That will smooth down the braid and marry the strings together. Next we will apply tallow once more to the whole length of the reata. Then we will draw it through this first hole in the board. I am making other holes, each slightly smaller than the one before. We will draw the reata through each of them. This will further smooth and tighten the braid."

Just then, a very large blue jay fluttered down from the ironwood trees and landed near their campsite. It cocked its head and looked at the two visitors. It squawked a greeting, and took quick, inquisitive glances around the area surrounding the fire pit.

"Dios mio, señor, I have never seen such a large blue jay before. He is nearly the size of a crow."

276

"Yes, Pablo. For some reason they are much bigger out here on the islands. They are almost twice as big as those on the mainland."

The blue jay squawked again and hopped around the fire pit, inspecting everything closely.

"He is hungry," said Inigua, "like us. He is looking for something to eat."

"He doesn't seem frightened at all, señor."

"No. It has been a long time since people lived around here. That jay has probably never seen a human before. He does not see us as enemies, and therefore has no reason to be afraid."

"Why is he so big, señor?"

"I do not know, just as I do not know why the foxes out here are so much smaller than the ones over on the mainland."

Pablo said, "I saw a white headed eagle circling while you slept yesterday. I can understand how the birds got here to Santa Cruz Island, but what about the foxes and mice and other animals? I think it is too far for them to swim. I know I could not swim twenty miles."

"Nor I. I don't know how they got here. Maybe they were always here. It is strange though. Many of the animals you find on the mainland are not here: deer, cougar, bear, coyote. And yet there are animals here that you do not find over there. It is the same way with certain plants. That is one reason there was a lot of trading going on in the old days."

"This seems like a very big island, señor."

"Yes, it is over twenty miles long and six wide. It is the largest of the eight islands."

"Eight islands? I thought there were only four."

"The four you know about are the northern Channel Islands: San Miguel, Santa Rosa, Santa Cruz, and Anacapa. There are four more to the south: San Nicolas, Santa Barbara, Santa Catalina, and San Clemente. You can't see them from here."

"Did you ever visit them, señor?"

"Yes, when I was young. We went mostly to Catalina, however. We followed the coast till we were opposite that island, and then made the crossing. We went there to trade for soapstone with which we made cooking bowls and platters. It was a difficult voyage... much hard paddling, and difficult conditions. Sometimes we met unfriendly Indians along the way, the Fernandeño and Gabrielaño. Some accused us of trespassing on their fishing grounds. Others simply wanted to rob us. We had to fight sometimes."

"Fight? That reminds me of something, señor. Do you remember when you were telling me about the knives we got from Albino?"

"Yes."

"You told me all about the different uses of the various knives, and showed me how to sharpen them. You also said that after a horse and a reata, a knife is a vaquero's most important tool. You said he carries it all the time and uses it for personal protection. What did you mean by that, señor?"

"I meant that when you get out in the world on your own you will find that not all people are friendly, Pablo. Some are bullies, like Tico, and some are just plain evil like Camacho and Cota. Others take offense over the smallest slight. You must always carry a knife with you, and you must be prepared to use it to defend yourself. If necessary, you must be prepared to kill with it. If you want to learn something about knife fighting you should talk to the stable master, José Sabino. He knows some nasty tricks."

These words disturbed Pablo, and made him feel even more uncertain about the future. He tried to dispel his unease by concentrating on the braiding.

When Inigua was finished drilling four holes in the board, he brought out the scraps of rawhide they had trimmed earlier from the whole hide, those parts which made up the leg and neck portions.

Looking up from his braiding, Pablo said, "What are those for, señor?"

"To make hondas. Two hondas will emerge from these scraps."

"Ah, bueno, señor. But why do we need two?"

"One I will make to demonstrate how it is done, the other is for you to work on alongside of me. San Juan hondas are intricate and difficult to construct. It is nearly impossible to explain how to make one. I must show you and you must do it yourself in order to understand. Doing it this way will help you remember."

From the two hind leg portions Inigua methodically cut two spirals, each about a quarter-inch wide and eight feet long. When he was done he carefully rubbed them down with tallow. From the front leg portions he cut two rectangles, each about five inches long and two inches wide. Placing them flat on the driftwood board, he cut narrow crescents from either end. He applied tallow to these now oddly shaped rectangles. Inigua noticed Pablo watching him with a puzzled look.

"These flat pieces will form the boots, or wear-leathers of the hondas. They keep the eye of your reata from wearing out. When the boots wear out it is much easier to replace them than make a whole new honda."

"That seems funny, señor, to put a boot on an eye? I would put a boot on my foot. Ha, ha."

"It is good you can make jokes, boy. You must be feeling better."

"Sí, señor. Much better. You were right when you said that I would feel less hungry after awhile."

"I am glad to hear it. You will feel better and better as time goes on – lighter and cleaner."

"But I have a horrible taste in my mouth, señor, and I think I have bad breath. And look here. Look at this." Pablo stuck his tongue out and angled it down to reveal a thick, pasty white coat. "Is this normal, señor?"

"Yes. That happens when you fast."

"But what am I to do about it, señor?"

"Do nothing. Or scrape it off if it bothers you. But do not feel alone. I have one too. See?" Inigua stuck his tongue out for inspection, and Pablo giggled at the sight. Inigua smiled and said, "Just be sure to keep drinking water, boy... plenty of water."

It was not long before the tamales disappeared altogether and Pablo was left holding four short strings in his hand. "Look, señor! Look here. I am nearing the end."

"Good boy. Leave about eight inches unbraided. Tighten your last bit of work with the fid, and then attach a holding tie. Congratulations, boy. It will be a fine reata."

When Pablo had finished, Inigua instructed him to stand up and coil the whole fifty foot length of rope. Inigua then led him over to the flat, sandstone ledge and showed him how to roll it underfoot. Starting at one end, they took turns rolling it back and forth under bare feet. While one of them rolled, the other drew the rope across the rock and coiled the finished portion. The reata twisted and curled like a live snake under these ministrations.

The sound and movement of their work attracted a pair of island foxes who were hunting nearby. Inigua spied their distinctive black, white, and rust-colored faces peering from behind a clump of bushes. The foxes' eyes darted back and forth between the contorting rope and the two strangers. Eventually, their attention focused totally on the squirming rope. They crouched with twitching tails, preparing to pounce. Inigua put his hand on Pablo's arm, and the boy stopped rolling and followed his gaze. Inigua gave a loud growl and waved his arms. The two foxes darted away through the underbrush.

"You must guard your reata from the animals, Pablo. Some will mistake it for food and try to eat it. When you are not using la reata, be sure to hang it up out of their reach."

"Don't worry, I will take good care of it. But those foxes, señor, they were very small, and clever too, eh?"

"Sí, compadre. One was a female with a round belly. She will have pups in a few weeks."

When the reata had been thoroughly rolled from one end to the other, Inigua and Pablo sat down facing each other near the fire with the coiled reata between them. Taking up rags dipped in tallow, they started at opposite ends and worked towards the middle.

By now the sun had dipped below the mountains to the west and a cold wind began to blow. Inigua stoked the fire.

"How are you feeling now, boy? Do you want to rest, or keep working?"

"I am fine, señor. And I am so excited. We are almost done, eh?"

"Sí, Pablo. So now we will draw the reata through the board. We can take turns. You do the first hole, and I will do the next."

Inigua took up the drilled board and directed Pablo to feed one end of the reata through the largest hole. The boy threaded the four loose strings into the hole, but had to undo the holding tie to get that part through. Then Inigua had him reattach the holding tie to the braid on the other side of the board. Now Inigua and Pablo stood facing one another on the blanket, the reata coiled on the ground between them.

"I will hold the board," said Inigua. "You pull."

Pablo pulled lustily hand and over hand, drawing the reata steadily through the hole. The rope passed easily from back to front, making a soft whirring sound as it went. When Pablo reached the standing end, the end where the strings had been doubled over onto themselves, Inigua removed the holding tie, and cut through the loops. Pablo then pulled past the braided part, and Inigua reattached the holding tie.

Now Pablo took the board, and Inigua fed the reata into the second hole, as before. Since this hole was smaller, it fit more snuggly, and was correspondingly harder to draw. Now the reata whirred with a higher pitch, hissing in short rasps as it passed. The third hole made the pulling even more difficult and gave the whirring sound an even more elevated pitch. By the fourth hole, the man and boy were gasping with effort, and the reata reluctantly whined through the hole in intermittent starts and stops. When the last hole was finally breached, Inigua and Pablo stood gasping for breath, their lean bodies bathed with sweat, and the chain of diamond-shaped patterns along the length of the rope lay gleaming at their feet.

Between heavily drawn breaths, Inigua said, "The reata…she is nearly finished, Pablo. She needs only an eye and a tail to make her complete."

42

THE STORM

As the day waned, Inigua brewed up a pot of Manzanilla tea. He and Pablo sipped it leisurely while they rested by the fire. Pablo found the hot tea delicious. It soothed and settled his empty stomach, and added to his contentment. As twilight approached, the two gathered their tools and materials and sat before the fire.

Inigua's attention was drawn to the evening sky. He remained transfixed for some time, his senses attuned to the great aerial canopy stretched above them. He slowly turned his face to the southeast and cocked his head. He listened, and then he nodded in confirmation.

"What is it, señor?"

"There is a storm coming."

Looking about him, Pablo said, "I don't see anything. How can you tell?"

"Observe the sky, boy."

Pablo gazed up and saw pink, puffball clouds streaming out of the northwest.

Then Inigua gestured with his head. "And listen to the sea."

Pablo became aware of the thunderous roar of waves pounding the shore below.

"And feel the wind, boy. It has shifted. The surface wind now blows from the southeast, and yet the clouds come from the northwest. These things should tell you we are in for a storm."

Looking about him nervously, Pablo said, "What should we do, señor?"

"There is nothing to do now. The storm will probably not arrive till late tomorrow. Since it is nearly dark now there is little we can do. But tomorrow we had better move our camp. We are too exposed up here on this ridge."

"But where shall we go? Where can we find shelter?"

"I know of a cave not far from here. It is a large cave, down by the sea. The villagers used to use it when bad storms came. I think this will be a bad one. Spring storms can be the worst. But there is nothing we can do tonight. Let us continue working. We will give your reata an eye with which to see."

Inigua handed the boy one of the eight-foot long strings of quarter-inch rawhide, and a small rectangle of leather with concave cuts at either end. He placed their twins at his own side.

"The San Juan honda was developed in Sonora, Mexico," he said. "It is an ornate yet very strong and practical honda. It will make a handsome eye for your reata, and give you years of good service. I will show you what it will look like…"

Inigua rolled the cuff of his left sleeve half way up his forearm. He then angled both arms down in front of him forming a circle. He clasped his left wrist with his right hand. Below the wrist his left hand was clenched in a fist.

"Look here, Pablo. Imagine that my bare arms inside my sleeves are the braided honda; the sleeves of my coton are the boot that protects the honda from wear; my right hand clasping the opposite wrist is a loop; and my clenched left fist is a Turk's head knot. You see my bare forearm? That is where you attach the working end of the reata." Inigua then relaxed his arms and rolled down his sleeve.

"This is how we shall proceed: first, we will each cut our string into four sections of equal length. Second, we will 'middle' each string." At Pablo's questioning look, he added, "That means we will cut little slits spaced evenly along the middle of each string. The strings will then be braided through one another using these slits. It is called slit-braiding. You shall see. It will yield a very strong and beautiful cord."

Inigua honed and stropped the sticking knife, and then cut his string into four sections, each of them two feet long. He lay them out on the wooden plank. Using the point of the knife, and starting several inches from the end, he began cutting quarter-inch slits along the middle of each string. The slits ran parallel to the edges, and were about a half an inch apart. He then handed the blade to the boy and watched him do the same with his, guiding him as he did so. When this was accomplished, Inigua laid his four strings one on top of the other, and showed Pablo how to thread them through the slits. He started near the half-way point of the strings. Using the fid, he pushed the top string down through the corresponding slits in the three below it. Then the second string was threaded down through the others in the same manner. It was the same with the third and fourth strings. He continued in this fashion, repeating the pattern, for several inches.

Whereas the reata braid formed a series of interlocking diamond shapes, this slit-braid slowly revealed a series of overlapping leaf-like shapes along its length.

"This part of the honda corresponds with my right hand," said Inigua, "the hand that clasps the wrist."

When they were done braiding the centers of their respective pieces, Inigua chose a straight, round stick from the stacked firewood, one that was about half an inch in diameter. He had Pablo hold it between his two hands while he looped his slit-braid around it. With the four dangling strings at either end, he began an eight-string slit-braid. He carefully braided a section about four inches long.

"This section will form the eye of the honda," he said. He then had Pablo remove the stick from the loop. Inigua held the stick while Pablo slit-braided his own eight strings.

"Now we attach the boot," said Inigua, removing the stick. He showed Pablo how to pinch the rectangular piece of leather together around the eight-string section, and to punch small holes through the overlapping sides. Then, using a short leather thong, he laced the boot tightly around the braid. When this was done, he bent the eye into a circle. Because the rectangle has concave edges, the inside of the eye did not buckle. Inigua then passed the eight loose strings at the end of the braid through the loop at the opposite end where the stick had been.

"Now we tie a Turk's head knot with the eight dangling strings. This will hold the eye together. It is the fist of the left hand." It took Inigua some minutes to accomplish this, and when he was done, he cut off the eight strings flush with the top of the knot. Pablo was amazed to see the resulting honda, which resembled Inigua's two-arm demonstration in miniature. The inside of the eye was about an inch and a half in diameter.

"*Qué hermoso*! That is miraculous, señor. I would never have imagined such a thing."

"It looks good, eh? And it is very strong. A honda like this can hold the strongest bull, or even a grizzly bear. Now, this part here, the part not covered by the boot, is where we attach the working end of the reata. Now it is your turn. You make your honda the same way."

It took Pablo much longer, but with Inigua's help he managed to complete the second eye. After inspecting it closely, and approving, Inigua suggested the boy keep it as a spare.

"If you don't mind, Pablo, I would like my honda on the head of your reata."

"I don't mind at all, señor. In fact, I insist. I would be honored to have it."

"Bueno. It will be a little piece of me that you can carry with you. And in this way I can keep an eye on you when I am not around."

"Ha, ha. Good one, señor. But don't start talking about not being around, for I will be keeping my own eye on you too. Ha, ha."

Inigua shook his head, smiled enigmatically, and said nothing. Instead he got up, rekindled the fire, and made another pot of tea. As they drank it, they discussed how they would move camp the following day. Then they sat side by side next to the fire to attach the honda to the reata.

"The fastening knot is actually a five-part four-bight Turk's-head, but made with four strings," said Inigua. Pablo looked perplexed. "Remember?" said Inigua. "That was a Turk's head that fastened the eye into a circle. It was the fist.

"I have an idea, Pablo. Why don't you attach your honda to the other end? Just for practice. You can take it off later to make a proper tail for your reata."

"But then my reata will have two eyes, señor."

"Not for long. It is easily removed. This is just so you know how to do it yourself. You can work alongside me. It will be good practice for you."

"All right, señor.

Inigua took up the four strings of the working end of the reata. They were about eight inches long and dangled free below the holding tie. He placed the end of the braid up against that part of the honda that was not covered by the boot. He threaded two of the strings through the eye from one side, and brought the other two through from the other. Pablo followed suite. Inigua then began 'crowning' the strings, explaining as he went.

"The Turk's head knot is tied back onto the end of the reata, surrounding it on all sides for an inch or two. This joins them, one over the other, and gives added strength to the bond with the honda."

Inigua went about tying the intricate knot, laying one string over another in braid-like fashion in a counter-clockwise direction. He passed each string through the bight formed by the previous string. Pablo mimicked his every move at the opposite end of the reata. These steps were repeated four more times, pulling hard each time to make the knot tight. Inigua and Pablo continued until their respective knots cloaked the reata for an inch and a half. Since the ends of each string passed under the bight of a different string, they were all held tightly in place. Inigua stopped then, and cut off the ends of each of his strings flush with the top of the knot.

"There," said Inigua. "The eyes are now married to the reata." Pablo looked down at them reverently. He hooked his finger through his own honda and tested it by pulling.

"Muy bueno, señor. It is very firm, very strong."

"Now that you know how to attach the honda, you can use the fid to untie it. It is not natural for a reata to have two eyes. It must see with only one."

Pablo did as was suggested, and then reattached the holding tie to the bitter end of the braid.

When he was done, Inigua said, "Now take your end and pass it through the eye, boy. That's right, one string at a time. Now pull it all the way through. That's it. Now you have your lasso. All that remains is for you to complete the tail, either with a knot or a flail. It will not take long. Have you decided on the shape of the tail?"

"Sí, señor. I want a Turk's head like you used to have."

"Bueno. I will show you how. You can always change the tail if you like. Just undo the knot with the fid and make it however you like."

The final knot of the reata was accomplished quickly, and Inigua showed the boy how to tuck the ends into the coils and out of sight. The knot

284

was a perfect oval of undulate cords with no apparent beginning or end.

The two castaways gazed down at the lariat for a long, silent moment. Then Pablo looked up questioningly at his mentor.

Inigua grinned at the boy. "Well, Pablo, we have done it. Your reata is complete."

The boy looked again at the glistening coils. He felt a confusing surge of emotions: gratification, relief, a twinge of sadness, and a growing exhilaration. He had never felt anything like it in his life. He reached out to lay an affectionate hand on Inigua's knee. The other hand found its way to the coiled rope.

In a voice cracking with emotion, Pablo said, "Ah, señor, how can I ever thank you for showing me how to make the reata?"

"De nada, joven."

"But, señor, you have given me so much. It is more than I deserve."

"No, no, not at all. And besides, you did most of the work. You did a fine job. But what is more important, you now know how to accomplish it from start to finish. This is vital knowledge for any vaquero."

"Muchas gracias, señor. I am grateful for this great gift." Pablo stood up then, a look of pride and anticipation lighting his face. He reached down and took up the coiled reata in his hands, looking down at it with admiration. He drew out a four-foot wide lasso, and raised it over his head. He began twirling it, slowly at first, and then gaining ever more speed. A portentous whirring sound ensued, joined with the chorus of crackling fire and the deep rumble of the surf. Inigua leaned back with a smile and watched the boy. Although the boy was not certain what lay beyond the firelight, he cast the lasso deep into the enveloping darkness.

*   *   *   *   *

They slept in the tent that night, the coiled reata tied by a thong to the tent post above their heads. Pablo had wanted to be sure no mice or other animals could get at it while they slept. When the boy first lay down he had thought he would be too excited to sleep, but fatigue and lack of nourishment soon tumbled him into a deep slumber.

They awoke on the third day of their fast to the flutter and flap of the tent tugging at its moorings. A dim orange glow lit the canvas. Pablo looked up sleepily at the suspended reata and smiled.

Inigua awoke with a start, and, instantly alert, said, "We are in for a blow, joven. The wind, she is rising. How do you feel?"

"I am well, señor," said the boy, smiling absently while running his thumb and forefinger over the well-oiled diamond skin of the reata.

Inigua yawned and stretched. "Look sharp, boy," he said, sitting up. "We must be gone from here."

They crawled out of the tent to behold a massive white cloud hanging over the mountains to the west. Its thick billow curled above the crest line looking like an enormous wave breaking over the island.

"Dios mio, señor, look!"

"I see, I see. The storm, she is coming. Drink some water. No time for a fire. No tea this morning."

Amid blustering winds, they quickly gathered all their belongings in one spot. Inigua lowered their food stores from the tree and added it to the pile. They dismantled the tent and rolled it up with the tent posts. Pablo carefully wrapped the reata into its final folds. Inigua led Pablo down the winding path to the shoreline, each carting one end of the rolled up tent.

They struggled along the beach for a quarter-mile to the east until they came upon the old sea cave. It was tucked into a steep, rocky hillside near the shore, a narrow strip of sand forming a doormat at its entrance. The triangular cave opening looked like a dark arrowhead, perhaps twelve feet wide at its base and narrowing to a point some fifteen feet off the ground. Brackish water seeping from the rock walls of the interior formed a small stream that trickled down across the sand into the sea.

Inigua led the way into the darkened interior. The cave narrowed and elevated somewhat as it lengthened into the hillside. Waiting till his eyes became accustomed to the dim light, Inigua located a flat, dry area about thirty feet in from the entrance. There they found the remains of an old fire circle.

"Bueno," he said. "Let's put the tent down here. This will be our new home for awhile, Pablo. We will be dry and out of the wind here. And look there. See? There are some Indian things left by the fire: a mortar and pestle, and some old abalone shell used as candle holders. We can use them once we are settled. But now we need to go back and bring another load.

"We need to bring the food and fresh water next. We could use the water in this stream, but it is not sweet. We need our knives and other tools too. Come."

It took them four trips in all to bring everything down. In his half-starved condition, Pablo nearly fainted from the exertion. Inigua moved slowly, pacing himself and conserving his energy. As they trudged back and forth they watched the veil cloud that covered the mountains break up and form whirling round cotton balls that scudded off the sloping sides of the islands and sailed off across the Channel.

"The wind has shifted," said Inigua. "It blows from the west now. It will swing to the northwest later on. This will be a strong storm, with much rain. We must hurry."

When all had been transported, they then set about gathering firewood. Several hours crawled by as they toiled with empty bellies up and down the deserted beach. They made several forays up the narrow valley interior too – Pablo to fetch firewood, while Inigua gathered herbs and buckthorn flowers. As they worked, the skies began to darken and the wind to increase. The veil cloud that had clung to the mountaintops in the morning reformed, but this time with a darker, more ominous aspect. Ponderous cumulonimbus scudded across the sky, their forefronts bending towards the mainland.

Inigua said, "It is time now, boy. We have done all we can. To the cave."

Pablo was never more grateful for an order in his life. He was dead tired. His tongue felt like a smoked hide, and every muscle in his body ached.

They repaired to the cave, where they built a fire against the drafty cold of the interior. Inigua kept feeding the fire until it blazed heartily. Then he directed Pablo to join him in a ritual sweat bath. Rain began to fall outside as they oozed sweat by the fire. They swept the glistening perspiration and dirt from their bodies with smooth pieces of driftwood. When they were done, Inigua led the boy outside into the pelting rain. They worked the buckthorn blossoms he had gathered into a frothy lather between their hands, and shampooed their hair under the chilling downpour. At last they returned, shivering but clean, to the welcoming fire.

43

MOMOY

Inigua sat cross-legged before the fire. The flames cast his shadow against the cave wall behind him, sending it dancing over the rock with each flare and flicker. Outside, the howling wind and driving rain lashed at the pounding surf in a darkened world of watery chaos. Pablo sat opposite the old man and watched the wavering wall-shadow mimic his own nervousness. But the boy did his best to disguise his unease and to ignore the raging storm outside.

Inigua set a pot of fresh water above the fire. He then dropped several large, round seed pods into the steatite mortar perched at his feet. Using the pestle, he carefully broke up the tough, spine-covered husks. Then, with gnarled, long-nailed fingers, he carefully withdrew the broken spines and cracked pods, leaving behind only the dried seeds.

"This Momoy comes from the Ojai Valley," he said. "It was given to me by Qupe, the grandfather of 'Akiwo. He gathered it last fall before the rains began. Qupe assured me it is very strong, very potent."

Inigua took up the pestle and pressed the rounded end down onto the clustered seeds. He crushed them slowly and deliberately. He then began rotating the pestle. As he ground the seeds he chanted in the old language, blending his words with the sound of the milling stones:

"Soon comes the time when time stands still.
Here lie the seeds from the magic vine.
We grind them close and steep them well,
Then drink the drink that makes us fly.
Be brave young one and fear no fall.
Soon comes the time when time stands still."

Pablo shivered involuntarily. He could no longer contain the outward manifestation of his dread. He knew Momoy was a deadly poison. His wanted to ask Inigua if he was sure he was using a safe amount. But he withheld this question, for he knew that Inigua had long experience at making and drinking Momoy. He also knew that Inigua would never harm him. Given this, there was nothing to do but trust his mentor's judgment. With this resolved, he felt calmer. Yet his ease was not complete, for he knew that his life would be forever changed – either for good or ill – by what was about to occur.

When the seeds were ground to his satisfaction, Inigua set the mortar and pestle aside. He bent forward to check the water pot, which was just beginning to steam. He leaned back then, and gazed affectionately at his young companion.

"It will not be long before the water boils," he said. "While we wait, I would like to take this opportunity to say what a pleasure it has been to know you, Pablo."

At the boy's startled look he added, "I mean by that… to know you as a boy. Soon you will have come of age. You have a good heart, young fellow, and possess many admirable qualities. I am sure you will grow up to be a man of strength, integrity, and kindness, and that your efforts, whatever they might be, will yield success."

With furrowed brows, Pablo said, "Why are you talking like this, señor?"

Inigua waved his hand as if to dismiss his own words. "It is only my clumsy way of expressing my affection and admiration for you. And I want to thank you too. I don't know what I would have done if you hadn't come along when you did. And now you have your reata."

Pablo nodded warily.

"During our time together I have come to appreciate you for what you are, and I now consider you like a son, or more fittingly, a grandson. Let me tell you a simple truth, boy. It is every parent's wish that their children, or grandchildren, if that be the case, grow up to be better than themselves. Better, and without the faults which burden the older generation. I have this same wish for you."

"How can I be better than you?" said Pablo, indignantly. "You are a grown-up and know everything. And you are very wise."

"No, this is not so. For one thing, I am well beyond grown-up. Just look at me. I am an old man, and I admit to you now that I am an ignorant and illiterate savage. I cannot read and write like you. Nor am I as wise as you think me to be."

Pablo shook his head, and started to speak, but Inigua continued, "Oh, I suppose I have learned a few things in my life, and I may even have been the author of a few good deeds, but I am certainly not wise. No, not wise, for I have always been governed by my passions. And, at an early age I sensed a certain darkness in my heart. I was not even conscious of it in the beginning. It grew slowly, over time. I think the dimming began when the Spanish arrived. From that time on I grew to be covetous, suspicious, resentful, and bitter. After awhile, these feelings wove themselves into an all-consuming hatred. This is not an admirable outcome to a lifetime dedicated to learning.

"Thankfully, I see none of that in you, Pablo. For this I am glad in my heart, and I hope for your sake that you remain as good and pure as you are."

"Don't say such things," said Pablo. "I am neither good nor pure."

"Yes, you are. But still, you are human, and only a child at that. This last will change soon, and I want to tell you what to expect."

"Tell me," said Pablo.

"Just a moment… look here, the water is boiling." Inigua removed the pot from the fire. "See how much water there is, Pablo? Just enough for the two of us." Inigua emptied the mortar of ground seeds into the steaming pot and covered it with the lid. "Now we let it steep. It won't be long now, boy."

"What were you going to tell me, señor?"

"For one thing, I would remind you of a sad fact, a fact you know full well. You are an orphan, Pablo. That makes your future more difficult than it might otherwise have been. If you had a family you could lean on them. But you have no one to lean on. You are alone. Therefore you must be twice as strong. But do not concern yourself about not having a family right now. When you are grown you will acquire one of your own. Until then you must stand alone on your own two feet, and be as brave as you are able.

"I want to give you some advice, Pablo. But first, an observation: two of your most endearing qualities are that you reveal your feelings honestly and openly, and you always speak your mind. While in a more perfect world these would be admirable traits, they can bring you grief in the world as we find it. The adults you encounter as you grow will not always be good or kind. You must learn to better conceal your true feelings and thoughts from those you do not know well, at least until you determine what kind of person they are.

"You are an honest and intelligent boy; you are healthy and strong; you can read and write. Use these gifts to your best advantage while holding your tongue and guarding your thoughts."

Pablo swallowed, and said, "I will try, señor."

"Good. And now I want to tell you what is about to happen. After you drink the Momoy you will begin to feel many things, Pablo. Some of them may not be pleasant. You may feel sick at first, but that will pass. It is important that you remain calm, and have patience. Keep sipping Momoy until you fall asleep. This is what is desired. In your sleep you will have many strange dreams. Pay attention to them, and go where they take you. You will travel in your mind, and mingle with people and animals in your dreams. Some of the things you experience will be real, and others not. At some point Momoy will beckon a special creature to you. I do not know what form this creature will take. Do not be afraid of it, Pablo, for it is your totem, your spirit helper. You will know your totem when it appears, for it will be like no other.

"Your totem will be like you in many ways, even though it is an animal. You should make friends with it, become companions. You will nurture one another and protect each other from danger, like a family would. Your totem will remain close to you for the rest of your life, even though you cannot see it. Just remember this: never hunt, kill, or harm the animal that is your totem. Never eat it if it is served as food.

"You may sleep for a long time, Pablo, but your mind will not be idle. You will eventually awake, only to sleep again. This may happen several times. Each time you will sleep less until finally you return to the time and place you know.

"Do you have any questions?"

"Sí, señor. Will I be a man when I wake up?"

"You will have changed. You will see things differently. You will be a man inside a boy's body."

"How will I feel, señor?"

"You will feel exhausted from having lived a lifetime in a day, and you will be hungry and thirsty. We have food and water here in the cave. Take care of yourself, Pablo, as any man would. Eat, drink, and rest. It may be several days before you feel yourself again. But when you do, you will begin to understand the changes that have taken place."

"And what about you, señor?"

"I will do the same."

"What is your totem, señor? Are you allowed to tell me?"

"It is up to the individual whether or not they share the identity of their totem. I choose not to tell you just now, but I will reveal it to you when you have come of age."

"Why do you want to drink Momoy, señor? You are not coming of age."

"There are other uses of Momoy besides coming of age. Shaman drink it seeking visions, visions which they can interpret in words, or in ceremonies or rock paintings. I am drinking it because I want to go somewhere. Perhaps Momoy will take me there. All will be clear soon. And now, I think our sacred tea is ready.

"Before we go into our separate dreams, Pablo, I would like to say one last thing: no matter what happens, know that I care for you, and that I wish the best for you. I know you will be fine, and will emerge from this experience stronger and more mature than you are now.

"I am happy to have shared with you some little knowledge of your ancestors, the Chumash. There is much more to tell. But this must wait for another time, another place."

Inigua lifted the lid of the pot and took a whiff. "Mmm. It smells good. Hand me those two cups, Pablo."

The old man filled the cups, and handed one back to Pablo. The boy watched as Inigua tilted his cup and poured a small libation onto the ground.

Inigua said, "Give Hutash a sip, boy, to honor her, and then drink."

Pablo dribbled a little tea on the ground, and then following Inigua's lead, sipped of the amber-colored liquid. It tasted bitter, and Pablo felt it grab his tongue in its astringent grip. He swallowed and felt the warm fluid glide down his gullet and settle in his vacant stomach. The tea, though bitter, had a pleasant weedy taste. He took a second, larger sip.

As he continued to drink, he felt a wave of heat sweep through his body. The heat was welcome, for he had felt chilled before. Slowly, as he sipped, the heat increased until he began to perspire. He noticed a curious red spot developing in the center of his vision. He turned his eyes towards Inigua and watched him sipping Momoy. The old man's eyes were open, and the pupils looked black and fathomless in the firelight. Pablo felt a sudden dizziness, and his own eyes seemed to have expanded so that they felt too large for his head. His vision began to blur.

When their cups were empty, Inigua refilled them. Midway through the second cup, Pablo felt an unwelcome wave of nausea sweep over him. The feeling grew stronger, and he was glad that his stomach was empty, for he was sure he would have vomited otherwise. His stomach muscles began to contract. Within a matter of minutes he felt them cramping. Pablo groaned and leaned forward holding his stomach.

"Keep drinking," he heard Inigua say.

The boy forced himself back into a sitting position. After several more swallows, the pain and nausea slowly eased, and then passed altogether. He continued to sweat, and the red spot grew until all he could see was tinted with that one color. His face felt hot and flushed.

Inigua poured them another cup of Momoy.

As he continued to drink, Pablo felt a wave of giddiness and the quiver of nervous tension rising within him. He shook himself like a wet dog. The cave walls slowly began to move, as if alive, their mottled surface ebbing and flowing before his eyes. Faces and shapes emerged and retreated amid the living stone. His ears filled with a myriad of sounds, sounds that seemed to come from every direction. They came faster and faster, growing louder until his ears were filled with a deafening roar. He rocked back and forth, his mind overwhelmed by the multitude of impressions and sounds.

He was vaguely aware of Inigua rocking from side to side and chanting softly as he continued to drink. Mechanically, Pablo swallowed the last dregs of his Momoy. Soon after, the cup fell from his hand, and he felt himself keeling over backward to land with a thump on the cave floor. The redness paled to black, and the roaring ceased.

44

DREAMING

Pablo slept all through the night and well into the following morning, dreaming all the while. His dreams had begun innocently enough – an array of geometric patterns and odd bug-like shapes writhing and twisting before him. What astonished him about them most were the brilliant colors. The colors he was familiar with, those at the mission, had always been rather drab. And the colors of the land and sea were commonplace and familiar as well. But these moving, three-dimensional images were in the most vivid hues the boy had ever seen. Their appearance was accompanied by intriguing sounds too: whistling wind, eerie music, moans, laughter, a distant drumming, and sometimes the muted buzz of human speech.

What followed, however, were dreams of an altogether different nature. At first they were simple little scenes, or vignettes, which he watched with growing interest. Soon these scenes reached out to engage him, and he began to be drawn into the action and dialogues which took place there. In time, these little scenes began to string themselves together into long, involved adventures that carried him along to places he had never imagined.

As one dream drew to a close, a new one emerged from the surrounding darkness. Each one grasped him firmly, pulled him along, led him on and on through incredible settings peopled by all sorts of strange and wonderful beings.

Sometimes Pablo walked upon the earth. Sometimes he rode astride animals, or was drawn along in peculiar, wheeled conveyances. Sometimes he swam effortlessly through the sea, either on top or under the surface. And sometimes he soared through the air like a bird.

Pablo had never felt so free. For all his young life there had always been someone standing over him, telling him what to do, giving him orders, presenting him with a never-ending series of tasks to perform. Now he was free, or so it seemed.

To Pablo's great relief, he discovered that he could sometimes influence the outcome of his dreams. By taking some necessary action, or by merely giving voice to his own thoughts, he could change the direction that certain of his dreams took. This was very gratifying when it worked, and highly distressing when it did not.

Out in the realm of his dreamscapes he mingled with both humans and animals. Some of the animals spoke with human words. Some of the humans spoke in languages he did not know, but somehow he understood them. He mingled freely with the inhabitants of places he visited, and came to know many characters: strangers, friends, lovers, and enemies alike. He talked and listened, debated and argued, embraced and fought. At times he laughed till his sides ached, and more than once he found himself running from some unholy terror until he felt as though his lungs would burst.

*   *   *   *   *

During Pablo's long drug-induced sleep he had one dream in particular that towered above all the others in its impact, a vision he would remember for the rest of his life.

It began with Pablo outside his own body, looking down at himself lying in the cave where all his dreams had begun. A bright light emanated from the mouth of the cave. Pablo wrongly assumed that both the night and the storm had passed. He descended into himself, then turned towards the light. He was surprised to feel himself rising slowly from the floor and turning over in midair. He was not afraid of falling, for he remembered Inigua's admonition to remain calm, and to go where Momoy took him.

Pablo saw the dying embers of the fire below him. He spread his arms and felt his body move laterally beyond the pit. He drifted towards the gaping mouth of the cave. Something was drawing him there, and he was glad to go. He wanted to be gone from this dark cavern, and to enter the light and the open spaces beyond.

As he passed through the arrowhead-shaped entrance, he entered a serene and expansive realm of sea and sky. He rose higher and higher in the sunlit air. Looking behind him he could see Santa Cruz Island floating there, covered in spring growth, and spangled with yellow flowers. He looked ahead across the Channel, and spied the blue mountains of the mainland in the distance. He felt drawn there. He felt an urgency too, a need to hurry to some as yet unknown destination. Glancing down he saw swirling sea currents fleeing behind him at an ever increasing rate. He tilted his body, lowering his left arm and raising his right. This steered him to the northwest. The wind whistled in his ears. Righting himself, he reveled in the exhilaration of flight.

In what could have been hours or mere seconds, he found himself bearing down on a seaside town growing up into the hills above a bay. There was a tall ship anchored offshore, and skiffs and canoes drawn up on the beach. He spied the adobe walls of a fortress, with a Mexican flag flying above it. He saw houses and cottages with tidy gardens scattered about the fort, and a white church perched on a rise some distance above the town. This, he realized, was Mission Santa Barbara, a place he had visited once with Padre Uria.

He felt himself descending, attracted to the town like a hummingbird to a blossom. He did not puzzle over this. It seemed the most natural thing in the world.

He found himself passing down a wide earthen avenue which led through the open gates of the fort. Soldiers and citizens passed to and fro, although, strangely, they seemed not to notice him. He came to a large, two-storied adobe house off to one side. He recognized this house. It was the home of Captain José de la Guerra, the *comandante* of the Presidio, and a good friend of Padre Uria. Pablo ascended the familiar exterior staircase at the side of the house and entered through an open door on the second floor. He came to a room filled with the cloying sweet scent of decay. And there lying upon a wood-framed bed lay Padre Uria.

His pallid face and flaccid features left no doubt that the spark of life had departed. His waxy hands clasped a wooden crucifix upon his chest. A blanket mercifully covered his swollen torso and elephantine legs. Arrayed at the foot of the bed were three figures in mourning: Don José de la Guerra, his wife Doña Maria, and a thin, elderly priest, the Padre-Superior of Mission Santa Barbara, who was just then making the sign of the cross over the remains.

"Ay, Dios mio!" wailed Pablo. "What has happened here?" He hurried into the room and stood at the side of the bed looking down at his former master. Strangely, no one in the room paid the least attention to him.

In a plaintive voice, Doña Maria said, "Oh, what a pity. He so wanted to die in his homeland. And finally, finally the ship he had waited for has come, anchored just now in the bay, the ship that would have carried him on his way. Ah, the poor, poor man."

Don José replied thickly, "At least his suffering is over now. He was a dear friend, and it troubled me much to see him in such pain. I will miss Francisco. I will miss him dearly. Can we bury him at the mission, padre?"

"Of course," said the Padre-Superior, "He was one of our most devoted and hard-working fathers. We will bury him at the mission with all the honor and respect he deserves. I will go now and make the arrangements. This afternoon I will send down a casket. Can you bring him to the church in the morning, Don José?"

"I will bring him."

Doña Maria turned to her husband and said, "You were the last one to speak with Padre Uria. What was he saying to you?"

"He was very distraught at the end. He despaired of ever reaching Spain. And he seemed most concerned about what was to become of the missions. He was also very worried about a former servant of his – a boy named Pablo. You may remember him."

"It is I," blurted Pablo. "I am here." But no one turned their head; no one seemed to hear him.

Don José continued, "I am sure you remember the boy, Maria. He came here once with the padre. It was last year, during the fiesta."

"Oh, yes, of course. He seemed like such a sweet boy. And he took such good care of the padre."

"Yes. But Francisco told me the boy is in some sort of trouble now, down at Mission San Buenaventura, and that Fernando Tico is out to get him. Padre Uria beseeched me to offer Pablo my protection."

"And did you agree?" asked his wife.

"It was the padre's last wish. How could I refuse?"

"I don't need your help," said Pablo, his eyes welling with tears. "I don't need anyone's help." But once again they did not hear him.

The visit to Padre Uria's death bed was one of many journeys Pablo would take during the night. Others would be as vivid, but none so heart-rending.

Leaving that somber scene behind, the boy's sadness quickly dissipated as once more he found himself flying. From these avian heights the problems and concerns of those who dwelt below seemed very small indeed.

But below too, lay the delightful Santa Barbara coastline. It beckoned him, drawing him westward. He found himself soaring over its foam-flecked beaches, passing by its steep bluffs, and hovering above its graceful curves and sensuous undulations. He flew for mile upon mile until he came at last to the windswept cape that the Spaniards named Point Conceptíon. From here, the coast veered to the northward. But Pablo steered out to sea, inspired by Inigua's tales of the legendary Shimilaqsha. He was curious to behold for himself the Land of the Dead. But in the far distance the boy spied a compact wall of clouds concealing all that lay beyond.

A strong headwind began to blow, slowing his progress. The wind continued to rise until he could no longer advance against it. He streamlined his body and tried with all his might, but he could make no headway. It became obvious to him that the sight of Shimilaqsha was reserved for the dead alone. Pablo reluctantly turned back towards the coast.

He passed over the shoreline and continued on over the ascending hills and peaks of the coastal range. Beyond this broken landscape lay the vast San Joaquin Valley, seemingly stretching forever to the north and south. The scooped valley throbbed with the color of lush spring growth. Gazing ahead through the immaculate air Pablo saw the rugged Sierra Nevada Mountains looming like a jagged barricade, a barricade which held back what he imagined were teeming hordes of Yankees.

He turned south, skirting the western reaches of the San Joaquin, and gazed down at circling condors, their black wings stark against the green and brown earth far below. Miles fled by until he saw the smoke of many fires rising off to the right. He steered towards them, crossing the coastal range once more and descended into the basin of *El Pueblo Señora la Reina de Los Angeles de Rio Porciúncula*. Here he came to earth and walked the dusty thoroughfares of the bustling secular town of Los Angeles. Among the many Spaniards, Mexicans and Indians plying its dusty streets he occasionally saw the lost-looking white face of an American.

During one of his many dreams he encountered the creature that would become his totem. The two were drawn to each other from the moment they saw one another. From that time forward they sojourned together in amiable companionship. On several occasions Pablo saved his totem from certain disaster, and more than once his totem pulled him from the very brink of the abyss.

     *   *   *   *   *

The storm raged over the island all through the night as Pablo slept. But by mid-morning the storm had passed on, and Momoy had begun to loosen its grip on Pablo. Groggy and besotted with half-dreams, he opened his eyes. He found himself lying on the cave floor. Someone had straightened out his legs and covered him in a blanket. The fire pit lay black and cold. He turned his head towards the gray light emanating from the mouth of the cave. There he saw the naked figure of a man standing with his back to him, a man knee-deep in the frothing whitewater.

The figure had long white hair cascading down his back. Pablo watched as he walked slowly into deeper water. Though Pablo could not clearly see him, he knew it had to be Inigua. He tried to call out to him, but found his mouth so dry his tongue stuck to the roof of his mouth. Feeling as weak as a newborn, he fumbled in the darkness until he found the bota of water. He rinsed his mouth and took a long satisfying drink. When he looked again the man was standing further out, his body now half submerged. An incoming swell curled over him, and the man dove deftly under it. Pablo attempted to rise, only to fall back, and though he struggled against them, the black wings of sleep closed over his eyes once again.

He awoke several hours later. He found himself alone in the cave. A raging thirst set him fumbling for the bota again. His thirst slackened, he looked again to the mouth of the cave. Bright sunlight shone down on a barren strip of beach in the foreground and the empty sea beyond. The sound of breaking waves echoed in the cave.

"Inigua!" the boy called. He waited, listening. But the only sound was that of surging water. "Inigua!" he called again into the emptiness.

Pablo felt very cold. He tried to rise, but found himself still too weak to stand. He crawled over to the stack of firewood and laboriously dragged pieces of wood into the pit. He tried starting the fire, but was once again overcome with exhaustion. He pulled the blanket over himself and slept once more.

45

TOTEM

In the late afternoon Pablo awoke again in the empty cave. He stood up weakly and laboriously donned his coton and trousers. He walked on unsteady legs out to the beach, squinting at the unaccustomed brightness. He found the strand deserted in both directions, but for the occasional scampering of snowy plovers, and the satisfied strut of sated gulls. He called Inigua's name again and again, but there was no answer. He reluctantly turned his eyes to the sea, scanning it somberly. Was it a dream, he wondered, or did he really see the old man entering the water? Was he bathing? Or just swimming? How strange.

His attention was drawn to a flume of water rising several hundred yards from shore. His pounding heart slowed when he realized it came from a pod of migrating gray whales. He watched them passing slowly on their long journey north – mothers escorting their calves.

Hunger and thirst drove Pablo back to the cave. He drank from the bota, and started a fire. Rummaging through their food stores, he came across the packet of nuts and dried fruit, which he ate slowly, savoring the delicious, long-forgotten taste of food. Food at last. How long had it been since he'd last eaten? Counting on his fingers, he decided five days.

The fire warmed and comforted him as the day slowly drew to an end. But he could not stop worrying about Inigua. Where could he be? He hated to think that he had drowned, or perhaps been taken by some creature of the deep. But his mind could not focus on Inigua for long, for it was filled with memories of the many dreams and vision he'd had. Their effect on him had been profound, and he could not help trying to sort them out. Each of them had meaning, of that he was sure. But what were those meanings? He sat cross-legged, holding his head in his hands, gazing into the fire. There was much to contemplate. The day slowly waned as he ruminated, and by the time darkness fell, he found his thoughts had grown dull with weariness. He lay down under a pile of blankets and fell into a deep and dreamless sleep.

The next day Pablo went fishing. On his way to the rocky point that Shup had shown him, he repeatedly called out to Inigua. Periodically throughout the morning he continued to call. Even though he shouted at the top of his lungs, the sound seemed to be swallowed up by the vast emptiness of sea and sky. He caught a good-sized rockfish and took it to the beach where he cooked and ate it ravenously. In the early afternoon he returned to the cave to rest. He decided he did not like it here in the cave. It was cold and dark. He would stay here today and tonight in case Inigua returned looking for him; then he would move his camp to a brighter spot.

Pablo felt truly lonely for the first time in his life. He could not understand why Inigua had left him. He was worried that if his mentor was not in the sea he might be lying injured somewhere on the island. Maybe he had gone foraging and fallen down. Maybe his leg was broken. Maybe he needs me, thought the boy.

After Pablo had rested, he roamed up and down the beach, calling into the steep hills that rose above the shoreline. He then hiked along the stream, searching the entire length of the narrow valley to no avail. Maybe Inigua decide to go off on his own for awhile, he thought. Maybe he is visiting some special place on the island. But it is such a large and rugged place. How will I ever find him? And then Pablo turned once more in the direction of the sea. He did not want to imagine what he knew in his heart was true.

The island sun set and rose again. Pablo spent the morning treading the trails among the hills, calling and searching for Inigua. Finding no trace of him, he spent the afternoon moving his camp back to the old spot on the streamside ledge above the beach. The boy hung his new reata from the tent pole out of harm's way.

He spent the next few days fishing and gathering shellfish and the eggs of seabirds. He gathered firewood. He explored the east end of Santa Cruz. On one of his expeditions he found a piece of discarded soapstone, flat and about the size of the palm of his hand. He took it back to camp.

Pablo spent long, lonely evenings by the fire. He passed the time grinding and carving the soapstone. With no one to talk to, Pablo spent many hours pondering his dreams and contemplating his totem. He also recalled the many tales of Inigua. He thought of Padre Uria too. He wondered if his friends and mentors had truly departed, as in his dreams, or if they would both turn up as hail and hearty as ever.

During the day, when not fishing or gathering food, Pablo practiced with the reata. After several weeks of diligent work, he found he could easily lasso anything within forty feet of where he stood. He nearly lost the reata once when he lassoed a young seal on the beach. If the seal had been any larger it would have dragged Pablo and the reata into the sea. It was with great difficulty that he was finally able to disengage the struggling animal.

Sometimes Pablo just sat on the ledge by his campsite and gazed out across the Santa Barbara Channel. He never saw a ship there, or a canoe – only sea life: migrating whales, cavorting seals and sea lions, and the occasional pod of dolphins loping far out in the Channel. He studied diving cormorants and pelicans, and watched seagulls beating against or sweeping along with the wind. The only sounds he ever heard were those of the wind, the surf, and the calling of birds. He took to talking or singing to himself now and then, just to hear another sound.

Pablo sometimes wondered if he was still dreaming. Or perhaps his whole life up to this point had been a dream, and now he had awakened for the first time only to find he was the last person in the whole world. While this last thought was unsettling, he found he actually liked being on his own. He enjoyed looking out for himself and seeing to his own comfort and safety. He liked doing things his own way.

One day Pablo found a five-foot long piece of milled driftwood on the beach. Using the hatchet and a knife, he carved it into a flat-nosed shovel. The next day he used it to dig a long, deep trench in the sand above high water mark. He spent the following few days gathering the scattered bones of the Chumash villagers, and burying them in this mass grave.

Pablo began to wonder if he had been forgotten out here on Santa Cruz Island. Perhaps something had happened to Shup. He was the only one who knew where he was. He decided he had better not count on anyone else. He needed to find a way of leaving the island on his own. While he enjoyed the freedom his solitude provided, he missed the company of others. He liked people, and would rather live among them than be alone all the time. And, more and more, he found himself thinking of 'Akiwo.

As the days passed, he began gathering driftwood logs in preparation for constructing a raft. Using the hatchet, he trimmed them so that they fit close alongside one another. There was one thing that perplexed him, however – how to bind them together. He supposed that if nothing else presented itself, he could always use the reata.

*   *   *   *   *

One day after his midday meal, Pablo sat on the upland ledge polishing his newly completed soapstone carving. He held it up to the light. "It is a good likeness," he said with satisfaction. He set it down in front of him and gazed out over the Channel. It was then that he caught sight of something bobbing far out in the water to the east. It was something small and red, something moving slowly towards him from the direction of Anacapa Island. Pablo stood up to have a better look. He could hardly believe his eyes. It was a tomol.

Pablo stood watching it until he was sure it was heading his way. Then he said to himself, almost regretfully, "At last, they have come." He turned and quickly tidied his campsite, then made his way down to the beach. As the tomol drew nearer, he could see two barrel-chested men working their double-bladed paddles. They were Malak and his son, Shup. Pablo raised his hand in greeting, and he saw Shup raise his in return.

Pablo watched them catch a low wave and ride it in till the canoe's flat bottom ground smoothly to a halt against the sandy bottom. "Haku, young one," called Malak. "Where is Inigua?"

300

"Haku, uncle," replied Pablo. He drew himself up straight, and said, "Inigua is gone."

"Gone?" said Malak. "Gone where?"

"He is swimming with the fishes." Pablo offered no further explanation, but instead busied himself helping them drag the bow up onto dry land. When the canoe was secured, the two mariners stood in the sand looking expectantly at Pablo. The boy seemed different to them somehow. He looked healthy enough – he was darker and stronger, and his hair had grown much longer – but there was something else. Pablo seemed no longer boyish and shy. He stood staunchly before them, looking back in their eyes with a level gaze.

"You say Inigua is gone, Pablo?" said Shup. "I do not understand."

"Nor I. Inigua and I took the sacrament, and when I awoke I saw him entering the water. I was not sure if I was still dreaming or not. Now I think I was not, for I never saw him again."

"How long ago was this?" asked Shup, looking out along the coast.

"Many weeks. I'm sorry, Shup. I promised you I would look after him. But…somehow I lost him."

Malak and Shup glanced at one another.

Malak sighed, and said, "Don't blame yourself, Pablo. If he wanted to go, that was his choice."

"I do not blame myself. There was nothing I could do at the time. But I will always carry a stone in my heart because of it."

The three turned their gaze to the sea, and after a few moments, Malak said, "We bring sad news of our own, Pablo. When we took fish to sell at Mission San Buenaventura last Friday they told us Padre Uria has died, in Santa Barbara."

Pablo nodded and murmured desolately, "I know."

Malak and Shup exchanged puzzled glances.

Pablo said, "You two must be tired after your long paddle. Come to my camp and I will feed you. Then you can rest."

When they had eaten and settled in the shade, Pablo said, "What other news have you from the coast? What of Don Tico?"

"We hear he is recovering well from his injuries," said Malak, "and that he is no longer searching for you and Inigua. One vaquero who bought some fish told me he carried a letter from the comandante of the Presidio addressed to Don Tico. Not long after it was delivered, Don Tico called off the search. I think it is safe for you to come back now, Pablo. That is why we are here."

"I am grateful, Malak. Your family has sacrificed much for us, and it will not be forgotten. When would you like to return?"

"Tomorrow morning, if the good weather holds."

"Bueno. I will be ready. You rest now, and I will go see if I can find us something for supper. Make yourself at home."

When he was gone, Shup turned to his father and said, "What do you think? Has he gone mad from being out here alone all this time? Or was it the Momoy?"

"Neither. There is nothing wrong with Pablo that I can see. I think he is just now settling into himself, the self that he will be. You were the same after the sacrament."

"And, father, did you notice? The bones are gone from the beach."

"I saw. But let us say nothing about it for now."

Shup walked over to the ledge to see where Pablo had gone. As he neared the edge his foot bumped against a circular, flat stone. He bent down and picked it up. "What's this?" he said. He held it up for his father to see. It was a round soapstone medallion.

"Be careful with that," said Malak. "That must be his 'atashwin. Look at it closely. Is there anything on it?"

"Why, yes, there is a carving of an animal here... a magnificent bull with great wide horns. It is a beautiful carving."

"A bull," said Malak, pensively. "How strange." He sat for a time in deep thought, and then shook his head. "Do you know what this means, Shup?"

Shup looked at him, puzzled. "N...no. What are you thinking, father?"

"I think this may be a very troubling development for Pablo."

"Why? I don't understand."

"Pablo wants to become a vaquero. How can he become one if his totem is a bull? He cannot hunt or harm or eat a bull. The bull is the father of all cattle. Does this mean he cannot harm or eat any of its offspring? If so, how can he be a vaquero?"

"I see what you mean, father."

"But of course it all depends on what Pablo believes, doesn't it, Shup? He may interpret things differently. Let us say nothing of this to him for now. Put his 'atashwin back where you found it and come rest."

*   *   *   *   *

In the early morning they packed up all the gear and loaded it in the tomol. They set out across the Channel destined for Hueneme. Pablo knelt in the bow and manned a paddle. Shup knelt behind him, paddle in hand, and Malak took the helm. The water was calm, and the crossing uneventful until they neared the mainland. Two miles offshore they saw a great stir of sea birds swirling above a large school of fish. Around the school circled a pod of bottlenose dolphins, jumping and slapping their flukes against the sparkling water.

"Those dolphins are feeding," said Malak.

"Shall we go there, father?" asked Shup. "We might catch a few fish of our own for our supper tonight."

"No. I am too tired. I just want to go home."

Without a word, Pablo shipped his paddle and stood up in the bow. He reached behind him and retrieved something from his pack. He placed one foot on the bow sprit and raised the object over his head. It was attached to a cord. He began twirling it over his head as the tomol continued to plunge through the rolling swells. As the cord lengthened the spinning bullroarer emitted a buzzing sound that quickly escalated into a loud hum. Pablo stood sideways to the bow, facing the birds and fish and dolphins. Shup turned around and looked questioningly at his father. Malak shook his head and motioned for him to keep paddling.

Pablo continued spinning the bullroarer. Shup and Malak, looking in the same direction as Pablo, saw two dolphins separate themselves from the circling pod and head towards the tomol.

They covered the quarter-mile that separated them quickly, breeching as they came on. They drew alongside the canoe and swam parallel to it. They held their position close to the bow, jumping in unison while eyeing Pablo. The larger dolphin, the male, had unusual striations running laterally across his dorsa. It made chittering noises and waggled its flukes, as if in greeting.

Pablo slowed the bullroarer to a stop and let it fall to the deck. "I knew it," he said to no one in particular. Then, addressing the dolphin, which continued breeching alongside, he said, "Haku, señor. I understand now. I'm glad you found her."

The scarred dolphin waggled its fluke once more and then retreated. It swam over on the opposite side of its mate and nudged her closer to the coursing canoe as though to give her a better view of Pablo. In mid-leap, the second dolphin waggled her flukes and made a trilling noise.

"Haku, Señora," said Pablo. "I am happy for you. Take good care of him."

The scarred one chittered one last time and veered away, leading its mate back towards the pod. The two dolphins quickly put the tomol behind them, leaving the three voyagers with the lingering image of their perpetual smiles.

Author's Note

A historical novel is by nature a blend of both fact and fiction. This book is no exception. It might be useful to the reader to know what liberties the author may have taken with historical fact.

Almost everything written about Mission San Buenaventura in this book is true. There was indeed a massive flood of the Ventura River in the winter of 1832. And it did destroy San Miguel Chapel and cause serious damage to the mission. However, there is no record of the dam at San Antonio Creek bursting, nor is there is any mention of fatalities.

The first mission church (a temporary structure) burned to the ground sometime around 1791. The cause of the fire is unknown, but in my account Inigua set the blaze in retaliation for the death of his daughter, 'Alahtin. Construction of the present-day church began soon after and was completed in 1809. Speaking of 'Alahtin – her story was adapted from a little-known narrative poem called "The Legend of Matilija" by M. Blickenstaff, circa 1937.

All the Spaniards portrayed in this book were modeled on actual historical figures, including Father Francisco Uria who was the Padre-Superior at Mission San Buenaventura from 1831 to 1833. He and his beloved cats were very much as described in the novel. He died in Santa Barbara waiting for the ship to carry him home. All other characters in the book are fictional.

I employed a good deal of license in my portrayal of the Spaniard, Fernando Tico. Although he actually was the mayordomo of Rancho Ojai and in charge of the whipping post at the mission, there is no evidence that he was a sadistic bully. But every novel needs a villain, and within the realm of this one, he was the obvious choice.

Inigua's description of the Spaniards' arrival in Ventura (1769) was accurate, taken from diaries and journals kept by members of De Portola's party and from other accounts. References in this book to De Anza's two visits (1774 & 1776), the founding of Mission San Buenaventura (1782), and other material related to the establishment of missions in California are matters of historical record.

I based Inigua's attempted suicide on a story told to ethnologist John P. Harrington by the Chumash informant Fernando Librado Kitsepawit. In it he states that during mission times a neophyte lost everything he owned while gambling. Despondent, he tried to kill himself by eating a tarantula. He failed, as did Inigua.

The descriptions of the amazing San Buenaventura Mission water system are as accurate as the author could make them, as are the intricate details of making the reata. The main departure from the everyday making of

305

a reata is that most vaqueros probably did not cure hides by staking them out in the sea. However, some may have used this method if they were near the beach. The usual method at the missions was to soak them in pits filled with brine, salt and oak bark.

The Chumash villages mentioned in this book did exist, and are shown on the area map. Only the villages visited or mentioned in the book are shown. There were numerous others, both on the mainland and on the Channel Islands. However, most of them had been abandoned by 1832. One departure from what is true pertains to the village of Huyawit in the Ojai Valley (the place where Pablo meets 'Akiwo). There was in fact a village there (near what is now Soule Park) but its real name is unknown. For expediency, I called it Huyawit, which is the Chumash word for *Condor*.

Inigua's narratives on Chumash culture and cosmology I gleaned from early Spanish diaries and journals, and the work of later anthropologists and historians. The Coming-of-Age ceremony utilizing Momoy was a common practice. Incidentally, the massive Sycamore (the Gatekeeper Tree) near what is now Foster Park really did exist, as described by Kitsepawit.

The marvelous plank canoes (tomols) and their uses were accurately described. And although Chumash voyagers were known to use rowing chants, those appearing in the chapter "The Crossing" were composed by the author. I also wrote Inigua's "Momoy" chant which appears later in the book. In the chapter called "Dancing" I gave as realistic a description of various Chumash dances as I was able. They are based on historical accounts.

Steckel Park (alongside Santa Paula Creek) was where I envisioned Inigua and Pablo slaying and skinning the steer. Just south of there, Mupu village later became the city of Santa Paula. Sa'aqtik'oy village became the town of Saticoy, and Hueneme is now Port Hueneme. Inigua's home village, Shisholop, was located near what is now 'Surfer's Point' in Ventura.

Swaxil village, on Santa Cruz Island, was situated at Scorpion Anchorage and it did in fact suffer at the hands of the Aleut Indians and their Russian masters. I altered the geography of Swaxil slightly to include a non-existent ridge overlooking the Channel, a sandy beach instead of the present cobblestone one, and a nearby sea cave where Inigua and Pablo took refuge.

While I did take these and other small liberties with the people, places, and events of the past, I tread as lightly as possible over the historical record. Having done so, I hope the reader caught a truer sense of the great and tragic drama that unfolded here in those early days of California.

TT

Made in the USA
Charleston, SC
15 April 2012